Captive ATTRACTION

Written by
Patricia Crumpler

Copyright 2022 by Patricia Crumpler

All rights reserved. No part of this book may be reproduced in any manner without the express written consent of the publisher, except in the case of brief excerpts in in critical reviews or articles. All inquiries should be sent to: contact Deana Charcalla at DeanaBean.com or DeanaBeanbooks@gmail.com

DeanaBean is a Registered trademark.

ISBN 979-8-9869396-0-5
Captive Attraction
paperback edition

Published in the United States of America by DeanaBean LLC
PRINTED IN THE UNITED STATES OF AMERICA
10 9 8 7 6 5 4 3 2 1

CAPTIVE ATTRACTION

The airship lurched. Aril-Ess didn't worry. *Temperature pockets.*

Jerr-Lan's muscles tensed. He put his hand on the pommel of his sword.

Aril, who sat across from him at the game table, eyed his weapon. "Don't be concerned. Just air currents."

"Perhaps currents. Maybe they're something else. I don't like it."

Aril-Ess smiled and gave a short huff. "Don't use an air current to mask the fact you've run out of strategy for the board game."

The airship smoothed. Jerr-Lan relaxed his grip, shifting his attention to the game piece.

She pointed toward the playing board. "Move!"

"Don't rush me. Besides, how can I concentrate on the board with you leaning over it, sitting so close… and your breasts so easy to see under that thin dress?"

"Shall I worry that the Master of the Guard can't concentrate?"

He met her dark eyes with his own green-eyed flash. "I can concentrate, and don't think for a moment I won't protect you with my life, Princess."

Aril-Ess cast a glance toward her cabin door. "Please, Jerr-Lan, don't call me Princess. On this airship, I'm an equal. My royal status means nothing and may cause complications with the other scientists. I'm an ordinary geologist on an exploration to map the southern regions."

The warrior leaned back in his chair and laughed. "Everyone knows that a princess of the first order is aboard. They step over me in the corridor as I sleep against your door."

"You don't have to do that. You shouldn't be so uncomfortable."

He raised his eyebrows. "At last! An invitation to share your bed? How much better can I protect you if I'm that close? You've finally given in to nature." He cocked his head and smiled. "I know I'm a match."

Aril-Ess sat up, firming her shoulders. "No. On both accounts. You know nothing about how much your scent attracts me. Males don't have the receptors."

"Maybe not, but there's a kit sold on the under market that—"

She stood and pushed her chair away from the game table. "There's no kit."

"There may be a few things on this planet you aren't aware of," he said, stretching his honed, sculpted arms.

She did not know for sure. But after sixty year's study in medicine, chemistry, law, and now her current research in geology, a kit to ascertain hormonal attraction could not have escaped her. She stood and turned her back to him. "No kit."

The warrior came to her side. His warmth stimulated her, heightened by his scent. He *was* a match. Not a perfect one but highly suited, and she could barely resist him. She stared at a line of rivets in the cabin's metallic wall. "No kit. Impossible."

Jerr-Lan laughed and took her hand. "No kit. I don't need one. I know by your reaction when I get close… or touch you." He moved aside a short dark curl and rubbed his hand down her neck. "I'm a match. I just don't know how much."

Aril-Ess gently nudged his hand from her neck. She needed control—of herself and what happened around her. By being in charge, she could keep her passion to learn headed on the right course and not let love or physical attraction divert her from her goal. "Well, I'm not going to tell you how much."

"See there. You just admitted it." He put his lips near her ear. "Princess—"

She stepped away. "Please. I'm not the great granddaughter of Jake Hill, the Planetary Prince, while I'm at work on the *Nautol*. I'm Doctor Aril-Ess of Cadmia, a simple geologist and cartographer on a mission to explore this area."

Jerr-Lan folded his arms over his chest "You shouldn't be here at all. We don't know much about this part of the planet, except that wild hordes still live here."

"We're only mapping the arid zones. We think the Hordesmen live in the wooded areas."

"Think? We don't really know what's here, Aril."

"And that's what makes it an important mission." She smiled at him. "And I have my own personal guard."

The warrior nodded. "Yes, you do."

She cocked her head. "By the way, how is it I rated a general in the Cadmian Special Guard?"

"What do you think?"

"My revered ancestor, Jake Hill, made you come with me?"

"Not exactly. I asked for an audience with the Planetary Prince to request the post."

"You don't need an audience to speak with grandsire. Besides, how did you know I was going?"

"Your brother told me about the mission. I asked Jake Hill for an audience to make the request official. I knew he would want you to be safe, so I volunteered."

She resisted toying with the crossed leather straps on his chest and looked up at him. "No rank insignia—only your medal of Excalibur. You want to appear as a mercenary?"

"My rank has no importance for this job—guarding you—and the Excalibur speaks for itself."

"Thank you for your … service. I don't think I need my own guard, but—"

Jerr-Lan took a step closer. "Jake Hill and I think you do."

Her slim fingers reached to touch his emblem. He covered her hand with his rough tanned fingers. "Aril, why won't you let yourself respond to me? Do you fear being with me will crack your closed heart? It might, you know. Would that be so terrible?"

She backed away, letting go of the shiny medal emblazoned on his harness.

"Aril, I don't have a single drop of royal blood. I have no right to even dream you would take me as your Life-Mate, but —"

She bit her lip for a moment. "You know grandsire doesn't believe in sovereignty. He would abolish it completely but the royals in place won't have it. He tolerates the title Planetary Prince for political reasons."

"He has said that many times, yes. But would Jake Hill, the Planetary Prince, feel the same way regarding his favorite offspring?"

"Grandsire will allow me to choose my Life-Mate with no restrictions. It's one of the reasons I don't wear the family insignia while I engage in my studies."

"How many sciences must you study?"

"I should learn as much as I can about our peoples and our planet."

"He wishes you to learn so you can be a qualified leader? A queen, or a ruling princess? Ruling means you will align with royalty."

"That is the theory. But in truth I do my studies because I want to learn. I'm young, not even eighty. I have plenty of time for a mate and a family." She liked Jerr-Lan. He would make a good mate, in time, when she was ready. And he was correct, she couldn't allow him to get any closer because she might fall in love with him. She couldn't afford a distraction. First, she must learn all she could to help make a difference on her planet, Cronanta, and continue to do what the Earthman, her grandsire, had done. She wanted a Life-Mate and a family but not yet.

The ship lurched again. Aril-Ess fell into Jerr-Lan's arms. He righted her and ran to the door. Loud hissing announced damage to one of the buoyancy tanks. A second lurch and the sound of dual hissing said the ship was in trouble.

CHAPTER 2

Jerr-Lan pulled Aril toward the rear of the cabin. He peered out the round window and scanned the arid dunes. "Lucky it's still daylight, but I don't see anything."

The airship listed and dropped, losing altitude fast on its way to touch ground. The skill of the pilots determined how well it landed—or crashed.

"Try not to worry, Princess. Our pilot and copilot are the best."

Her arched eyebrows came together. "You know them?"

He firmed his shoulders. "Warriors. Handpicked by me."

Her lips tightened.

He held up his palm. "The Planetary Prince takes no chances with his family."

She sniffed derisively. "Little good a few fighting men would do when an airship is unarmed."

He winced. "Not exactly unarmed." Patting the sword on his hip he added, "Plus—"

"This is a peaceful mission," she said through clenched teeth.

"And it can remain peaceful if no one bothers us. But our buoyancy tanks have been breached, and only a powerful weapon can penetrate the *Nautol's* hiltite cladding." Jerr-Lan peered out the window again. "We're between high dunes. Who knows what waits beyond them?"

"The wild hordes? Against three—you and the pilots?"

He shook his head. "And the stewards, cooks, engineers…" A deep breath expanded his toned chest. "They are my men, well trained. I know they prepare for defense as we speak."

An explosion from beneath the airship shook the craft. The vessel plummeted, slamming them against the cabin wall.

Jerr-Lan's jaw muscles twitched. "Wild hordes don't possess steam missiles."

The airship hit the sandy terrain. The hiltite cladding screamed as it scraped over rocky outcroppings. The *Nautol* twisted to a stop, then turned on its side. The starboard wall of Aril-Ess's cabin became the ship's bottom. Jerr-Lan kicked the crumpled door open. With a firm grip on Aril-Ess's arm, he pulled her through the canted corridors. Railings became handholds and foot braces. Jerr-Lan's strength brought both of them up and out through the emergency door to the top of the craft, once the port side. The crew-turned-warriors waited with swords and a small steam cannon. As the noxious propellant gases spilled from the damaged tanks into the hull, Members of the exploration team crawled out of the airship.

Movement from the top of the nearest dune heralded figures riding gants, the swift four-legged mounts used by the military. The oncoming mob, dressed like Hordesmen, didn't look right. Too small. Hordesmen were tall and sat high on their gants. These marauders were men, Commonfolk. As they approached, the bright flash of metal from the setting sun indicated the enemy cannons had been made from alnata, the strongest and most lightweight metal on the planet. Some of the riders brandished swords and spears; others lowered their cannons.

Alnata weaponry was difficult to fashion, but because its strength could use smaller steam chambers, making them formidable arms. Top quality meant extreme expense. Even Cadmia's army possessed few of them. These challengers had the war gear of a well-funded army.

Volleys of shot whipped dust swirls around the derelict *Nautol*, raining grit all about. Cannon shells shattered the hull and crashed windows. The enemy drew closer.

Jerr-Lan slid his sword from the leather sheath. He tensed as he took a defensive stance in front of Aril-Ess.

The cook, now cannoneer, aimed his thin tube at the shiny alnata weapon in the hands of the point marauder. The enemy's device exploded in a cloud of smoke and steam. Bits of flesh and alnata flew in all directions. The gant sagged at its knees and fell to the sand.

"One down, dozens to go," Jerr-Lan muttered. "Good work," he shouted to the cannoneer.

It took a short time to reload. The warriors on the downed airship evaded the shots, and in turn pummeled the on-comers. When the enemy reached the side of the downed airship, the warriors jumped from their position to the ground.

"Stay here," Jerr-Lan said.

Aril-Ess shook her head firmly. "No. I'm going with you."

Arrows flew and swords flashed in the battle.

Inside the *Nautol,* gasses mixed into clouds of black mist that hung like a curtain over the downed craft. The exploration party, no longer safe on the *Nautol's* hiltite skin, climbed down and cowered behind the warriors.

Jerr-Lan dispatched three opponents at once. Around him, the adversaries piled in a bloody heap. With a whoosh, multiple arrows hit their mark on Jerr-Lan's chest. He fell clutching his sword.

Aril-Ess screamed, "Jerr-Lan!" and kneeled at his side. Her shoulder stung as she bent over her friend, the warrior who took arrows for her.

"I'm sorry, my princess," Jerr-Lan whispered.

Aril-Ess moved her lips but no words escaped. Her body turned tight. The last thing she saw as her vision narrowed was the bleeding body of the man she could have loved.

CHAPTER 3

The foul smell and the crying brought Aril-Ess from her drugged sleep. The rattle of chain attached to manacles sounded, and her arm couldn't move to her forehead. The light of Cronanta's three moons, in a rare conjunction, allowed her to see where she was—slumped on the first-row bench in a weather-beaten open-air speeder. The pilot sat in a protective bubble guiding the craft above sandy terrain. Crammed and weeping, the other occupants were the female members of the exploration team.

A gravelly voice yelled, "You!"

Aril-Ess turned to the direction of the shouted words. Still muddled from unconsciousness, her mind conjured the image of the Yaytoog, mythical creatures, large, ugly, and fat, said to feast on wayward children. An unattractive beast-like woman matching the description of a Yaytoog, stood over Aril on a small platform behind the clear pilot shield. Before Aril-Ess could understand what was happening, the revolting woman shoved a sting stick into Aril's arm, causing a jolt of pain.

"Now I have your attention?"

Aril-Ess nodded.

"Sit up, where I can see you."

Aril-Ess sat up. The pain of the stick brought her to full awareness, and she assessed the situation. The overfed beast wore a typical leather harness; her ample flesh surged around a metal-studded breast cup that dimpled her waist where the bottom leather shorts barely fastened. She held the pain stick in one hand, and a safety strap attached to the craft in the other. The hide strap remained taut as the woman fought to stay upright and balanced against the wind of the speeder. The Yaytoog female grinned each time she pricked a captive.

One prisoner, the *Nautol's* artist, searched the aircar with her gaze, focused on the pilot's bubble, and cried out, "Help us!"

He didn't twitch.

The Yaytoog threw her head back in laughter. "Don't bother, stupid." She touched the stick to the implorer's cheek. "He's accustomed to this, and he gets a fat fee. Now shut up."

Aril-Ess's eyes darted between the cruel supervisor and the artist. Aril-Ess whispered to her neighbor, the former botanist, with whom she shared a chain. "Let me have the slack. Don't pull, all right?" The girl nodded; her eyes unfocused from her drugged haze.

"You're a brute!" Aril-Ess shouted to the Yaytoog beast.

The woman's mouth dropped open. Her eyes narrowed, and the edges of her thin lips curved upward. "The wind must be playing tricks on my hearing. What did you say, bitch?"

"I said you're a brute. No, I take it back. That would insult brutes everywhere."

The Yaytoog blanched and raised her stick. As she brought it down, Aril-Ess grabbed it, avoiding the stinging end, and in a flash, upturned it, ramming the stinger straight into the beast's left eye. The beast let go of the leather safety strap to put both hands to her eye. Aril-Ess flattened her palm and chopped the vulnerable spot behind the woman's knee, causing her to bend and lose balance. With a tug on the chain, Aril-Ess gained enough height to reach the Yaytoog and heave her from the craft. The dreadful screams from the woman died away as the craft sped on. The screams did not affect the pilot, confirming what the woman had said earlier.

The captives who were jammed into the craft glanced around, confused. Soon, one smiled, and as they caught on to what had just occurred, the murmuring increased. The woman behind Aril-Ess pointed to the stick. "Throw that away."

Aril-Ess scowled. "It's a weapon. We'll keep it." She carefully placed the sting-stick down on the floor with the tip against the speeder's metal wall.

Moving through the night, with wind as background to the distressed mumblings, Aril picked at the manacles, trying to see the mechanism in the moons' light. She thought back to her studies in engineering, then closed her eyes. Pulling stored information from her memories, she identified the lock's components as her fingers slid over the catch. With more time and a pick, she could free the fetters. Aril wished she wore her dress leathers instead of her casual dress. The formal harness would have had adornments, pins and insignia, plus the hidden defensive blade that Jake Hill required all family females to carry and be adept in using.

She searched the scene and spied the tip of a writing pen sticking from the work coat of the botanist. "I need your pen."

Without permission, Aril bent her head over the pocket and grabbed the instrument with her teeth. "Thanks," she said, the word muffled by the pen. She dropped the pen in her lap. The length of chain links allowed her enough room to guide the point into the mechanism. Working the lock by feel, she glanced over her shoulder toward the ground.

The terrain had changed with bits of green, and in the light of the moons, lakins grazed below. The speeder angled down slowly. The terrain went from verdant patches to pastureland. The craft dropped low enough that it skimmed over the bawling lakin herds. Past the meadows and approaching more dunes, the transport slowed. Aril leaned into the wind, catching sight of lights ahead. As they approached, a structure came into view, a two-story building and landing dock. She hadn't had time to pick the lock open.

The craft stopped and hovered at the dock. The pilot opened the protective bubble and hopped out without a look back.

Harsh lights flooded the dock. Odd that this place would have the expensive strongium lights instead of the soft light of common steam bulbs.

Mumblings from the captives increased as the craft stayed moored with the buoyancy rays still engaged. Since the pilot left, they had not seen anyone. Hurriedly, Aril worked on her cuff locks. The pen point was bent but it still had some picking life. She needed time.

A door of the building opened. Another Yaytoog-like woman, large and unkempt, approached the hovering transport. She held her sting stick tightly and made a sucking noise with her tongue. With her hands on her hips, she snarled, "Where's Grund?"

Aril spoke. "Gone."

"Where? With that swine Gaf-Lox?"

"I'm not sure who she's with," Aril answered. "I guess she had her eye out for someone."

Grund's twin scoffed. "Just like her. You, then," she pointed at the nearest captive. "Hold up your hands." The supervisor stuck a key into the captive's lock. Simultaneous snapping and clicking on all the locks released the manacles.

Aril's hands were free. She smiled. This Yaytoog was alone, armed only with a stick. Aril had a stick, too, and the advantage of surprise. She closed her hand over the sting stick, tensing her muscles for attack.

A door on the side of the building hurled open, spewing a group of men, each armed with a stick. The moment was lost. Deep shadows in the transport hid Aril's movements while she jammed the point of the stick against the metal side—it would never cause another person pain again.

Aril stood and left the craft, clenching her teeth. She joined the coterie of scientists and marched toward the building. They made a wide berth around the guards who pointed sting sticks at the moving queue.

The interior of the building looked like lakins had been there. The eston rock construction showed its age. Rows of stone benches obviously had never been cleaned. These benches didn't have the luxury of Illie fur, the other herd animal used for food, hide, and hauling.

She took in the large room while keeping the captives ahead in her lateral vision. Each prisoner, after being frisked, received a wire slave belt, the kind that were illegal throughout the entire planet. Aril held back her words when a grimy man wearing a soiled white robe of a poor trader, felt around her smock. Grinning, he gave her another pat-down, slowing over her breasts. She tensed and pictured this man facing grandsire, explaining both his handling and the unlawful slave belt he connected at her waist.

The main control for the belt wires had to be nearby because the spectral waves that controlled the belts didn't carry far. No one would try to escape. If the pain didn't stop an escapee, the blindness and brain damage from prolonged delivery did.

The man directed Aril to a nearby bench. She sat next to a pale, delicate creature, a sylph. Sylphs usually kept to themselves, not wanting the company of the other sentient beings on Cronanta. Their small stature and slight bodies didn't lend them to tiring activities, such as labor or the military. One sylph out of a hundred, a scanner, could read minds, and of those, a few rare ones called chiefs could go deep, discerning truth from deceit. Under Jake Hill's planetary rule, major courts kept a chief on staff, used only for capital crimes--death as the penalty. With a chief sylph's ability to know the truth, no innocent person had been executed.

The sylph scooted over, giving Aril room, and moved once more to make sure she made no contact. Then she turned her face away, the unspoken gesture for wanting privacy—impossible under these circumstances.

If this sylph could read the mind of at least one of their captors, the information could help Aril increase the odds of escape. She needed her neighbor's attention. Aril pretended she had just seen a hanta, a disgusting disease-carrying rodent, and directed the thought toward the sylph. The small pinkish silver female didn't stir. She wasn't a chief or even a scanner. Aril-Ess, high princess, descendant of the Planetary Prince, would have to use her wits and skill to flee and bring justice to these kidnappers.

The wire at her waist kept her there for now, but she would get free. Somehow.

CHAPTER 4

"You sent for me, Prince?"

"Look around, Ray-Tan. Notice anything?"

The warrior placed his hand over his crossed leather straps, feeling his metal insignia.

Prince Tim-Ell chuckled. "No threat, friend. You touch your metal when you are ready to fight. Tell me what you see in this apartment."

Ray-Tan relaxed and scanned the room, slowing his gaze at the plain walls and the sparse furniture. He leaned around Tim-Ell to check the small kitchen and turned to see into the open door of the bedroom. "Nothing. Quiet. We're alone?"

"Yes. I gave my slave to Sen-Mak."

"Your brother?" Ray-Tan nodded. "I saw him leering at her during the reception in the palace last week. Maybe you shouldn't take pretty slaves to your events."

"Why not? It's great to have a gorgeous girl on my arm. And it keeps the other women away. I want to focus on my military career."

"So, you *gave* her to Sen-Mak?"

Tim-Ell put up his hand. "I know. She was lovely, eager to please, and worth a lot of money. But I grew tired of her constant nagging for me to take an apartment in the palace. She didn't like this place."

"I don't like these apartments, either," Ray-Tan said. "I'm only here because of you."

"What's wrong with this place?"

Ray-Tan sneered. "For one, the landlady. What a—"

"She's nice to me."

"Of course, she is." Ray-Tan rolled his eyes. "You're the Crown Prince."

"True," Tim-Ell said.

Ray-Tan fingered his insignia. "Now that you don't have a slave, we can return to the barracks."

"I don't want to live in the barracks. What I want is a new lady. What are you doing tomorrow?"

Rolling his lip, Ray-Tan thought. "The usual. Inspection, sword practice, exercise—"

"Good. Have your assistant see to the duty. Eppo-Zim told me there was to be an auction in the Vant Valley tomorrow."

Ray-Tan glowered. "Eppo-Zim."

"You don't care for our country's Vizier? How can Protar function without him?"

"You know I don't like him. He's…"

"My father's choice."

"When you take the crown, you can replace him."

"I could," Tim-Ell said. "But he knows everything about running the country. My father sits in the palace with no worries."

"And as long as he stays there, his life is safe. But, is that a good life?"

Tim-Ell shrugged. "He likes it. I don't want to think about ruling Protar. I want a new companion—one that's beautiful, talented, and has an interesting personality. Go with me?"

"If that is your command, Prince."

"It's not my command. I'm asking as your friend."

CHAPTER 5

Aril's stomach turned. The hard eston bench hurt her butt. The place reeked of vomit and urine, most likely the result of waist-wire reprimands. She had to modify her belt. Thinking back to her law studies, she remembered a trial where a man had abused his slave using the same illegal control. From that trial, Aril knew how the belt worked.

Among the refuse littering the floor, she found a thin flat stone and lodged it under the connecting clasp. The stone fit between the belt and her skin; its coolness shielded her.

Aril stood up to count the number of guards and get a better idea of exit possibilities.

"Sit down." One of the leather-harnessed male guards held up a control as a threat. Aril continued her reconnaissance, unafraid of the control's menace. In unison, the captives around her screamed. The poor sylph turned from rosy gray to deep purple and contorted into a fetal position. Hands grabbed Aril and pulled her down. Their captors used the strategy of group control. Everyone was punished for an individual's misstep. Aril's single-mindedness had brought injury to the other captives, especially the frail sylph. Now, she had no allies, no one to protect her. She pictured Jerr-Lan's arrow-pierced body and his words. Her stomach twinged. She hung her head and whispered his name. Never had she felt so alone. Fear nipped at her thoughts. She took a breath. *Be brave.*

A few minutes later as the sylph uncoiled and the purple faded to gray, one of the guards shouted, "Stand. Starting from the first bench, line up and follow me."

The guard led them to a dining room. Benches had been carved along two sides of the high eston rock walls. Long tables faced the benches, leaving room between them for servers to move around. Round windows near the ceiling gave the impression of eyes peering down. The captives stood until told to sit, and then took their place at the tables. Grease shone on the dishes, and the cups showed soil from many users. Redgrain bread tasted surprisingly good. Tashberries, weeds that easily grew in poor soil, provided berries for the jelly, and a paste made from the mature seeds formed the filling for the bread. Tashberry butter and jelly offered a nutritious and tasty substitute for meat. For generations, impoverished people and the military had thrived on it. The food relaxed her—a bit. Aril chuckled to herself over the irony of the situation. She had been sent to explore and gather information about this unknown area. She now knew the geology and the soil content based on what sat on the plate before her.

After the meal, they marched to a filthy latrine. Several times, Aril walked faster to be near the sylph to apologize. "I need to talk to you."

The female wouldn't make eye contact. "No," she said in response to Aril's words. Finally, she slowed but didn't turn. "Leave me alone. I hate you."

On their way back to the main benches, the grimy robed man who had felt Aril's breasts grabbed her arm. "Come with me." He shoved her into the first clean place she'd seen since she arrived. The grimy escort lounged in the open doorway.

A man dressed in a medical doctor's coat swept his hand, indicating an examining table.

Aril slid onto the table.

"I am Doctor Al-Mot," he said in a monotone. He lifted her smock and pressed on her abdomen. "Where are you injured?"

"I'm not injured." For the first time she noticed the blood smeared on her garment. Jerr-Lan's blood. She hung her head, took in a staccato breath, and let it out slowly.

Doctor Al-Mot backed away a step. "I need to examine you. Remove your clothes."

Aril crossed her arms over her chest and set her jaw. "No way. Tell me what is going on. Why have I been brought here?"

"You don't know?" His face and voice remained flat. "You and the others will be sold as slaves."

"Slaves? No judge? No trial? What crime did I commit?"

Doctor Al-Mot dropped his gaze to the floor and spoke in a whisper. "The same one I did—my ship flew into the wrong place, blown off course in a storm."

Aril leaned toward him. "You are a slave?"

He made eye contact. "I might as well be. I can never leave here. I know too much, and my wife and family are with me. I must do what I'm told." Still whispering, his voice modulated to an appeal. "Please. Moss-Tow told me to examine you and give him the report."

"Who is Moss-Tow?"

"The slaver who owns half of this estate. For my family's safety, please let me do my job."

Aril cast a glance to the soiled man in the doorway, and back to the doctor.

Doctor Al-Mot nodded. "Ick-San, Moss-Tow said to notify him when I've seen the girl. Tell him I'm examining her now."

Ick-San glowered. He hesitated then left.

Aril removed her smock, the blood smears bringing the nightmare back. Doctor Al-Mot adjusted the pressure lever on the wall to energize his instruments. A light puff of steam misted from around the metal dials. He pulled wires and tubing from their recesses toward the table and checked her vital signs.

He returned the devices to their niche and came back to the table. "Unfasten your thong."

Aril let out a breath, checked the doorway, and unfastened the clasp on her leather bottoms.

Doctor Al-Mot gasped and took a step back. He met her eyes with his widened stare. "Jake Hill! The Earthman's gene for body hair…You're a relative—a princess."

Aril followed the doctor's gaze to her groin. A line of sparse dark hair pointed to her thighs.

The doctor opened his mouth and shut it, making only stuttering sounds. He found his voice. "Who *are* you?"

"I'm Aril-Ess, great granddaughter of the Planetary Prince."

"If *they* find out," he looked over his shoulder as his words became whispers, "Your life is in danger. They would fear retaliation from Jake Hill and would destroy every bit of evidence that you were here." He pressed his eyes shut. "Oh, Goddess, protect us." He bent close to her ear. "Most of the people here are too uneducated or stupid to know about the gene for body hair but Moss-Tow is shrewd and doesn't miss anything. He might know. And he will demand to see you—completely."

Aril pulled out a pubic hair and flinched. "Well, he won't see any of these." She gritted her teeth and pulled another.

"Don't do that. I'll get you a shaver." He opened a drawer and removed a razor.

"Thank you," she said. "Did you learn about Earth genetics in your medical training?"

Doctor Al-Mot nodded. "Yes. Hurry, Princess. Moss-Tow enjoys making people wait, but when he saw you in the dining room from his office window, he wanted to see you in person. He might not delay."

"Keep my secret, Doctor. Please don't call me by my title. If I'm to be a slave, call me that."

"Of course. I'm sorry. Uh, slave."

She finished her task then handed him the razor. "When Jake Hill comes here, which he surely will, speak to him personally. Use the code, *Alas Babylon*. He will spare you because of those words. Memorize them. They are the title of his favorite Earth book, and only someone close to him would know that."

Doctor Al-Mot mumbled the code words.

Noise in the hall alerted them of company. Aril pulled up her leather thong.

Ick-San stopped at the door and bowed. "Moss-Tow."

A large man dressed in a blue and gold striped robe, the garb of a rich trader, strode into the examining room. White teeth grinned from his dusky face under a black brush mustache. A red turban touched his eyebrows, bushy things that shadowed his dark, evil eyes.

Moss-Tow's robe swished as he approached the table. "Ah. She is more beautiful up close. She is well, doctor?"

Doctor Al-Mot swallowed hard. "Yes."

"Such a handsome woman will fetch a good purse. But I could not sell something so valuable until I have made sure she is worth her price, no?" He threw his head back and roared a laugh implying he didn't care if anyone shared his humor. He glared at Doctor Al-Mot. "I want a *full* medical report and afterward, have her wait in the holding room. I'll send for her once I've talked with Gual-Gur." Ick-San followed his employer out.

"Who is Gual-Gur, Doctor?"

"His partner."

"I've not seen men slaves. Where are they?"

Doctor Al-Mot shook his head and let out a deep breath. "They probably don't live to become slaves. Men will fight back. The traders don't deal in male slaves—except for Gual-Gur—if the males are the right age." His face hardened. "He likes them young."

"Young?"

"Right out of the egg."

"How can that be?"

"Gual-Gur trains them for special…buyers, I suspect he purchases eggs ready to deliver."

"What mother would sell her egg after she fed and incubated it?"

Doctor Al-Moot's shoulders sagged. "You are not in the north now. Horrible things go on in this territory. You can't imagine." He looked at the floor and then to Aril. "I'm sorry, Prin…uh, slave, but I must examine you completely. I pray to the Goddess that you suffer no harm from Moss-Tow."

Aril narrowed her eyes. "Save your prayers for Moss-Tow…and Gual-Gur." She removed her thong.

The doctor turned the wall lever, releasing steam energy for his instruments. He checked the dials. "Right, then. Let's begin."

CHAPTER 6

In the holding room, the captives lounged on the uncomfortable eston benches. Some slept; some looked as if they had gone into a trance, heads hanging, bodies flaccid and slumped. The rosy-gray sylph squatted on the bench rolled up, sphere-like.

Ick-San escorted Aril to the place where she had been. The sylph uncurled and bared her teeth, letting loose a high-pitched rasping scream. Most of Cronanta's inhabitants spoke the same language. Aril had never heard that sound before, but the snarl on the sylph's face communicated perfectly.

Aril turned her back on the gray female and glanced over her shoulder. The creature rasped again.

"Oh, shut up," Aril said. "We're all in this together. It doesn't do any good to hate each other. Focus your hatred on those guards."

Guards. Aril thought about *her* guard Jerr-Lan. Tears stung her eyes. He had been a fixture in her family, best friend to her brother. His last words were of her. Had his body been found? She didn't know if the ship's communications officer had sent an emergency call. Even if he had gotten out the message, the spectral waves didn't always travel the right direction. Air communications weren't dependable. Certainly no one who was left at the crash site survived. Eventually Jake Hill would send away-teams to search. How long would it take to locate this place? From what she had seen, it looked like any other large estate owned by a wealthy trader. But Jake Hill *would* find her. She must take care of herself until then.

Ick-San, still in his soiled robe, walked heavily toward the bench. "Come with me."

Aril hesitated. The sylph stiffened and glared.

"All right," Aril said.

A wave of fear coursed through Aril. She had so little control over what was happening. Was her courage slipping? No. She'd wait to see what lay in store before she succumbed to fear. Straightening her shoulders, she followed the man out of the building to the dock where the speeder still hung in the air. She smiled to herself—no one had turned the buoyancy element off. Maybe this craft could be her getaway. There was no way of knowing how much of the anti-gravity rays remained in the tanks. If the tanks expended their anti-gravity rays, the transporter would fall to the rocks below. Not far, but enough to cause damage. She shut her eyes for a moment, wishing she could rely on something, but she didn't believe in Cronanta's All-Knowing and All-Powerful Goddess, Golonka.

"Stop lagging," Ick-San said. He showed her his waist-wire control. The stone lodged in her belt would prevent a punishment, but she feigned fear and sped up.

Although hours had passed, the pale approaching daylight gave Aril an idea of how long she'd been at Moss-Tow's site. Ick-San led her to the back of the building and up eston stairs to the second story. He held the door, and followed her into a large room. Papers and books littered a desk by the entrance. The rest of the room did not hint of business—the smell of spicy incense hung in a cloud in front of crossed diaphanous curtains. Soft lights caressed the fabric. The veil of curtains did not completely conceal the bed.

Ick-San hurried out, slamming the thick metal door behind him. A gust of steam preceded the metallic sound of the lock sliding into place. The sturdy door with large bolt heads in horizontal lines meant no one could break that door down.

A hand split the curtains. Moss-Tow sidestepped the silky fabric and swaggered past Aril to the desk. He took a form from the top of the papers. "Your medical report, Aril-Ess. Lovely sounding name, almost regal. Fit and hardy. And unknown to men." He pulled a blank document from the top drawer, examined it, and scratched his head dramatically. He dipped a pen into the inkwell and began to write. "Let's see now. I'll make you so perfect buyers will fight over you. Sixty years old, youngish, trained as a cook as well as a… uhm, skilled at herbal remedies." He laughed. "My father was a used air-speeder salesman, so this is in my blood."

Strangely, his assessment correctly described her skills, but fell short of the scope of her knowledge.

"Never had sex… Of course, it's true now according to the doctor's report, but won't be true when I present you to the buyer. By the time your new owner learns that little fact, it will be too late. No returns on merchandise!" He wrote more on the form. "We should have a good sale tomorrow just going by the reservations. There are always more bidders who come unannounced." He turned his head toward her. "By the way, the door is locked, and even I can't open it from this side. When I wish to leave, I'll call Ick-San to unbolt." He pulled at his beard and leered. "Let's have a look at the package, eh?"

She stepped back. "What if I scream?"

"The stone walls are thicker than the door. Do you think anyone would hear? I wouldn't mind, though. As a matter of fact, screaming stimulates me." He stepped closer. "Just think how lucky you are, lovely slave. You get to spend time in my soft bed. How many of your sisters in the holding area would trade their hard benches with you? But I have chosen you, my dear."

She stiffened her body and clenched her jaw. "Don't touch me."

Moss-Tow stuck his hand into his robe and brought out a waist-wire control. "If you don't cooperate, I'm afraid I must use this. You won't like it."

Aril tilted her nose upward, the last vestige of fear overcome by anger. "And you, such a large man. You can't handle a girl? You rely on a magnetic pulse?"

Shadows darkened his face. He threw the control to the carpeted floor. "No. I don't need anything but these." He held out his two hands and grabbed her. She pulled away and he grabbed her again, chuckling, teasing with his superior strength. She felt him lessen his grip, thinking she was weak. She wrenched from his grip, went down on her knees and threw her weight against his legs. He fell onto the bed. She flew on top of him and pressed her knuckle into a soft spot just above his ear. He screamed and thrashed his head. His turban tumbled away. The pain of her grip almost immobilized the man. She twined her hands around his neck and forced her knee into his midsection. Sour breath expelled from his lungs. She squeezed her hands over the movement of his throbbing neck in just the right spot until he stopped breathing.

In the lavatory, Aril washed her face and looked in the mirror. She noted her jaw line inherited from Jake Hill and silently thanked him for the defensive training that he had required all palace females to learn. Using her fingers, she combed the dark curls that lay close to her face. Usually, she kept a hair ornament to flatten her curls. The ornament contained a thin, strong blade, a last resort for defense. But it wasn't there, no doubt stolen when she had been asleep from the drugged dart. A bubbling sound caught her attention. She ran to the bed. The noise came from the steam generator. Temperatures dropped at night in the desert. She hadn't noticed the chill. Moss-Tow's body didn't feel as warm as before. She quickly undressed him, heaved him into a resting position, and pulled the covers over him. She didn't relish sleeping with a corpse, but he had been correct—a soft bed surpassed the floor or a bench. From her military training, she took sleep whenever she could. And she would need her rest for the day to come.

Light from the windows woke Aril. Moss-Tow's cold body had turned blue. After a trip to the lavatory, she used the communication device on his desk. "Something has happened," she blubbered. "Send for the doctor. Quick!"

The door lock hissed and clicked. Ick-San pushed the metallic portal open and ran past Aril to Moss-Tow's body. He stared at the corpse and then shot an accusing glare at her. "What happened here?"

Aril put her hands to her face. "We tussled last night…" Her gaze dropped to the floor. "He… He—"

Ick-San rolled his hand. "Yes, yes, I know what he did. Then what?"

She shrugged. "He was cold when I awoke."

Doctor Al-Mot joined them. He touched Moss-Tow's naked body and checked his neck and face.

Ick-San bent over the body. He straightened and turned to Doctor Al-Mot. "What killed him? Better be natural causes."

Al-Mot's expression turned solemn. "By my physician's oath, Moss-Tow died from cessation of circulation." He shot a look at Aril. "He should not have tried to be so lively. The man couldn't handle the activity."

Ick-San bit his lip and nodded.

Doctor Al-Mot pulled the cover over the corpse's head. "We should call Gual-Gur."

Ick-San placed the call. The room stayed silent until footsteps ringing in the eston hallway made the men stiffen. Ick-San's face tightened. Doctor Al-Mot took a few steps backward. Gual-Gur had an impact on them, and he hadn't yet arrived.

Ick-San swallowed hard. "Gual-Gur," he announced and bowed.

Gual-Gur was Moss-Tow's opposite in appearance. Short, slim, and light-colored, his sparse hair almost matched his yellow eyes. His plain leather harness exposed a bony, pale body, looking more like a hanta than a man. Aril tensed.

The small man's movement reminded her of a vicious serpent Jake Hill had once killed on a family outing. Gual-Gur cast a quick glance at Moss-Tow. No emotion played on his face. "I don't care about the details of his death, so don't bother. Now the business is all mine." He cocked his head. "Ick-San, there is to be an auction today?"

"Yes, Gual-Gur."

"Then proceed with it. I'll put you in charge for the sale. Report to *me* from now on."

Gual-Gur left the room and the two men relaxed.

Ick-San stood straighter and braced his shoulders. His face angled upward. He glared at Doctor Al-Mot. "I'll take her to the holding room. You, return to your office, and don't have any more interaction with this slave."

Aril arrived back at the holding area and took her place on the eston bench. The sylph hissed and turned her back. Aril sighed. She had gotten through the night, but what lay ahead? Well, she had handled a detestable slave trader and survived. She would handle the auction, too.

CHAPTER 7

The Yaytoog twin who had met them at the transport walked along the benches, handing out clothing. Most of the garments were typical light and airy white smocks, made from elga fibers, threads made from stalks of the redgrain plants. For a few captives, however, she had something else.

The woman reached into a straw bag draped over her other arm and drew out an intricate leather corselet, decorated with shiny metal studs. She pointed to Aril and handed her the elaborate harness. "Put this on."

Aril turned the harness over for a better look. The top was mostly twin concentric circles of thin leather cords ending in studs over her nipples. The bottoms, starting across her hips, had a studded diamond-shaped opening over her navel. The meager strips barely covered skin, except for a solid crotch. She scowled. "How vulgar."

"Put it on!" the sylph hissed. "Don't get us stung."

The captives stared as Aril removed her blood-marked covering, and her plain leather bottoms, the pain wire still in place. With her eyes on the Yaytoog woman, Aril stepped into the new, more revealing bottoms and adjusted the fastener. The bodice connected in front, utilizing the shiny studs. She sat down, wrenching soft creaks from the newly tanned leathers. A quick glance around the room gave her the opportunity to see three other women wearing similar tasteless garments. Aril tried to make eye contact, but their downcast gazes indicated they did not want friendship.

The tension wrought by the other women in the holding room increased her apprehension. She tried to connect visually with a few of them who still stared. Each one glared, relating blame for the painful reminder they had suffered, and fear for the shocks to come if Aril didn't cooperate.

The Yaytoog shouted orders to the captives. "Line up. Follow me."

Starting at the first bench, the captives fell into line and followed the beast. Aril hesitated—trying to overcome the bits of fear taking root in her mind. The botanist gave Aril a strong push into the queue.

After a short march, the women halted at a room resembling an amphitheater. The captives sat in the slanted benches on one side, and what appeared to be potential buyers, sat on the opposite side.

The first slave auctioned, the Sylph, whose name was announced as Kye-Ren, dainty and attractive, elicited no bids. Ick-San opened the bidding again, with a lower starting price.

"No Sylphs!" a bidder shouted.

"Too delicate," another said.

"Bring out the pretty ones," a gruff voice insisted.

After a few more insults from the bidders, Ick-San took Kye-Ren off the stage and moved on to the next sale—the woman who had been the artist on the *Nautol*. One by one, the captives took the steps to the stage, and each stood under the ray of light shining down from the roof window. When the beast woman pointed to Aril, only the fearful stares of the remaining few captives motivated her toward the shaft of light. Hoots and cheers from the buyers brought a smile to Ick-San's face. Before the man could start the auction, two men, dressed as warriors, stood and quickly approached the platform.

"Stop the auction," the taller of the two demanded.

Aril sighed deeply, letting her breath out through a wide grin. "At last! I am so glad to see you."

The shorter, more muscular warrior cocked his eyebrow at her.

The taller man turned to Ick-San. "I need a word with you."

Ick-San looked him up and down, stopping his gaze at the man's third finger-ring as it rested on his sword. "Of course." Ick-San shuffled away, assisted by the warrior's grip on his elbow.

Aril smiled at the warrior left on the platform next to her. "I hoped we'd be rescued. What about the other girls? Some have already been taken, I think."

The warrior fingered the emblem on his crossed straps. "What are you going on about?"

Aril pointed to his emblem. "Thank goodness you're an Excaliburian Knight. You can shut down this revolting business.

He palmed over the emblem and looked away in the direction of Ick-San, whose flailing arms suggested he was losing an argument.

Aril leaned toward him. "Well? How long are you going to make us all wait?"

The man turned to her. "What are you talking about?"

"Do your duty. You are sworn to uphold the land and end corruption. This nightmare has lasted long enough.

His cheeks tinged red. He swallowed hard and twisted away from her glare. "All I know is. . . I've come with Crown Prince Tim-Ell of Protar to buy a companion. I believe he wants you."

Blood drained from Aril's face. For a moment the world spun. She clenched her jaw and stared at the back of his head. When he cast a glance back to her, she pointed her finger at his face. "Slavery is a punishment decreed only by a judge. We have been abducted. Suffered cruel treatment. You wear the badge of Excalibur, the highest honor a warrior can earn—founded by Jake Hill himself and awarded to the best and most moral men."

The warrior's face reddened.

Aril's upper lip curled thick, and her words turned into a snarl. "You are not fit to wear that insignia."

The crowd began to hoot and demand the auction continue. Shaking his head, Ick-San put his hands in the air until the booing abated. "This slave is sold." The jeers increased, bouncing off the eston walls. Ick-San held his arms up again. "Good folks…we have others, just as exceptional." He shouted over the noise…to no avail.

Gual-Gur came into the amphitheater. By the time he reached the platform, the din had diminished to an angry murmur.

"What is this?" Gual-Gur asked.

"This is Prince Tim-Ell," Ick-San said.

Gual-Gur nodded. "I recognize him. Good day to you, Prince."

The prince squinted at Gual-Gur. "You look familiar. Do I know you?"

"We've not met before, but I know who you are."

Ick-San cleared his throat and pointed to Aril. "The prince has demanded we take this slave out of the auction. He wants her."

"How much has he offered?"

"Uh," Ick-San shrugged. "We hadn't gotten that far."

Gual-Gur's face didn't flinch. "Fifty-thousand limbels."

"Robbery," the prince said.

"Well, then, perhaps we should see what price she gets among them." Gual-Gur swept his arm at the muttering crowd. He turned to Ick-San and whispered, "Why is the sylph still here? I told you to sell her first."

Ick-San swallowed hard. "No takers."

"Well, then, my good prince. I'll make you an offer of a lifetime. Two beautiful slaves for one price."

"Two?"

"Ah, yes. This exquisite slave," he gestured toward Aril, "and the lovely silver girl in the front row."

Prince Tim-Ell shook his head. "I don't want a sylph."

"That's the deal." Gual-Gur's face showed no emotion. "Take it or leave it."

"But," Ick-San interjected, "he's the Prince of Protar."

"That is true." Gual-Gur's mouth turned into an evil smile. "So, for him, only forty-nine thousand limbels."

Prince Tim-Ell stared at Aril. He looked away and faced Gual-Gur. "Very well. Bill the Palace."

"Happily, my Prince. See Eck-Brut," he pointed to the beast woman standing next to the first bench of the captive area. "She'll give you your slaves and their gear."

Aril's nails dug into her palm. Her anger, outflanking her fear, intensified when Ick-San shoved her in the direction of the benches. "Get your hands off me," she growled.

The Yaytoog-like woman held the pain button high. "You! Troublemaker! Stop that."

Aril threatened, "Just wait until—"

The remaining captives screamed, and the sylph went down, turning purple.

"Hey! Stop," the prince said.

The shorter warrior grabbed the control out of the beast's hands. "Don't do that." He put the control on the ground and kneeled to check on the sylph. The crowd, with their low sounds of anger, went silent.

"Perhaps," Ick-San said, "you should take your slaves and go, Prince. Eck-Brut, give them their set of traveling belts."

"Ray-Tan, you'll help the sylph?" Prince Tim-Ell said. "I don't think we'll need these belts."

Ick-San pointed to Aril. "I'd recommend it, sir. I believe this one will bolt at the first opportunity."

The Yaytoog removed Aril's wire belt. The small stone fell, making a muted thud. She sucked a quick breath. No one reacted. Aril let out the breath as the beast-woman attached a new leather belt with flat metal discs on the inside around Aril's waist. Ray-Tan picked the sylph up, her deep purple fading, and held her while the beast-woman disconnected the punishing wire. He carried her as the four of them left the amphitheater.

Aril, ready with a tongue-lashing for the fraudulent knights, suppressed her words. Once again, the specter of fear crept into her mind. She had never been out of control of her environment. She wanted to do something. Although the sylph no longer wore a control belt, enough damage had been done. Aril would bide her time and wait for an opportunity to escape. One was certain to occur.

CHAPTER 8

After a few steps, the prince snapped a lead on Aril's belt. She snarled, making the sound of a baccur, the common four-legged pet, as if she had been in need of a walk.

Ray-Tan carried the sylph down a hallway and on through the holding room. They exited through the door that led to the landing dock.

The transport! Maybe it remained hovering, and the tanks had not been depleted. She could grab the belt control from the prince's hand, wrench the lead from him and bolt to the speeder. In her military stint, she had served as a pilot. She could fly almost anything…even that transport…if it was still there. Not a strong escape plan, but something. She readied for her move as they walked outside.

The transport may have been there, among the scores of speeders moored hovering alongside the dock, the parking area for the bidders. Aril shut her eyes and shook her head.

"Ray-Tan," Prince Tim-Ell said, "stay with the women while I get the speeder."

Ray-Tan nodded. "Are you able to stand?" he asked the sylph.

"I think so," she said in a tinkling, sweet voice. Not the voice she had abused Aril with back in the holding room.

Ray-Tan lowered her to a standing position. "All right?"

She moved her head with a quick shudder. The movement caught the sun's light making her silvery hair shine like strands of silinin, a precious metal used for jewelry. "Thank you," she chimed in a thin musical voice. "My name is Kye-Ren."

Aril rolled her eyes and turned her gaze to the parking lot where the prince stepped over the final speeder and popped into a small craft. The classy little ship, a four-seater, new and sleek, rose above the others and made a transit around the mooring poles. Aril's belt tingled, meaning the belt had a short range. No stone protected her now. She would have to do something about that.

The speeder slowed and hovered just above the dock. The three had to step up to get in. Ray-Tan sat in the back with Kye-Ren, leaving the front passenger seat for Aril. The speeder accelerated softly, gained a low altitude, and sped east, with the sun slightly at their backs. Aril studied the terrain as it passed beneath. The patches of green amid the arid ground turned into fertile valleys separating shiny white cliffs of seensite, the valuable stone used for statuary and architectural decoration. This stone had fine properties, worth a lot of money. The frequent cloudy puffs emanating from the land suggested geothermal pockets, making it easy to harness the power for the mining rigs. Yet, there were no huge steam machines with loud pistons cutting into the cliffs.

As they proceeded, they left the valleys and came upon flat ground, where dark soil gave way to yellow swards of moss, indicating the presence of several ores. Once again, she realized the irony regarding her mission on the *Nautol*. The geology and biology of the area identifiable by the colors and the flora, indicated a topography rich in ore and minerals. But why weren't these areas being mined?

"What is your name?" the prince asked.

Caught off guard, Aril said, "Me?"

"Yes, you. I read it in the sales program, but I forgot. Those programs are usually made up, anyway."

Aril's eyes shifted from the prince to the terrain. Why should she answer him? What problem could her resistance cause? With *her belt* disconnected, that nasty little sylph wasn't going to suffer. Give no quarter, take no quarter, the military way. Perhaps, though, she should take a different tack.

"Aril-Ess." She surprised herself at the hateful way she said it.

"I'm Tim-Ell."

"I know. I heard. Crown Prince of…"

"Protar. What is your problem? You have been purchased by a prince. You only have one person, me, to take care of. All of my slaves have been happy."

Aril flushed and shot him needles with her eyes. She stifled her comment describing his heritage and intelligence.

They flew long enough that the sun had moved to midday position. The slaver lived far from Protar, but Aril formed mental notes of the direction and terrain. When Jake Hill came…

They passed over the outskirts of a city. Tim-Ell piloted the craft to a lower altitude. Most of the structures illustrated the older type of architecture common in Protar. A few buildings were more modern. The craft slowed and dropped again, and soon it landed on the ground next to a two-story square apartment complex.

Tim-Ell turned to Aril, then the passengers in the back. "We're home." He returned his gaze to Aril. His light blue eyes sparkled in the light. Ash blond curls framed his square jaw. His face reminded her of Jerr-Lan, but his body, taller, was slightly less muscular.

The parking area faced the back of the complex. A wall of openwork eston shielded an atrium-like patio. They passed through an arch in the decorative eston and headed for the closest apartment. Tim-Ell fingered a small keyboard, and the glass doors in the back of the apartment slid apart.

Aril backed up into Kye-Ren, who hissed and bared her teeth.

"Whoa," Tim-Ell said. "We'd better keep these two apart. "Here, Ray-Tan. You take the sylph. You don't have a slave."

Ray-Tan's eyes widened. "I don't need a slave."

"Well, you've got one now."

"But, Tim, I, I…" He cast his eyes away for a moment. "Yes, Prince."

"Oh, come on. I'm not giving a command here. I'm giving you a gift."

"A gift I don't want."

The sylph folded her arms over her chest.

"No offense, Kye-Ren," Ray-Tan stammered. "I've never had a slave, and…"

"My gift to you," Tim-Ell said with a laugh. "Enjoy. Now, come with me, Aril-Ess, slave with an attitude."

Aril hesitated, watching the sylph disappear with her new master into the adjacent apartment. Squaring her shoulders, Aril entered the dwelling, hearing the whoosh of steam pressure on the door's mechanism.

Tim-Ell unbuckled his sword and clanged it on the eston table. He removed his crossed leather chest harness and placed it next to the sword. He stretched his arms and rubbed his neck. His back muscles flexed; his biceps tightened. Aril widened her nostrils and looked away, unimpressed. Jerr-Lan's body surpassed this man's physique. Jerr-Lan! Gone. She had had her chance with him, many times. Other women her age took mates, started families. Why hadn't she?

"This is the kitchen," Tim-Ell said, strolling into the next room. He opened the metallic cold box and removed a glass bottle. After twisting off the cap, he waited for the foam to subside and took a long drink. Holding the bottle up, he pointed to Aril. "Care for a bit?"

"I don't drink erbate."

He nodded. "A man's drink."

Thirst parched her throat. She went to the cold box and peered in. "There's only erbate. Is that what you eat, too?"

He laughed. "There's some other stuff in here." He pulled out several stalks of green lunt; most of the leaves had turned brown. "This has to go." The lunt made a thump in the waste can.

"So, what do you eat?"

"Whatever the landlady fixes in the dining room. That's why I took this place—so I don't have to fool with food. None of my companions have been good at cooking." Tim-Ell pointed. "That's the living room."

Aril swiveled her head to look at the next room. Bare, except for wall sofas padded with Illie fur. The same fur lay on the floor in front of a fireplace. A lack of ash suggested it had not been used. Undecorated, the place seemed cold, echoic.

"That's the bedroom," he said, pointing the other way.

"Where do I sleep?" Aril asked.

Tim-Ell chuckled. "Well, it's only one bedroom, you see."

"What I'd *like to see* is a place for me to sleep—away from that room." She indicated the one bedroom.

He narrowed his eyes. "You can sleep on the couch. If you want privacy, I have an empty pantry. Use the cushions from the couch and sleep there. My door will be open to you."

Aril sniffed. "Not a chance."

He laughed harder. "Why wouldn't you want to sleep in that fine bed?"

Aril lifted her chin. "I can think of one, big, ugly reason."

"Ugly? I've been called other things, but never that. Besides, I'm the Prince. People don't talk to me like that."

She regretted her comment. He wasn't ugly, in fact, he resembled Jerr-Lan but he participated in illegal slave sales and mocked the knighthood.

Tim-Ell put his hand on his hip. "What is your problem? I'll treat you better than those other men who wanted to bid on you. I'm a high warrior and a prince."

"High warrior?" She ran to the dining table and picked up his leathers. Tapping the Excalibur insignia, she sneered. "How did you possibly get this? Did you ambush a true knight, or maybe fifty of your men took him down? Then you stole his medallion?"

Prince Tim-Ell walked hard to the table and snatched the medallion out of her hand. "I earned this. I have studied many years to win Protar's swordsmanship award."

She shook her head and shot him her worst look. "A knight must be excellent in swordsmanship, but there's more to it, and the official who awarded this would know the proviso."

"My father, the king, awarded me that honor."

"I see. How did he get the medals to award? They only come from Cadmia, directly from—"

"Yes, yes, I know from the great and powerful Jake Hill."

His voice had contempt when he spoke of the Planetary Prince. Aril stifled her urge to attack him, to go for his head, then his neck like she had against Moss-Tow.

"Not that I answer to you, slave, but Protar is a member of the Planetary Alliance. The Cadmia ambassador gave us these medals."

"Oh, but he didn't describe the requirements needed to win the medals?"

"Enough," Tim-Ell said. "I'm hungry. Come with me."

Food. Aril realized how hungry she was, and it wouldn't accomplish anything to further aggravate the imposter knight. Her military training told her to eat when she could, sleep when she could. Maybe she would sleep with another corpse this very evening.

CHAPTER 9

"I'm starving," Aril said. "But…" She looked down her body at the skimpy leather bra and bottoms. "Is there something I can put over this?"

"I like that," Tim-Ell said. "It looks good."

She blew a quick breath out of her nostrils. "And you want every other man to ogle at me?"

"Do I mind?" Tim-Ell furrowed his eyebrows. "Not really."

"Suppose someone spills hot food on me, and I get burned. Then I can't work efficiently."

Tim-Ell laughed. "You have an attitude, don't you? I should make you eat with only your bottoms on for that."

Aril flushed. Modesty wasn't a question. In the private apartments of Cadmia's palace, the residents frequently wore scant clothing. Her near nakedness offended her now because she couldn't choose. She wanted control even if over what she wore. Crossing her arms in front of her chest, she stared at him.

He sighed. "In the closet of the bedroom, you will find slave smocks. My other companion didn't use them. She *liked* to wear the skimpy things. But hurry, I want to eat before the landlady stops serving."

Aril dashed into the bedroom and threw open the closet door. Next to a warrior's dress uniform of leather and silinin, hung three plain fabric tunics—white, pink, and blue. She pulled the blue one from its hook.

Aril followed Tim-Ell across the sandy patio to the front quad of the building, where a large kitchen and dining room took up the space of two apartments. A few residents ate at stone tables. Tim-Ell sat and pointed to a seat across from him.

An older woman wearing a dirty apron smiled. "Good afternoon, Prince. Who is this?" The woman looked at Aril.

"My new girl," Tim-Ell said. "How about some food?"

The woman slogged away, shuffling fabric slippers on the eston tiles and returned with two plates and two small bowls balanced on a grimy tray. She put a mug with utensils next to fabric napkins with holes in them.

Tim-El and Aril had entered from the rear glass doors. Across the room, a crack of light seeped through the front door.

"Do a lot of people eat here? Aril asked.

"Most of the tenants," he said, cutting a piece of meat. "Why?"

"Just curious." She eyed the door. They had circled the building before landing, allowing her a good look at the front. There were enough nearby buildings to shield her if she could get free. But the belt...she would have to get the control for it or convince him to take it off her waist. She'd have to be a little nicer to charm him into trusting her.

"Are you looking at the door?" Tim-Ell asked. "Planning your escape?"

Snagged. "Truth is," she said, looking straight into his eyes, "I *will* escape, so why don't you live up to your Excalibur values and free me?"

"Free you? I just bought you at an exorbitant price, and I had to take a worthless sylph in the deal. Forget it. But I'll be watching, so you won't get a chance to escape."

"How well do you think you can keep guard?"

He smiled. "Please...I'm a warrior. I think I can keep a girl..." He eyed her for a moment. "...even a strong and fit one, from running away."

"You don't think I'm a threat?"

"You could do some damage, or cause trouble, but nothing I can't prevent."

"Think so?"

"You have quite a mouth. Your words could get you in trouble."

Aril slumped and nodded. She'd been told that, many times by Jake Hill. She ran her finger under the belt. "If you are so good at watching me, will you take this belt off?"

"When we are in the apartment, you don't have to wear it. The door locks are coded—you aren't going anywhere when we're in there. Why don't you keep quiet and eat something? Let me enjoy my meal."

Aril took a spoon and tried the thick green liquid in the bowl. She barely recognized the taste, but after a few mouthfuls, she identified it as grain soup.

The meat on the plate had shreds of gristle surrounding the chunks. The tuber still had granules of soil on its skin.

"You enjoy this? I can't eat this slop." Her spoon hit the stone tabletop.

"Maybe…" He struggled to chew, "Not enjoy, exactly, but… it's filling."

She crossed her arms over her chest. "Do you think the food is fit for royalty?"

He took another bite and shrugged. "Food *is* better at the palace."

"I should think so. Do you have baccurs there?"

"Of course, big hunting baccurs. Why?"

"Maybe you should take this meat to them. My bet is the baccurs would sniff and walk away because *they eat* better than this."

He took a breath and let his shoulders drop. "This is what the landlady serves. What do you suggest?"

"I suggest you take me to the market tomorrow to buy decent food."

"You know how to cook?"

"You didn't read the sales brochure?" She twitched her jaw.

He laughed. "I told you I don't believe most of the stuff in the catalog. It's like buying a used speeder…they tell you what you want to hear."

"I'll cook from now on. I don't want to be poisoned." She looked around and sneered. "Why would you, a prince, live in a place like this?"

"My needs are few as living quarters. And living here is better than being in the palace. Prince Tim-Ell took another bite, made a face, and spit the meat out. "Pass the butter and bread."

Aril handed him a slice and held up a dish. "If this is lakin butter, I'm… well, it's not. I don't know what it really is."

He bit into it, looked at it, and put it down. "The market it is. Tomorrow." He wiped his hands on the threadbare napkin. "I'm done here. You can make me tashberry butter and jelly sandwich."

They returned to the apartment via the patio, and he keyed in the lock that opened the glass doors. Aril saw the first and last digits. Four more to memorize.

"Now that we are in the apartment, take off my belt," Aril said.

"Excuse me?"

She modified her tone. "Please remove my belt as you said you would."

Tim-Ell took the small key from his waist pouch and touched it to the lock. Aril's restraint strap unlatched and fell on the floor. She kicked it aside and scorned it.

In the kitchen, Aril rummaged through mostly empty cabinets until she found a fabric bag with hard bread. On the shelf below, she found two small earthenware pots, one with tashberry butter and the other the jelly.

"I'll need a knife. A sharp one," Aril said, "to cut this bread. It's as hard as eston."

Tim-Ell left his place at the table and came to the kitchen. He pulled at his chin. "Yeah…I don't think it's a good idea for you to have a sharp knife. I'll cut it." He took three knives from a drawer, selected one, and set the others aside. The bread cracked and flaked as he forced the blade through. He tossed the bread chunk into the trash with a thunk. "Just give me a spoon." He took the knives and disappeared into the bedroom, closing the door behind him. When he returned, Aril brought the pots and two spoons to the table. They ate in silence.

While she washed the utensils, the whoosh of the steam lock caught Aril's attention. Ray-Tan entered. "Pardon the interruption, prince."

"No interruption," Tim-Ell said. "What's happening?"

"A problem at the barracks. I need to go there."

"I'll go, too." Tim-Ell said. "Give me a minute." He withdrew into the bathroom.

Feeling Ray-Tan's stare, she wiped her hands smartly on a dishcloth. "What do you want?"

"To tell you that escaped slaves suffer a harsh punishment."

"And what's that?"

"Death," Ray-Tan said.

CHAPTER 10

Aril swallowed hard. A prickle of fear ran down her spine. She kept her face passive, something she could control. "Thanks for the warning."

Tim-Ell came from the bathroom, strapped on his sword, checked the dagger at his ankle, and adjusted his chest harness. "Ready?"

Ray-Tan turned to the glass doors. Tim-Ell joined him, but as the door whooshed open with a gust of steam, the prince turned to Aril. "Don't do anything stupid. All right?"

Stupid. Jake Hill was the last person to use that term regarding her choices. No one else would dare. Her mother, sweet and sensitive, rarely raised her voice. Her father, who gave her the Earthman's gene, was quiet and studious. Even in spats with her brother, Hin-Cal, she hadn't heard that kind of disparagement. But she had no time to waste being offended. She needed to check out the apartment. And the door locks.

She started with the kitchen cabinets, this time slowly and deliberately, not the hasty search for the tashberry products. Finding nothing of use on the shelves, she next gave her attention to the equipment—standard cooking apparatuses—steam-heated oven and stovetop, cool-box. Cronanta's plentiful geo-thermal fuel ran everything from air temperature, cooking, refrigeration, and regulating the planet's most precious resource, water. She didn't see anything in the kitchen, short of spreading knives, forks, and spoons. She went to the bedroom.

Two nightstands flanked the large bed with lamps attached to the wall above. The prince left the soft glowing steam lights on, wasting precious energy. These lamps used soft steam light globes, but a switch by the doorway illuminated a ceiling strongium bulb, the expensive glowing powder coating a glass globe that burned bright with applied heat. Only the richest homes had these, and this apartment complex was a dump. Curious. But not what she needed to focus on.

The knives. Where would *she* have hidden them? Pulling away the unmade sheets, she kneeled and examined the levin-wood bed frame. A barely noticeable crack made her smile. She pressed on the wood and it popped open, a hidden drawer—with the three knives. Speaking of *stupid*...was the Crown Prince as dense as he was immoral? She'd better leave them there until she was ready. Good, she was making progress. Now to the closet.

A dress uniform hung on one of the hooks. Typical of high military ranks, its leather breastplate and paneled skirt used ornaments fashioned in silinin and tellas, the soft yellow metal that all of Cronanta's financial system was based upon. On a shelf above the hooks, the prince's helmet gleamed with the shiny precious metals of nobility, the same kind helmets worn by the officers of Cadmia's guards...like Jerr-Lan's helmet. She closed her eyes. Jerr-Lan had been such a good friend. If he were here...What would he say? He'd tell her not to grieve and get busy with exploring her escape options. Right, then. She checked the closet. Nothing useful there.

In the living room, the bare walls and plain furniture offered nothing. She needed to examine the door locks. From the inside, the locks appeared to be standard, the kind most apartments and homes used. Theft was uncommon in most nations, but not unheard of. On Cronanta, where inhabitants lived as long as a thousand years, assassination was more frequent than theft.

This tenant, a high prince, needed better security. Anyone with a small steam cannon could enter from the open doorways to the patio and blast the door locks. If an assassin took him by surprise, the prince didn't have a chance. Did the prince depend on his neighbor, Ray-Tan, for backup? Crown Prince Tim-Ell was not safe in this location. Why had no one noticed that? While she didn't care about the safety of that arrogant fool, she lived there now, and it wasn't safe for her. Perhaps she should point out the lapse in protection to the prince. Perhaps she would enjoy that.

After another sweep of the apartment, she realized how tired she was. It had only been slightly more than a day since the *Nautol* had crashed. She lay down on the Illie fur cushions on the wall sofa and fell asleep.

She woke to sound of the steam lock then, voices. It took a few moments for her to sit up. She stretched and noticed the dim lighting. The sun's slanted rays turned the white eston walls a pale orange. The metallic sound of weaponry clanging on the table startled her. She hit the floor and sped to the dining room.

Prince Tim-Ell grinned. "Still here, I see."

Aril stifled her words.

Ray-Tan looked out the glass doors. "Dinner time." He sighed. "I wonder what slop the lovely landlady will regale us with tonight."

Aril smiled inwardly. At least someone else agreed with her assessment of the fare.

"Why didn't you stay and eat at the barracks?" Tim-Ell asked.

Ray-Tan gave him a questioning look. "I go where you go. Plus, Kye-Ren needs to eat. She's probably rested enough by now."

Rested? Kye-Ren. That nasty little sylph… And this warrior cared. These Protarians were a mystery, paradoxical. The prince said that Protar was a member of the Planetary Alliance. She doubted it; she hadn't heard that country's name in any of the official assemblies she'd attended. But that didn't mean anything. She attended those meetings off and on at the behest of grandsire. Only the most provocative incidents with countries had interested her. If Protar *was* a bona fide member, then a Cadmia ambassador lived here. If an ambassador from Cadmia resided in Protar, then he would be aware of the illegal slavery and the mockery of the Excalibur. She would find out.

Tim-Ell held up the anti-escape belt. "Supper?"

"I'd rather eat tashberry butter and jelly," Aril said with a sour face.

"From a spoon," the prince teased.

"Why not?"

"You are going with me. To dinner. In the dining room. Stand still while I fasten this belt."

What could she do? She elevated her elbows and let the prince snap the belt. He touched the keypad on the glass door locks, and the three of them, the prince, Aril, and Ray-Tan, went next door. The sylph came out with her silvery hair pulled back and her smock clean. She must have washed it while she *rested*. Her upper lip raised at the corner when she cast her gaze to Aril.

Aril sneered back at the delicate creature. The four of them headed to the dining area.

The dinner of unidentified meat, gooey tubers, and marginally edible green vegetables tasted as bad as the previous food. The bread, without the unknown butter-stuff, bested the meal. The landlady wore the same grimy apron and approached Tim-Ell and Aril with a pitcher of wine. "Special for you, my Prince." She glowered at Aril. "And, you, too, I suppose."

The prince quaffed it down in several sips. Aril had never experienced inferior wine—until now. Aril stopped at few sips. Tim-Ell took another offered by the less-than-clean landlady. *How can he drink this swill?* A prince, the highest noble, next to the king. What kind of class was that?

One taste of the dessert, a chalky, thin-flavored custard, proved the final insult. Aril shoved her bowl away.

Tim-Ell took another bite and did the same. "Supper's over." He rose. Aril followed. Ray-Tan and Kye-Ren walked behind.

"Good night," Tim-Ell bade his friend when they got to their apartment door. The prince walked on.

Aril took a last look at the sylph, who made an ugly hand gesture.

"Pleasant dreams," Aril said nastily. She caught up with the prince, who was keying in the lock code.

In the apartment, Aril cocked her head and caught the prince's eye.

His eyebrows pulled together. "What?"

"Remove my belt. Please."

"Hmm. Right. It wouldn't be good if you got that wet."

"Why would I get it wet?"

"Because you will now draw my bath."

"What?"

"Your sales description does not mention a hearing problem. Do you require motivation for obeying orders?"

Motivation? The shock belt? The twin emotions of fear and fury fought for words in Aril's mind. "You'd hit the control and shock me for asking a question?"

He scratched his head. "I've never shocked a slave in my life. But I've never encountered one so…"

"Recalcitrant?"

"I'm not sure what that means, but—"

"You're the Crown Prince. Didn't you go to the university?"

He stuck his chin up higher. "Of course, I did."

"But you were out cavorting during vocabulary class?"

His eyes narrowed. He jerked the belt from her waist. "Go…draw…my…bath…Slave."

His tone surprised her. She turned and headed for the bathroom. The fixtures were standard, hot and cold. The water flow concerned her. It gushed into the tub, rather than the trickle agreed by the Planetary Council to preserve the precious liquid. Even if this area, Protar, had plentiful stores, the planet's needs outweighed the pleasures of one country. And, that patio…dry and pebbly…why wasn't bath water diverted, draining into the area for grass, or important plants?

Aril filled the tub one third, as the amount agreed upon by the council for bathing. She placed towels and soap on the small table near the tub.

Tim-Ell came in and stripped his leather harness and bottoms. He stretched his arms outward. "I'm a bit drowsy. I think I'll go to bed early."

She tried to avert her gaze and found it impossible as he stood before her. She could see why he had no problems interesting ladies. But not this lady. She forced herself to look away.

"Ahem," the prince said. "That's all of the water?"

"You need more to get clean?"

"You are not a very good slave," he said, he removed his ankle dagger, putting it under a towel, and threw one leg over the edge of the tub. He slid into the water. "Wash me."

"What?" This time she questioned him because she felt sleepy.

"There's that hearing problem again. If I have to get out of the tub…"

She stepped nearer and dipped a cloth into the water. The soap smelled pleasant as she rubbed it into the cloth. It lathered immediately when she applied it to his shoulders. Keeping her facial expression uniform, she washed his body, including his many attributes, assuming an air of disinterest, which, in fact, was true. She rinsed him with the spray hose. He stood, and she dried him.

"Now, that was nice, wasn't it?" the prince asked, yawning.

"For you? Yes." She left the bathroom and sat on the wall couch in the living room.

Prince Tim-Ell obviously slept without clothes but had his ankle dagger in place. He came into the living room and announced. "I'm going to bed now. Feel free to join me. It's a comfortable bed." He yawned and stretched.

"I'll never be that uncomfortable," she answered with quiet disgust.

"You know, I'm so weary I'm not up to dealing with you tonight. But my door will be open if you get tired of those cushions and furs on the floor."

He walked into the bedroom and swung the door wide.

Aril took the bedding from the couch and threw it onto the pantry floor. She reclined on the soft Illie fur and immediately fell asleep. That night she dreamed someone stood over her. She dreamed of whispered male voices and several figures who crept around the apartment.

CHAPTER 11

The sun shining through the glass doors cast a beam of light into the pantry where Aril slept. She woke and sat up. The still of the apartment contrasted with her dreams of men wandering about the place. The dream memories pricked her with unease.

In the kitchen, a kettle for brewing sat on the counter, but there was nothing there to make fresh keela. During her search the day before, she hadn't noticed any ground keela beans to brew, the morning staple for most of Cronanta. Perhaps she had missed the necessity in her hunt for an escape item. She checked the cabinets.

"What are you looking for?"

Tim-Ell's voice gave her a start. He obviously knew how to move like a warrior. She'd grant him that. And, obviously he liked to walk around sans garments, except for the ankle knife. She thought of her own ankle dagger and wished she had it.

"Keela. Don't you drink that in the morning?"

"Of course. In the morning, and afternoons, sometimes. We can get some at breakfast."

Aril felt her top lip moving into a sneer. "In the dining room, right?"

"Either that or go without. I'm going to have some. If you don't want any, you can sit and watch me drink my cup." He turned toward the bedroom, this time his steps sounding on the eston flooring. She'd have to give the landlady's keela a try.

He returned to the kitchen in his Crown Prince leathers. "Here," he said holding the slave belt, "I'm putting this on you."

She huffed a quick breath through her nose and then raised her arms to let him fasten the belt.

In the dining room, the smell of brewing keela gave Aril a small but tangible sense of comfort.

The landlady served Tim-Ell his cup and glared at Aril. "Get your own, slave."

Gladly, you ugly... As Aril served herself, she noticed an old woman sweeping the floor. She wore a slave tunic and must have been six hundred years by the look of her. "Excuse me."

The woman looked up with rheumy eyes. "Yes?"

"Aren't you too old to be a slave?"

The woman's face sagged. "Apparently not."

"How long do you have left in your slave term?"

"Slave term? What's that?"

"The number of years you were sentenced."

The old woman shut her eyes and shook her head. "You're new, aren't you? From somewhere else. There is no *term* in Protar. Slavery is forever."

Aril lost the grip on her cup, spilling the keela. "Forever?"

The landlady gave the old woman a smart slap. "Stop talking. Do your work." She turned to Aril and pointed toward Tim-Ell. "He's too good to his slaves. But," she poked Aril's chest with her finger, "when you are near me, you will do as you are told. Understand? This is my only warning. Clean that spill right now."

Aril took the rag the old woman offered and wiped up the keela. She refilled her cup and returned to the prince's side. Sipping the bitter, low-quality brew, she considered what she'd just heard—a lifetime of slavery. Now she had a new motivation to escape.

Soon Ray-Tan and Kye-Ren came into the dining room. The time the sylph spent in Ray-Tan's care had produced beneficial effects. She looked groomed. Her silver hair was arranged in curls on top of her head. She wore a clean tunic with a leather tie, her tunic gathered to emphasize her breasts. She smiled at Ray-Tan, wide enough to show her pointy little incisors. Then her gaze caught Aril, and her expression changed into a death-wish glare.

Aril did not allow her emotion to show, but it became harder when she noticed that the sylph still did not wear a slave belt. Kye-Ren's glare moved to Aril's waist and her grim-lipped look turned into a nasty smirk.

Aril turned to the prince. "As soon as we're done with this…breakfast…we should go to the market."

Tim-Ell took a swig from his cup and made a face. He pushed the half-eaten plate away. "I don't see how your cooking could be worse than this, so let's go."

They left the dining area, walking through the patio. Aril halted at the apartment's glass doors.

Tim-Ell stopped and turned. "What are you waiting for?"

"Two things," she said. "Your royal leathers might intimidate people at the market. And I don't want to wear this belt."

"I don't mind intimidating people. And I do mind you trying to escape."

"Leathers that don't indicate your status would be better among the common folks. And, this belt…It isn't safe for me. If we separate too far, the mechanism will shock me."

"That's the point," Tim-Ell said.

"If the market is crowded, we may accidentally—"

"So, stay close."

Aril put her hands on her hips and glared at him. "I don't want to take the chance. We'll just have to eat that swill instead of good fresh keela and soft breads, and tender meats, and—"

"Stop. You'll wear the belt, and you will come with me to the market."

Aril held up her hand. "How about if I swear that while we're at the marketplace, I won't try to escape."

Tim-Ell shook his head. "How do I know I can trust you?"

Aril's face flushed. "I'm no liar. If I give my word, I'll not go against it." She put her hand on his Excalibur insignia. "I pledge it on the most honorable institution on the planet." Even though *he* didn't live up to the vows of the Knighthood, she thought better of pointing that out at this minute.

The prince pulled at his chin. "I don't know."

She took a step closer, grabbing his attention with her eyes. "Hasn't someone ever pledged on that emblem for an oath? Have you?"

He nodded.

"Then take my pledge today. Just for the market."

Tim-Ell let out a long breath. "I hope I'm not sorry for this. You know what could happen."

"I know," Aril said. "Horrible." Once again, she stifled speaking her opinion of Protar's slavery laws.

They entered the apartment, and she stood with her arms lifted. He pressed the control and released the belt.

"Your leathers?"

He pondered for a moment, nodded, and headed for the bedroom to change.

In his plain leathers, he walked to the back door. She touched his shoulder. "Aren't you going to take your purse?"

"I charge all things to the palace. The vizier pays my bills."

"The vizier?" She sniffed her distaste. "Don't you have limbels of your own?"

He nodded.

"Take them. You aren't wearing the prince's dress now. Do you usually go around without money?" She withheld her opinions regarding a king still using a vizier, a single person who speaks for a king. Too many viziers had become corrupted. Jake Hill abolished the practice long before.

Prince Tim-Ell fastened a hand sized leather pouch to his waistband and opened the glass doors. Aril, without the hated shock belt, accompanied him to the patio and out past the open, unguarded portal. They emerged in the back of the complex where the snappy new speeder waited. They got in.

The craft flew over fields of redgrain, the tallest and most luxurious Aril had ever seen. The dark blue cast of the soil, and the redgrain's fertility suggested the ground contained—

The aircar accelerated slamming Aril back into the seat. "What are you doing?" she screamed.

"Going fast!" He tilted his head back. Laughing, he said, "Get used to it!"

CHAPTER 12

The aircar set down smoothly on the grassy lot, next to other crafts. Aril and Tim-Ell headed for the tents and noises of the marketplace, entering through a gap in the fabric pavilions. Aril took in the surroundings and noted the ease with which she could slip away from the prince. Her oath not to escape nagged her. She must get free at all costs, even if she had sworn on the symbol she held dear. The symbol, she rationalized, that did not carry the same weight of honor here in graft-ridden Protar as it did in the cities and countries of the globe that adhered to the Knighthood principles.

People moved in all directions, stopping at the seller's stalls, sometimes blocking the currents of moving shoppers. This was her best chance. She tensed, waiting for a break in the line.

Just as she gauged her movements to blend in with the crowds, someone screamed. The masses of people moved aside, and a young man dressed in a slave's sarong bolted past. A man dressed like a trader chased the boy, yelling for him to stop. The youth's pace increased. The man halted, calmly took aim with a dagger and let it fly. The dagger embedded into the boy's back, its bloody tip emerging through his chest. The boy's legs crumpled. He fell.

Aril turned to Tim-Ell with her arms flailing. "Do something!"

"What do you think I can do?"

"That man is a killer. Arrest him."

He shook his head and grimaced. "Such a shame, but the police will take care of the problem. Besides, what it looked like to me was a slave attempting to escape. Stopping a slave by any means is legal."

"Any means? Murder is murder."

He sighed. "That boy could have lived for a long time. However—"

Aril got close to the prince's face and spoke with clenched teeth. "Don't tell me murder is justified when apprehending a slave."

Tim-Ell pushed her back a few inches. "All right, I won't tell you that, even if it's true and unfortunate. But see? If the boy had a slave belt on, he wouldn't have tried anything so stupid." He cocked his eyebrows at her.

She got the message. Would he let his dagger fly if she bolted? Did she want to find out? She dropped her shoulders and let out the breath she'd held since the boy fell. Perhaps she would wait for another opportunity to take her freedom, thus keeping her promise.

The crowd moved a bit slower and talked with less enthusiasm. Would anyone complain about the abuse? Would it make a difference? Aril's need to leave clashed with her less-than-confident feeling she could get out with her life intact. She hated Protar; she hated Tim-Ell. She hated the swill she'd been consuming, and *that* situation she had control over. Her attention focused on the booths.

She found spices and condiments at one merchant, fresh fruits and vegetables at another. The smell of freshly roasted keela beans made her mouth water. She inhaled the perfumed aroma as the merchant scooped warm grounds from the hopper. For a moment, she closed her eyes and banished reality to imagine sitting at the large table in the palace with her family. The image lasted for a few moments, until the logical part of her personality insisted she return to actual circumstances. The fantasy ebbed and she opened her eyes. The merchant held a cloth bag for her. His expression asked for the payment. She looked from side to side but didn't see Tim-Ell. *He wasn't there. She could make her break!*

She held up one finger to the merchant to tell him to wait. Crowds of shoppers ambled by. If she didn't run, just blended in, would she be obvious?

"Looking for your escape route?"

She flushed. Tim-Ell came from behind her, took a bite of buttered bread, and handed her a second piece. Aril didn't answer the question.

"Excuse me," the keela merchant said and wiggled the bag.

Tim-Ell held the bread piece in his teeth and opened his money pouch.

The bread was delicious, still warm, and the rich lakin butter had sunk into the soft white interior. Aril almost went back into her trance. Instead, she followed Tim-Ell into the current of shoppers until he stopped at a meat vender.

Aril stepped up to the display case. A large hunk of lakin meat hung on a hook. The price was as attractive as the roast.

"We'll take that one," Aril said.

The merchant squinted at Aril and then looked to Tim-Ell who nodded assent. "I'll bring it into the back and wrap it."

Aril leaned over the display case toward the butcher. "Wrap it here."

He pointed to the interior of his tent. "I wrap the packages in there."

Aril increased her volume. "Bring the paper out and wrap it where I can see you."

He glared at Aril and looked expectantly at Tim-Ell.

"Wrap it," she said, "where I know I will get this piece and not some inferior meat you will switch."

The butcher's face turned red. "Warrior! Your slave has gotten out of control. How dare she speak to me in this way? Punish her for impertinence."

Aril stepped between the merchant and Tim-Ell. Her glare caught the merchant's eyes. "This is Crown Prince Tim-Ell. He doesn't discuss his personal business with common merchants. You will deal with me, and I have told you what to do."

Tim-Ell let out a mild chuckle.

The butcher eyed the prince. When he spied the royal signet ring, he bowed his head. "My apologies, Prince. I will bring the paper out and wrap this meat for you." He scurried to the back and brought back a length of paper. Handing Aril the package, he asked, "What is the prince doing here at the market?"

Aril took the bundle. "Checking on his people like all good sovereigns should. He is making sure the merchants are honest and fair."

The butcher swallowed hard. "That will be 30 limbels."

"Charge it to the palace," Tim-Ell said.

Aril turned to him. "I think you should pay him in limbels now. Who knows when or if the palace will pay? Although he tried to cheat you, he needs his money now."

Tim-Ell flinched at her words but nodded. He dug into his pouch and gave the money to her, and she passed it on the butcher. The merchant muttered, "Thank you."

As they walked away, Tim-Ell complained. "I'm almost out of limbels."

"I think we're done here," Aril said. She held out half of the packages to him. He paused, looked at both of his hands, then carried the bundles out to the speeder.

The craft touched down in the back of the apartment complex where two men leaned against a tree and watched Aril and Tim-Ell unload. The men scrutinized their movements as they took the purchases into the patio.

Aril peeked around the openwork wall of the back entrance. "Do you know those men?"

"What men?"

"You didn't notice the men who watched your every move?"

Tim-Ell looked through the stone lattice surrounding the entrance. "No. Not familiar."

"This place is unsafe," Aril said. "Anyone could enter this atrium at any time. A small steam cannon could take down the glass doors."

"What do you know about steam cannons?"

"I know they shot down the ship I was in." She glared at him. "After which I was illegally abducted and sold."

"You are a prisoner of war, subject to slavery."

"Who said? What war? And enemy warriors aren't made into slaves anymore."

"Protar still takes slaves of enemy warriors. And I only know what your sale papers say: that is, you are a prisoner-of-war slave."

They stopped at the glass doors. Tim-Ell punched in the code and the doors opened.

"So," Aril said, "all of a sudden you believe what the sale papers say?"

He put his part of the burden on the stone dining table. "Make keela. Do it now. Do it without talking."

Aril sighed. She could use a cup herself, and the conflict had wearied her. She put the grounds in the kettle and turned on the steam. Movement from the patio caught her eye.

The two men had left the tree near the parking lot. They sat under the shade of a tree in the patio, a place where they could see into the apartment. They strained their necks to see through the glass doors.

CHAPTER 13

Aril placed two cups of keela on the table. The smell permeated the apartment. Tim-Ell came from the bedroom, sat at the table, and took a long sip from his cup. "Tastes good. Did you do something special?"

I would have if I'd had a chance to buy poison. She shook her head and tried hers. The rich taste trickled down her throat, and the flavor increased as she breathed deeply. She put her head back to enjoy what she had longed for. When she brought the cup to her lips again, she glanced outside and noticed those men, one tall and thin, the other short and stocky, still watching the apartment. She shuddered from memories of the dreams she'd had the night before.

Tim-Ell drank the rest of his cup in silence. He stood. "Cook dinner. I'm going to find Ray-Tan." He keyed the glass door and it slid open. The two men outside looked at each other and ambled away.

As soon as Tim-Ell disappeared beyond the openwork portal, Aril tried the doors and the windows, including the high ones in the living room. All were locked tight, even the window in the bathroom. The knives were still in their hidden place imbedded in the mattress frame. They'd be there when she needed them.

She'd have to be patient regarding her escape back to Cadmia, but not now. She focused on the meal.

By the time Tim-Ell returned, the apartment smelled of roasted meat and savory vegetables.

"Uh, huh," Tim-Ell took a deep breath. "Your exorbitant price may yet pay off."

They ate without speaking. It had to be the finest meal Aril had ever had. Of course, it wasn't, but the quality of the food brought a bit of stability, and more important, some control over her existence.

Tim-Ell patted his furrowed abs. "Delicious. After you clean up, you can polish my sword and dagger."

A wave of energy surged through Aril's body. She sat up straight.

"Just kidding," he said with a smirk. "Later, I'll take my things next door and let that sylph clean them. Ray-Tan says she's meticulous at caring for his weapons."

Aril's nostrils flared. Very funny. But, if she couldn't get hold of the weaponry, at least Kye-Ren would have extra work to do. Small payback, but something.

After Aril cleaned the kitchen, she sat down at the stone table. A noise at the glass door made her turn. The landlady stood outside with a tray.

"If you give me the code," Aril shouted into the living room, "I can answer the door."

"Sure," Tim-Ell said on his way to the back door. "I'll be giving you that code right away."

The landlady stepped into the kitchen. "I noticed you weren't in the dining room tonight. And such a shame, Prince." She smiled sweetly, "I made a special wine toddy for you." She took a glass from the tray and offered it to Tim-Ell. "Since you weren't there to enjoy it, I've brought it to you." A smile still on her lips, she turned her gaze to Aril. "And one for you, too, my dear. Enjoy."

My dear? "Thank you," Aril quickly took the tray. "We'll enjoy it later and return the tray." She gave Tim-Ell a quick glance and moved her eyes to the door.

"Yes, uh, thanks," Tim-Ell said, and opened the door.

The landlady huffed twice before she left.

"So, what was that about?" Tim-Ell said.

"Don't drink it."

"Why not?"

Aril took the glass from him. "Throw it out and go to bed as usual."

He laughed. "Ah, I see. Eager to join me? And no wine? I guess I'm the stimulant!"

"I'm serious. And I will never join you. Are you the type of brute who rapes helpless women? Do you force your slaves into—?"

"Enough. I've never forced a woman into my bed, ever. And as for the drink, if it's poisoned, wouldn't that suit your purposes?"

"Indeed, it would. But I'm not going to drink mine, and if something happens because you drank your draft, I don't want the blame put on me."

Tim-Ell paused. "Smart." He dumped both drinks down the sink. Shaking his head, he went into the bedroom. The door swung wide.

Aril made her bed in the pantry, leaving the door cracked so she could keep watch in the dimly lit apartment. From her vantage point, she could see the glass door facing the patio. She didn't worry about falling asleep; her instinct said something would happen.

Within a few hours, the glass doors whooshed apart with little sound. Two shadows moved past the pantry door. Aril left her bed and peered through the crack. Two men, one tall and thin, the other heavy and short, proved her intuition accurate. She pushed the door further open in time to see them edge toward the bedroom. They crept in.

A scuffle punctuated the quiet, and then a muted cry. A thud against the door, sounding like a body, slammed against it, closed it, and prevented Aril from seeing or helping. A high-pitched scream preceded a prolonged howl. As she put her hand on the door handle, Tim-Ell rushed out of the bedroom and snapped on the steam bulb in the hall. "Are you all right?"

"Yes," Aril said. She glanced into the bedroom where two bodies lay on the bedroom floor, unmoving. "Those were the men we saw this afternoon."

"I know," Tim-Ell said. He made eye contact with her. His expression communicated his gratitude for her advice, but he spoke no words.

The door slid open, and Ray-Tan dashed in, sword drawn, wearing only his ankle dagger. His neck glistened and as he passed, Aril caught a whiff of his scent, a slight match. If he was giving off scent, it meant he had been aroused. *By the sylph?*

"Thank you, friend." Tim-Ell wiped his blade on a corpse's shirt. "I've taken care of it."

Ray-Tan nodded. "For now." He placed his sword on the stone table with a quiet clink. "We should discuss this."

Tim-Ell let his sword bang on the tabletop. "We will, but right now I need you to go to the call station and contact the police. That call better go through. I don't want these bodies here any longer than necessary."

Aril understood his concern. The communication waves must work as poorly here as in Cadmia.

Tim-Ell looked at Ray-Tan's body and laughed. "I suggest you put on a tunic before you leave the complex. And...uhm...clean your..." He made a gesture to his neck.

Ray-Tan paled. He accepted the dishtowel Tim-Ell offered and wiped the glistening oil from his neck. Taking up his sword, he left the apartment.

"I wonder who these men are, or were, and what they wanted here?" Tim-Ell said. "They didn't have their weapons drawn. In fact, all they had was their ankle knives."

Aril avoided looking at the bodies. "Robbery?"

Tim-Ell shook his head. "I don't keep anything of value here." He rolled his eyes and chuckled. "You are the most valuable possession in this place."

Possession? "You can make a joke now?" She pointed in the direction of the bedroom. "Two men are dead."

"Do you think they shouldn't be?"

"Well, yes, they deserved it. But this situation isn't humorous. You should be worried about someone watching you and coming into your home."

"I don't think it's humorous. It's puzzling. Why would they take such a chance? Unless—"

"Unless they thought you'd be in a deep sleep. The landlady brought you a special toddy. She's in on it."

"You're right," he said. Carefully avoiding the bodies, Tim-Ell returned to the bedroom and pulled a white shirt over his naked body. He reached for his leather breeches.

They sat opposite each other on the wall couches without speaking until the rosy glow of dawn turned the room pink. Soft light broke through the high windows. Noises at the front door meant the police had arrived.

Tim-Ell admitted two policemen dressed in red tunics with leather breastplates, sectioned skirts, and mid-calf boots. They carried short swords and daggers on their belts. Thin metallic skullcaps had a squat row of red feathers running from the pointed tip at their foreheads to the rounded back. They appeared ferocious compared to Cadmia's blue-shirted, non-helmeted force.

The lead officer questioned Tim-Ell. "Do you know these men, Prince? Can you think of a reason for them to come into your apartment?"

The prince couldn't answer why the men broke in.

Ray-Tan, Tim-El, and the policemen moved the corpses to the police craft. Aril stood and tiptoed on the couch, to see out of the high windows. The police climbed into their open craft, bodies in the back seat. One of the landlady's young male slaves ran to them. The policemen again hopped out of the aircar.

The five men then rushed toward the patio. Aril went to the glass doors in back in time to see the men hurry into the main dining room of the complex.

CHAPTER 14

Tim-Ell and the others ran through the open door of the dining room. An old woman slave lay in a pool of blood. He recognized her as the elderly slave.

"What happened?" one of the policemen asked.

The landlady, standing over the slave said, "She fell."

Tim-Ell squatted next to the injured woman. "We should get her to a facility."

The landlady put out her hand. "No. I won't pay for that. There is a doctor who treats slaves and doesn't charge much."

"I'll pay for a facility," Tim-Ell said. The landlady shook her head.

"No…I can't accept that. You, policeman, you will—"

"We'll notify the doctor on our way back to the station. I know the one you speak of. Doctor Fil-Set."

"Hurry, then," Tim-Ell said. "This woman needs attention."

The officer nodded, got the doctor's information, and left.

Tim-Ell and Ray-Tan headed toward their apartments.

"Want some keela?" Tim-Ell asked.

"More than usual," Ray-Tan said. "But we need to talk about staying here. I'm not sure, but I think I have seen one of those men before…"

"One of the men I killed?"

"Yes, he looked familiar, and I think he brought a message for you from Eppo-Zim."

"When?"

"I can't be sure, but, several weeks ago. You weren't there." Ray-Tan leaned against the doorjamb of his apartment. "What are we going to do about this place?"

"It isn't safe," Tim-Ell agreed. "We need to find another apartment. I'll go to the palace and—"

Ray-Tan put his hand on the pommel of his sword. "Um, Prince?"

"What's on your mind, friend?"

"I don't like the idea of alerting the palace."

"My father?"

"Not the king, Tim-Ell. Do you recall, it was Eppo-Zim who found you this place? Perhaps we should search on our own."

"You suspect our venerated vizier?"

"I'll not say that exactly. Although what would it hurt for us to wait before informing Eppo-Zim?"

"It wouldn't hurt anything. But I'd have to request money. I recently asked for fifty thousand limbels for the aircar, and then I bought that slave."

"Two slaves," Ray-Tan said. "Kye-Ren and—"

"Aril-Ess."

"Right."

Tim-Ell smiled. "You don't want to go back to the barracks?"

Ray-Tan bit his lip. "I'm adjusting to apartment life. I'll give it some more time."

"Who knew?" Tim-Ell patted Ray-Tan on the shoulder. "That you would want to have a slave, and a helpless sylph at that."

Ray-Tan stiffened. "Helpless? Not exactly, even though she's never done manual labor. She's willing to learn new things."

"Is that right?" Tim-Ell said with a smile.

Ray-Tan, warrior, one of the strongest in Protar, great swordsman, and man of few words, blushed.

"Come to my place," Tim-Ell said. "I bet there will be keela for us." He took his friend by the arm and walked to the next apartment. When the glass doors parted, the smell of freshly brewed keela gusted outward.

They sat at the stone table. Tim-Ell caught his slave's eye. He twitched his head toward the keela kettle.

"What was the disturbance?" Aril asked as she put the cups in front of them.

"The landlady's slave fell. They are sending for a doctor."

"Why don't they take the woman to a medical station?"

Tim-Ell let out a sigh. "The landlady felt it could be handled by a doctor. One is on the way."

The scowl on Aril's face mirrored his own feeling. When he became king, he would make some changes. His father let the vizier make the decisions now. He'd deal with that later. He sipped the keela and then put down his cup with a clink on the eston tabletop. "So, what do you think we need to look for, Ray-Tan?"

Ray-Tan thought for a moment. "Somewhere near headquarters."

Aril took a seat. "You speak of new living quarters?"

Tim-Ell shook his head. "Why did I suspect you would have an opinion on this?"

"I do have an opinion," Aril said. "At least listen to what I offer."

Tim-Ell folded his arms on his chest. "Speak."

"Buying?"

Tim-Ell rolled his lip. "Why not? Yes, then."

"You want a place arranged in a square, with apartments in three sides, the fourth part, closed parking for the speeders. The patio should only have access through the quad's back doors. All bathwater should be routed to the patio—"

"Wait a minute," Tim-Ell said. "The layout makes sense but why do we care about the bath water?" He had to admit she showed remarkable intelligence yet said some odd things.

"Patios should be used to their best advantage. Portion it so a part is cool and refreshing with trees and shrubs or at least a small garden growing medicinal herbs. Part out the rest of the patio for exercise, like sword practice."

Ray-Tan nodded. "That makes sense."

Tim-Ell couldn't disagree. It made sense. However, should he encourage this slave, smart, tanned, and so lovely, to be more assertive?

"Plus, one more, very important necessity," Aril said.

"And," Tim-Ell said, suspecting something contrary from her tone, "what would that be?"

Aril narrowed her eyes and looked at him. "Two bedrooms in each apartment."

A blur of white distracted the discussion. A man dressed in a doctor's coat ran past.

Aril hurried to the glass door. "I hope that old woman will be all right."

Ray-Tan stood. "Yes, how unfortunate for that slave."

Ray-Tan left, and Tim-Ell asked for another cup of keela. He accepted it and stared at the dark contents. "About looking for a new apartment—" His words were interrupted by the banging on the glass doors. Ray-Tan stood with what looked like a ball clothed in a white dress. It took a moment, but Tim-Ell realized the ball was Kye-Ren, her silver skin paled white.

Ray-Tan shouted through the glass. "Help me!"

CHAPTER 15

Tim-Ell keyed the lock and Ray-Tan rushed in.

"Help me get her to the hospital. She's cut herself trying to peel vegetables."

Aril stared at the dark stain expanding against the white fabric. "Put her on the tabletop and let me see."

Ray-Tan held the sylph closer to his chest. "No."

Aril pushed close, thinking back to her medical training. "She's bleeding and she might not last long enough to transport. Let me see. I may be able to help."

Ray-Tan turned to Tim-Ell with a question in his eyes.

Tim-Ell shrugged slightly. "Let her try."

Ray-Tan put the unconscious sylph on the eston slab. Purple-red viscous fluid stuck to his leather breastplate and smeared over the white dress. Aril wiped away the blood from the oozing area on Kye-Ren's upper leg. "She's cut a major vessel and has gone into stasis to slow the blood loss."

Aril pinched the area and grabbed Tim-Ell's hand. "Press there and don't let up."

She hurried to the spice cabinet, took out three small jars, pulled a pan from the bottom shelf, and put it on the cook top. Quickly, she measured the ingredients with a spoon from each pot into the pan. Next, she put an empty cup into the cool box.

"What are you doing?" Ray-Tan asked.

"I'm making something to help."

Ray-Tan fingered his medallion. "Stop! She needs medical attention."

"I'm giving her medical attention."

"Wait, Ray-Tan," Tim-Ell said. He patted his friend on his shoulder. "It will be all right."

Aril removed the bubbling concoction from the heat and poured it into the cooled cup. She took out three butter knives and on each dull blade lifted a bit of the clear viscous liquid. "Move over," she told Tim-Ell. After touching the drops of liquid from the knives to Kye-Ren's wound, she pressed the gap together. The wound sealed. "Now," Aril said, "go see if that doctor is still here. This will hold for a while."

Ray-Tan rushed out the door.

Aril put a wadded towel under Kye-Ren's head.

Ray-Tan returned. "He's still here and will come as soon as he can."

"How is the old slave?" Aril asked.

Ray-Tan shook his head sadly. "Not very good." He wiped a strand of silver hair back into place on Kye-Ren's forehead. "She," he looked at the sylph, "was trying to make us breakfast." He checked the wound. "There's just a trickle of blood. What did you do?"

"I glued the wound together. It's a temporary fix."

Within a short time, the doctor stood outside the glass door. Ray-Tan let him in. The doctor hurried to the table and bent over the pale figure lying on the eston slab. He opened his bag. "I'm Doctor Fil-Set. Would you mind stepping back? I need room." He examined the wound. "Who treated this?"

Aril stepped closer. "I did. I can assist you."

"Good," he said.

Doctor Fil-Set took out medicines and needles from the bag. Ray-Tan put his hand to his face. "I can't stand this."

Tim-Ell looked puzzled. "You're a hardened warrior. You've seen much worse than this."

"This isn't a battle wound. It's a woman. It's Kye-Ren."

Tim-Ell put his hand on his friend's arm. "Come with me." He escorted Ray-Tan outside.

"This is amazing," the doctor said. "What did you use?"

Aril pointed to the counter where she left the ingredients. "Equal parts of dodio, potess, and alco boiled."

He laughed. "All common kitchen ingredients! The only place I've seen this done is in Cadmia. They taught us this emergency method in medical school. The Cadmia soldiers use it on the battlefield."

"You studied field medicine in Cadmia?"

"Yes."

Aril deliberated whether to question him. It seemed odd that this doctor had trained in her country. She thought for a moment and decided to go slowly and slip in a few questions. "You are from Protar?"

He nodded as he deftly stitched the wound. "I'm curious how you learned this technique."

Aril looked away, thinking. "I've had some training."

"I see you are wearing a slave's tunic."

"Yes." She let out a long breath. "I'm a slave. How is it you trained in Cadmia?"

"I came from a poor family with no prospects. Cadmia ambassadors came here and offered a program for underprivileged children who had promise. I qualified. They accepted me with all expenses paid under the condition that I give my services to the poor. I'm one of the few doctors who treats the poor or slaves when the masters don't want to pay."

"How kind of you, Doctor." Aril's internal voice wanted to trust this man.

He pulled the thread neatly and snipped the knot. "There, done." He smiled at Aril. "So where did you learn this procedure?"

She sorted her words carefully. "Um. How is the old slave?"

He grimaced. "Dead. She should have been taken to an infirmary."

Aril shook her head. "The poor thing fell?"

"Hmph." Doctor Fil-Set didn't conceal his disgust. "So, the owner said."

"You don't think she fell?"

"I can't prove that." He looked away.

"Please tell me," Aril said. "I want to know."

Doctor Fil-Set bit his lip and let out a long breath. "Not that you could do anything about it, but that old slave's head wound matched the bloody ladle lying next to her. There were no other signs of falling."

The conversation ended when the two warriors returned.

"How is she?" Ray-Tan asked looking at the sleeping sylph.

"She'll recover. It doesn't look like she lost a lot of blood, but sylphs don't have that much to spare. She would have never made it to an infirmary." He looked at Aril. "This slave saved the sylph's life."

Ray-Tan shot a look of gratitude to Aril and lowered his head.

Doctor Fil-Set took pills out of his bag. "She will come to in a while, when her body has made enough new blood. Starting tomorrow, give her one tablet a day in the morning for five days and put this salve on the wound. No hard work until the stitches have disintegrated."

Ray-Tan scooped Kye-Ren up in his arms. "Thank you, Doctor." He looked at Aril uncomfortably and nodded a single gesture of appreciation.

Tim-Ell stepped to the door to let his friend out. Aril got a clear view of the lock and saw the missing numbers she needed for the code. She smiled.

CHAPTER 16

At sunrise, Ray-Tan knocked at the glass door.

Tim-Ell held his hand up, indicating he was ready, drank the rest of his keela, and buckled on his sword belt. His leather harness creaked as he moved. He hesitated at the back door and turned to Aril. "Don't bother trying to get out. I changed the lock before I went to bed last night."

How well Aril knew, because on the night before, when she heard the regular sounds of his breathing, she tried the combination she'd memorized.

The doors swished open. Tim-Ell keyed the lock. "I'll be back early afternoon once I've taken care of business at headquarters. Clean my dress harness before I return."

Aril gritted her teeth at these orders but nodded. After her escape attempt had failed last night, she'd decided to make the best of this situation until she found an opportunity to flee. Of course, she wouldn't be totally compliant, but at least she'd try to lessen her antagonism. Perhaps if she instilled trust, the prince would give her more latitude.

She cleaned up after breakfast and found the leather-tanning oil. The prince's dress leathers hanging in the bedroom closet were similar to Cadmia's design, wide crossed straps across the chest, a thick belt with sturdy straps for weaponry, a studded paneled skirt over short leather pants, and wide metal wrist cuffs. Sandals with crossed straps to the knees bore his heraldry emblem, a rampant tollus with a shaggy mane, its teeth bared, and claws extended. Aril stared at the emblem, strangely like her own family's crest, a tollus ready to pounce. Jake

Hill selected the image after saving a princess, the beautiful Arba-Lora, when her flier crashed. Aril smiled. That princess became Jake Hill's mate, the two forming a union so powerful that most of the planet joined the alliance.

Although slaves in Aril's palace were charged with oiling the harnesses, she had always cleaned her own, a result of her military service. Jake Hill encouraged the females of the family to serve and demanded it of the men. All children raised in the palace lived up to his standards, or they could not wear the family emblem. She chuckled. Was that such a big deal? Not wearing a simple badge? But Jake Hill made it important, and only one member had failed the grade.

Aril cleaned the dress harness until the leather was supple and the metalwork shone. A movement outside caught her eye, Kye-Ren, still pale, and walking with effort. She sat in a patio chair facing the sun. Aril remembered her medical training about sylphs needing sunlight to heal. Kye-Ren would recover. She basked on the patio, free, with no slave belt to hold her there.

The metal cuff Aril held hit the stone table with a clang. She watched the sylph for a long moment and wished she could lounge in the sun, too.

How much had happened in the few days since the *Nautol* crashed! And what was to come? If she could stay alive, Jake Hill would find her. And what he would do to the corrupt nation of Protar made her smile. She sighed, thinking about the innocent people who would suffer. Didn't innocent people always suffer when a rotten few were in control?

Aril glanced out the glass door again. Tim-Ell and Ray-Tan approached Kye-Ren. Aril angered as Ray-Tan lifted the sylph up in his arms. She had walked to the patio table and now she was being carried?

What was it about Ray-Tan's actions that bothered her? Aril couldn't identify what bothered her, but fury pulsed inside her.

Tim-Ell strode into the apartment. "I was going to ask Ray-Tan to go with me, but I'll take you instead."

"Take me where?" she asked.

"To look at a few places. An agent will meet with me later after I've seen the one I've chosen."

"You want my opinion?"

He laughed. "I'd get it anyway, wouldn't I?"

She nodded. If she didn't hate him so much, she would have smiled.

He took the slave belt off its hook in the kitchen and held it up.

Aril put her hands on her hips. "No belt."

Tim-Ell cocked his head. "Right. I'll be focused on details and looking around, and you'd be off in a flash. Or, maybe you've decided not to run off?

She looked away. "No, I haven't decided not to flee."

"Then what do you expect?"

She let out a long breath. "I'll give you my word. When we shop at the market, and this time looking at places, I'll not try to escape."

He put the belt back on its hook. The smile left his face. "Don't make a fool of me."

They stood for a moment staring at each other. He broke the stare. "My dress leathers look good." He picked up one of the cuffs. "Excellent. You've had experience with military dress?"

She didn't answer. The less he knew about her the better. If anyone found out her true status, a direct descendant of Jake Hill, her life could be counted in minutes.

"I'm hungry," Tim-Ell said.

After she tidied from the midday meal, the prince keyed the door and they headed for the sporty aircar. Tim-Ell sped the craft above the rooftops, darting between house spires with frightening precision. He set down at the outskirts of town near a small complex.

Aril shook her head.

"What's wrong with this place?"

"No courtyard. Don't you want a private area where you can exercise? Have a small garden? Get fresh air?"

"Yes." He put in the coordinates for the next property and engaged the buoyancy drive. The ship rose and raced away.

As they approached the next property, Aril shook her head, and Tim-El didn't land.

"Too small," Aril explained.

On the third property, he set the speeder down in the grassy atrium. He hopped out of the craft and looked around. Forgetting her slave status, Aril extended her hand to be helped out of the flier.

Tim-Ell laughed and opened the small door of the open craft with a flourish. He took her hand to assist. She flushed at her action, and it deepened at the prince's response.

"This property's layout should suit you," she said. "The apartments are long, with all the rooms spread out, double units on each side of the square. And it has a covered hangar with a decent stall for gants." She caught his eye. "Two bedrooms?"

"Absolutely," Tim-Ell said.

They peeked through the glass doors opening onto the atrium. Inside, the quarters were furnished like most apartments, with couches carved out of the stone walls, an eston dining table, a stone bench, and wooden chairs. The kitchen mirrored those of other apartments using steam fueled appliances.

"It looks like you can get to the atrium only by using the back doors," she said.

He nodded. "That's why I landed inside."

"Good. That's safe. No one can gain admission from the outside." She turned to him. "If the bathwater can be diverted to this part, and the price meets your criterion, I'd say you've found what you need."

Tim-El flipped his hand. "I don't bother with price."

"Why not?"

"I tell the vizier to handle the deal. He takes the money out of the treasury and pays."

"You aren't serious?"

"Why not?"

She shook her head with her lips parted, incapable of responding for a moment. "So, the vizier deducts the amount, negotiates a lower price, and keeps the difference? Why don't you just beg him to rob you?"

The prince looked confused for a moment. "Eppo-Zim has been the vizier since my father took the throne."

"Really? Graft and corruption can last a long time. So, who checks up on the vizier?"

"The treasurer." His eyebrows pulled together. "I think."

"Who is rock-solid honest, right? But you, the heir apparent, don't know for sure who checks on whom or how your government works? You should know these things."

"You're a slave. How do you come up with these questions?"

"Even a slave knows when rotten things stink."

Squaring his shoulders, he faced her.

Aril swept her arm toward the building. "Why don't you do your own negotiation, ask for the money, and pay for it yourself? It will be good for you to have the experience. Take the responsibility and leave the vizier out of it."

A knot in his jaw moved; his lips tightened. He took her by the elbow and walked to the aircar. "Get in." He did not open the door for her.

This time Tim-Ell sped high over the roof tops well above the spires. He didn't speak when he landed the flier, nor did he say a word on their way to the apartment backdoor. He keyed the lock in silence. Tim-Ell waited for Aril to enter, closed and locked the door behind her. He left stomping hard toward the speeder.

CHAPTER 17

Crown Prince Tim-Ell guided his speeder into the royal hangar of the palace. He felt accomplished and shrewd. He'd met with the property owner and negotiated a lower price. It surprised him how that gave him pleasure.

He pressed the low-hover button and hopped from his aircar. A guard dressed in the palace uniform stiffened, put his hand to his chest, and brought it out smartly in a salute.

"At ease, soldier," Tim-Ell said. "Put my speeder in its mooring slot."

"Yes, sir." The soldier eyed the craft with admiration. "With care, sir."

Instead of going to the living quarters, Tim-Ell headed for the Treasury.

A wizened old man with thick spectacles and thinning hair looked up from his desk. "Why, if it isn't the young prince!"

"Good afternoon, Ark-Dal. I need 175,000 limbels."

"Directly to the point, I see. Well, now. Have you spoken to the vizier?"

"I don't need to speak with him. Unless my father objects, which I doubt, I will take a treasury certificate for the amount."

Ark-Dal scratched his shiny bald spot. "I doubt the king would object. He never does, but Eppo-Zim—"

"Eppo-Zim has no say in this. Or does he?"

The old man's eyes widened. "Well, not officially, but…What's gotten into you, boy? Why don't you leave money decisions up to me and the vizier? Let us do our jobs."

"I'll let you write that certificate. How's that? You don't oppose me, do you?"

"Well." The old man stumbled for the proper words. "Not exactly oppose, but this is irregular. Our vizier handles all of these business transactions, you see."

"Yes, I do see. Perhaps as the heir to the throne I should learn more of how our ministers operate and not put all of the responsibility on poor, overworked Eppo-Zim."

"But Your Highness—"

"I think that is exactly what I should do, make a study."

Ark-Dal took out the register and raised his pen. "How much did you say you needed?"

"One hundred, seventy-five thousand. No, one hundred and eighty thousand limbels. Give me five thousand of that in specie. Put the check in my name."

"Yes, Your Highness. A check and five thousand in specie." The old man scratched away at the account book, sprinkled a bit of powder on the ink, blew on it, and tore it from its pad. He muttered to himself as he opened a wooden box and removed a bag of coins. Handing the specie to Tim-Ell, he said, "I must report this to the vizier."

"Do what you want. I'm the prince. Eppo-Zim works for me."

The old man bowed his head. "Of course, Prince. Yes."

Tim-Ell strode away feeling light-headed. He folded the document and tucked it into his money pouch along with the coins. He nodded to the palace workers on his way to the living quarters, where the servants told him his family was in the throne room, sitting at council.

At the great doors outside the throne room, the guards saluted smartly, hand to chest and out again. Tim-Ell returned the gesture. The sentinels pushed open portals decorated with the rampant tollus, his family crest. All heads turned his way as his steps tapped softly on the stone floor. The guards standing in a line leading up to the throne each stamped their feet sharply and put their hands to their leather breastplates as he passed.

King Jess-Reet sat on the tall, extravagantly bedecked throne. Next to him in a smaller, but not less decorated chair, sat Queen Ran-Cignar.

Queen Ran-Cignar smiled wide. "My handsome son! How long has it been since you've come home?"

A tall woman approached Tim-Ell and looked him up and down. "Not since the last ball."

"Greetings to you, too, Sister," Tim-Ell said.

The woman stared at him for a long moment.

Tim-Ell stared back. "Well, Nah-Sar, what's wrong now?"

"Why don't you wear your dress uniform when you come to the palace?" She pulled a scarf of sheer fabric from her waist. It shimmered in the shafts of sunlight beaming from the high throne room windows. "We dress properly. You should, too."

Tim-Ell rolled his eyes. "I don't dress to visit or impress anyone."

Queen Ran-Cignar left her seat and came to him. "He'll wear his military best on the Longest Day Celebration." She smiled at him. "Won't you, dear? Our First Prince and Commander-in-Chief will start the Grand March."

Tim-Ell rolled his eyes. "Longest Day Celebration? I don't have an interest in that."

"Oh," the Queen said. "But you do this year. Make sure to come. Everyone will be here."

Tim-Ell cast his glance to his father. "Is this a command summons for the Celebration, Father?"

"If your mother says it is, then it is."

Laughter chimed in the halls from the attendees and the family. Tim-Ell chuckled and nodded in agreement. Everyone knew who had the real power. The merriment rapidly dwindled when light shone from the parted doors. Eppo-Zim, resplendent in bright purple and blue robes, the dress of an important administrator, made hard steps that rang out on the flooring.

He approached the king and bowed his head. "Your Highness." He gave a short bow to the Queen. His eyes searched the crowd as if he sought a culprit. He stopped his gaze on Tim-Ell. "My young Prince. How good to see you so fit and sound." Eppo-Zim smiled thin lips at the king. "Might I have a word with your son?"

The king assented with a head movement.

"Prince?" Eppo-Zim said and waved his arm toward the doors.

The polite but threatening summons triggered a stab of mistrust in Tim-Ell. Instantly the image of his sharp-tongued female slave loosened a bolt of daring aimed at the vizier.

"I'll speak with you later," Tim-Ell said. A jagged breath of surprise echoed from the crowd. That small sound gave the prince encouragement. "That is, if I have time."

Eppo-Zim turned red; his nostrils flared. He pivoted, almost with a stomp, leaving without a word.

In his near one hundred years, Prince Tim-Ell had never seen anyone, not even the king, refuse Eppo-Zim. Would there be a price for that?

Well, bring it on.

CHAPTER 18

Aril, bored, alone, without the possibility of escape, spent the afternoon cleaning and polishing all of the prince's leather and metal. By the time she put the harnesses back into the closet, the atmosphere in the apartment had filled with the delightful smell of tains oil. Tains, horrible predators and carrion eaters she wouldn't want to meet in the desert, rendered fantastic curing oils from their hides. The scent brought back memories of sitting on Jake Hill's knee when she was young.

By nightfall, she had eaten alone and bathed. The last bit of water gurgled down the tub drain when she heard a noise in the kitchen. She dried her wet body quickly, donned a fresh smock, and hurried to ensure the person in the apartment belonged there.

"Good evening," Tim-Ell said. "I'm tired. I hope there's something good to eat. And tomorrow we move."

"What?"

"I bought that complex. In the morning, after I return from headquarters, we'll pack up and relocate."

"Well, I only have a few smocks, so my part is easy."

"Good. I'll have some of my soldiers do the moving. I'm hungry and then I'll want a bath."

Aril had a comeback but reconsidered and headed to the cool box. She brought out a bottle of erbate.

"Ah, yes, the essentials first." He downed the drink and wiped his mouth with the back of his hand. "And?"

"Your meal will require a little while to heat. I already put the supper away."

Tim-Ell pulled a chair, sat his elbows on the eston tabletop, and waited for his meal without talking.

Minutes passed before she set the plate before him.

"Looks good." He took a bite. "While I eat, draw my bath."

As muscles in the back of her neck bunched, Aril searched her mind for tranquility. "Yes, Prince," she said barely moving her lips. She retreated to the bathroom and filled the tub to one-third before returning to the kitchen.

He pushed the empty plate away and stretched. "I want my bath. You can clean the kitchen later."

In the bathroom, Tim-Ell removed his harness and the few clothes he wore underneath. He took off his ankle sheath and slid into the steaming bath. "Ah, perfect. Now the soap."

Aril-Ess, High Princess of the Hill Family, froze for a moment. Had she ever treated a slave like this? Her hand trembled while thinking. Yes, she had slaves to bathe her, but they did so willingly, happily. Didn't they?

"Well?" he said.

She dipped the cloth, rubbed the soap into lather, and applied the suds to his shoulders, arms, and chest. She washed his face and back. Aril avoided staring at his groin, although she couldn't avoid that area completely. All right, his body fit the description of perfect, and his face matched. What he offered would most likely thrill some other woman, but the thought of intimacy with a captor disgusted her.

She soaped up the cloth. "Here, wash yourself. I won't touch it."

He took the cloth and laughed. "Ah, what you are missing, slave."

She didn't respond but stepped away from the tub. "What? What are you staring at?"

"You. How lovely you appear in your wet smock."

Aril grabbed a towel and dabbed at her smock, but the thin white fabric clung to her breasts like a veil. She put her hands on her hips and, with her glare, dared him to stare.

He dared. She stomped out of the bathroom.

"Get back here. You're not done."

Aril stopped, counted to five, and returned.

"Massage my neck."

She stood behind him, her hands hovering over his neckline. His eyes were closed, and his dagger lay on a stand next to the tub. She could…

"What are you waiting for? Massage me."

She had killed before. Moss Tow hadn't been the first. But in those times her safety hung in the balance. What would be her reason now?

Tim-Ell trusted her, and he posed no threat or harm right now. On the other hand, she was his captive and at this moment, she could use the dagger and flee. Aril swallowed hard. If she eliminated Tim-Ell, perhaps she could pry the lock off the door with the hardened metal of his sword. She could take his speeder, a craft so fast few could match it. By her reckonings, Protar lay south of Cadmia. She would set the coordinates for north and see where it took her.

She pressed her eyes shut. Death for the prince in return for her freedom.

"Slave!"

His words shook her. She clasped his neck and moved her fingers.

His muscles relaxed in her touch. "Ah. Just right."

Aril sighed. What would Jake Hill have her do? Could she turn into a cold-blooded killer? This man, her keeper, whom she disliked so deeply, did he deserve to die?

"That's good," Tim-Ell said, and sat up away from her grasp. "Towel."

She'd lost her opportunity. There would be other times.

Taking a towel from the stand, she held it to him.

Tim-Ell stepped out of the tub onto a furry rug. Water rivulets trickled down his body, spreading through myriad muscle indentations. "Why do you think I have a slave? Dry me." He chuckled. "And don't be afraid to rub. Rub. Everything."

Looking away from her activity, she dried him, trying to take little notice of the areas she rubbed.

Wait just a minute. Why should she act like a frightened purceen, mewing and cringing? She was no furry pet. She turned her head, looked straight at the man, and studied him as she dried. Maybe he would be the one to feel uncomfortable.

"Dry," she said. "You're done."

He locked his eyes on hers, unblinking. "So, I am. That's a good slave." He smiled crookedly. "You're dismissed. Until I call for you, of course."

Aril could play that game. Except, she couldn't force a smile. Without moving her stare, she said, "Thank you, Prince. By your leave, I'll clean the kitchen." Without waiting for his response, she turned on her heel and left.

Tim-Ell, dry and ready for bed in his usual sleep attire, clad only in his ankle dagger, came into the kitchen. "Get good rest tonight. It's a busy day tomorrow. But if you aren't able to sleep, my door is ever open."

Several words surfaced, but she buried them in her mind. She tidied the kitchen and retired to the pantry, her makeshift bedroom, shutting the door firmly.

Morning came with a soft rap on the pantry door. Aril had overslept, not a usual thing for her. The smell of freshly brewed Keela rushed into the small chamber. She rose from her pallet, stretched, opened the door, and glanced around the kitchen. An empty cup waited next to the pot.

"Sleepyhead slave," Tim-Ell said, raising his cup to her. "I've already been to headquarters and back."

His joviality opened the portal for her unpleasant attitude. Aril poured a cup of keela and sat at the table. Sipping the brew, she thought about the move. Perhaps in the turmoil of activity she could slip away.

Tim-Ell left the table and stepped to the glass doors. He wore a red tunic, and an empty sword belt slung low on his hip. "Ah, Ray-Tan and the other men are here."

She riveted her stare on the sword that lay on the tabletop until a large metallic open transport softly landed on the scant turf of the patio. Ray-Tan and five men dressed as soldiers hopped from the craft's gunwale.

Tim-Ell turned to Aril. "You'll stay at Ray-Tan's while we pack. There isn't much, mostly the furniture in the bedroom and the kitchen things. It shouldn't take us long." He glanced down at his sword. "I'll just take this." He slipped the shiny weapon into his sheath. "And one more thing." He removed the wire belt from its hook on the wall. You'll need to wear this." The anguish on his face apologized as he fastened the belt on her waist. "Come." He keyed the lock. "Next door."

Spending time with that bitchy little sylph was the last thing Aril wanted. No, that wasn't true. Her slave status fulfilled the number one spot for that category. In a few steps they reached the back door of the adjacent apartment. The dainty sprite *unlocked her door.* No belt, no boundaries, no slave smock. Aril's anger escalated.

Ray-Tan caught up with Tim-Ell and Aril, following them into his apartment. Kye-Ren immediately lost her radiant look as soon as she spotted Ray-Tan and sighed as if she could barely stand. Tim-Ell handed her the belt control. With a breathy sigh, her wrist dipped as if the weight strained her grasp.

"Here, Kye-Ren." Ray-Tan pulled a chair from the table. "Sit down. You need to keep calm until you recuperate."

"Hmph." Aril grumbled under her breath. Did Ray-Tan know about his dainty slave's hours outside taking in the sun? Kye-Ren didn't seem to have a problem moving around then.

Ray-Tan hovered over the sylph. "Can I get you anything before I leave?"

"No, thank you," she answered breathlessly. "I'll be all right."

Even if Aril wanted to, she could not utter a sound. *Ray-Tan offered to serve the sylph, his slave!*

Tim-Ell put his hand on the door. He caught Aril's eye and winked at her. Perhaps he found it amusing, but Aril didn't, and if she compressed her jaw any harder, her back teeth would surely crack.

Aril relaxed her jaw and sat down at the table across from Kye-Ren.

The sylph immediately stood and moved away, swishing her white dress embroidered with silver and pink flowers. The filmy outfit tied in the back with a pink sash knot Jake Hill called a bow. The color matched a ribbon woven into silvery curls pulled to the back of her head. Kye-Ren looked like an ornament, so delicate and pretty.

But as soon as they were out of view, the sylph's expression hardened, eradicating all indications of fragility. Kye-Ren picked up the belt control in one hand, and the other pointed to Aril, in a rude, aggressive gesture, often meant as a threat. "I want no trouble from you."

Aril refused to allow that gesture or the threat of the belt to get a rise out of her; she blanked out any trace of emotion, pointed her finger back at Kye-Ren. In a calm voice she said, "Then don't start any."

CHAPTER 19

Kye-Ren's lip turned up in a crooked sneer. She tossed her head, sliding a few of the perfect curls around the silky pink ribbon. She moved to the glass door. Her attention focused on Ray-Tan who carried a heavy piece of bedframe. His muscles flexed and strained. As she watched, the sylph's angry face changed from anger to unmistakable pride.

Pride! How long had they been together? Just a few days, and now he cared about her wellbeing and she admired him?

Aril forced a swallow. Odd feelings stirred within her. What troubled her? Regret? Envy? Was she jealous? In the past she used her studies as an excuse to reject many suitors. Would-be lovers called her cold, snobbish, unfriendly, the same words she applied to Kye-Ren. Yet the sylph had entranced Ray-Tan, and she returned the sentiment.

Aril slumped in her seat and rested her chin on her hands. She had to get control of herself. Was that the problem? Did she value control too much? Maybe, but right now control would help her escape. All she had to do was—

A rap at the glass door took Aril by surprise. The doctor who treated slaves stood outside. Kye-Ren let him in.

"I've come to check on my patient," Doctor Fil-Set said. Although he referred to Kye-Ren, his eyes didn't leave Aril.

Kye-Ren pulled aside her dress to show the bandaged area. Aril moved closer to observe. The doctor returned his attention to the sylph's wound. He removed the bandage and handed the cloth to Aril, as if she was his assistant.

"It heals well," he said, and returned his gaze to Aril. "You might want to expose it to sunlight."

"I am." Kye-Ren's voice took an edge. "Thank you for saving my life."

"You're welcome, but I can't take credit for your life."

"What do you mean? You stopped the bleeding."

As the doctor pressed a new dressing on Kye-Ren's wound, he nodded toward Aril. "She stopped the flow before I came. Thank her."

"I don't believe it." Kye-Ren paled. She pulled her dress over the bandage. "You've checked on me; now you should leave." She keyed the lock with exaggerated action, and the door whooshed open. The sylph turned her face away, dismissing him.

Without taking his gaze from Aril, he backed to the door. She stepped next to him. He paused for a moment, gave a quick bow with his head, and left. Before the door shut completely, Aril crammed the old bandage into the lock. A corner piece stuck out. She stood in front of the door, hoping Kye-Ren wouldn't notice

Kye-Ren turned and stared at Aril for a long moment. She folded her arms on her chest; her silvery cleavage elongated at her neckline. "It's not true. That crazy man is a fool." She grabbed the belt control and stomped into the living room. She plopped on the wall couch.

Through the glass door, Aril watched the doctor cross the patio. He stopped when Tim-Ell came from the apartment with an armful of kitchen objects. At first, Tim-Ell displayed his usual blasé facial expression. She couldn't see Fil-Set's face, but when he spoke, Tim-Ell's face changed. He shook his head vigorously and glared at the doctor. Fil-Set didn't move. Tim-Ell spoke angry words and, although Aril couldn't hear the conversation, clearly the doctor left disappointed.

Three warriors brought armloads of household items from the apartment and stowed them in the large transport. The six men boarded the craft, which lifted up and away.

Somehow, Aril would have to get the belt control from Kye-Ren. She returned to the seat at the table, put her head down, and pictured life in the palace at Cadmia. Where were the search parties right now? No doubt her father, brother, and Jake Hill himself combed the planet for her whereabouts. They would find her. She knew that for certain.

Kye-Ren came from the living room. Aril sat upright and stared at the sylph for a moment. In return, the pale creature studied Aril, then glided to the couch.

Aril returned to her thoughts of Cadmia. When her family found her...What retribution would the Planetary Prince impose on this corrupt part of the planet? Guar-Gul's band of killers and his slave trade would be shut down forever. No punishment could be enough to pay for Jerr-Lan. The slave outpost was just the beginning of reprisals. Protar would have to answer for the many transgressions committed by their rulers, including the exploitation and abuse of slaves, plus the misrepresentation of the Excalibur honor badge. These people had a lot to answer for.

And, if that overindulged haughty little menace in the next room tried to press the belt control, Aril would pull her apart piece by piece.

Surely, there were objects in this apartment that would help her get the control from that nasty little sylph. And, since Tim-Ell had left with the men, his speeder waited for her in the parking area.

Aril bit her lip. Grandsire had insisted his offspring learn methods for escape and survival, including bypassing the starting mechanism of transportation vehicles. If she could get to the prince's speeder, she could fly it.

Plans ran through her mind. She sighed. Each plan resulted in harm to Kye-Ren. As long as the sylph didn't threaten Aril's safety, how could she justify the violence? Could she be patient and wait for her rescue by the Cadmians? Control and escape, the two subjects constantly in her thoughts. And Tim-Ell knew that. His intelligence proved higher than she'd originally thought.

Aril lay her head back down on the stone tabletop and banished all thoughts. She napped. This nap had a dream, and the dream showed her how to escape. She woke, smiling.

Quietly, she rummaged through the shelves in the kitchen. Selecting a few containers, she mixed granules and put them into the kettle. Now to get the mixture into Kye-Ren. Sylphs had acute olfactory abilities. She sprinkled a tiny bit of fresh keela grounds in the sink. Aril returned to her seat, hoping the smell of the grounds would attract Kye-Ren.

As expected, Kye-Ren came out of the room to check on Aril.

Aril smiled. "How about some keela? I'll make it."

Kye-Ren grimaced as if Aril had insulted her, but then she paused, considering the idea. "All right, but I'll make it. I don't trust you."

The sylph ran water into the kettle and placed it on the heating surface. Before long, the smell of freshly brewed keela filled the kitchen.

Kye-Ren shoved a filled cup toward Aril.

"Thanks." Aril put the cup to her lips and pretended to drink. Kye-Ren took her cup into the living room, as Aril expected. Voluntarily sharing keela with someone was considered friendly behavior. Kye-Ren would surely not want that.

Aril poured her cup into the sink and waited. She peeked into the living room. Kye-Ren lay asleep on the wall couch. Gently, Aril removed the belt control, which lay in the sylph's outstretched fingers.

In the kitchen, a firm, steady tug on the bandage tip dislodged the partially engaged fasteners. She put her shoulder to the door and moved it open enough to squeeze through. Once she crossed over the threshold, the soft hum of the transport echoed in the patio. The transport craft made a shadow over her. She tried to dash back through the door opening, but the glass panel had closed and wouldn't budge. She grumbled and waited at a table until Tim-Ell put the craft down nearby.

He hopped out first and strode toward her, a grim stare boring a hole through her.

Aril sighed and placed the belt control on the table. He was the prince, but by Goddess, not her master.

Ray-Tan caught up. Glancing at the control, his eyes accused her. "Where's Kye-Ren?"

Aril thumbed over her shoulder toward the apartment. Ray-Tan ran. Tim-Ell put his hands on his hips and glared. Aril shrugged. Without conversation, he grabbed the control, and escorted her back to Ray-Tan's apartment.

Low conversation rose from the living room. "I'm sorry, Ray-Tan, I guess I'm still weak from my injury. I fell asleep," Kye-Ren said.

"It's all right," Ray-Tan answered in soft words. "We're going to pack our stuff now."

Our stuff? Of course, Tim-Ell would want his right-hand man at his beck and call. Perhaps that wasn't completely fair. The men shared a deep friendship.

Ray-Tan waved his hand at Tim-Ell. "We have enough help."

"Good," Tim-Ell said. He took the control from the tabletop and turned his gaze to Aril. "Let's go to the new complex."

She walked next to him.

He held up the belt contol. "Aril, you aren't taking this seriously."

Aril. He called me by my name, not slave. She sneered at the control. "Oh, yes I am."

He shook his head and grabbed her gaze with his stare. He put his hand on her shoulder. "Don't you understand what could happen?"

"You'd kill me? Throw your knife at my back?"

His eyes questioned hers. "You think I'd do that?"

She held her head up at an angle and threw him a glance. "Ah, well, you paid so much for me, probably not."

He winced and his usual smile faded, twisting into grimness. Then, what was that expression, that unreadable glaze in his eyes? Was he insulted? Hurt?

"Will you please take this belt off me while we are together?"

He nodded and undid the belt.

They didn't speak for the rest of the short walk to the parking area. Tim-Ell threw the belt and control unit in the back seat of the little craft, helped Aril into her seat and hopped in. He pressed the starter. Smoothly and quietly, the trim little vessel lifted over the few trees and, with a burst of speed, dashed through the air.

They flew over fields of redgrain, the feathery tops undulating in the wind. A flock of brightly colored birds, their long tails glistening iridescent green in the sunlight almost collided with the speeder.

Tim-Ell swerved the craft. "Hmmm. Look, a flock of greentails. Delicious. I wish I had my bow and arrows."

Aril sniffed. "You think you could take down a game bird with an arrow?"

"Yes," he said with confidence. "I hit the moving red circle all the time at practice. Why should a moving greentail be different?"

Aril had hunted for food during survival training. She had pursued the bird for its fine taste. Experience taught her to throw a net instead attempting the difficult task of using a bow and arrow.

"You really think you could hit one of those birds with an arrow?"

"I could bring down more than one. Perhaps you'd enjoy cleaning some greentails for dinner?"

She laughed. "Cleaning a greentail would be unpleasant, but I'll happily clean as many as you can bring down. With a bow and arrow, that is."

"You're on. Not today, but soon, I'll hunt for greentails."

Maybe I won't be here to clean them if by some chance you could hit one.

The fields of waving redgrain gave way to sparse meadows and then the bluish rocky terrain Aril had seen before. On the far right, the spires and slender high domes of Protar curved around a gleaming crescent-shaped lake, a body of water rare on Cronanta. Most cities pumped their water from springs deep below the surface.

"Pretty, isn't it?"

"What?"

He pointed to the water glistening in the sun. "Lake Golonka."

While he admired the shining lake, Aril's arm snaked behind her back until she curled her fingers around the wire belt. "Oh, named for your goddess." She tossed the belt over the side.

The prince scratched his nose. "Um, not exactly *my* goddess."

"You don't believe Golonka mated with the great sky beast and delivered an egg she called Cronanta, and it's still waiting to hatch something great and powerful?"

Tim-Ell laughed. "Not really. You said 'my goddess,' so you don't believe, either, right?"

"I don't believe in Golonka."

"So, what do you believe?"

Aril enjoyed the wind in her short curls and closed her eyes for a moment. "A Great Spirit keeps watch over us, expecting us to live our lives in a way we would want to answer for when we meet it after death."

"You're a Hillian?"

"What's a Hillian?"

"Someone who believes that Jake Hill, the Savior, was sent here to rescue our souls."

Grandsire will rescue me. But... "Jake Hill? A savior?"

Tim-Ell sneered. "He claims he's divinely come to Cronanta and leads us to his god."

A flash of heat ran through Aril. "He claims no such thing!"

"You declare yourself an expert on Jake Hill?"

Although she could prove her expertise in the subject, she didn't know what to say. She spoke carefully. "I have some knowledge of the Earthman. He doesn't claim to be anything but a man who thinks a Great Spirit had a hand in the creation of every living thing. He wants each person to have a private opinion on religion and wouldn't inflict his beliefs on others."

Tim-Ell didn't respond to her explanation. He swept his hand to the left and put the craft in a downward spiral. "That's where we're going."

The aircar descended, hovering just above the grass of an atrium. Aril got a better view of the square complex. The fourth side of the complex provided covered parking. Riding a knee-high cushion of air, the craft advanced slowly until it stopped in the parking garage.

Tim-Ell extended his hand to Aril to help her step over the side. "That one," he said looking at the left-hand side. "Ours." Aril felt odd at the word *ours*.

He keyed the lock, and it opened with a soft puffing sound.

She stood outside for a moment and looked around. No gates to the outside. The atrium could be accessed by the aircars, a strong gate, and by the doors in the rear of the apartments. Getting to the speeder would be easier here. She couldn't keep her smile from forming. She would get away for sure.

CHAPTER 20

The design of the building impressed Aril with its simplicity and efficiency. The glass backdoor of the apartment opened into the kitchen, with a living room beyond. A pantry on one side and a large bath on the other flanked the kitchen. Two opposing doors in the living room opened to the bedrooms.

She walked into each room, assessing the work needed to get the rooms in order. Dishes and other items lay about the kitchen. The bedroom near the bath had Tim-Ell's bed strewn in pieces. She chuckled to herself, wondering if the three knives were still hidden in the frame. In her bedroom, she found a military cot, where three other slave smocks and the hideous metal-studded harness she wore for the auction had been left.

Aril hung her few items in the closet. Although tempted to toss the ugly harness, she suspended it on a wall peg. Perhaps the prince's next pet slave would enjoy the revolting garment. While she put sheets on her cot, clinking sounds came from kitchen as Tim-Ell stocked the cool box with his erbate bottles.

Before long, she had all of the kitchen items washed and stowed then started to prepare the midday meal. Sounds from the bedroom, including a few oaths, testified that Tim-Ell's assembly skills did not match his self-proclaimed archery abilities. She knew the type, like her brother, Hin-Cal, who once he started on a manly task, would spend hours working, rather than ask for help. She could have put that bed together in one-third the time he'd already spent. Good. Let his meal get cold. Yet a small voice in her head tugged at her conscience.

Aril stood at his bedroom doorway apparently unnoticed. Tim-Ell kneeled on the floor, warring with a tool to connect the bedframe. How she wished she could take the knives from their hidden niche and show him how to use the connecting tool. Hadn't he learned basic hand tools in military training?

"What?" Tim-Ell said.

"Need help?"

"No. Anything else?"

"Lunch is ready. Are you?"

"I'll eat when I've finished."

She put her hand to her mouth knowing she didn't cover the smile. "Perhaps you will be ready at suppertime."

Tim-Ell threw the tool on the floor. "Maybe I need a break." He brushed his hands together and followed her into the kitchen.

Outside, Ray-Tan helped the warriors move the few items he had into the adjacent apartment. Kye-Ren supervised their labor.

After the meal, Ray-Tan rapped at the glass door.

Tim-Ell let him in. "Erbate?"

"Sure, thanks."

Tim-Ell looked to Aril and glanced over at to the cool box.

An unspoken order. She reached for the cool box and took out two brown bottles, beaded with moisture. "Would you like me to unscrew them?"

Tim-Ell frowned for a swift moment. Apparently, he understood the dig regarding his war with the screw tool and the bedframe. "Yes. Do."

She jerked in surprise. He didn't get as insulted as she had planned, and now she had to open the bottles. Using a dishcloth to steady the bottlenecks, she twisted the top and handed the foaming bottle to Ray-Tan, the guest, and then Tim-Ell.

The two men drank in silence, then like a precision drill, wiped their mouths with the back of their hands.

Ray-Tan set his empty bottle on the tabletop. The glass clinked on the polished stone. He patted the sword at his hip. "How about some fencing practice?"

Tim-Ell put his bottle down and stretched his neck first left, then right. "Great. That's what I need." He went into his bedroom and returned with his sword belt.

Aril watched through the glass door for a short time. She had seen plenty of swordplay. Not a champion, her skill with blades matched the average male warrior, but no woman could touch her. Bored with the masculine displays on the patio, she went into Tim-Ell's bedroom and picked up the tool. She put the bed frame together easily. She'd let him put the mattress on, but she couldn't resist checking the hiding place hinged in the frame. When it popped open, she found a note that read, "Looking for something?"

She crumpled the paper and threw it against the wall. Then, realizing her mistake, retrieved it and smoothed out the wrinkles, hoping he wouldn't notice if he checked. And he would check. Oh, Goddess! Aril cursed herself for being so careless. She changed her mind and pushed the mattress on the frame. First, it would show Tim-Ell that she was strong, and second, having the mattress just hanging over the frame near the hidden drawer would deter him from checking on the note. Maybe. She'd have to look again for those knives.

When she returned to the kitchen, she got a good view of the patio, where Tim-Ell and Ray-Tan sparred with swords. Tim-Ell riposted, instantly stepped aside, and parried. Ray-Tan's blade twirled away, glinting in the midday sunlight. Ray-Tan bowed his head in a noble gesture, granting the contest to Tim-Ell.

Even though the sword practice had initially bored her, the movements of the exercise bothered her. Aril wished she had seen the entire bout.

Both warriors, slightly out of breath, clasped wrists, the typical contest end between men who were not enemies. Aril had seen this, done this, many times.

Tim-Ell returned to the kitchen and sat at the table. "Erbate."

Aril hesitated long enough to get a glare from him, and then she took unhurried steps to the cool box. She didn't offer to open the bottle this time and clinked it on the polished tabletop.

Tim-Ell opened it and took a long drink. He put the bottle down and drummed his fingers. "A man will come this afternoon."

"So? You'll have a visitor."

"Um, actually he is coming for you."

A streak of fear assaulted her. Coming? For her? *Control.* "What do you mean?"

"You'll see. I need a bath." He held up his hand. "I don't need you to help. Not this time."

Control. She bit her lip, holding back questions. Fear crept on little feet, making her take short breaths.

Tim-Ell left the kitchen. He returned with a puzzled look. "You put my bed together?"

"Who else?"

He scratched his nose. "Thanks...I think." He turned and went back into the bedroom.

From her seat at the table, she saw him, clad only his ankle dagger, walk into the bathroom. Ankle daggers were the last thing a warrior removed, and the weapons were never far from reach. The thought of Tim-Ell's dagger brought back the question of what happened to the three knives that disappeared from the bedframe hiding place.

She tried to block her thoughts about weaponry and fighting, but she couldn't banish them completely. Her fear thinned to apprehension. Who was coming and why? She needed something to do, to focus upon something mundane; perhaps peeling tubers would help. After retrieving the root vegetables from the cool box, she searched the drawer of cooking utensils hoping to find a peeler. There, among the bottle openers and spatulas, were the three knives that she'd seen hidden in the bedframe. What did it mean?

Adding to her anguish, a visitor was coming to see her. Using the smallest of the sharp blades, she peeled the first large vegetable and then the second. Aril-Ess, a High Princess of the Hill Family, held a knife, but at the moment, lacked the fortitude to wield it.

She stabbed the tuber and cut through. That felt good. She cut the other way, slicing until neat small cubes of white lay in front of her. That short spell of trepidation eased; she impaled each cube and threw them into a pan of water she had boiling on the heating surface. She whispered, "I'm Aril-Ess of the Hill Family. I can face whatever comes my way."

Tim-Ell, dressed in his red tunic with the simplest harness and weapon belt, came from his room.

"Is that all we're having?"

Aril went to the cool box and pulled out a hunk of meat. She threw it onto the hot surface, where it sizzled and hissed.

"I see you found the knives," he said.

"I did, but I don't understand why you hid them, and now you've put them out for my use."

"You aren't going to hurt me with them."

She flinched. "And how do you know that?"

He smiled. "You've had a couple of opportunities, like the dagger while I closed my eyes in the bath, for one. My sword on the tabletop, for another. And I'm pretty sure it's not that you are afraid of being caught. But just in case you think I'm lax, don't."

She looked away for a moment. What could she say?

A rap on the door jarred her.

"Here's your visitor," Tim-Ell said.

CHAPTER 21

An overweight, small man with a flattened forehead held a thin case and stood on the other side of the glass door. Tim-Ell let him in. Aril couldn't take her eyes from his hair. Not hair, but fuzz. Grandsire had told her about Earth women giving birth. Their babies began like the children on Cronanta as an egg fertilized by their fathers. However, unlike Cronantans, the babies of Earth emerged from their mothers fully formed but about the size of a pet purceen. They were unable to do anything and required constant attention. While Cronantan children were born with full heads of hair, Earth children were often born with fuzz.

The short brown fluff on this man's head appeared exactly as she had imagined fuzz looked like on Earth babies. She stifled a laugh. If he had come to take her away, she could best him in an instant.

The man stepped inside and brushed his garish robe with his hands as if he had walked through a dust storm.

Tim-Ell, standing behind the man, rolled his eyes. "Slave," the word came out playfully, as if addressing a beloved pet. "This is Leb-Brit." He paused then added, "The Royal Dressmaker."

Aril threw a questioning look at Tim-Ell.

"I'm taking you to a palace function. You need something to wear."

Leb-Brit walked around Aril assessing her. "Uh huh," he said, then, "Hmmm." He touched her waist.

She narrowed her eyes, threatening him, and he stepped back.

"Prince, how can I do my job if she doesn't cooperate?"

Tim-Ell smiled wide. "Answer that question, and you'll win a great prize." He looked at Aril. "He needs to…well, whatever dressmakers do."

"What if I don't wish to go to the palace for a…function?"

Tim-Ell looked puzzled. "What?"

Aril thought for a moment. Perhaps it would be a good idea to see the palace. She could evaluate the security, look for weaknesses in the guards, gather information for her Cadmian rescuers, and bring those corrupt rulers to justice.

"Never mind, I'll go," Aril said.

The dressmaker cleared his throat as his message of disgust. "Slave!" He said the word like he would a curse, not the friendly way Tim-Ell had said it. "You do not speak unless questioned."

Tim-Ell offered a quick smile. "Leb-Brit, I'll be in the living room if you need me and will stay out of your way for now."

"Yes, Prince," the little man said like the sycophant he clearly was. He opened his case and pulled out a lightweight screen with a stylus attached. He began to sketch. He stopped and held a measuring tool at Aril's sides, breasts, and hips. Each time he pressed the button a line of blue light wrapped her body and displayed measurements. When he pressed the second button, the machine recorded the dimensions. He hastily sketched an outfit and by manipulating the controls, changed the colors.

"Ah," he said. "Perfect."

Aril snatched the pad from him. She gasped. The dress had swaths of orange and purple cloth crossing her chest with gaps exposing her nipples. Lengths of cloth draped down her back in a train.

Her muscles went rigid. "Absolutely not." She seized the stylus and removed the design before the man could respond. She had her own ideas. On the body image, she redesigned the garment using her favorite Cadmian outfit. "This is what I want. Light blue gossamay, crossed over the breasts, with one scarf over the left shoulder, and pointed edged hem on the short skirt. No sparkles."

Leb-Brit looked as if someone had stabbed him. "What?" His mouth hung open for a short time while he took in a breath. "Gossamay? Who do you think you are?"

Aril rethought her choice of gossamay, the lightweight fabric made from the large cave spiders' webs. The webs were huge and softly colored, depending on the cave environment. Heated, the webs contracted into wondrous bolts of fabric, expensive and frequently worn by royalty and wealthy people. She wasn't the princess here, and a slave with a gossamay gown wouldn't be received well. In fact, even in Cadmia, if a mere commoner wore that fabric, the gossip and indignation would be heard for a long time. She flushed. Perhaps Cadmians weren't as magnanimous and cultured as they thought.

"Prince!" the dressmaker said.

Tim-Ell left the couch and faced the small man.

"You need to do something with this... creature. Never have I been so—" He sputtered, searching for words. "You should chastise her."

Aril handed the screen to Tim-Ell and folded her arms in front of her chest. "And is this the way you speak to the Crown Prince? Are you not on the staff of the royals? Don't you *work* for them?"

Leb-Brit went pale. "Oh, I beg your pardon, my Prince. I meant no disrespect."

Tim-Ell studied the drawing. He turned to Aril. "I like this dress. What's wrong with it?"

"Nothing," she said. "I like it, too."

He nodded and handed it to Leb-Brit. "It's lovely. Good work, Dressmaker."

Leb-Brit bowed his head. "Thank you, Prince. I'll get on it right away. Of course, I'll have to get approval from Eppo-Zim to purchase the gossamay."

The gossamay would cause a problem with the ladies of the court. Aril thumped the screen lightly. "How about a light blue sheer fabric instead? That would do."

"Well, I'll still have to clear it with the Vizier."

Tim-Ell slammed the screen on the table. "And just why do you have to clear this with Eppo-Zim? What possible reason would he have to be involved with a dress?"

"Well," Leb-Brit took a step backwards and fumbled for words. "Anything that involves you or your...um, or what you do."

Tim-Ell held his finger in front of the small man's face. Leb-Brit's eyes expanded, taking the action as the threat it clearly was.

"You," Tim-Ell said, "are not to report anything to Eppo-Zim. I gave you and no other person this address. Where I live and what I do is for me alone to report. Do you understand? If the vizier asks you for information, tell him what I said. If he has the nerve, he can ask me questions himself."

For the first time since she'd met him, Aril felt some respect for Tim-Ell, the Crown Prince.

Leb-Brit trembled. "Yes, Prince. I understand. May I go?"

Aril pulled the screen from the table. She carefully handed the device to Leb-Brit, hoping Tim-Ell's rough handling didn't disturb the phosphor-bacteria culture inside, the microbes enclosed in the device producing the light. The dressmaker took the screen and gently placed it in his case. He backed up toward the door, his eyes on the floor. Tim-Ell suspended his hand over the door lock. "Make me a new tunic. Light blue. We'll match."

The dressmaker moved swiftly out the door.

Aril sat down at the table. "What is the palace function?"

Tim-Ell waved his hand, dismissing the subject.

"Is Ray-Tan attending?"

"Yes," Tim-Ell said. "It's some kind of important announcement, and all the upper ranks must attend."

Aril thumbed in the direction of the adjacent apartment. "I wonder what silver-girl will wear."

Tim-Ell scratched his nose. "Uh, she's not going."

"She refused?"

"Sylphs aren't allowed in the palace."

Heat ran up her neck and into her cheeks. Protar discriminated against sylphs. She thought about her palace in Cadmia. Sylphs were welcomed. Weren't they? They rarely visited the palace and then only Hall of Justice Chiefs in matters of law. Although the sensitive chief sylphs were allowed into the palace, Aril couldn't remember seeing a female sylph, ever. But everyone knew their kind were reclusive, didn't like society. It was their nature. Of course. That was the reason, wasn't it? Logic tapped her on the shoulder. Did sylphs decline society because they felt the discrimination? She realized they were looked down upon not just in Protar, but in Cadmia as well. In spite of Aril's feelings for Kye-Ren, she couldn't dismiss the injustice of those people.

When she returned to Cadmia, she would have a thing or two to say about intolerance. Ray-Tan didn't have a problem loving a lower-class woman. Lower class! How could she think that way? She forced a swallow. The Cadmians, herself included, could take a lesson from Ray-Tan.

She closed her eyes because the Cadmians would never be able to do that. When Jake Hill rescued her, he would kill Ray-Tan and anyone else responsible for her abduction and slave status. Ray-Tan had done nothing but accompany Tim-Ell. Tim-Ell. He would surely die at grandsire's hand. She dropped her gaze to the floor. If they fought, grandsire could get hurt. No, she had seen him in action. No one man could defeat him. His Earthly muscles and body structure had made him stronger, faster, and more adept than the finest Cronantan warrior.

She rested her elbow on the tabletop and cupped her chin. Tim-Ell brought a box of books and put the box on the table. "Lost in thought? Bored?" He pointed toward the shelves cut into the eston walls on either side of the wall couch. "Help me put these up."

Aril shook off her deliberations about discrimination and death. She glanced at the titles as she slid the books into the ledge that suited their height. Books on weaponry, military procedure, and hunting manuals were tall, so they went on the bottom shelf. Picking up a book on local plants, she abandoned her chore and flipped through the pages.

She held open a page. "You should have some of these plants out there." She nodded in the direction of the patio. "Not just herbs for taste, but medicinal plants."

Tim-Ell responded with a blank stare.

"If you aren't interested in plants, why do you have this book? All of the plants mentioned are available in the fields. You could just dig them up."

Tim-Ell's blank stare changed little. "Is that what you want to do? Dig up plants?"

"I wouldn't mind a day out in the clear air. And having fresh herbs for cooking would make the food better. Crisp greens, juicy tubers, fruits."

"You'd take care of a garden?"

"Well," she studied her fingertips. "For as long as I'm here, why not?"

"As long as you're here? What does that mean?"

She could have smacked herself. Escape would be more difficult if she constantly referred to it. What she should do is keep her own council and lull him into trust. After all, he did return the knives to the drawer. Did that mean he didn't worry that she would stab him while he slept?

Tim-Ell put more books on the shelf. "Seriously, you want to dig up plants and transfer them to the patio? How do you do that? And where?"

Aril handed him more books. "Remember those valleys we flew over from that horrible place?" She hesitated. "That," she sneered, "slave auction."

Tim-Ell didn't react to her tone. "I remember."

"And that area we flew over when we came here. What can't be found there can be bought at the bazaar."

"So," he placed the last book on the shelf. "I'd fly you to the area, you'd dig and bring the plants back here?"

She cocked her head. "Not exactly. We would take a shovel and pots to the valley, and I would show you what to dig up. Then, when we got back here, I'd tell you where to plant them."

He put his hands on his hips. "Me, the Crown Prince of Protar would dig?"

"Like a slave?" She bit her lip and let out an amused sniff. "Yes." She stepped back and looked him up and down. "You've never had to dig? Even when you camped or were in battle?"

He hung his head and nodded slowly. "I've dug graves."

Aril's conscience tugged. This man had lost friends, and he still mourned them.

He raised his head and gave her a sad smile. "Bad memories." The smile faded. "I don't mind digging for plants. Maybe next week or so. We'll make it a picnic. Out in the fresh air and sunshine. It sounds like fun."

She frowned. She didn't want to have fun. Not with him, her captor. The captor who wouldn't see the light of day once she was rescued. Her scowl deepened. For the rest of the afternoon, she put away the last items from the move. Tim-Ell spent his time reading a thick sheaf of papers, which looked to Aril like military reports.

Around suppertime, when Aril began preparing the meal, a knock at the front door startled her. Tim-Ell answered. A man in full dress harness, including his metal of Excalibur, came in, followed by a woman wearing a conservative, but stylish gray dress with dark green trim and belt. Aril liked her immediately just by the way she dressed.

The man stomped his leg and saluted. "Cal-Eb reporting as ordered, Sir."

Tim-Ell returned the salute. "At ease, Captain. And I see you brought your mate."

"Yes, Sir. May I present Del-Am, my Life-Mate, Sir."

Tim-Ell bowed his head in acknowledgement. Then he took the young woman's hand and pressed it between both of his. "So very glad you meet you, Del-Am."

Del-Am appeared a bit apprehensive. "Thank you, Prince."

"Don't be worried." Tim-Ell smiled at the woman. He turned to Cal-Eb. "Would you like to live in one of the apartments? The one over there?"

Cal-Eb's gaze followed Tim-Ell's hand direction to the apartment across the patio. He went to the glass door and stared. "Us? I don't understand."

Tim-Ell laughed. "I'm looking for good neighbors! You are an outstanding officer, Cal-Eb, loyal, quiet, and hardworking, not to mention an excellent swordsman. I'm offering you the apartment, and like Ray-Tan, you will serve as a part-time bodyguard." He sent Aril a quick glance.

And slave guard.

"Bodyguard, Sir?"

"Nothing official, but while you are here, if I need you…"

Cal-Eb stiffened. "It would be official, Sir. And I would defend you under any circumstance."

Tim-Ell put up his hand. "Exactly why I asked you to take the other side of the complex." He turned to Del-Am. "What do you think?"

Del-Am swept her head to look at the apartment. "Thank you, Prince. I would love to live here."

"Settled!" Tim-Ell's hand hovered over the glass door lock.

Cal-Eb stepped around Tim-Ell and blocked the door. "While I'm here, Sir, I might as well ask you about the choice we've made."

Del-Am put her hand to her heart. "Oh, Cal-Eb." She took steps to stand alongside her mate.

Cal-Eb cleared his throat. He glanced to Aril with a questioned look.

"Feel free to speak in front of my slave. What is it, Captain?"

"Sir." He hesitated, then squared his shoulders. Del-Am linked her arm in his. "Because you are the Commander-in-Chief of the Army, you can give permission." He pulled a small scroll from his waist belt. "Will you sign this permit?"

Tim-Ell took the scroll. "Let's see." He read it and nodded. "Of course. Wonderful. Will you have a celebration?"

"No." Cal-Eb looked lovingly at his mate. "We will sip the nectar privately. Perhaps soon."

Tim-Ell scratched his name on the scroll. "Congratulations," he said and led them to the back door.

Aril's neck muscles tightened. She glared at Tim-Ell as he returned to the kitchen.

He spread his palms out as a smile left his face. "What?"

"Lest I heard that wrong, enlighten me. Did that man and his mate get a *permit* to have a child?"

"You heard correctly. How should that offend *you?*"

She blew her breath through her nose. "It's an offense to Cronantans everywhere. Outrageous."

"If it is important, I'll explain to you, my slave. In Protar we keep the population controlled by permits."

"Why?"

"The same as other countries. To save resources."

"I doubt that."

Tim-Ell's expression turned serious. "What does that mean?"

"Well, on Cronanta water is the resource most controlled and yet Protar has a lake. I haven't noticed water conservation."

"Food."

"With all those redgrain fields? I've never seen better crops. Protar must have a surplus of flour. And those huge herds of lakins in the valleys? At the marketplace, booths overflowed with vegetables." She swept her hand toward the kitchen appliances. "Steam is plentiful here, so what resources are in danger?"

He scratched his nose. "Well, then, we require a permit to collect the tax from the couples who sip the nectar. Why is that wrong?"

"A tax?"

"It's the only tax we charge."

"How can that be?"

His jaw tightened. A cheek muscle flinched. "I don't know. It's how it is."

Aril crossed her arms in front. "So, your parents got a permit to create you?"

Tim-Ell pulled at his clenched jaw. "I doubt it. I can't see Father taking out a permit. And Mother…well…" He shook his head vigorously. "No. Besides, it's pretty obvious when the king wants children, who would he ask?"

"Does a prince get a permit?"

"I wouldn't think a prince would have to apply for a permit. I'm certainly not planning on producing offspring anytime soon." He pressed his lips together until they became thin lines. "Enough questions."

Tim-Ell picked up the thick report he had been reading. "Cook dinner. Quietly."

Aril stood in front of him for a long moment, but he didn't look up. She returned to the counter, where vegetables waited to be cut. Taking the medium sharp blade from the drawer, she appraised it for balance, assessing its weight in her hand.

She turned fast and caught Tim-Ell's eye. He had watched her. With raised eyebrows, the hint of a smile pulled the corners of his lips.

CHAPTER 22

The next morning after he finished his keela, Tim-Ell rose from his seat and stood behind Aril-Ess. "I assume since you can do most everything, you can ride a gant."

"What if I can't ride?"

"Then you will have a day of pure misery. Wait! I know. You can ride in the saddle with me. That will be fun."

"I can ride," she said, teeth clamped.

"Aw, I thought you might enjoy a day in my embrace."

"Enjoy?"

"Well, then, perhaps you would enjoy camping."

She didn't look up from peeling a tuber. "What does that mean?"

"It means I'm taking you on a camping trip to the south. We will be on gantback one whole day in the desert. At the end of the day, we reach a beautiful oasis. Nothing like it."

"The Commander of the Army takes a last-minute vacation? Figures."

He stood inches behind her. She continued her work as if he wasn't so close.

"It's a business trip. I'm going to the border of Protar to look at gants for the Army."

"You don't need me. You and your soldiers have a good time on your little trip."

He spun her around. "I'm going with *you*."

She caught her breath.

He laughed. "Are you afraid? What do you think I'll do? If I was going to hurt you, I've had plenty of reason before this."

"Why do you want *me* to go?"

"Because I want your company. Ray-Tan will fill in for me at the fort. You'll love the oasis. It's beautiful there."

She pushed him away, not too rough, but enough to let him know she wouldn't put up with the way he touched her. Maybe a trip would be good—getting out in fresh air, a chance to escape. "When?"

"Tomorrow. I have bed rolls and equipment. You pack food. Enough for two days. I'll get fresh food at the gant ranch for the trip back."

For the rest of the day and night, she imagined the opportunities for escape and how she could get away. Her mind churned at daybreak, none of the ideas being adequate. By the time they mounted the gants, she concluded it would be spur of the moment, and she should be on guard.

They kept a light pace, swift on downhill slopes, slow and even on the upsides. The partial green subsided, turning to vast plains of tashberry bushes, then to sand. As the day passed, Aril marveled at the terrain. Puffs and flurries of sand moved in random swirls. Swarms of fine dust, at times almost invisible, turned the turquoise sky into bronze, dulling the sun. Blurred by whirls of sand eddies, columns of grit danced like erect serpents in irregular directions, raw and unpredictable. By late afternoon, the sand turned from tan to bluish, and as dusk descended, the sand shone with deep blue sparkles from the sun as it lowered on the horizon.

Aril recognized the ore-rich ground. "Where are we?"

"Nearing the border with my mother's country."

"I thought you said your mother's country merged with Protar when your parents married."

"That's true. I guess it's Protar."

"You don't know? Where is the border?"

"I'm not sure." He waved his arm. "Around here somewhere. Near the oasis."

"You aren't sure of the border? You are supposed to be king someday and you don't know your borders?"

He pulled the gant to a stop. "The north is bordered by a dense forest and a stream. In the south the shifting sands make it difficult to be certain. I use the shape of the horizon, the hills, to ascertain our border."

Aril slowed. "The shape of the horizon?"

His jaw tightened. "Correct. See that?" He pointed to a group of tall hills far off. "It looks like a woman lying on her back.

After regarding the horizon for a few seconds, she saw the similarity. "No marker?"

"No marker. It would get abraded to nothing after a few sandstorms. I know where I'm at, heading between her breasts. The oasis is right over that ridge of sand."

"That blue sand? Do you know what blue sand means?"

"Not really. But I suppose you'll tell me."

Aril halted her gant and put her head back. "You want that blue sand inside your border." She checked her next words to close the door to questions about her background. "I think it means metals. But I haven't seen any foundries in Protar."

Tim-Ell clucked to his gant to join her. He scratched at the back of his head. "There are some mines near the gant ranch. I'm not sure if they are in Protar or in Ambel, my mother's country."

"Which has become Protar now, right?"

"I think so."

"You think? If the ore is alnata," She was sure the color meant alnata, "then it is worth a fortune. Is Protar smelting ore into metal? Who owns the mines? The foundries?"

"I don't know. That's what we have a Vizier for."

"Really? Do you hear yourself? You don't know who gets the money for the ore? You don't know where Protar joins with Ambel. Borders are important. If you don't mind them, you might lose them. It looks like you have already lost the income from the rich ore." She caught herself before she said too much. "Or what may be ore."

"I'll check on it when I get back." His face showed a mixture of anger and disgust at her insinuations. "Come on, the oasis is nearby." He slapped his gant, which took off in a gallop, leaving her in a cloud of fine dust.

She gave her gant a kick in its side, surprising her with its swiftness, catching the prince and passing him. On top of the sandy blue ridge, she lost her breath at the beauty of the trees swaying over two crystal blue fountains. One line of water bubbled from the middle of a rock ring. Another glittering flow gushed from a cavity in a rocky outcrop into the other, joining into a ribbon shining in the late rays of the sun. The combined stream ran for half a mile, then disappeared into another group of rocks. Lush green vegetation flanked the watercourse until it dipped into the sand abruptly at the rocky end.

A soft breeze preceded the sound of a gant struggling up the slope. The prince halted the animal next to her.

"Isn't it pretty?"

"Yes," Aril said. "Do you know if it belongs to Protar?"

He let out a breath. "It does." Then he kicked the gant's side and let it have its head. He whooped a high-spirited yell at the speed.

Aril patted her gant's neck. "I guess he rides like he flies. Fast and wild." She fought the temptation to let her gant go in the reckless pace the prince had enjoyed. But she wouldn't let him think she enjoyed anything he offered.

Tim-Ell set up the tent while Aril unpacked the meats and redgrain bread she wrapped in small towels. Accompanied by a skin of wine and dried fruits, the meal with its rich assortment of tastes equaled many meals she had in many palaces.

The prince finished the last of the wine. He stood and stretched. "Now for the best part."

She eyed him. "What's that?"

"The spring." He shed his clothes except for his ankle dagger and ran to the spring. Putting his toe in the stream, he pulled it out with a jerk and moved farther down the watercourse. He tried it again and moved once more. The third time he tried the water, he waved to her.

The sun had set, and shades of orange and purple cast dreamlike light over the valley oasis. The air cooled, and the wind blew in little gusts. While she watched, Tim-Ell unbuckled the ankle strap and put his dagger on a small rock. He entered the stream and beckoned to her again.

She stood with her arms in front of her, torn between not doing what he wanted and enjoying the water. A bath. All right, she could stand to get rid of the dust from the day's ride. She slowly made her way to the rock with the dagger. Small wisps of white appeared in the cooling air over the water. She removed her sandals and stuck her toe in the water. Warm. Perfect.

She took off her top smock but left the under smock on. She entered slowly, a few feet from Tim-Ell. "A hot spring?"

"And a cool one. Adjust the temperature by getting close to where they join."

A wind picked up, bringing a scent delicious with the perfume of blossoms. Sweet, tangy, and powerful. She couldn't resist taking in a deep breath, letting the fragrance renew her.

Tim-Ell moved closer, the last rays of sunset showing a Vee-shaped wake behind him. He breathed deeply, too. "Perfect timing. The Burnettia is in bloom."

"Burnettia? The trees that produce the dark fruit?"

"Yes. Oasis trees. The branches almost break from the amount of fruit."

Aril loved the tasty, dried fruit, but because of its scarcity rarely got to enjoy it. "Those trees like a special kind of soil." Sandy, wet, alnata-laced soil. She took in the watercourse and the trees that lined it, the pink petals dropping and floating in the wind. "So many trees. So much fruit!"

Tim-Ell sighed. "It's a shame hardly any of the fruit gets picked."

How could that be? "What do you mean?"

"It's so far out in the desert that no one wants to ride for a day to get the fruit. It dries of its own accord and birds eat it."

"Then you should get a caravan out here in time to harvest. It not only would provide nutritious food but also, it's easy to store, the perfect food for armies. What is the matter with Protar? You? What waste."

"I come out here once in a while and bring back a bag of the dried fruit. I hadn't thought about using it for camping food. Even though it's delicious, it's not that well known."

Aril pictured the delicacy served on ornate trays at the palace in Cadmia. Each precious morsel was taken in tiny bites and savored. Being practical and not given to luxuries, the Hill family rarely indulged in the treat. And here in this degenerate country, the trees were ignored and unappreciated.

Tim-Ell scanned the trees, thick with blossoms. "Maybe I'll come back in a few months and get a bag and you can taste some."

She held back her excitement. The thought of the thick creamy interior, the sweet, rich flavor, made her mouth water. "Not on my account," she said, and turned her back on him. She silently made a wish that he would get a bag. But by then she would have escaped, and it would do her no good.

After an early breakfast of fruit and what was left of the packed food, they left the oasis.

Tim-Ell showed Aril a landmark, which from the top of the first rise looked like a religious symbol. "See that? We head for it, but halfway there you'll see it's really two rock formations, far from each other but look as one. We will turn a bit east after reaching the first tall rock, and then the second one will point the way."

"Point the way where? What is the purpose of this trip?" Aril asked.

"I am ordering gants for the army. We are heading for the best gant ranch in Protar."

Aril sniffed. "Or maybe in some other country."

Tim-Ell glared at her. "It's in Protar!" He put his mount into a gallop.

His ire gave her a bit of cheer. She urged her animal to catch up.

Within two hours, they passed the second rock formation that didn't look at all like it did from the rise at the oasis. An hour later, the terrain changed, with bits of green and low bushes that turned into tashberry fields, then gave way to rows of tall plants that produced nubbly brown ears. The fruit of the plant was dry and hard, fit for fodder, nutritious and long-lasting to store. Aril admired the neat, extensive rows, where multiple ears shone in the sunlight. Cadmia had permia, the fruit that Jake Hill said reminded him of a food called maize from Earth. But these fields put Cadmia's farms to shame.

She pulled up next to Tim-Ell. "How are these fields watered? The plants need a lot of moisture to do this well."

Tim-Ell looked from side to side. "Underground streams. See those structures?" He pointed to waist-high metallic devices where spokes had cup-like endings. "Wind-catchers. The wind turns the device that pumps the water."

Again, Aril admired the setup. Protar, so backward in some ways, excelled in others. Punctured pipes under the soil irrigated the roots of the permia. The plants thrived, offering great amounts of fodder for a lot of animals.

Beyond the vast permia fields, the trail took them to a huge farm. Green hills were dotted with gants in the typical shades of gray, but a few were black, white, or spotted. Aril had been brought up with gants, and these were some of the finest she'd seen. Tim-Ell had been wise to make the trip to this place. She grudgingly and silently wished Cadmia could buy these animals for their army.

For the rest of the day, Aril roamed the farmland, not far from view of Tim-Ell as he negotiated with the rancher. They stayed at the ranch that night, two adjoining rooms where Tim-Ell kept the door between them open. Even if she could have escaped, she didn't know where she was, except that behind them lay a sizeable desert and she didn't know the landmarks.

The loss of control continued to irritate her. Adding to that, the resources of this rogue country annoyed her. Bad government and wickedness should not be rewarded with wondrous resources. Her mouth watered at the thoughts of dinner at the ranch, where Burnettia fruits lay in heaps in a basket next to rich redgrain rolls. The ranch workers hardly touched them as if they had been common to the point of boredom. Aril took a few fruits from the basket and kept them in her room for the ride back.

The return to the city annoyed her the most. Heading north and east, they trotted along a road that took them past the shining lake and into the city in three hours.

When she saw the spires of the tallest building peeking over the horizon, she caught her gant up to the prince. "Why did we spend a whole day in the desert to go to that ranch?"

He shrugged. "I like it that way. I get to spend the night at the oasis."

She shook her head in dismay.

"Hey, you liked it, too. You have a handful of Burnettia to show for your trouble."

Her face burned. She had been so careful not to be seen shoving the fruits into the folds of her smock and pinning them next to her elbow to take into the room. She was sure he didn't see her wrap them up in the small towels that lay in the knapsack. Damn that man.

CHAPTER 23

Back in the apartment, Tim-Ell's steps, light slaps from his leather sandals, echoed on the stone floor from the hall into the kitchen. He pulled a cup out of the cabinet and leaned over the stove for the keela pot next to Aril, where she stirred the grain cereal bubbling in the pan. She had always enjoyed food preparation, often taking over the kitchen in the palace in Cadmia. But being forced to cook rankled her. Even so, if she hadn't insisted on moving, they would be eating the horrible slop served by that repugnant landlady. Aril tasted the cereal. It needed sweet crystals, just a pinch.

After breakfast, Tim-Ell, dressed in his military harness, stood at the backdoor.

"I have a little work to do at headquarters. I'll be back by midday with a shovel and such, and we'll dig your plants." He pressed his hand against the small screen of the handprint lock. The door whooshed open, and he left.

This apartment had a handprint lock. She had watched as he programmed it, but the privacy shield had deprived her of the code. After she cleaned up, she had a couple of hours to try random combinations. Maybe she'd get lucky, and she could record her own palm.

When Tim-Ell returned, he left the speeder on the grass outside the glass door. He stepped inside. "Ready?"

Aril cast her glance to the insulated bag on the tabletop. Tim-Ell peeked in and rifled through the contents. "Ah, you included three frosty bottles of erbate. Good slave!" He picked up the bag. Before laying his hand on the screen, he keyed in a code and studied it. "I see you've tried 96 combinations on the palm lock in hopes of registering your print." His chuckle at her efforts annoyed her. He pressed his hand on the screen and the door moved quietly apart. She followed him to the craft.

The aircar hovered for a moment, disturbing the higher clumps of grass. The shiny vessel ascended. Aril's shoulders jammed into the seat as the craft sped forward. She forced her body away from the upholstery. "You're a maniac."

His grin grew wide. "I have a fast aircar. I need to keep it finely honed, like my sword." He swerved to miss a spire by inches.

"Hey!" Aril yelled.

Tim-Ell climbed his craft above the building tops. "Better?"

"You could slow down."

"I could but, nah." With the buildings behind them, he increased the speed. "Tell me where you think we should land."

A wide valley shimmered ahead in the direction of sunsets. As they approached the plain between low mountains, details emerged. Green swatches hugged small water courses. Beyond the swards of verdant growth, an arid plain caught her attention.

"There." She pointed.

"What? I'm not sure where you're directing me."

She leaned close and pointed, her arm close to his face. "There."

He kissed her neck. She glared and pulled back. "Don't," she menaced. "Land in the place with the tan and dark blue soil." She moved as far away as she could and crossed her arms over her chest.

Tim-Ell descended slowly until they reached the area Aril indicated. The little craft landed as if it sat on an invisible pillow. She admired the vessel and had not seen one better. The low sides made for easy exit. Tim-Ell hopped out, and quickly took the shovel and rough sacks from the back seat. He came to Aril's side and extended his free hand. She ignored his offer and stepped over the small door.

She took a few steps and stopped at a squat bush. "Tashberry. Dig that one. Get the root ball."

Tim-Ell, Crown Prince of Protar, hurried to the plant and bore down on the shovel. He held the plant, the soil ball sprinkling grains on his fine leather sandals. A wave of humor passed through Aril. *Who's the slave now?* She nodded. He put the plant in one of the sacks.

As she moved about, she called out various names, and stopped in front of the plants she wanted. Like an obedient servant, Tim-Ell dug and stored them in the sacks.

"Look at this one," he said standing over a rounded bush with delicate white flowers. He bent to pick one.

"No! Don't touch it!"

He flinched and stepped back. "Aw. That's nice. It's poison and you care about my health."

She strode toward the plant. "You're joking."

He looked around as if to ask an observer the answer. "I thought the flowers would be pretty for a garden."

She shook her head and hoped her dismay and disgust had been properly displayed. "Recently you signed a permit to sip the nectar. And now you claim not to recognize the flower that produces the nectar?"

"Flower?"

She couldn't keep her eyelids from fluttering at his offering of ignorance.

Tim-Ell shrugged silently.

"You really don't know about these flowers?"

His usual cheery expression faded. "No. But of course *you* do and will be sure to inform me."

She tilted her head up and looked away. "Only if you want to be informed." She took a long breath and turned back to him. "About something any schoolchild knows."

He stepped to the plant and kicked it. Bits of leaves and flowers went in all directions. "You test my patience!"

She had been told that many times. Punishment for insolence and rude attitude had been swift and sure in the Hill Family. She needed to alter her tone.

After a pause she let out a soft breath. "The white flower on that plant you just ruined contains the nectar needed to procreate. In most countries it is protected, and against the law to destroy." Her insolence made a minor comeback.

"Good thing I'm the prince." He paused. "Look, here in Protar we don't pick flowers. We take the permit to a pharmacy, and the chemist dispenses a small bottle of liquid. Couples share the liquid one night, and a while later they are ready to...you know the rest."

"A *liquid* from a *pharmacy*?" The insolence was in full bloom. She rolled her eyes. "What kind of country do you run here?"

Tim-Ell closed his eyes. His rigidity released. He showed no anger, an Excaliburian technique. "Please tell me what happens in civilized countries when nice people sip the nectar."

"Gladly. When a Life-Mated couple decides to have a child, they usually follow an age-old tradition. They formally announce their intention and set a date so everyone can celebrate with them. The couple spends a day picking the flowers that grow wild and *are protected*. They boil the flowers and make a syrup, which they drink at a celebratory dinner. Different timing for each couple but later, when the effects manifest, they…you know the rest."

"Whatever," Tim-Ell said. "I'm taking these bags back to the speeder. Look around and see if there's anything else you want."

She barely noticed his footfalls fade; her attention focused on a dark blue rock with bits of sparkle catching the sunlight. Unbelievable! As she picked up the fist-sized piece, the color and amount of shining mineral amazed her. It was unusually pure, rare, and valuable. Bits of shining rocks lay scattered about. She hurried to another sample, and one beyond that. Rocks stretched out in a long path in front of her, each as rich as the last. Movement in a mound of boulders distracted her search. More movement, slinking, crouching, and hunkering. Then she heard them, the unmistakable hissing growls of tains, viscous pack-hunting, meat-eating, sharp-tooth, long-clawed villains of the wild.

Instinctively she reached one hand to her dagger, the other for her sword. Her heart skipped beats. She was unarmed. Searching the ground, she found a stick with a forked point. Picking up the stick signaled the attack from the yellow and black spotted animals larger than hunting baccurs. A dozen of them formed a circle around her. The bulky leader, with teeth bared, lunged. She kept it from her throat by stabbing it with the stick. The other tains moved closer, and one on the left took attack-stance. A blur of spots leaped upon her, ripping her shoulder. The leader bit the stick away, and another tain took flight toward her. Its weight pulled her down. A pain ripped through her hip. Then another strike, more painful, in her shoulder. The smell of her blood heightened the beasts' energies. As she flailed, pushed, and defended, she allowed a fleeting thought that she would die being ripped apart by disgusting beasts, and nothing would be left of her. No one, including Jake Hill, would know what had happened.

The fierce growling turned to screams. The weight of the animals lifted as the snarling diminished in what felt like slow motion. One by one, the tains were silenced, taken off of her. When a break in the fur permitted light, Tim-Ell's face, nostrils flared, his teeth pulled back in a resolved clamp, loomed over her.

"Aril!" He kicked at the last growling tain, which let out a scream. The animals fled.

Tim-Ell squatted next to her, his expression grim and concerned. He lifted her gently. She barely noticed the walk to the speeder where he placed her in the seat with a soft touch. Ripping a ragged piece from her smock, he got close to check her. "Let's see." Gently touching the fabric to her face, he wiped the blood away. "Bloody but shallow. Good." He cleaned her shoulder. "That needs attention." He looked her over. "A lot better than I thought, but you need treatment." He hopped into the driver's seat. The speeder rose and shot forward, but not so fast it caused her distress.

Aril assessed her injuries. Her shoulder started to throb, and a knife-like pain shot through her hip. She had been wounded far worse than this. From what she could tell, the principal wound was a gash on her shoulder, with others on her hips requiring stitches. Tears formed. She tried to suppress them by swallowing and willing them to cease. Her diaphragm shuddered. An emotion she had not felt for years forced its way to the surface. She wept.

Tim-Ell gently brushed her cheek with his fingers. "It's all right. You're safe."

No. She wasn't. Her tears weren't because of the injuries, the hammering pain, or fright. She hadn't been able to defend herself. She had never been vulnerable before. And now, because of him, and others, too, she needed protection. It burned her worse than she could have imagined.

"There's an elite hospital near the palace."

Aril wiped the tears from her cheeks with her wrist. "An elite hospital won't treat a slave."

He locked eyes with hers. "*Yes*, they *will.*"

Something pricked her memory. The doctors and assistants would treat her if the Crown Prince told them to, but she'd have no say in her care. If they examined her completely, and one of the *elite* doctors knew about the Earth gene for body hair…

"I would prefer that slave doctor. Please, Prince. Contact him." *Did I say please?*

He must have noticed the change in her tone. He patted her hand. "What if he isn't very good?"

She wished her voice didn't quiver and tried to enunciate in monotone. "He's fine. A good doctor. I want to go back to the apartment and have him look at me there."

Tim-Ell nodded. "All right. I'll find a call box. What's his name?"

"Fil-Set."

The speeder slowed and gently set down near a call box. Tim-Ell placed his call and came back to the speeder. "He'll be right there."

"Thank you," she said in a whisper.

The edges of his blue eyes crinkled kindly. "You're welcome."

The craft landed a step from the glass door. Tim-Ell hopped out and bent over Aril's side, ready to lift her.

"No," she said. "I can walk." The anguish of her inability to defend herself had passed, and anger replaced it. She wanted him to leave her alone. In the apartment, she went into her room, closed the door, took off the tattered smock, and lay on the cot clad in her leather underwear.

Shortly afterward she heard a knock on her door.

"It's Doctor Fil-Set. I'm coming in."

CHAPTER 24

Doctor Fil-Set poked his head into the room. He hurried in and set his bag next to the cot. Aril sat upright.

Fil-Set went down on his knee, took a cylinder from his bag, snapped on the light, and peered at her shoulder. "Let me see here. Nasty gash, but not bleeding. Stitches." He brushed dark curls from her forehead and checked the scratches on her face. "Ointment." The beam of light moved down her neck across the leather bra harness and down to her hips. He ran his finger next to the gash over her navel. "Bandage." Small gashes angled under her torn leather shorts. "Take your pants off so I can see."

Aril unsnapped the fly and slipped them off. Fil-Set cast the light about, pausing at the red jagged wounds scattered on both hips. "Stitches." The light beam zig-zagged across her pelvis and then stopped. The line of hair over her pubic bone, shaved at the slave station, was now a stubble, and in the beam, clearly visible.

Doctor Fil-Set gasped. His mouth paused, gaped. "Ah, ah…" He dropped the light. "Who are you?" he whispered. "Cadmia?"

Aril nodded.

"You are a princess."

Aril put her finger on his lips. "Don't say a thing." She moved close and spoke in low tones. "I'm Aril-Ess of Cadmia."

He bowed his head. "Princess."

"Please. I am Aril-Ess, Slave of Protar's Crown Prince, and if anyone thought otherwise, my life would be worthless."

Doctor Fil-Set covered his mouth with his hand. His eyes widened, and he nodded, turning head to the door. After clearing his throat, he increased his volume. "Tell me how you incurred your injuries, Slave." He put his finger up and slanted his head to the door.

"I was attacked by a pack of tains."

While she spoke, he crept to the door and quickly pulled it open. Aril leaned to the side to see beyond. Tim-Ell sat at the table reading.

"Prince," the doctor said, "do you have wine? I think it would help your slave."

Tim-Ell let his notebook fall and stood. "Of course. I'll bring some right away."

Fil-Set returned to the cot. "Good, he didn't hear us." He reached into his bag and took out his needle kit and a vial of topical anesthetic. "I'll need to stitch that gash on your hip, too."

Tim-Ell brought a glass of wine and handed it to Aril.

"Drink that," Fil-Set ordered. "It will help you relax." He looked at Tim-Ell and without words ordered him out of the room.

Fil-Set shut the door. He dabbed the anesthetic on her shoulder.

Aril pulled her up knees. The doctor sat on the end of the cot.

Fil-Set lowered his voice. "And to think I tried to buy you. A princess!"

Aril flinched at his statement. "What?"

He removed a threaded needle from a glass tube. "When I was here checking on—I forget her name—the sylph. You were such a good assistant."

Aril twirled her finger. "And?"

His lip quivered into a sneer. "I asked the prince if I could buy you because I need an assistant."

"Really?"

"He got angry and said the richest man in Protar couldn't afford you. But even if I could, he wouldn't sell you."

Great. When the Prince tires of me, I could be a slave owned by a serving-class doctor.

"I tried to reason with *him* that you would be helping me bring medical help to poor folks and slaves. I thought he might attack me."

"Can you travel to Cadmia?"

Fil-Set didn't respond. Only his eyes moved, as if in thought. His lips parted but no words came out.

"Doctor Fil-Set?"

"I haven't traveled since I returned from my medical training."

"Do you have contacts in Cadmia?"

Fil-Set looked away. "No."

Aril leaned toward him and grabbed his arm. "You must get word to Cadmia. Jake Hill will reward you with more riches than you can imagine."

He let out a long breath. "You want me to get word to Jake Hill, the Planetary Prince. He would come to Protar. Take you back."

She leaned closer and detected a faint scent. This man was not a mating match for her, but why was he scenting? Dismissing that thought, she whispered, "And he will clean this foul place up."

Fil-Set jerked. The faint scent Aril had detected disappeared. "You mean war?"

Aril pressed her lips together. She nodded in one deep move.

A quiet knock on the door made them both turn. Tim-Ell stuck his head in. "How are things going?"

"Fine," Fil-Set answered. He pierced Aril's shoulder with the needle and brought up the thread.

"More wine?"

Aril downed the last of her glass and offered the empty to Tim-Ell. "I don't want any more." She almost said thank you. The effect of the wine? No, the thought that with this doctor she had a chance to contact Cadmia.

"Call if you need anything." Tim-Ell left the door cracked a few inches.

Fil-Set drew another stitch.

Aril watched him pull the gash together with each suture. Luckily, she only had one such injury. Luckily? More than luck. Tim-Ell had saved her. She hadn't asked if he needed treatment.

The wound was closed, and the doctor pressed a bandage over the sutures. "Almost good as new." He put a tin of salve on the cot and applied the medicine to each wound. The larger spots got bandaged. "Use this ointment each morning and night. I'll be back to remove the stitches in a few days."

She engaged his eyes, hoping he'd understand what she really needed.

"I'll see what I can do about contacting Cadmia."

Aril took his hand and pressed it to her cheek. "Thank you, Doctor."

She followed him out of the room. As Tim-Ell placed his hand on the screen lock, she saw a bloody puncture on his thumb. Looking closer, she noticed scratches on his arms and legs. A small tap inside reminded her she should show concern for his damage, but a larger tap said he held her captive, and he could speak to the doctor himself if he needed care.

The doctor left and she retreated to her room to nap on the cot. A knock awakened her. Tim-Ell pushed the door open. Soft light from the steam bulbs filled the dark room.

Tim-Ell stood over her. "Hungry? There are leftovers from lunch. I've put them out on the table, but I could bring something in here."

Aril moved her stiffened shoulder and winced at the pain. "I'll come out there." She ignored his hand offering to assist her. Taking a seat at the table, she eyed the sandwich still wrapped in a hand towel.

She needed comfort food. "No, you can eat that. I want tashberry butter and jelly."

"Easy." He turned to the cabinets. Small earthenware pots, one with the butter and another with jelly, clinked as he placed them in front of her. Next, he gave her a half loaf of bread.

The biggest knife she had seen in the hiding place, and later, in the drawer, stuck out of the bread. The serrations appeared bigger and sharper than she remembered.

"I'll cut it for you." He chuckled. "Not that I don't trust you. You shouldn't distress your shoulder."

Aril reached for the knife. "I can cut my own bread." Something inside tugged at her. She angled the knife handle toward his hand. "But I would like two slices. Please."

CHAPTER 25

Day after day, Aril's shoulder mended. She eased into the daily routine of the new apartment, the one with the palm identifier lock. Each day she tried combinations in hope of stumbling onto Tim-Ell's code.

A week after the tain attack, Doctor Fil-Set came in the afternoon to remove her stitches.

Tim-Ell let the doctor in and swept his hand toward the dining table. "I think you will have better light here."

Clearly Tim-Ell didn't want them in the bedroom. He sat down, leaned his elbows and hands on the eston top, and stared at the doctor to take his suggestion.

The doctor placed his bag on the table and sat down next to Aril. He searched his bag. "Um, I keep small towels to soak up antiseptic, but I don't seem to have any. If you tell me where you keep them, I'll get one."

This was normally a chore for Aril, but as she moved to get up, a sharp nudge at her ankle stopped her.

Tim-Ell's eyes darted between her and the doctor. He paused, frowned, and narrowed his eyes. "I'll get one."

As soon as he was out of range, Aril whispered, "Did you get in touch with anyone in Cadmia?"

Fil-Set bit his lip. "I don't think so. It's not that easy. I don't trust communication spectral rays. It would be easy for someone in Protar to capture one. Then what would you do?"

She tightened her jaw. "Worded correctly, spectral rays sent to Cadmia would make sense to only Jake Hill. *Alas, Babylon.* If you said that in a message to the palace, no one in Protar would have a clue. Understand?"

Tim-Ell appeared and handed the doctor the towel. "She understands about what?"

Obviously, Fil-Set did not practice subterfuge—he flushed.

Aril flattened her expression. "That I'm not going to have much of a scar."

Tim-Ell's mouth turned down. "Good news." His eyes scanned her shoulders and neck.

The scan was as palpable as a caress.

Tim-Ell broke his gaze when Ray-Tan rapped his knuckles on the glass door. He entered and stood for a moment, watching the doctor clip and pull out a stitch on Aril's skin.

Ray-Tan patted the pommel of his sword. "We haven't practiced for a few days, Prince. Maybe we better get some exercise."

Aril stiffened and then softened the look she shot at Ray-Tan. He suggested, without words that because of her injuries, the prince had neglected his duties and Ray-Tan would at least keep him in shape.

"Good idea." Tim-Ell turned to the doctor. "How long will your work take?"

Aril kicked Fil-Set under the table. He jerked and stammered, "Uh, it will be a good while. I have to see to her hip, um, too."

Ray-Tan palmed his Excalibur medal. "Prince, the light won't last for much longer. If we are going to work out, then we should get to it."

"Right." Tim-Ell glowered at the doctor and put on his sword belt. The two warriors left the apartment but took their fighting stance close to the glass door.

Aril winced when Fil-Set pulled hard on an embedded suture. "You will contact someone in Cadmia?"

"I will most likely have to travel there, or at least to another country and send a courier."

"How long will that take? Ow!"

"Be still. Um, I mean, I'm sorry, Princess."

"Don't! You must forget that title. Well, remember it for your message."

Fil-Set put up his hand. "Sorry." He bit his lip. "Please don't move. I'm afraid I'll hurt you."

"All right." She turned her head to watch the swordplay, hoping it would give her something to focus on. And it did. She studied the moves and forgot Doctor Fil-Set. Her eyes dashed back and forth while the duelists dodged and deflected. Tim-Ell, taller and with a longer reach, defended almost every step.

Ray-Tan, steady and sure, had barely broken a sweat. Aril bit her lip, waiting for the first blood, the nip from the blade that would end the contest and cause the Crown Prince of Protar to bend his head to the common-class warrior.

The pace quickened. Ray-Tan had the prince backstepping and tensing, moves intended to demoralize the opponent. Aril's fencing master had pounded that maneuver endlessly until she gained the skill. Ray-Tan made it look easy. Easy, but Tim-Ell kept defending. The friendly combat became serious. Tim-Ell's lips pressed into thin lines. Aril held her breath. It wouldn't be long. Her mouth dropped open as Ray-Tan's blade tipped for a second. Tim-Ell took the advantage and brought his sword up engaging Ray-Tan's blade, which spiraled away. Ray-Tan bowed his head in defeat.

Both men squatted under the small tree and leaned on either side catching their breath.

"There," Fil-Set said. "All done." He ignored the towel Tim-Ell provided and wiped the antiseptic drips with a small cloth he took from his bag. From the glass door she saw Tim-Ell lean to see inside. Fil-Set jerked his head and sniffed. With crisp movements, he packed his medical bag.

By the time the doctor snapped his case closed, Tim-Ell came in and held the door for him to leave. Fil-Set passed Ray-Tan who disappeared into his own apartment.

"So," Tim-Ell said with a grin. "Did you see me work out?"

"Indeed, I did." She said with pious irritation. "I also saw Ray-Tan allow you to win."

Tim-Ell's eyes widened. He tightened his jaw, saying his words from barely moving lips. "I won that match fairly."

She crossed her arms. "If that's what you wish to think, go ahead. I *know* what I saw."

"You don't know a thing. You're just a woman, and a slave at that."

"Really? Even a slave can see when something isn't right." She examined her fingertips for a moment. "Do you want to know for sure?"

"I already know." He looked away, out at the patio.

"Well then, you wouldn't be afraid to test it, would you?"

"How would I do that? I just bested the one man in the entire Protar Army who comes close to my skill."

"Do you have slaves from other countries?"

"What?"

"Ask around. I'll bet you there are a few who work for you who are skilled at fencing but not allowed to have a sword."

"You're crazy."

"Perhaps. But it doesn't change what I'm saying. Offer a prize. Make it freedom to anyone who can draw first blood from you."

He narrowed his eyes. "Make dinner." He stomped off to the bathroom, followed by the sound of water splashing into in the tub.

CHAPTER 26

Tim-Ell pitched his sword against the bathroom wall. The loud clang caused him to swat at the air, annoyed. *She* would hear it and know he was vexed. With a savage twist of the handle, he turned the water off. After tossing his clothes and leathers about the floor, he fumbled with the buckle on his ankle, freed the strap, and placed the dagger on a small table next to the tub. Sliding into the water, he winced at the hot temperature. Aril's attitude could not be tolerated. The last slave he had prepared his bath with perfectly warm water and added a pleasant-smelling oil that floated on top, soothing his body. She stood by waiting, wanting, to scrub him, anywhere and everywhere he liked. But the one out there in the kitchen! Who did she think she was?

Why did he allow her to talk to him like that? How could she think he didn't win that match? Would Ray-Tan throw the contest? It made no sense.

Tim-Ell sunk beneath the hot water. Did the unpleasant heat come from the water? Or from that sharp-tongued, cold-hearted, woman? He sighed. Aril, lovely and different than any other slave. Different? Unbelievably so. But she was a slave, one for whom he paid a huge sum, even though she acted like a spoiled princess-brat. He had met a few of those. They were always trying to snag him as a Life-Mate. After all, he would wear the crown one day. Not that he wanted that. His brother, Sen-Mak yearned to ascend to the throne and complained Fate tortured him to be born second son.

If Sen-Mak wanted the crown, he should have it. All Tim-Ell wanted was… What? That harsh, opinionated slave who irritated him? He felt a stirring in his groin. His other slaves couldn't wait to join his bed. But not *her*. She was not the most beautiful, but she was the most attractive woman he'd ever met. Her face, those perfect breasts. His erection increased. Damn it. He needed to get better control.

That woman! She was wrong about the fencing match. But she had been right about the merchant in the marketplace. And breaking away from Eppo-Zim. She had advised him about this apartment building. His head dropped back against the edge of the eston tub. *She had saved Kye-Ren's life.* And why was his slave pleasant to that insignificant doctor who wanted to buy her? How insulting was that? He was the highest-ranking prince in Protar. Maybe he *should* sell her. His stomach lurched at the thought of another man touching her. Set her free?

But he couldn't let her go. She was the one he wanted. Soft full lips, flawless skin. He wanted to run his fingers through her dark curls and...The water parted around his full erection. He sat up. The swollen appendage dipped beneath the surface. He couldn't afford to let her to see that. She would most likely laugh at him. He needed to control his desires and his thoughts.

The Excalibur training. That's it. He took deep breaths and imagined a meadow, one with sweet-smelling flowers. No! Not *those* flowers. She had shamed him. He mumbled the words, "Like any school child knows." His mind jumbled, reviewing the past. And now she said Ray-Tan threw the match. How could that be? The question bothered him. He had to disprove her accusation. Could he challenge a good swordsman for a prize?

He remembered a conversation about a slave who had been Swordmaster in his country. Ray-Tan discussed using his skills to teach Protar warriors, but they both thought better of putting a sword in the hands of a slave who knew how to wield it. Perhaps a match with that man would prove *she* was wrong, verify the best swordsman in Protar.

Tim-Ell jumped out of the tub and quickly dried. He put on his ankle dagger and strode into the kitchen. "Very well. One of the slaves who works in the stables was the Swordmaster in his own country. I'll challenge him to first blood. Then you'll see."

Aril dropped her gaze to the sink and smiled as if she'd notched a new win. She turned and stared at Tim-Ell. "Why should the slave compete? He might get injured. What will you offer him? Freedom is the only thing worth fighting for."

Tim-Ell's lips pressed thin. "Then that will be the prize."

Aril closed her eyes. The word "freedom" floated from her lips in a hushed longing.

It disturbed him. He yearned to hold her, take her in his arms, whisper sweet words, but the soft word she'd just spoken meant she wanted to be away from him. His face tingled as it heated. He stomped into the bedroom and snatched a clean tunic from the closet. If he converted disappointment into anger, he could handle his emotions. His anger didn't dissipate while he dressed. He stamped hard steps through the apartment until he reached the door, where he slammed his hand onto the lock screen and pushed the door ajar before the mechanism had a chance to fully open. Grunting, he pushed against the lock a second time. As Tim-Ell neared Ray-Tan's apartment, a motion-detection strongium light over the back door illuminated. Tim-Ell rapped on the glass door. Ray-Tan held the door open.

Tim-Ell stood inside the doorway quietly, thinking. How could he ask if Ray-Tan threw the last contest? And if the man had, what did that imply? Had he done it before? Of all the warriors he knew, Ray-Tan had the most integrity, honor.

Tim-Ell chose his words carefully. He would never insult his friend. "Ray-Tan, do you remember the groom who claimed to be a Swordmaster in—"

Ray-Tan nodded. "Linter, I think. Yes, because we fought over that valley and took him as prisoner. What about him?"

"I want to speak with him." Before Ray-Tan could ask questions, Tim-Ell left. Instead of returning to the apartment, he sat on the patio table bench to think.

Two moons rose, casting their light on the courtyard planted with herbs at the direction of her, his slave, the thorn in his side, the woman he had to admit he cared for. He had to prove …what? What should a Crown Prince prove to a mere slave? He shouldn't have to prove anything. But he would show her he didn't need anyone to throw a match. He had earned his prowess and skill with hard work and wouldn't accept a dishonest victory. There was no more to consider. He would find a worthy opponent and best him. He left the patio and headed for his apartment. Without any conversation, Tim-Ell went straight to bed. He left the next morning without words or breakfast.

CHAPTER 27

As she finished her housework, Aril-Ess hoped her words had irritated Tim-Ell, and he would react as she'd planned. With the chores finished, she scanned the shelf of Tim-Ell's books and chose a familiar title, *Field Positions for Battle,* standard reading for warriors. Flipping a few pages, she let out a sigh, snapped the book shut, and traced her finger over the embossed hide cover. The book wasn't pristine, even though the fancy binding meant it was a presentation piece. The well-thumbed and soiled pages revealed its owner had used it many times. All right, he'd studied his craft. Study didn't mean skill.

Similar to the scuffed hide of the book, Prince Tim-Ell's harness and warrior's leathers, were worn and well used. She thought back to the sword practice the day before. It was true, he had skill. But how much skill did he need if the opponent let his blade drop, allowing the winning stroke? Ray-Tan didn't seem the kind of man who would be dishonest, but then, Protar was rife with deceit. The Excalibur insignia indicated Protar had been admitted to the Planetary Alliance, yet in Protar the medal could by worn by anyone. By planetary treaty, slaves were to be wards of the court, their services auctioned for the duration of their sentences, and they were to enjoy the care and protection of the purchaser. Contrary to the planetwide Allied Agreement, Protarians attended slave markets and allowed slaves who attempted escape to be murdered. She snapped her eyes shut. Planetary law would wreak justice on this corrupt nation just as soon as she attained liberty. If Doctor Fil-Set couldn't get a message to Jake Hill soon, maybe Tim-Ell would arrange a match, and if the slave sword master won, the prince would free him. Then Doctor Fil-Set could get the man to take a message to Cadmia.

Movement outside caught her peripheral vision. The glass door provided a view of the grassy atrium centered in the complex. Tim-Ell's flier buzzed low and settled outside the hanger. Two military fliers hovered and softly landed on the grass near the patio.

Ray-Tan and three warriors escorted a large man who wore tattered leathers and a ragged slave's tunic. Kye-Ren approached Ray-Tan. He motioned her away. Aril smiled. The scowl on the arrogant little sylph's face gave Aril a moment of pleasure. Kye-Ren tossed her head and sat on a bench outside the apartment. Based on the expressions of the warriors, including the huge slave, serious business loomed.

Aril hit the glass with her palm. *I want to be out there, not here watching from behind a glass door!*

Ray-Tan accompanied Tim-Ell to a spot on the grass where Aril had an excellent view. Three warriors escorted the large slave to the same area. Ray-Tan gave the man a sword, and after Ray-Tan stepped back, the man swung the blade in the air to assess its weight and balance. As if he leisurely batted a fly, the man reached upward. The sword almost floated in his hand. A cursory check of the blade produced a nod and a slight smile. He went through a few more moves as the people in the atrium watched the practice in awe. Then he spread his feet in an unmistakable stance and nodded to the prince. Tim-Ell and the slave faced each other in the customary two sword-arms' space. They bowed, the official start of a duel. The slave took the initiative wielding the sword, flashing in the sun's rays like lightning. Tim-Ell side-stepped the move.

Aril gasped. For so big a man, the slave moved like a feather in the wind. Tim-Ell riposted with a forward thrust, but the opponent took a dance-like step backward, avoiding the point. The slave tossed the sword to his other hand—an insult to Tim-Ell—and lunged. Tim-Ell evaded with a twist and parried but on the defensive. The slave flaunted his skill by allowing Tim-Ell to gain the offensive. Aril held her breath; she suspected what would come next. *Don't fall for it!* The huge man dropped to his knees; Tim-Ell's blade cut through air where the slave's head should have been. The man thrust his blade upward. Tim-Ell backed away in time.

Aril's heart beat hard in her neck. The duelists fell into a short burst of attacks. Tim-Ell feinted, and the slave stepped backward. This time Tim-Ell's offense played hard and fast. The slave lost his momentum. Three, four, five retreats. Just as he made his attack, Tim-Ell stumbled. His forward motion caused an imbalance. He went down. The slave burst forward to hold the sword over Tim-Ell. Ray-Tan and the other warriors with drawn swords rushed the short distance. By the time they got there, the slave had cut a tiny nick on Tim-Ell's neck.

Aril leaned against the glass struggling to breathe. The slave extended his massive arm to help Tim-Ell to his feet. Then he reached down, grabbed the spherical stone that the prince had tripped over. He threw it up, caught it, and handed it to Tim-Ell.

The Crown Prince of Protar had been beaten by a stone.

Aril sat on the bench at the kitchen table, no longer watching. Tim-Ell had positioned the duel so she could see him win. Staring at the wall, she reviewed her part in the humiliating event. Tim-Ell had been winning with the slave on the defensive but for a stone! No matter what the reason, the prince had been bested by a slave. So, he wasn't the prime swordsman in Protar. Why didn't that make her feel good?

She stood and went back to the glass door. The atrium, now empty, looked like nothing had happened. Kye-Ren still sat on the bench her face pinched in anger. She rose as if she had been made of wood and stomped into her apartment.

Aril gazed around the room, her comfortable prison. She must be patient. The slave Swordmaster won his freedom. Maybe this was her chance to get her word out.

Tim-Ell, his eyes like eston, made his way to the apartment, his stride tired and slow. Ray-Tan caught up to him. As they talked, Tim-Ell's kept his head down. When they reached the glass door, Tim-Ell nodded and Ray-Tan left. Aril stepped aside as Tim-Ell, his knuckles as white as the stone he gripped, passed her without words on his way to the bedroom, his face drawn and grim.

Aril followed him. Should she soothe his feelings? Reduce his mortification? Hadn't she orchestrated this scenario? Yes, her fault, but why would she want to make her captor feel better about his obvious shortcomings? Words failed her. She stood in the doorway as he ripped the Royal emblem from his harness. His fingers paused at the Excalibur medal. He shrugged out of the harness and tossed it on the floor. Without looking at her he marched toward the door. She stepped aside as he left the room in long strides. Picking up his pace, he put his hand on the palm reader lock and left the apartment.

CHAPTER 28

Tim-Ell strode past the now empty courtyard of his apartment complex to the hangar, passing the expanse near the freshly turned dirt, the new herb garden. He threw the stone into the garden with enough thrust to cause small geysers of dirt to shoot knee high. The stone matched the others outlining the turned soil. Overstepping the flier's door, he got in and hesitated at the controls. He didn't know where he wanted to go. He wouldn't stay here. The palace was out, and headquarters was the last place he wanted to be. He set the coordinates to town. Surely there would be a tavern in whose company the Crown Prince of Protar would not be recognized without his royal emblem.

He put the flier down in a shabby parking garage and walked the nearby streets. He didn't recognize this dirty and unkempt area. At the end of the block, a building with music blaring would most likely offer him what he needed—alcohol and company who wouldn't care about his shame, and folks who wouldn't ask questions. Through the open door, smoke and the sour smell of long-dried spilled drinks assaulted him. He entered, and the thought that he didn't carry much cash made him wince.

An attractive woman approached. Even in the dim light, she had a used look, perhaps had taken too many trips on the back of a sweating gant, as the saying went.

The woman put her hand on his shoulder and gave an admiring squeeze. "Hi. I don't remember seeing you here before."

Tim-Ell ran his fingers through his hair, rethinking his choice of taverns. "I haven't been here that I can recall."

"Have a seat," she said. "I'll tell the barman what you'd like to drink. I'll bring it to you."

Tim-Ell took out the coins from a small pouch attached to his sword belt. "Yeah...I don't know..."

A squat man with a grim face forced a smile and pulled a chair opposite the prince. "Allow me," he said and pulled a limbel from his jacket. "We'll have two scuppers."

The woman smiled derisively. "I'm not sure they serve anything so fancy here, but it will be interesting to find out." She raised her hand and summoned the barman.

"Wait," Tim-Ell said pointing to the woman. "I don't want scupper. That's for celebrating. I'll have erbate." He ran his finger over the coins. "I can cover that."

"No need, friend," the squat man said. "Two erbates, on me." He stuck his fist forward, waiting for the almost-touch, the sign of accepting a friendship, even a temporary or drinking bond. "And, whatever the lady is drinking."

Tim-Ell didn't want a drinking buddy, but the man held out his closed hand. Maybe it wasn't such a bad idea. Tim-Ell eased his fisted hand out near enough to make the gesture.

"How about making that three erbates?" The woman turned to the prince putting out both closed hands, the female version of introduction. "My name is Gar-Vost."

The small man put his fist out in a greeting to touch. "And I am Car-Pin."

The noise of the music became garishly loud as the two waited for the third name.

Tim-Ell took in a breath. "You can call me Tee," the nickname his sister had given him. He barely remembered the tutor trying to teach him to talk, and that name had been the best he could do at the time.

The first round of erbates went down fast and Car-Pin ordered another. As the afternoon wore on, round after round of drinks didn't lighten Tim-Ell's mood. Later, a man named Vas-Sar, tall and wiry, friend of Car-Pin's joined them, and he took over the responsibility of providing erbates.

Vas-Sar introduced subjects, elaborating on the ones in which Tim-Ell faked a mild interested. They talked about hunting, and Vas-Sar said it was good for a man to hunt once in a while to strengthen his manliness, to return to the primitive ways.

Gar-Vost eyed Tim-Ell and smiled a come-on look. She ran her hand down his bicep. "Hmm, Tee, I enjoy a bit of primitive action myself."

Car-Pin and Vas-Sar laughed, nodded, and elbowed Tim-Ell.

Tim-Ell cleared his throat. "Uh, not tonight, but thanks. I think I've had enough erbate."

Vas-Sar stood up with a clatter of his chair. "Oh, come now, we're having a good time. Can the lady help it if she finds you to her liking?" The man turned his view to Gar-Vost. "I'm interested. I can provide all the primitive action you could possibly enjoy. Leave our downcast friend here alone for a while. Maybe he's not in the mood for someone new, even a lady as attractive as yourself."

"Yes, that must be it," Car-Pin said. "Is there someone you want and won't respond the way you'd like?"

Tim-Ell didn't answer but cast his gaze to the floor.

"You hit on the problem, all right," Vas-Sar said, his voice low and soothing. "Who is this she-devil who tears at your spirit? A beauty? A princess, far above your station?"

Tim-Ell did not want to discuss his problems, especially his swordplay debacle. He could suppress that. Now, with the right amount of erbate in him, the other, equally disheartening problem, surfaced. He shook his head. "My slave."

The three guests sitting with him at the table laughed. Gar-Vost's eyebrows grooved into a V-shape. "What slave would dare to refuse her master?"

Shaking his head, Tim-Ell downed the last of his bottle. "This one."

The barman had kept the drinks fresh since they sat down. He hurried over with a new bottle while the other three gave their opinions on uppity slaves and how they should be treated.

CHAPTER 29

Aril ate dinner alone. In the quiet, she thought about what she had done to bring about her plan to contact Jake Hill. Her actions had brought shame to Tim-Ell.

So, what was wrong with that? He kept her as his illegal slave. He belonged to a corrupt government in a kingdom that claimed to be part of the Planetary Council but didn't follow the rules.

She tried to, but couldn't, dispel her guilt about goading him into a match to prove his worth as a warrior.

Ray-Tan knocked on the glass, then let himself in. Her guilt dissipated. Even the little bitch-sylph had the handprint and combination of the lock. Why did she feel sorry for instituting her plan, a strategy that might get her freedom?

"Have you heard from the prince?" Ray-Tan asked.

Aril sniffed her disgust. "You are more likely to hear from him than I. Why do you ask?"

Ray-Tan let out a soft snort. "Because he left here in a terrible mood, and I'm usually the one he drinks with. I don't like it. When people see his Royal Emblem, they could cause problems."

"They won't see his emblem," Aril said. "He took it off and didn't wear the harness anyway."

"He took his sword?"

"Certainly." She put her chin up. "He wouldn't leave it here for me, now would he?"

Ray-Tan muttered garbled curse words.

Aril stared at Ray-Tan's face, drawn into frown lines of concern. "You really care about him, don't you?"

"Of course." Ray-Tan held back his words.

"Tell me what you're thinking. I won't say anything."

Ray-Tan nodded. "People assume he's just another corrupt royal, but he's not. He cares about the people, especially us, meaning the soldiers. We get ahead on merit, not who we know."

"Oh, really?" she said as snotty as she could. "Like adhering to the principals of the Excalibur?"

Ray-Tan looked away. He returned his attention to her. "It is impossible to keep the ways of the Excalibur Knights." He shook his head. "Prince Tim-Ell will try to change things when he becomes king." He dropped his head and took a breath. "But he might not last long on the throne. There are too many people, officials and relatives, who will try to stop him putting right the things that have been wrong for so long."

Usually adept at comeback comments, Aril-Ess didn't know what to say. The thought about getting a message to Cadmia emerged. She chose her words carefully so it wouldn't be obvious how much she knew or what role she played in prompting Tim-Ell into the contest. "I saw the prince spar with the man in the tattered clothing."

Ray-Tan crossed his arms over his chest. His nostrils flared. "Yeah. I don't know what possessed the prince. All of a sudden, he wanted to have a go at that slave."

"That slave seemed to be very skilled. He bested the prince."

Ray-Tan let out a long breath. "But shouldn't have. Prince Tim-Ell is the best swordsman in Protar."

Here was her chance. "Not as good as you, though."

"Me?" Ray-Tan cocked his head. "Why would you think that?"

"Oh, come on, warrior. I saw you train a few days ago. You let your sword tip drop, allowing the prince his opening. You let him win."

"Not so," Ray-Tan said. "I did let the sword tip down, but not on purpose." He pointed to a scar on his forearm. "A few years ago, I was injured in battle. Sometimes my hand goes numb for a moment and I lose control."

A wave of self-reproach flooded through her. "An injury? Have you seen a physician?"

"No! I want to stay in the military."

"And you're afraid if the prince knew, he would end your career?"

"The prince knows and keeps my secret. He's helping me. Each time we spar I get a little better."

Her self-reproach increased. "I see."

"The slave who won the match did so by default. The prince slipped on those rounded stones, the kind he helped you put in the herb garden." He threw her an accusatory glare.

A stone she had been responsible for? How dare this common-class soldier accuse her? A swordsman had to be responsible for where he stepped. Then her thought slapped her in the face. Common soldier? How many times had she denounced the way royals looked down upon the common folk? The twinge in her stomach brought her back to where she was now—a slave. She needed to focus on her goal, freedom. "Ray-Tan, what will happen to that slave? The man who fought with the prince?"

"He has been granted freedom."

"Oh. When will he leave for his homeland?" This was important if she was going to have Doctor Fil-Set give the man a message to take to Cadmia.

"He can't leave. He is granted freedom from his slavery, but not freedom to leave the kingdom."

"What?" All of the self-reproach and guilt melted away. Her body stiffened and anger filled her mind. "What kind of freedom is that?"

Ray-Tan touched the pommel of his sword. "The safe kind. What do you think would happen if that man, taken as a war slave and who knows the details of our army, goes back to his family in an enemy country? One, who most likely is considered dead."

Aril spoke with little movement to her lips. "Right. The Protar version of freedom." She stepped toward the door. "It's time you left, Ray-Tan."

The warrior's mouth opened and closed. "A slave who gives orders. I don't understand how he tolerates you." He turned toward the door but paused and threw his words over his shoulder. "You saved Kye-Ren's life and for that I owe you, but here's some advice. Watch your tongue." He keyed the lock and left.

CHAPTER 30

Sooner or later, Jake Hill would find her. He would challenge anyone responsible for her captivity. She rarely allowed herself the luxury of thinking about retribution or vengeance, but the image of those Yaytoog beast-women exchanging the sting sticks for mining picks gave her a slight mood boost. The thought about the men who ran the operation, the ones who bought newly hatched males to train in who knew what? She banished the image before it took place. Those men would go to the harshest mining settlement, maybe even in this area since this kingdom was rich in ores. New thoughts emerged. The planetary mining organization didn't know about the ores in this area, yet Protar was a member of the Planetary Council, including the Mining Union, and able to bestow the Excalibur medal, as shoddy as it was here.

She didn't think Tim-Ell knew about the minerals. She sniffed a quick laugh. He didn't know much about commerce in general, let alone the specifics of economics and mineral trade. The Vizier knew, she would bet. And the treasurer.

Many hours passed. Looking out of the glass door, she saw no lights in the adjoining apartments. Everyone had gone to bed, and she should do the same. The tongue-lashing she had for the prince would have to wait until the next time she saw him. Maybe he would never return to the apartment and stay at the military headquarters. That would be just fine with her. She fluffed up the slim mattress on her cot and retired for the night.

Her rest however, departed like a thunderbolt crack as voices laughed and echoed around the courtyard. Tim-Ell's voice was garbled and slurred as he thumped and jiggled the lock and released the door. She didn't suffer fools or drunks. He would receive no help from her. From the open door of her room, she had a clear view of the kitchen entrance. The outside light highlighted the hunched and swaying figure of Tim-Ell and the darkened outlines of his companions.

Two men helped Tim-Ell through the door. One patted the prince on the back. "Well, Tee, we had a good night, didn't we? But don't let that slave woman off so light. You own her and you can do what you want. So, do it! Be a man. Take what's yours."

Although Tim-Ell's answer did not come out as words, his tone clearly agreed with the stranger's admonitions. The men laughed again and left. Tim-Ell staggered through the kitchen to her door.

Tim-Ell steadied himself by gripping the door jamb of her room. "S-slave," he intoned with imprecision. "M-m-mine," he managed before he stumbled in and fell upon her.

She was ready to give him a throttle, a blow to his windpipe, or a jab against the bridge of his nose. Her muscles tensed; her mind sharpened. As she took in a deep breath to charge her muscles into action, a change swept her, something she'd never experienced. Her muscles tightened in a different manner. Her heart beat wildly and an unfamiliar but stimulating jolt rocked her. She didn't dislodge him on top of her. Not because she lacked strength, but her body wouldn't obey. Instead, she rolled with him off the cot and onto the floor, her breath coming fast and shallow. A wild tremble punched like a shockwave roaring through her body. She pulled his head close; the moisture of his hot breath met her lips. He moaned. Her mind screamed, *no!* but her body wasn't listening. The soft puff of oils glossing his neck emitting the mating scent took over. A perfect match! Her hard-won strength from years of training meant nothing. In this battle she lost the will to fight.

"Aril," he whispered, barely able to speak when she pulled her lips from his.

She had no words, only her drive to have him. She tore at his clothes, deftly unbuckling the harness.

He needed little prompting. His mouth captured hers like a fierce warrior. She parted her lips to invite his tongue. She couldn't breathe. A mind-blurring spin swept away her rage of the hours before. Kisses produced a rush of heat. His fingers brushed her breasts, sending a pulsating wave of desire through her body. Her excruciating need for him intensified with each moment, with each touch of his body. Her breath came in short gasps. Desire burned, opening a part of her deep within, a part that she required him to fill. She couldn't and wouldn't stop.

He rolled on top of her, nipping at her neck and at her breasts. She groaned, pulled at his harness as he brushed his lips against her cheeks, and back to her breasts. His knee parted her legs and he pushed against her as she positioned herself to receive him.

"Now," she said in near desperation. He pushed inside her, and she cried out. Pain, then uncontrollable passion increased, mystifying her mind as he thrust over and over. He moaned, then rolled away, muttering disoriented words.

She pulled him back on top, her body throbbing. "Again!" she demanded.

He exhaled a low, soft breath and pushed inside her. His rhythmic motion increased, and with it, concentrated sensory stimulation, exhilarated her body with blossoms of pleasures. The pulsing built until she didn't think she could stand it, then a part deep within her burned with a white, hot light, made barely tolerable by her scream, muted by pushing her lips into his shoulder. He slowed, moaned, and collapsed on top of her. Spent, she took quick shallow breaths until they slowed, her ardor diminished, and she was able to push him away.

He lay next to her, asleep, his chest rising and falling in regular and sonorous breaths. She blanked her thoughts not allowing logic or understanding to enter her mind. But that didn't last.

What had she done? For years, she'd avoided relationships affected by the animal attraction of scent. Tim-Ell, Prince of Protar, her captor, her owner, was a perfect match, and she would be unable to resist him when he was aroused.

She washed in the bathroom and pulled herself together. Her emotions whipsawed as she reviewed the scenario. Her first time, and it had not been the romantic coupling considered traditional, loving, gentle, with the man who won her heart. Instead, she had given herself to a man who bought her, her master, the degenerate heir who would rule the dissipated and immoral nation of Protar. She rolled with him, demanding he take her. On the floor!

Gathering her strength, she returned to her room and lay her blanket next to Tim-Ell. The sturdy fibers of the cloth would be put to the test. She moved him onto the blanket and slowly, gently, pulled him into the living room. Rolling him from the blanket, she left him near the couch, fetched his few clothes and gear, strewing them about. She arranged the room as if there had been a struggle. She hoped this and his drunkenness would explain it all to him.

Returning to her area, she vowed to stay there until after he awoke the next morning.

CHAPTER 31

In the morning, noises from the apartment suggested Tim-Ell showered then left. When she heard the door lock make its distinctive click, she peeked out of the room and hurried to the glass door. Tim-Ell headed, hard-stepping, to the hangar. He came out again and went to Ray-Tan's apartment. Aril couldn't hear the conversation, but when both went to Captain Cal-Eb's, and the three of them turned toward to the hanger, she assumed Tim-Ell's slick little flier had been left somewhere else. Tim-Ell wore his full harness, but from the distance she couldn't tell if he had reattached his royal emblem. She went into his room. After a bit of searching, she concluded he had assumed his official role as Crown Prince. She wasn't sure why she wanted to know that, or if she cared. Clearing it from her mind, she returned to the kitchen and made her breakfast.

Late that afternoon, Tim-Ell palmed the lock and entered. He checked the pot on the stove, lifting the lid and setting it back down without a sound. After depositing his harness and sword in his room and washing up, he sat at the table with an expectant look.

Aril set his place and served the meal. They ate, neither one speaking.

After she had cleaned up the dishes and headed for her room, he called out to her. "I want to talk with you."

She'd been dreading it, but knew it had to be. "All right." In the living room she sat on the couch as far away as the seat allowed.

"I know I came back last night, in a bad way."

"You were drunk."

"Yes. I was. But I distinctly remember us being together."

What should she say? She had hoped he wouldn't remember anything. "You were drunk. You don't know what you recall."

"I remember. I didn't dream it."

She would have to do some word-dancing. She couldn't possibly admit the truth. "Have you forgotten I said I would never willingly come to your bed?"

"Yes. You said that. But I came to you, and you…well, the details are what have escaped me. Fill me in, so to speak."

His innuendo about filling in was meant as a humorous stab at what occurred. She didn't appreciate it, nor did she smile. He waited for her reply.

"You came into my room, drunk and out of control. What happened, happened."

He shook his head solemnly. "No. I don't believe it. I wouldn't do *that*."

"Believe what you want. Your kind of person believes what they want." She couldn't admit the truth.

He looked down at the floor, deep in thought. "I couldn't. I wouldn't do that. My kind? What does that mean?"

Their conversation ended when the bell from the complex entrance rang. Tim-Ell rose from the couch and went to the call box next to the door. He pressed the button to open the gate and leaned against the doorjamb, his cheeks taut and his brow furrowed.

The light over the glass door illuminated, and Tim-Ell admitted the visitor, Deb-Brit the Royal Tailor and a teenage boy dressed in a slave's smock, who carried a large package. The prince tossed a glance to the table in the kitchen. Deb-Brit's head bobbed in a shallow movement and headed in that direction.

Deb-Brit spoke fast words, as if anxious to leave and be on with his business. He put the package on the table and unwrapped the brown paper that had been tied with string. Holding up a light blue garment embroidered with gold designs, he proudly announced. "Your new tunic, Prince."

Tim-Ell jerked his head, acknowledging the dressmaker and muttered, his words like low growls, showing his foul mood, unusual for him. The young assistant's eyes widened, and he took a step back from the prince.

Deb-Brit frowned. He took another wrapped garment from the bundle and held it out toward Aril. "And you, *slave*, the dress your *master* ordered."

Being in a similar foul mood as Tim-Ell, she refused to bite at the dressmaker's barb. No games, not with this snot.

"Don't you want to see it?" Deb-Brit asked with a whine in his voice.

Of course. He would be proud of his work, no matter the circumstances or who would wear it. Pride. A sentiment way too common in this backcountry cesspool. She curled her lip "Whatever."

The man's face pinched. Like many artists, praise meant more than payment. Would he want praise from someone he considered the lowest of the low? The man did not attempt to hide his disgust that a slave could manipulate her master. Manipulate? A flash of regret came to mind that she did have sway over a powerful person.

"Very well," Deb-Brit said, almost spitting the words. He took the dress from the wrapper and held it up. The soft fabric unfolded, showing pale blue in various layers, some almost transparent, some studded with small sparkling gems.

Aril-Ess stood and sucked in a quick breath. The dress exceeded her expectations. In fact, she had forgotten about it until Deb-Brit walked into the apartment. Reluctant to give this arrogant man credit, she took the garment from him and examined it in detail. She couldn't help from saying, "It's beautiful." She swallowed hard and engaged the man's stare. "Thank you. It's absolutely without compare. You are a true artist."

Deb-Brit, clearly shocked and touched by her unexpected sincerity, managed to put his nose in the air and said, "Of course I am. You don't need to tell me that." He turned to Tim-Ell. "Might you try on your tunic in case I need to make adjustments?"

Tim-Ell picked up the item, saying nothing, and went into his room. When he came out, Deb-Brit smiled with pride. He regarded the prince from all angles and proclaimed nothing more was needed.

The color perfectly set off Tim-Ell's light hair and blue eyes. The hue complemented his tan, and the cut showed off his physique in a way Aril hadn't appreciated, even though she had seen him naked many times. His long-ago comment about never needing to seduce a woman came back to her. Many women would seek him out, especially since he was the Crown Prince. What would happen at the ball when he appeared in this suit? Heads would turn.

Deb-Brit pursed his lips as he took a last look at his creation. "I'll be going now." He didn't ask to see Aril in her dress. It must have cost him a lot of pride, but his desire to insult her apparently overwhelmed his moment of gratification of seeing his art displayed.

Deb-Brit jerked his head to the young slave, who stepped to the table to unpack blue sandals studded with glistening gems for Aril, and soft tan boots with interwoven leather designs to match the color of the prince's outfit on the table. The young man gathered the paper and placed another small bag on the table. With everything collected, the young man toddled behind his master, who waited for Tim-Ell, still wearing the tunic, to unlock the door.

After the Deb-Brit left, Tim-Ell went into his room. The door clicked as it shut behind him.

Aril gathered her pieces and hurried to her room. After she removed her smock, she slipped the piece over her head and fastened loops over sparkling buttons on the side. The dress fit like a second, elegant skin. Long scarf-like pieces crossed over her breasts, showing enough cleavage to be attractive, but not so much to be vulgar. The silky strips crossed again at her back then came around front and tied snugly under her breasts, holding them up and out. The dress matched her design, but more, better than she had indicated. She chuckled to herself. Perhaps when Jake Hill rescued her, Deb-Brit would be spared. Never before had she seen or owned such a lovely garment. But the artist! Who would tolerate such an arrogant man? Ha! Five minutes with grandsire would cure that man of his haughtiness. And then some.

Extra ribbons matching the fabric puzzled her. Along with sparkling faceted stones that studded the dress, several of the stones were attached to hairpins. That nasty little man, as talented as he was, wouldn't have added those to the ensemble on his own. Tim-Ell must have told him to add accessories. But he was a warrior, not a fashion-lover. She pulled her hair up and inserted the ribbons and stones. Not that she was a fashion lover, either, but she yearned to see the effect.

Wanting to see how the dress and accessories looked, she waited until she heard Tim-Ell's door open and listened for his steps as he went into the bathroom. She scurried into his room to look at the full-length mirror next to the closet. Turning to see the sides and back, she repositioned the hair accessories.

The prince came in. He stopped mid-step and caressed her with his stare. She tensed, half expecting him to touch her, to take her in his arms. Their eyes met. He froze, turned heel, and left the room. The sound of the door opening and lock clicking meant he left the apartment.

She let out a sigh. The look he gave her as he stared at her in the dress made her blush. She had seen that look on grandsire when he sent silent messages to his beloved, Arba-Lora. Her father did the same when he cast his eyes to his mate, her own mother.

Returning to her room, she removed the lovely soft gown and accessories that a horrid man, an artist, had created just for her. As she donned the light smock, the apparel for slaves, thoughts about the ball surfaced. How could she avoid his touch if he insisted on dancing? What kind of a ball? Specifics had never been discussed, other than the ball was the celebration of the Longest Day.

Did he take his bedecked slaves to balls to fend off noble ladies with Queenship on their minds? He probably had to fend off noble and commoners alike. A thought crept into her contemplation. Isn't that what she had done? All those years of study when she dodged the advances of men who sought her? A tear took her unaware and slid down her cheek as she thought about Jerr-Lan, the warrior who had protected her with his life.

Memories of many balls at Jake Hill's palace in Cadmia came to mind. She could picture her grandsire's wife, the lovely and elegant Arba-Lora, wearing one of Deb-Brit's creations. Folding the dress with care, she put it on the shelf in her closet. *Her closet!* As if it wasn't a prison, and she, having a magnificent gown for a ball, wasn't a prisoner. A prisoner who had practically raped her captor just hours earlier.

CHAPTER 32

In the hangar, Tim-Ell stood in the place his flier usually occupied, sorting out the previous events. He couldn't reconcile his memories of having torrid sex with the woman he most desired, to her claim, believably so, that she would never willingly submit to him. *What happened?*

He would not have forced her. He was sure of that. He recalled that day, the day he had been defeated by a slave who had not held a sword in his hands for five years. Was it just the stone that caused his defeat? He'd had the man backing up, defending vigorously. The slave, Linter, skilled and experienced, gave a good fight. No! Linter the slave had been *losing*. It had been a matter of moments before the end.

The memories of the defeat and his shame followed the mental reenactment of the duel. Weak men drink and whine when they lose. What did that make him, Crown Prince and head of the Army? Weak. He sniffed in anger at his behavior.

Those men at the tavern, he couldn't remember the name of the tavern, nor would he be able to find it again, or his flier. Great. Prince Tim-Ell would have to ask the police, who were an off-shoot of the military, for help getting his flier.

He leaned against a post in the hangar and searched his memory. Who were the people he drank with? A woman, most likely a prostitute. He'd never engaged the services of a lady of the evening. Just like he would never…*No.* He wouldn't have done *that* to Aril-Ess. He slammed his fist against the post and nailed his eyes closed. He remembered telling those people, two men, one woman, that he pined for his slave woman.

Oh, Goddess, what a weakling, a fool. Pathetic. *I've dishonored myself.* Heat crept up his face. Those people, they had provoked him to "take what was his." He remembered agreeing with them, wanting to bring Aril-Ess into his bed. Flashes of the trip back to the apartment surfaced, but not enough to recall the experience. Those men must have brought him home, but he had bits of recollection entering the house…or her room. Did he bring her to *his* room? Absolutely not; it wasn't his way, even if he did make the stupid comments about taking her. But he *had* made love to her, passionate, torrid love, and *that* he remembered vividly. None of it made sense. He rode in Cal-Eb's craft with Ray-Tan and spent the morning seeing to military matters so he could force away the images of the night before. At headquarters he cringed as he asked the chief of police to find and return his flier.

He pushed up from his desk and paced the room. It wouldn't happen again. Ever. Perhaps he should free her and let her be on her way. To where? He didn't know anything about her except what the certificate described as a *prisoner of war.* That was possible. The woman wouldn't be afraid of anything. Some kingdoms and principalities had women warriors. But they didn't look like Aril-Ess. The female warriors he'd seen all looked like Linter, the slave swordsman. The man who beat him. The man who had earlier that morning accepted a position in the Protar Army as a combat trainer. With his ability, and now his reputation as the best in the land, how long would it be before he worked his way up to Protar Swordmaster, with all the benefits and grants that went along with the title? And why shouldn't the man be allowed the status? The swordsman earned it. All because of her, the slave Aril-Ess. The woman he couldn't let go. He cleared his mind, not wanting to explore the reasons. He needed to stay away for a while and let things settle. The ball. How could he get out of it? That wouldn't happen because the King, his father, had insisted Tim-Ell attend. Aril looked stunning in that dress. Beautiful or not, he'd find a way to avoid her.

He made a bed on the cot in his office and ate at the mess hall with his warriors. How many things could he avoid? He didn't want to spar, and he certainly didn't want to go back to his apartment.

CHAPTER 33

To keep from focusing on her many problems, Aril kept busy by cleaning and polishing Tim-Ell's harnesses and equipment. She thumbed through every book on the shelves, but most of them were battle-oriented, the kind of reading that interested a military man. The books on flora and fauna held her attention, but she knew most of the content.

A small area off the living room, like an enclosed garden, offered a place for sunshine and fresh air, the roof a lattice and the side that faced the outside was mortared with open brickwork. She had wanted to get potted herbs and a few chairs but hadn't seen to that yet. The space would make a good exercise area. Using the kitchen knife as a practice blade she performed maneuvers she had done for years at the palace in Cadmia. Next, she used a broom handle as a sword. Later it became a pike as she took deep lunges at an imaginary opponent. She ran at the walls, jumping and propelling away until she gulped in air. Blood coursed through her veins and provided a workout that left her spent but pumped with the aftereffects of adrenaline. How long had it been since she experienced the joy of movement? This would be her new routine. Except, not in front of *him*. No one needed to know about what she could do. Dr. Fil-Set knew the secret of her bloodline. She sniffed. He had yet to do anything about getting a message to Jake Hill.

She went down on one knee to catch her breath. At this level, through the open brickwork she focused on two men across the street. They were watching the building with a deep concentration. Could they see she had been practicing defense movements? Weapons maneuvers? One, leaning against a tree was squat, the other sitting on a knee-high boulder was tall and wiry. She couldn't hear their words. The tall man spoke; the other nodded. They didn't take their gaze from the apartment while they conversed. Jake Hill told his progeny many times "go with your gut. If something doesn't feel right, it probably isn't." Those men didn't feel right. They were spies.

Later that afternoon, Ray-Tan knocked, then let himself in the glass door. Aril offered him part of the leftover meat and tubers that she was eating.

"Thank you, but Kye-Ren made our meal," he said.

Our meal. How nice. Still, how could Ray-Tan, a warrior, a general in the Protar Army, be in love with that vile silver bitch? The female who bared her pointy little incisors at Aril every time she could. Scent? Was it possible that the pheromones of a subspecies of the Cronantian line would attract a member of the dominant species? A few studies had indicated pheromones crossed species. Aril hadn't studied much about the pheromones other than what she had learned as a field medic, and that hadn't gone much further than the chemical reactions regarding male-female attraction levels.

"Do you need anything?" Ray-Tan asked, breaking into her thoughts.

"Other than not being kept prisoner in this place?"

Ray-Tan put his hands on his hips. "Leave it alone. Can't you appreciate the fact you are in the best place a…"

"A slave? Say it, a captive held illegally."

"Look, you aren't being abused." He held up his palm to stop her protest. "I've been sent here to check on you. I see you're alive, and in your normal state of cheer. Now I'll go back."

"To *your* slave?"

He pointed at her accusingly. "To Kye-Ren, who *does* appreciate her position and is happy with her lot."

Aril tossed her head and laughed. She wasn't going to win her point. "And who still hates me?"

Ray-Tan relaxed and smiled. "With a passion."

Aril spread her hands. "Whatever. Go back to your little silver girl. I don't need anything."

He turned to leave.

"Ray-Tan?"

He stopped but didn't face her. "Yes?"

"Thanks for asking."

He nodded, put his palm on the lock, and keyed the number.

The routine continued for the next three days, with Ray-Tan checking on her at dinnertime. Aril kept the apartment in order and did her exercises, with a sheet over the open brickwork so the men who were often across the street watching could not see her. She prepared her meals and ate alone.

The third night Ray-Tan checked on her, he reminded her to prepare for the ball, which would be held the following evening. He pulled at his Excaliburian emblem. "Look, the Prince most likely won't require you to wear your wire, but please don't try anything foolish." He paused to let the meaning set in.

"You mean I shouldn't try to escape."

"Precisely. The palace is full of guards. Most people won't know who you are."

"A slave."

"Yes. But some will. It's dangerous and foolhardy to think you could flee."

"The prince will kill me?"

He shook his head. "You have him all wrong. But it doesn't matter. There are many dangers at the palace. Promise me you won't do something stupid."

"Ray-Tan."

"On your honor, Aril-Ess. Promise."

"Whatever. I wouldn't want to get my fancy dress bloody."

"Good." He left.

The following afternoon, Tim-Ell returned to the apartment. "I won't be long. Please be ready within the hour." He dressed for the evening.

Aril took her time getting ready. She wondered if the royal affairs in Protar would be like the ones in Cadmia. Jake Hill didn't like his guests to wear their royal insignia, tiaras, crowns, or wreaths made of precious metals. He invited people from every stratum, even as he attempted to eliminate strata. Guests included family, friends, inter-kingdom dignitaries, and people who distinguished themselves in society, including brave warriors and their mates. The dress code was fancy, but not mandatory. Jake Hill said he wanted the company of good folk, not a fashion show. His Mate, Arba-Lora, always looked gorgeous and wore lovely, but not overdone, gowns. Her age, not known by many as over four hundred years, retained her beauty and elegance. Aril resembled Arba-Lora in face and figure. Maybe that was one of the reasons Jake Hill favored her, although he claimed it was because Aril had Arba-Lora's spirit. The tale had always amused her. Perhaps she refused advances because she waited for her own Jake Hill.

Aril put the finishing touches on her dark tresses, which were long enough to be swept into a pile of curls supported in place by crystal-ended pins and ribbons the color of deep ice. She stepped away from the mirror and stood in the doorway to the living room.

Tim-Ell didn't say anything, but he caught his breath twice. He nodded and ran his gaze over her several times.

He buckled his ceremonial sword. "Time to go."

They walked across the courtyard and met up with Captain Cal-Eb. His wife, Del-Am, wore a gown of soft sunset orange with matching sandals. Del-Am's eyes widened when she saw Aril. Although protocol dictated not speaking to a slave unless to give orders, Del-Am said, "You look beautiful."

Aril cast her eyes down and answered in low tones. "Thank you." She added, "My Lady," the proper response for a slave. *What should I do? I don't know the protocol for a slave who is being escorted by nobility. I know how slaves would address me a ball in Cadmia.* When she returned to Cadmia, she would discuss some things with Jake Hill. Being a slave put a new light on being a slave's master. She would like to tell Del-Am how pretty she looked, too. Aril's status meant she wasn't supposed to speak to the woman in such a friendly manner.

Captain Cal-Eb held Del-Am's hand and stood back, letting Tim-Ell approach the flier. Tim-Ell opened the low door for Aril to take the seat. The captain and his wife sat in the back seat. Tim-Ell raised the windshield to protect the women's hairstyles, reversed the craft out of the hanger, and as usual, immediately put the fast little ship to speed.

The rooftops flew by in a blur. In a few minutes, the unmistakable spires of a palace appeared on the horizon. According to Ray-Tan, this was a dangerous place to be.

CHAPTER 34

Prince Tim-Ell parked his sleek craft in an area near the top of one of the spires. The few elegant ships moored there suggested a private area for royalty. The Prince and Aril, along with Captain Cal-Eb and his mate Del-Am, walked down several long ramps that ended in a courtyard with trees cut in a variety of shapes. The Longest Day celebration coincided with the conjunction of the planet's three moons. Softly whooshing fountains tinkled; the waters sparkled in the light of the largest moon. The other, smaller, moons would make their appearance that night.

They walked through a landscaped area illuminated by soft lights on posts. At the end of the garden, four warriors with tilted pikes guarded double doors. Tim-Ell stopped at the doors, put his fist against his chest twice. The guards came to attention, snapping their spears upright.

"Well done, men," the prince said.

"Yes, Sir," they replied in unison.

It was similar to what would happen in Cadmia, except the doors would be open, and the guards wouldn't tilt their weapons. Would there be four guards on the other side of the doors keeping the guests in? Two of the guards, spears upright, opened the door. On the inside, two guards thumped their vertical pikes on the floor as Aril and the Prince entered. The prince gave the same greeting to these guards. Aril thought about the warning Ray-Tan had given her about not escaping. Tim-Ell would not hurt her, but Ray-Tan knew who would.

They passed through a corridor into an open archway. The smell of incense amplified as they approached the ballroom. This huge room did not look like the party room in Cadmia. Precious metals embossed immense columns. Swags of expensive cloth, intertwined with flowering vines, added a gaudy touch on already overdone architecture. This palace contrasted to the stately design of Cadmia's castle, with its clean lines and unadorned polished stone. Jake Hill's home, designed by him, housed his family and many members of the generations that followed.

The archway's stone walk turned into another corridor, where echoes of laughter and music signaled the ball's proximity. Couples in fine dress waited in a line to be announced. The couple at the front stepped up to a man dressed in the uniform of royal household service. He took their invitation. That uniformed man handed the invitation to the Reception Master, who announced them. The male guest put his hand over the lady's hand, and they entered. The uniformed man spotted Tim-Ell, hurried to him, and signaled the Reception Master, who, with a broad smile and rapid steps, approached Tim-Ell.

"Give way for the prince," the Reception Master said and bowed.

Tim-Ell nodded to the Reception Master with a sigh, as if he didn't want his presence to be announced. The Reception Master guided them to the front of the line, where he said to the crowd in the ballroom, "May I have your attention." He paused for the laugher to hush and the music to stop. "Presenting Crown Prince Tim-Ell, and his companion."

Companion? The Reception Master didn't ask her name. Did the Prince always bring slave companions who were of such little importance they didn't have their names announced? Aril did not put her hand out and the prince did not make a move to touch her. She could feel the crowd staring as he moved forward. She stayed slightly behind him.

"Stay next to me," he whispered.

She took a quick step up. They walked across the expansive room toward the double throne. A man, an older version of Tim-Ell, and a woman with dark hair and a stern face, sat on ornate chairs with tall backs, upholstered in purple and gold. They wore gem-studded crowns.

The woman, obviously the Queen, kept her face expressionless, but the man smiled.

"My son!" The King said.

Tim-Ell stopped a few feet in front of the throne. He gave a quick look at Aril. As he dipped to kneel, she did as well.

With his head parallel to the floor he said, "Sire." Then he added, "Mother."

"Rise, my boy," the King said. "It's good to see you."

Tim-Ell rose. "Thank you."

The prince didn't lie and say, *Good to be here.*

Aril rose.

"And who is this lovely creature?" the King said with pleasure resonant in his words.

"May I present Aril-Ess, my companion."

Aril let out the breath she held, then held the next one. Would the king ask where she came from? If she came from their kingdom, the obvious query would be her family name.

"Aril-Ess, may I present the Queen."

The Queen, her expression suspicious and stern, snapped, "Don't tell us this is one of your…women…a slut you have the nerve to present at court and bring into our home."

"Then I won't." He clasped Aril's hand and whisked her away from the throne area. Picking up speed, he steered her to a cushioned stone bench. "Stay here." He strode away.

Aril sat with her back straight, knees held primly together with only her eyes moving from side to side, taking in the details of the people and the room.

A young woman in a gauzy white smock came to her and bowed. "May I get you a plate, ma'am?"

For a moment, Aril relaxed, accustomed to the service. She smiled, ready to give her request but stayed her words at the sight of the bright red splotch on the slave's face. Someone had struck the girl. Tears rimmed the slave's eyes, and her hands shook. Aril's muscles tightened as if she readied to take on an opponent. But for Tim-Ell buying *her,* she, High Princess of Cadmia, direct heir of the Planetary Prince, might be in the same predicament as this unfortunate young woman.

Aril whispered. "Who hurt you?"

The slave girl's eyes went wide. Her head shook slightly. She could not reveal that information to an elegant guest in the ballroom.

The girl, her expression blank asked, "Might I serve you a drink? Punch? Scupper?"

The conversation would go no further, and Aril could not do anything for the unfortunate girl. "Scupper, please."

"Cheese and a bit of fruit?"

"Yes, that would be wonderful."

The girl bowed, weaved through the crowd, and scurried into an open doorway, which in Cadmia would be a preparation room. Aril leaned back. What happened in that room beyond that door? She had been to many parties and balls and had a multitude of servants attend her. Never once had she considered the activities and demands behind the service. Now it became important. When she was back in Cadmia, she would see to detailed investigations concerning the treatment of slaves and what went on behind the scenes.

I am slave to a prince, but have gained valuable knowledge about people and things I would not have learned otherwise. I will use this experience to make sure abuses come to a halt all over the planet.

A young man wearing a uniform with the royal crest, the royal household garb, approached her. "Miss? The King requests your presence."

Fear hit her like a bolt of lightning. "The King?"

"Yes, Miss. Will you please come with me?"

Speaking with the King didn't bother her as much as the fact he sat next to the Queen. Aril nodded and took the page's arm. As she crossed the floor, she looked for, but didn't see, Tim-Ell. Turning the corner into the ballroom, she breathed relief at the Queen's empty seat.

The King smiled. "What is your name, again, young lady?"

"Aril-Ess." She bowed with bended knee. Protocol demanded she not make eye contact. Her gaze caught sight of a satiny foot pillow to the side of the throne.

"Aril-Ess. Lovely. Your name matches your appearance. You are a cut above the other young women my son has brought to our events. They are just cover, so court ladies leave him alone. But you are different."

She rose and met his gaze. *I won't call you sire, the title reserved for my great grandfather, Jake Hill.* "Yes, King."

He laughed. "King Jess-Reet."

The custom regarding the foot pillow was for the highest-ranking female to offer the pillow and place it under his feet. Since the pillow remained untouched, that meant no woman had offered it. Even though Jake Hill didn't like the notion of nobility, he had also admonished his family when guests to honor customs. Aril reached for the pillow and held it next to King Jess-Reet's feet. "Your pillow?"

The King tipped his head forward with eyes wide and raised eyebrows. "Ah, my son has taught you well."

Aril stifled the deriding chuckle forming on her lips. Prince Tim-Ell probably didn't know the quaint gesture and, like Jake Hill, would not have such foolishness as a pillow underfoot.

A young page placed a goblet on a small table next to the throne. "Your drink, Sire." The boy bowed his head and backed away.

The King leaned toward it, but Aril held the goblet up. "Do you have a taster, King Jess-Reet?"

"In the kitchen."

"The kitchen! If your taster is in the kitchen, how can you be sure the test is carried out? How can you see its effect?"

"True. My Vizier said a taster appears vulgar and would be better hidden away. You don't agree with that?"

"Here," she said, "is what I *would* agree with." She told him her opinion to which he laughed loudly and called the nearest page.

"Summon Eppo-Zim immediately," the King said.

Aril stood next to the seated King while they waited for the Vizier to come. A man in rich robes with a bald head sauntered through the crowds. Since viziers had positions of power as advisors to royalty, Jake Hill suggested they take small wages as a token of their service, making sure they weren't tempted to become addicted to riches and become corrupt. As the man neared the throne, he kept his eye on the King. He swept low.

King Jess-Reet said, "Rise, Eppo-Zim. I have a mission for you."

The man in the elaborate dress brandished a wide smile. Aril jerked in recognition. Where had she seen that evil grin? This was her first meeting with the Vizier of Protar, Eppo-Zim.

"What mission, Sire?"

King Jess-Reet pointed to the goblet in Aril's hand. "You can be my taster tonight. And I may call upon you other times in the near future."

Eppo-Zim lost some of his tanned color. "You want *me* to taste the wine?"

"Wasn't I clear?"

Aril handed the goblet to Eppo-Zim. He took it and smelled it. "Do you think there's anything wrong with this wine?"

"Do you?" the King asked.

"Of course not. Your taster is in the kitchen."

"I don't want a *kitchen* taster," King Jess-Reet said, enjoying the banter. "I want a *throne* taster, and since I don't have one, you and Epog-Mal, our Royal Treasurer, will be my tasters until I find someone I trust at my side."

Eppo-Zim's mouth opened as if he would speak. Instead, he took a delicate sip and handed the goblet to Aril with a glare. His evil glower caused that familiar feeling of recollection to return. He did not question who she was, either. Her gut said he already knew.

"The wine is safe, Sire," Eppo-Zim said, his nostrils flaring on his stiff face.

"Very well. You may leave."

Eppo-Zim fled.

King Jess-Reet's smile radiated up his rounded cheeks to form small crinkles around his eyes. "The King has a few pleasures now and then." He stood and extended his hand. "Dance with me, clever young woman. I haven't danced in years, but I want to now."

"I would enjoy that." And she meant it.

He led her to the dance area. Chuckling, he said, "I hope I remember the steps. I may be a bit rusty."

She winked. "Well then, because you're the King, I'll let you tread on my toes."

He laughed again. Dancers around them backed away, leaving Aril and King Jess-Reet as solitary dancers. Aril and the King extended their left arms over their heads and grasped right arms, moving in a circle to the count of four, then they reversed arms and directions. The King did not miss a beat.

"You are a treasure," Jess-Reet said. "And obviously not from Protar, or I would have become aware of you earlier. I want to do something to please you. Name what you desire." They turned, taking the back-to-back stance.

Freedom. Her opportunity to go home. Not possible. He knows I'm from another kingdom. I can't tell him the truth. Before they turned face-to-face, she wiped the disappointment from her expression. "Thank you." She took two steps away and two steps back to meet him. "I would ask for," They separated, turned in a circle and met again. "for your slaves' good health."

They touched palms, turned away, and back again. He took her arm and strode four steps forward. "We have good healthcare for everyone."

When she could catch his gaze again, she said, "Do you know that for a fact? Have you seen for yourself?"

She dipped; he bowed; they locked arms.

"I never leave the castle. I have the word of…"

They reversed positions. "Eppo-Zim or Epog-Mal?"

"I see," He waited until they faced each other, "your point."

In this part of the dance, they locked arms and moved forward touching each other's hips.

"I've heard you have three sons, and I know one of them is a great warrior. Why not invite the three of them to accompany you for a single day to look at your kingdom? Keep it secret until they arrive at the palace. Leave quickly and have an army guard go with you for extra safety. If no one knows where you are going, there can't be any plans for…"

"An ambush," he finished.

"Yes, a threat on your life."

The music ended. The people who had relinquished their places on the dance floor applauded. The King nodded.

"Lovely woman, rumors and gossip travel faster than arrows. By now the Queen must have heard a tale far blown from the truth and will be back shortly." He cast a glance at the empty throne. "Of course, perhaps you would like to be presented."

"No!" Aril said without thought.

He laughed. "I understand completely. I will escort you back."

"To that corner," she pointed to the place she been, hidden from the throne area.

King Jess-Reet guided her around the corner where Tim-Ell now sat alone. He stood when he saw them, surprise in his expression.

"My son," the King said, "thank you for sharing this lovely lady." He dropped his head and sagged his shoulders. "I'm so sorry." He let out a breath. "Truly I am." He turned and left.

"You spent time with my father?"

"We danced," she said.

"Good. Then we've been noticed as being here. I've made my rounds, and after some big announcement that's supposed to be proclaimed soon, we can leave. I hate these things."

He sounded a lot like Jake Hill complaining about social events.

"I'm ready when you are," she said.

The music stopped. The Reception Master strode to the center of the ballroom, waited for the crowds to hush, then read from a scroll-like paper. "His Royal Highness, King Jess-Reet, and his wife, her Royal Highness, Ran-Cignar, announce the engagement of Crown Prince Tim-Ell to the High Princess, Sari-Van of the kingdom of Crocess. The Princess will arrive in Protar in five days. Their engagement party will be one week from tonight, and the marriage will follow the next day."

People applauded and cheered. Not all people.

Tim-Ell shot up from the bench.

The crowd cheered and applauded louder.

Aril put meaning to the King's apology. He hadn't regretted taking Tim-Ell's companion for the dancing—he lamented the blindsided attack of the arranged engagement.

People rushed to congratulate the prince. Aril got behind the bench and pressed against the wall, away from the crush of well-wishers. A number of attractive young women frowned and wiped away tears, their dreams of catching the Crown Prince dashed.

Two hours later, the prince sat on the bench unmolested by his supporters. He hung his head and swore softly.

CHAPTER 35

Tim-Ell didn't speak on the walk back to the flier. He said nothing as they buzzed close to the spires and rooftops of Protar. The only sounds came from the light chatter between Cal-Eb and Del-Am in the back seat. Quiet dominated the trip until the prince eased his craft into its place at the apartment hangar.

After the Captain and his wife bid them good night, Tim-Ell and Aril continued in silence past the courtyard and into the apartment. Instead of the usual, cheery reminder about keeping his bedroom door open to her, Tim-Ell said nothing, entered his room, and shut the door. A few minutes later, only the noise of running water echoed in the chilly stillness.

Aril removed her dress and undid her hair in slow, deliberate movements, stretching the sensation of elegance. It had been a long time since she had enjoyed the luxury of feeling like a feminine, stately woman. She cleaned up in the bathroom and readied for bed. Sleep evaded her. She imagined how the prince would marry and be out of her life. The thought hit her like a spear. What would happen to *her?* No Princess, no wife, would tolerate a slave like Aril around. She would be the first change in the prince's life. Would he give her away? Key-Ren had once taunted, saying the prince would tire of Aril and give her away like he did his other girls. Now it had the sting of truth. Would Tim-Ell give her to his brother? The Swordmaster from Linter, perhaps? Or maybe another worthy soldier who had acquitted himself in weaponry trials?

After a few hours of speculation, she went into the kitchen and mixed herbs from the cabinet with water and put them to boil.

Tim-Ell came out, wearing his usual sleeping attire, the ankle dagger, and let out a long breath. "What are you doing?"

"Making a sleeping draft."

"Is there enough for two?"

She reached into the cabinet and brought out the herbs again. Pinching from the small containers, she threw the ingredients in the boiling liquid. "Yes. Now."

He took two cups from the cabinet and set them on the table.

Aril removed the pot from the stove top to cool. "Will you be staying at your headquarters?"

He ran his fingers through his hair. "I don't know. I hate questions. There will be a lot of questions. I only know what I heard tonight." He spat the last word as if produced a bitter taste on his tongue.

"You don't know this princess? Wasn't this arranged when you were small?"

He released a string of curses, ending with, "Nothing. Never. And not."

His scowl and tone of voice said clearly he did not want to marry.

"Can you refuse?"

He looked at her, then cast his gaze to the wall. "If I want to renounce citizenship, relinquish my Army rank, and defect from my kingdom." He shook his head. "What country would take me in? Offer me a place to live?"

Slow words in her mind screamed. *Not Cadmia.* Yet, she pitied the man who did not want to be forced into a relationship. Like she had been. The question most important to her, surfaced. *What will happen to me?*

Tim-Ell poured the draft, now cool enough to drink, into the cups and they sipped the tangy liquid. While they finished, Aril stared into the cup with visions of what lay in store for her future. The deep sighs from the prince brought her out of her thoughts. His gaze dropped to the floor. The effects of the brew took a few minutes to work, but drowsy, they both went to their separate beds. Aril slept, dreaming of Jerr-Lan as he bled from the arrows in his chest, then rising to rescue her from the nightmare. Part of the nightmare was the fact she needed rescuing.

When she awoke, the sun's rays slanted through the glass of the back doors, meaning late morning. She dressed in her usual smock and headed for the bathroom. The door was closed, and noises indicated Tim-Ell occupied the room. He had never slept this late. She quickly put on the kettle to make keela.

The prince hurried out of the bathroom, scrambling for his harness and the accoutrements of his position. In the kitchen he poured a cup of keela and drank it in a few gulps. As he put his hand on the door's palm device, the bell from the complex's entrance rang. A palace courier said Tim-Ell had an urgent dispatch from the King. Tim-Ell pressed the button to admit the messenger. With a brief glance at Aril, the Prince placed his palm on the lock reader. The device clicked and he left. As usual, the door closed, leaving her at the glass. He sprinted toward a man in a uniform who had been part of the palace household from the night before. He spoke to Tim-Ell for a moment. The prince nodded, headed to the hangar accompanied by the palace courier, and both men hopped in the flier. After he started the craft, it floated to the middle of the courtyard and hovered. The flier left the area like an arrow and gained altitude.

Aril spent her day as the ones before. Would the Prince stay at headquarters? At sundown, the flier appeared in the courtyard and with little sound, whooshed into the hangar. Minutes later, Tim-Ell let himself into the apartment.

Aril brought out another place setting and served what she had cooked for the day.

Tim-Ell cut the tender meat with his fork and stabbed a piece with a speed of a hungry man. After a second bite, he said, "Tomorrow, Ray-Tan, Cal-Eb, my two brothers, and *my father* are spending the day with me." He shook his head. "I have to get up early and find a Rotner Monk." He took another bite. "The kind that wears a full robe." He sliced through the meat with his fork.

"I know what a Rotner Monk is. They don't talk much, tell the truth, give aid to poor and helpless, and are forbidden to take more payment than they need to subsist." She added with a sneer, "A group much needed in *this* kingdom."

He stopped the loaded fork inches from his mouth. "Whatever." He scraped the utensil clean in one bite.

"And?"

"The point is they wear full robes. I am to bring in one monk and carry an extra robe. One monk in, two monks out. Get it?"

"Your father is posing as a monk?"

Tim-Ell twisted the cap from a bottle of erbate.

"Oh, your father is leaving the palace incognito."

"I don't know what has gotten into him. He wants to see as much as he can, using his words, *looking at things*, but I'm not sure what those *things* are. No one in the castle can know about it until we leave, and Mother will find out when she gets up and reads the note he'll put on her pillow."

"Why are you telling *me*?"

He pointed the fork at her. "Because I think you said something to him."

"It's not like we sat for hours talking, Prince. We danced the Prelata for ten minutes, which you might not know, but the movements don't facilitate much conversation."

He didn't respond but kept eye contact with her.

She cleared the empty plate. "You don't want to spend time with your brothers and father?"

"It's not so much as *want* to be with them but it will be interesting. I rarely see my brothers, and we've never gone out together. From what I gather, this might be a training session for a King. Me."

"That sounds strange to you? People must learn their craft. They take training, go to school, learn from mentors. Why wouldn't rulers learn skills to run a kingdom?"

He took a long pull from the bottle and wiped his mouth with the back of his hand. "Like King school, eh? Come on."

She took the empty plate away. "The name is foolish but not the reasoning behind the training. How did you father learn how to rule?"

Tim-Ell regarded the almost-empty erbate bottle for a long moment and shook his head. "He didn't. He married my mother by arrangement of the former Vizier, so Protar could gain the land of a small principality, which included that lake you saw. Protar grew because of their union. But neither one knew anything about how to make decisions, or how to run a kingdom. That's why Protar has a Vizier."

"Your parents have been satisfied to pose as figureheads and not be decision makers?"

He ran his fingers through his hair. "I guess that describes it."

"You aren't going to be that way, right? You want to know what is happening in your land."

He finished the erbate. "I don't want to be King. I hope I can get the chance to talk the old man into helping me get out of marrying that princess."

Aril devoted most of the rest of the night thinking about his marriage, too.

The next morning, when Aril got up, Tim-Ell was already gone. She remained alone all day, often staring out the window for his flier or his figure striding toward the apartment. Late that night, she prepared for bed, no longer waiting. What kind of day had the King experienced? Did he see what really went on in his kingdom? Muted noises at the back door meant Tim-Ell had returned. Although curious about the King's secret field survey, she stayed in bed, not wanting to appear too interested, or involved.

CHAPTER 36

At breakfast the following day, Aril placed the prince's plate on the table in front of him. "Will you take me to the market today?"

Tim-Ell reached for his cup of keela, sipped, then nodded. "We'll go to the marketplace to the north. It will take about an hour."

"Not that I know much about the geography of Protar, but why so far away? The other markets didn't take that long to travel."

"We'll go to that market because Princess Sari-Van of Crocess's entourage will be coming through the northern woods on its way to the city."

"Entourage? Won't they fly a large airship to the palace?"

Tim-Ell rolled his eyes. "It's old-fashioned. Crocess wants to send Sari-Van in the traditional way, a wedding gant-train."

"A gant-train! How quaint. I'd like to see that."

Tim-Ell put his cup down with a clink on the stone table. "You will. I thought I'd take a flyover. I'd like to see what a gant-train looks like, too."

His voice dropped, as if he spoke of a tragedy happening to a loved one. "I suppose she'll have her own guards, but I should get an idea as to what kind of security I'll need to provide."

Usually, the Head of the Guards would arrange for foreign visitor's security. But for guests of this nature, the Queen-to-be, Tim-Ell, as Army Commander, would be expected to handle it personally.

He rose. "Get ready as soon as you can."

Aril snatched the empty cup from the table and whisked it with the other dishes into the sink. She cleaned up in a blur of motion, eager to shop, but more eager to see the silly procession she had only read about in history studies. A gant-train, a stupid spectacle, suited for a stupid marriage in a stupid kingdom.

She had been contemplating her escape, what she would have to do before Tim-Ell's bride banished her or … worse. Maybe a trip to the outlying woods in the north would provide a strategy. She had been studying his battle books, trying to locate Protar in its position to Cadmia. From what she learned from the maps, Cadmia lay to the north and west. Protar was a small kingdom situated on the lower eastern hemisphere. She had watched the prince input numbers on the flier's ignition and memorized the code. If he had not changed the numerical sequence, her experience with other craft would enable her to steal the flier. She grinned to herself as she dressed. Crown Prince Tim-Ell would miss his precious little ship. She'd have to fly at full-throttle. Ha! That flier could go faster than most of the pursuit-craft the army or the police had if they chase her.

Her smile faded when she reached into the closet to choose clean clothes. The only things she had, beside her gown, were slave smocks. She wore them double because the ones Tim-Ell liked were gauzy, not the kind of fabric she would ever allow the Cadmia slaves to wear.

Dressed in the two smocks, she came out into the living room. He put down the book he held and headed for the back door.

As she climbed aboard the four-seater Tim-Ell's hand hovered over the keypad. "Promise you won't try to escape while we are at the market."

"I promise." A chill raised bumps on her arms as she pictured the brutal treatment administered to wayward slaves on Protar. She shoved her hands into the pockets of her smock., The scene in her mind turned to one of future retribution.

As usual, Tim-Ell flew like a maniac, skimming spires at breakneck speed, missing rooftops by inches. He treated flying like a challenge. If he misjudged his skill, she would go down with him. However, hurtling through the sunshine and fresh air at times was fun.

Shopping took longer because she did not know her way around this unfamiliar market. Eventually she loaded Tim-Ell down with cooking and cleaning supplies. She had to take a few packages herself to the speeder.

After everything was stuffed into the back seats, the cargo area lid was shut. Aril barely contained her excitement to see the woods she pinned her escape plans on.

An hour later from a high altitude, dust on the horizon suggested the presence of the gant train. They descended to see details. The dust cloud came from a wide dirt path that had been disturbed by a large contingent of animals. Tim-Ell handed Aril a pair of field glasses. He dipped the craft and flew lower, to the side, not in a direct path.

"I don't want them to spot me," he said. "Take a look and tell me what you see."

Aril took the device, noting how light it felt. Alnata. Cadmia didn't have these. How was it a piss-ant kingdom could afford instruments of this quality? She gazed at the dry ochre ground and remembered the dark blue strata of alnata ore in the spot where the tains had attacked her. The presence of ore was one thing, smelting it another. Alnata needed high heat to be manufactured. Did Protar have geothermic cannulas capable of producing foundries?

Tim-Ell elbowed her gently. "What do you see?"

Her thoughts faded. Tim-Ell knew little about his country. Her questions about how the army got their high-quality gear would likely go unanswered. She focused the binoculars on the gant-train that had entered an open area, making it easier to spy. She moved the viewscreen over the scene, turned her head for a moment, and looked again. Three flower-bedecked wagons, pulled by four harnessed gants each, were flanked by guards. On one side, two riders on handsome gants, one a uniformed man, the other a woman in riding clothes, trotted side by side. She smiled, rolling her lip inward.

"Land the flier," she said.

"Why?"

"Just land. I have a plan that might help you." *And me.*

Tim-Ell pulled the little craft into a clearing a mile south of the slow-moving procession. "Okay, what is it?"

Aril pointed through the trees to the rocky road. "When they get close, you need to go out there and speak to the princess and the captain of her guard."

Tim-Ell's eyes squinted, and his lips pressed into a silent question.

"And this," she leaned in as if she was about to tell him a secret, "is what you will say."

CHAPTER 37

Tim-Ell crossed his arms over his chest. "I see. You want me to leave you in this clearing, which I doubt can be seen from the road, and you will wait here in the flier?"

She nodded.

"Right. As soon as I am out of sight you'll key in the code and steal the flier?"

She remained silent.

"Come on. I'm not that stupid. Besides, I changed the code last night in the hangar. By Goddess, I can practically feel your eyes burn a hole in my hands every time I hit the numbers. How many codes have you memorized?"

Aril closed her eyes and slumped into the soft leather seat.

"Look, I'll do what you suggest, but you come with me."

She smiled to herself. "All right. I'll stand with you."

Tim-Ell helped her out of the aircar. They walked through the trees and bushes until they came to the path paved with sand and rocks. When the procession turned the bend, Aril grinned at the sight of the traditional bride convoy. Two vans, both with arches decorated in wreaths and flowery garlands, trudged forward, each pulled by enormous tan gants bred for drayage. Ten warriors, mounted on trim, muscular war gants, held back their military mounts to stay in a circle around the train. In front of the first wagon, two riders on fine gray dappled gants, the kind of personal animals a rider would own, paced the wagons, almost touching sides.

Tim-Ell and Aril left the cover of the woods and stood in the middle with their hands in the air. The caravan slowed, then halted. Ten warriors hopped from their mounts and ran in front of the first wagon, the decorated covered van where a dozen well-dressed women leaned in their seats to peer out the sides. The man and woman who rode the elegant mottled gants alongside the wagon halted their mounts.

"What's your business?" the warrior with the longest pike asked as he pointed the lance at Tim-Ell.

"I would like to speak with Princess Sari-Van." With slow, deliberate movements, the prince unbuckled his sword belt, then shrugged out of his harness. He threw the harness a few feet in front and used his foot to point at the harness that landed emblem-up. "I'm Prince Tim-Ell, Princess Sari-Van's betrothed. I'm unarmed, as you can see. This is a peaceful request."

The warrior mulled it over and looked at the man riding the larger dappled gant. "Sir? It's the Prince of Protar. He wishes to speak with the Princess."

The woman on the smaller, spotted gant urged her mount forward. "I am Princess Sari-Van. Is this how Protar welcomes its royal visitors?"

Tim-Ell approached the gant and bowed low. "No, Your Highness, not usually. But right here, we are outside the border of the kingdom." He pointed to where the woods started again on the road ahead. "I wish to have a brief, unofficial meeting before you cross into Protar."

Aril tensed, praying he would follow her instructions.

"Princess, I have the power to grant sanctuary in Protar to you and anyone in your party. I can't grant you your title; you would be an ordinary citizen, but I would accept your warriors and give them a place in the Protar Army. In addition, I would give the captain of your guards," he pointed to the man on the dappled gant, "a captain's commission."

Princess Sari-Van turned in her saddle and looked at the captain, whose jaw had dropped at Tim-Ell's words. Sari-Van turned back to Tim-Ell and pursed her lips but no words came out.

Tim-Ell took a few steps closer to the Princess. From that distance his words were muffled, but Aril smiled. Tim-Ell had followed the script she'd given him, telling the Princess she didn't have to marry a stranger, like him, but could live in peace as a commoner and marry the man she loved. Aril moved closer.

Sari-Van put both hands to her lips then turned to the captain.

He kicked his gant's flank and made it to her side in two leaps. "What is it, Princess?"

"Fin-Dal," she said, swallowing and taking a shallow breath. "The Prince of Protar has offered us sanctuary. I must abdicate, but we..." She closed her eyes, and opened them, relief blossoming with a smile. "Fin..."

"You wouldn't be a princess," he said in a strained voice.

"I could be your wife, and that is a much better title."

Fin-Dal jumped from his gant and strode to face Tim-Ell. They spoke no words for a moment, then his arm came across his chest in a tribute salute.

Tim-Ell returned the salute.

The captain retreated to Sari-Van's side and helped his princess to dismount.

Fin-Dal dropped his head, took a breath, and head, held high, escorted Sari-Van back to Tim-Ell, meeting the prince's gaze. "Prince of Protar, what do we need to do to accept your offer?"

Aril strode to Tim-Ell's side, partly to make sure he didn't botch the negotiation but more importantly, so that Sari-Van and Fin-Dal saw her —knew *she* was part of the solution.

Tim-Ell cleared his throat and spoke so everyone in the Princess's entourage could hear his words. "To anyone who wants to join the Princess in Protar, gather your possessions and stop at the border. I will send fliers to take you to a safe place. The members of your party who wish to return to Crocess will continue to the palace and deliver the Princess's dowry to my father, King Jess-Reet."

Aril nudged him with her elbow. She suspected the marriage refusal would be easier for the Queen to swallow if the dowry didn't return to Crocess.

Tim-Ell added, "Oh, and do you have copies of the list of treasures you offer in your dowry?"

"Of course," Sari-Van said.

"Make sure King Jess-Reet has that list before the dowry gets into the hands of the Royal Treasurer. When your people are ready to return to Crocess, an escort will guide them back under our protection. You and those who stay will be safe."

Fin-Dal slipped his arm around Sari-Van. He looked at Tim-Ell. "Thank you."

Tim-Ell picked up his harness and sword belt. He put the leathers back on. "Be at the border in two hours." He jerked his head for Aril to follow him.

She folded her arms and stared at the gant train.

He spoke in a low voice. "Are you planning to have the people going back to Crocess to take you with them?"

"I'm not telling you anything." She headed to the flier. "But it's nice that you worry."

With his hand almost touching the ignition, Tim-Ell turned to her. "How did you know? Are you some kind of witch?"

"When I saw them in the field glasses, a fine instrument by the way, I noticed the elegant gants were touching. Gants don't like to be close. They often bite and kick others that get in their space, but those two gray ones had bonded, meaning they were accustomed to being together."

"Excellent observation, but how did you know the woman rider was the Princess?"

"Her bearing. She rode like a she'd had an excellent Gant Master to train her. And I saw the riders pass a sad glance between them, as if that would be their last ride together. Fin-Dal couldn't stay in Protar."

"You saw all of that when we flew over?"

"I went with my gut feeling."

"Gut? What's that? I've never heard of gut. Like intestines?"

"Oh!" Aril said. Gut had been a term Jake Hill had shared with his family, an Earth expression. "I meant I had a *good* feeling about it and how could it hurt to offer them sanctuary?"

"What if you'd been wrong?"

She laughed. "If I had been wrong, then you would have looked foolish. Sari-Van would just find it out early, *before* she married you!"

He responded with a half-smile. "Thanks."

Tim-Ell pushed the speed lever forward, making the air sing along the streamlined fuselage of the sweet little ship. They landed at the fort, the army headquarters. "Stay in the ship," he ordered.

She nodded. There were too many armed men about for her to cause any trouble. She had seen many forts in her years as a soldier. Jake Hill required family members to fulfill at least five years of military service. If a Hill relative became a leader and had to give the order for combat, he or she would need to know the horrors and traumas of battle. Negotiations always had to be the first attempt at peace, but Jake Hill also understood stubborn folk sometimes needed an incentive to consider peace, what he called "facing a big stick."

Protar's soldiers were the same as other Cronantians, young men in their prime who learned to follow orders and were willing to give their lives for their kingdom. A wave of sadness formed a lump in her throat. How many of these young men would die when Jake Hill got the message she was captive? For that, she was certain her grandsire would bring down the big stick first, then do the talking.

Perhaps Fin-Dal shouldn't accept the position in this army. He would feel loyalty to Tim-Ell, and Sari-Van may end up being a widow. But, if the Princess married Tim-Ell, widowhood would be her lot for certain.

Would Aril's people and family be so happy that she was returned to Cadmia, they would overlook ravaging Protar? But then, Jerr-Lan. Protarians hadn't killed him; the slavers had attacked their ship. The slave center was located somewhere out in the desert, away from city outside the borders.

Now anger replaced her worry. Tim-Ell knew where the slavers had their stronghold, and he knew what they did to the slaves .

Tim-Ell beat on the hiltite side of his flier. "Hey, what's wrong?"

She swallowed and turned, their eyes meeting. "Just thinking."

Pulling at his chin, he eyed her sideways. "Not usually a good thing." He leaned closer. "I'm arranging quarters for the people in the Princess's caravan."

"You're going to lodge Sari-Van in an army base?"

"Where else can I put her?"

"There's an extra apartment in your complex."

Tim-Ell ran his fingers through his hair. "They aren't married. She'd be alone."

Aril shrugged. "You could invite a Rotner Monk to be conveniently outside the complex. He could wait where your spies stand. Then he could pray for their sins. And yours, too."

"What gets into you, Aril-Ess? I don't have spies watching you."

She shot him her best accusatory glare. *What a liar.*

"Maybe putting the Princess in the apartment is a good idea," he said. "She probably wouldn't do well here. She's accustomed to being taken care of."

"Having slaves? Poor little Princess. She'll have to learn how to cook and clean and take care of herself."

"Come on, that's a drastic change, from Princess to commoner."

How about from a princess to a slave? Although she will be an outcast from her family, perhaps never seeing them again. I know how that feels.

"You can help her, right?"

Aril glared at her fingernails. "Oh sure, you could give her the code to the glass door, and she could come over for lessons while being my warden. Oh, wait, I know! Let little silver-bitch teach the Princess."

Tim-Ell laughed. "Yeah, that won't happen. Ray-Tan said he choked on her first meal, so he cooks. He shows her the things she needs to do in the apartment. She can't do anything. Remember what happened when she tried to peel vegetables?"

"I remember. I keep hoping she'll try again." She chuckled quietly. "I'll help the ex-Princess Sari-Van convert to common-hood. After all, she's so sad at her engagement being cancelled."

Tim-Ell shook his head at her jibe. "I haven't time for sparring words. I've got to get a convoy together to pick up the Crocess people who want to stay. I'll be back in a few minutes to take you to the apartment."

While she waited in the flier, she organized her plan. Now that she had manipulated Tim-Ell into giving his ex-fiancée an apartment, she refined her strategy regarding getting a message to Cadmia. All of Sari-Van's guards wore the Excaliburian emblem. Most Knights would love to visit Cadmia, where the Knighthood began. As soon as she returned to the apartment, she would write notes ready to give to the soldiers when they said goodbye to their Princess. When Sari-Van was safe, the ones with families would return to their country, knowing they would never see her again. Aril was confident she could convince at least one of them to smuggle a note to Jake Hill, earning his gratitude, not to mention the riches he would give as a reward.

Tim-Ell emerged from a door on the side the building where he had parked the flier, most likely his office. He took long strides with tightly closed lips. Stiff-jawed, he hopped over the gunwale of the ship into his seat. Aril braced for his customary exit, up and off in a blur. The flier whooshed into the cloudless sky, at a speed that blurred details below.

He touched down next to the apartment, not bothering with the hangar. Unloading the goods from the market they had purchased hours earlier, he gave her the light ones and struggled with more than he should have handled. He leaned against the glass door to balance and unlocked the panel. Inside, he placed the packages on the table and hurried out.

Aril sat on the cold bench, alone. Well, there was always silver-bitch next door. Maybe she would come by for a visit. Aril laughed aloud. Didn't they say he or she who controlled, controlled alone?

After storing the purchases, she exercised in the sunroom. Breathing hard, she wiped sweat from her brow and pushed back the sheet hung against the brickwork to check across the street. The spies weren't there. Did they get the information they needed? Had Tim-Ell pulled them away? She didn't think so— he had too much on his plate with his royal defector and her lover. Fin-Dal would not share living arrangements with Sari-Van until they wed. Old habits are difficult to break, and princesses were supposed to keep their sex life quiet. Once the population of Protar knew Sari-Van had broken the engagement, she would need to maintain a low profile. No one cared about a common woman's escapades, but it would take time for the ex-royal to dim the celebrity light.

Just before dusk, when the sky turned softly orange and the insects sang their night songs, two fliers, Tim-Ell's and a larger four-seater, set down in the courtyard. Tim-Ell and Ray-Tan got out of the small one. Three people emerged from the closed four-seater. Fin-Dal helped Sari-Van, and from the front, a robed Rotner Monk disembarked.

Aril sucked in a breath. She had been teasing about the monk. Tim-Ell had taken it seriously. And so, it appeared, had the defecting couple.

Aril chuckled. Sari-Van would not be lonely tonight. Would the bride notice there was only a couch in the living room and a stone table with a bench in the kitchen of their apartment? From what she could see, Sari-Van flashed a shy smile at Fin-Dal, whose eyes sparkled. No, they wouldn't care about the sparse furnishings. Not tonight, anyway.

The Monk wasted little time. Aril remained locked in her apartment prison, where she could see but not hear. Within a few minutes, the Monk raised both arms as his lips moved with the pronouncement of their union.

The Monk slipped the token coin from Fin-Dal into a hidden pocket and hurried to the four-seater. The pilot would return him to the dun-colored crenellated stone monastery where the Rotner Monks lived their austere lives. The Prince and Ray-Tan sauntered toward the flier, alternating steps with claps on each other's shoulders. After hopping into Tim-Ell's marvelous vessel, the flier shot into the air like a missile from a steam cannon. The newly married couple disappeared into their apartment. Aril sat alone with only her own company for the rest of the night. She had to get free.

CHAPTER 38

The next day, Tim-Ell came home early. He slammed his sword belt on the table, unusual for him since he took good care of his equipment and weaponry. Aril-Ess had begun preparations for dinner, kept her back to him, and waited.

"We have a summons to the palace tomorrow."

She didn't respond.

"I think I'll be reprimanded for not marrying Sari-Van."

Aril kept her eyes on the vegetables she scrubbed. "How could anyone know you orchestrated the Princess's change of plans?"

"No one knows I *offered* the sanctuary. But my parents and the Vizier feel I should have challenged Fin-Dal to a public duel. Plus, it is known I *granted* them sanctuary." He let out a big sigh. "Now I'll have to wed another hand-picked princess to make the kingdom bigger."

"Maybe not," Aril-Ess said. "Does your kingdom acknowledge national or planetary law?"

"What's that?"

"You don't know what law system your country uses to rule?"

His jaw tightened. "We have laws." He looked away for a moment, then back at her, spreading his hands. "I don't know what they're called."

Aril-Ess rolled her eyes. "Some king you will be. It's probably a mixture, seeing that you wear the Excalibur Insignia but have illegal slavery."

"Look, this isn't a good time to insult the ways of my kingdom. Besides, what's it got to do with me being set up for a second arranged marriage?"

She dried her hands and turned to face him. "It might mean a great deal. You need to consult someone, like a True Witness Scribe." Her voice went a notch higher. "I assume you have them, Witness Scribes, for small matters that don't require a court. You *do* have courts and judges, right?"

"Yes." He crossed his arms over his chest. "We have a legal system. And we have True Witness Scribes. And before you ask, yes, they are dependable and honest."

"Even the ones at the palace? Do they associate with the Vizier?"

"All right, the ones the populace use are trustworthy. Is that enough for you?"

She nodded. "You went to the University, right?"

"Yes."

"Was there a legal program?"

He pulled at his chin. "I don't remember a program of law."

"Then your legal students went to a larger university somewhere else, and most likely your kingdom operates under planetary laws." Lowering her voice she added, "Except when it suits them to violate the laws, like—"

"Get on with it, Aril. What are you talking about?"

"According to Planetary Law, if someone has a contract for marriage and it is broken, that person is not obliged to participate in a second similar contract. Find a True Witness. Check the laws."

Tim-Ell paced the room. "I'll check it, but my mother might not recognize any laws. She makes them up as she goes. And Father does what she tells him. A few days ago, with me and my brothers, he had a good time as we toured the kingdom. I saw a new side of him."

"Great. Maybe there's hope for Protar yet."

"Be careful of what you say, Aril. It's bad enough how you talk to me, but you could get into real trouble at the palace. Trouble I couldn't get you out of."

Aril returned to her duty at the sink. "Thanks for the warning. I'll be on my good behavior. Wait a minute. Why am I going with you to the palace tomorrow evening?"

He whispered in her ear. "Father added that to the summons, something like, 'bring that lovely companion of yours.' You caught my father's eye." He snorted. "*That* is sure to thrill Mother."

Aril sucked in a quick breath. "Oh, Goddess."

CHAPTER 39

"What am I supposed to wear at this meeting?"

Tim-Ell took a long sip of his morning's keela. "I don't know."

"What did your other slaves," the word caught in her throat, "wear when they went to the palace?"

"Gowns. They only time they went there was to a ball. I don't know what ladies wear to a, tea, or dinner, or whatever."

Aril-Ess put the keela pot down hard on the stone tabletop. "Well, I'm not going to wear a light slave smock, that's for sure."

Tim-Ell chuckled. "The slave tells the master what she will and won't do, eh?"

"Have I ever referred to you as *master*?"

"No. You are the worst slave I've ever had."

"Really? One that got you out of a marriage you didn't want?"

"Yes, and one who arranged to make me the second-best swordsman in Protar."

A wave of guilt passed through her. She had been responsible for that. Words surfaced, but she wouldn't let *I'm sorry* out. Instead, she said, "How about taking me to the market? You can buy me something suitable for the palace that won't embarrass either of us."

"Now?"

"Yes."

"Then I guess it's now. I have things to do at the fort later this morning, so put something on and make it fast."

Aril hurried into her room and pulled two smocks from the closet. She removed the worn one, her everyday garment, slid the fresh ones over her head and tied a thin leather thong at her waist. In the apartment, she usually went barefoot, electing to save the plain sandals she'd been given at the slave station. How long ago was that? The lovely blue sandals made to match the gown were still on the floor of the closet, where she'd taken them off after the ball, the one night where she hadn't looked like a slave. She tossed her head. Today she'd see that the prince bought her a good pair of sandals, along with something fitting for a palace.

They had long come to the arrangement where she promised not to escape while shopping, so she didn't bring up the subject. She couldn't have discussed it right then, anyway, because Tim-Ell was gone. Aril sat at the table and finished her keela. Impatient, she checked through the glass to see the courtyard empty. She poured another cup and sat at the table, tapping her finger.

As she finished her second cup, Tim-Ell came through the door. "Ray-Tan will handle things for me while we shop." He waved his hand for her to rise. "Ready?"

"Where's your purse?"

He sighed.

Her gaze tracked him as he went into his bedroom, took out a small leather bag from the top drawer of his bureau, fastened it to the sword belt, and pulled his tunic over the bag. He returned and stepped before her. "So," he said, fingering the royal insignia on his harness, "am I the Prince or just a mercenary out with his slave?"

She answered him flatly." I don't care who you pretend to be."

He smiled. "Ow, that hurt."

"Good."

She followed him to the hanger and allowed him to hold the door for her on the sleek little flier. As usual, he flew at breakneck speed, aiming for and just missing spires and tall rooftops. Aril had become accustomed to his dangerous piloting, but she didn't join in when he let out whoops of laughter at his near misses.

When they landed in the parking area of the market, she finger-combed her dark curls back into place. He stared as she smoothed her smocks into place and retied her belt. He watched her movements a lot lately, not like before when he kept an eye on her to prevent her from escaping.

Being morning, a cool breeze rippled the colorful pennants that topped the merchant tents. Aril breathed in the clear fresh air of the turquoise sky that displayed dotted puffs of clouds. It rarely rained on Cronanta, but she had witnessed two good rainstorms in Protar, seen them from inside the apartment and wished she could bask in the moisture, as many children did to play and feel the raindrops in a storm. Two lush episodes of water from the sky, most likely added to the beautiful lake she had seen from the flier. Protar had so many natural resources—ore, redgrain fields, and water. Why didn't Cadmia know about this kingdom? Protar could be prosperous and hold great esteem with the Planetary Council. They were rich. The prince said they had no taxes, other than the ridiculous tax on artificial nectar. A tax to have a child! That certainly didn't occur in Planetary Law. What a strange kingdom this place. When she escaped...

"Aril?" Tim-Ell shook her shoulder gently. "Are you awake?"

She came out of her thoughts and stared at him. "What do you want?"

He scratched his head. "This shopping excursion is for you. Remember? Which way first?"

"Oh," she said, and pointed left. "Foods that way. Goods," she pointed right, "that way."

Tim-Ell turned right, and she had to double-step to keep up with him. They stopped at a stall with garments of all colors dangling on hangers blowing in the wind. Tim-Ell leaned against a sturdy tent post as Aril examined a few of the outfits.

"Nothing here," she said. "Next."

He nodded and followed her past a few stalls. Passing by other stores, one stall caught her eye. This place had permanent wooden racks with the clothing displayed in order of the colors. Aril pulled out several garments in soft orange-pink, the color of her favorite melon. She selected one that had sparkling beading on the front.

The merchant came to her. "This one will look good with your coloring."

"Do you have one like it without the beading?"

"You don't like the beading? That's what's so special. You won't find another like it."

Aril rolled it over in her hands and rubbed the fabric. "It feels so soft." She turned it inside out and checked the seams. "Well made. Do you have a skirt to match?"

The merchant eyed her slave smock for a moment and looked over at Tim-Ell, who nodded to the man. If the piece hadn't been so lovely, she would have left the stall. She hated the constant reminder she wasn't free and had to get permission from the *master*. The merchant tried to take her hand to lead her to the rear area where the skirts hung on their rack. She pulled away and gave him as dirty a look as she could while wanting to have him show her the other pieces. He brought out several skirts that would go with the tunic she still held. One had mottled shades of melon, blended with pink and cream. The filmy material had been sewn in sections, giving it a fluid look, ending in a hem that hung in points flaring out as it went down. She held it to her waist. Some of the points touched her knee and alternate points came down to her calves. Perfect. Back in Cadmia, she'd had beautiful clothes, and this outfit equaled them. She found what she wanted and didn't need to try it on.

Tim-Ell came to the rear. "Pretty. Do you want them?"

Once again, her annoyance surfaced. But what could she do? "Yes. I want them. Now I need shoes."

He didn't balk. They waited while the merchant wrapped the purchases in brown paper and tied them with a string. Across the grassy aisle, there was a stall with many shoes, mostly sandals, displayed on pedestals. Aril saw the pair she wanted before she crossed the path. Made from silky-soft lakin hide, the white sandals had a strip running up the length of her upper arch, where thin bands rose from the sole and met the wide strip. A loop at the ankle accommodated laces that reached mid-calf. Small painted flowers adorned the wide strip and back loop. Aril got the merchant's attention and pointed to the sandals. She took a seat, and like royalty, waited for the man to bring her the shoes. He hesitated, but Tim-Ell motioned, and the merchant hurried to serve her.

While the merchant slipped the shoes on her feet, she became aware how the prince stared at her, first her hair, which ruffled in the light breeze, then her face, and then his gaze traveled up and down.

"Nice," Tim-Ell said. Standing next to her, he leaned on a table and knocked something over. Picking it up, he laughed. It was a wooden replica of a foot. "Look," he pointed. "The toes have paint on them."

While the merchant wrapped the shoes, Aril took the wooden foot. "Toe paint. Didn't your slave girls paint their toes?"

He shrugged. "I don't know. Maybe. They ordered all kinds of stuff for their hair and such."

Aril regarded her feet. It had been a long time since anyone had given her the pampering she had once taken for granted. In Jake Hill's household, hairdressers, laundresses, cleaners, and other workers took care of them. When family members served in the military or spent time away from home, they fended for themselves, but in the palace, they had been cared for in the finest fashion. Something made her long for nail paint. She called the merchant over and asked for a pot of dark orange, a color to match her new outfit. Tim-Ell said nothing as he reached into his leather bag for payment.

They purchased a few items for the kitchen stores, then returned to the apartment. Tim-Ell made a hasty retreat, saying he had important matters at the fort.

After a light lunch, Aril got to work with needle and thread. She turned the beaded garment inside out and made new seams, hiding the gaudy decorations on the inside and turning the soft lining into the front. She pulled the tunic over the flowing skirt. With the tasteless sparkles hidden, the outfit looked classy, allowing the elegant colors to present an understated beauty. This combination would look fine for a palace event. With her new sandals, Aril felt like a princess, which came a lot easier to her than trying to accept the status of slave.

CHAPTER 40

Tim-Ell hurried to the fort, arriving in time to try the new gant he'd chosen months ago. The supplier had fine animals and also charged the highest prices. But the cavalry needed the best mounts available. When he had become the commander of the army, Tim-Ell vowed to keep his soldiers supplied with the highest quality of everything, and he'd been able to keep his promise.

He had chosen a well-proportioned animal, one that could run and had a smooth gait. Those requirements didn't often go together, but it looked like this gant had it all. Today he'd know for sure. The mounts were being delivered that afternoon, and he could barely wait to try out the animal. Tim-Ell had assigned the best Gantmaster, the royal trainer, to work with the mount. It would take a few weeks to ease the animal into his control, but he looked forward to the challenge. Ever since he'd taken his first ride at his father's side, Tim-Ell had been a natural gantsman. The day they'd been attacked by bandits, just able to ride back to the royal stables to save their lives had been one of change for both of them. His father decided to stay safe inside the palace. Tim-Ell decided to make the country safe.

He arrived at the fort as the gates swung wide to allow the animals through. Soldiers lined up around the parapets to see the herd that caused geysers of dust to show for miles.

Tim-Ell handed his flier to a hangar man and rushed to the building that housed his office. The steed had been tied near his office door. It stamped and pulled at the lead, unhappy to wait while the tumult of activity went on without it. Tim-Ell smiled at the animal as it pawed the ground with its pliable but sturdy hoof. He stroked the supple male's neck all the way down past his shoulder. When he rubbed the animal's rump, the thick, leathery tail lashed at the prince's touch.

"Whoa, there, boy," Tim-Ell whispered. "You're all right." He pulled out an orange tuber he bought at the market that morning and held it to the gant's mouth. The gant sniffed it, eyed the man offering the treat, and bit, mouthing the thing for a time before taking it whole and crunching slowly. "There. See, boy? You are the finest gant I've had. You and I will be one."

Tim-Ell took his time, talking and stroking the spirited animal. He led the mount up and down the paths between the barracks, letting the creature get accustomed to his touch and voice. Every so often, he offered a treat, which the animal no longer sniffed, but took immediately, giving trust to his new master. The gant had already been broken in but personal gants needed time with their new owner. After a few hours, Tim-Ell ordered a saddle, fastened it, and allowed the gant to relax. Then he slipped the bridle into the gant's mouth. When he thought the time was right, the prince swung up to the saddle and let the gant buck and heave until it tired and knew it couldn't shake the rider. Tim-Ell took the animal through the usual paces and then had the gate opened so he could see what his new ride could do. He wasn't disappointed. When he gave the animal its head, the gant galloped long smooth strides until Tim-Ell slowed him. They had traversed far from the fort, and although the gant still had spirit and energy, the prince led it to a small oasis, where they rested under a tree with the sound of flowing water.

Tim-Ell wondered about what he would face at the palace in a few hours. *I need to consult a True Witness about the laws.* The trip back to the fort did not impart the same joy as the earlier trip, heading out into the arid lands surrounding the army headquarters.

Well satisfied with Wind Master, the gant's new name, the commander of the army turned the animal over to a groom and, feeling a bit of gloom as to what may happen that evening, headed home in his slick air vessel.

When he arrived at the apartment, the look Aril gave him made him aware of the dust that covered his uniform. With no directive from her, he headed for the bathroom, where she drew his bath and put soap and towels on a table near the tub. He had hoped she would bathe him because he liked that attention, but he no longer demanded the service, taking satisfaction from the times when he asked her politely and she acquiesced. He chuckled. The worst slave he ever had!

The day had been a long one, and the ride had left him tired but content.

He slipped into the bubbly water. Aril-Ess had put unguents and oils in with the soap. At least he would smell nice for his appearance at the palace. This woman, this reluctant slave, so unpredictable. He washed his face with a soft cloth, thinking about her. Dunking his head beneath the surface to clean the dirt from his hair, he thought about how her hair had shone in the morning light. What could he do about her? He felt bad about her confinement. She wanted to be free. He couldn't bear the thought of her leaving. But if she escaped, she could be killed. Even if she got out of the kingdom, she would face worse dangers—wild animals, harsh terrain. Many people perished in the unforgiving lands surrounding Protar.

Lately, thoughts of her surfaced during the day, affecting his concentration. The memories of that night of passion haunted him. Although the recollections were incomplete, he knew she had wanted him, just as he knew she'd been a virgin and cried out when he entered her. But she did not try to make him stop. He could not make sense of that night. Illogical. She wanted him then, of that he was sure, but after that, she rejected him.

Damn that woman. Why couldn't she be like the other girls? They were happy to be with him. They never insulted him or assaulted him with sharp words or nasty looks. Maybe that's why he loved her. Did he just say that, even in his mind? He could not deny it. He pictured her at the ball, the dress that covered her but showed everything. He needed to calm down. He could not face the evening in this mood. He got out of the tub and shut the bathroom door.

Cursing his erection, he tried to think of other things. His new gant. What a beauty. A beauty? Aril's beauty was incomparable. Maybe he could give her more freedom, around the apartment complex? She could work in the garden, get outside. That might help. Perhaps he could give her the lock combination, set up with her palm. How could he convince her if she escaped it could mean her life? He had to try.

He wrapped a towel around his waist, willing the bulge in the fabric to deflate.

CHAPTER 41

In her bedroom, Aril-Ess slipped the new tunic over her head and tugged it past her breasts. She turned at the sound of Tim-Ell entering.

He stepped close. "It's pretty, but, different."

She stepped into the skirt. "I turned it inside out to hide the beadwork."

"Why?"

"Why do you think? It looks better this way."

His expression radiated admiration, as if to say no matter what she wore, it would be beautiful. Although he hadn't spoken the words, he approved and thought it looked elegant.

"Right," he said. "It's nice."

"You have such a way with words, Prince."

He spread his arms for moment and stepped closer.

A wave of something hit her like a hot wind. Tim-Ell was stimulated. Her receptors caught his scent, and she felt the *wham* again. Her mouth parted but no sound came out.

"Aril-Ess," he said, "I know what you want."

I don't think you do.

"Look, I want that, too."

What?

He came next to her.

If you touch me, I'll lose control. I will slam you to the bed, and rip off that towel. In five minutes, you won't have a single brain cell left. Her nipples buzzed and her insides throbbed. Her mind screamed, *No!* But her body wasn't listening. A war raged between her head and her body. Her insides quivered, knowing what they wanted.

He reached out to touch her. She backed away using all the will she could summon.

The rap on the back door took Tim-Ell's attention. He hurried to the glass and put up a *just a minute* finger. He dashed back to the bedroom. "Aril, please, promise me you won't do anything to escape. I'll let you out and you won't have to stay cooped up. Promise me."

Her mind and words responded to what was happening inside her, not to the words he said. She whispered, "No."

"Oh, Aril, don't you want to work in your garden, shop, visit, have friends?"

He was far enough away that the attraction effect subsided a few notches. She'd just said no to her responses but what was he saying?

"Aril, it's dangerous to try to leave Protar. Don't you understand? Here," he reached for her hand. "I'll input the lock and press your hand on the screen."

She pulled her hand away and stepped back. "I can't promise you, Tim-Ell." She just called him by his name. Had she done that before? She couldn't remember. He shook his head, sighed, and returned to the back door. She heard the lock whirr and then sounds of conversation.

Aril could breathe again, but her body was on fire. She let out a long blow of air. Peeking out her door, she saw Kye-Ren outside, waiting for Ray-Tan. Maybe she should have made the promise so she could run out and knock that little demon on her silvery ass. Ray-Tan and his half-sized woman were happy, sleeping together. A wave of anguish flooded her thoughts. She didn't need to waste her time thinking about other people's sex lives. Why not? She had plenty of time, and after that brush with Tim-Ell, what else could she think about? She ran to her cot, threw herself down on the mattress, and let out a low, guttural moan. Then she wept and cursed the place that made her cry, twice, something she hadn't done since was a little girl. Aril allowed a few minutes of self-pity, regained composure, and added another coat of paint on her toenails. Sounds from Tim-Ell's room suggested he had finished dressing. They emerged from their rooms and met in the living room. The Crown Prince looked royal in his formal uniform, tan with red trim and golden embroidery. His sword hung at his side. The royal emblem cast in precious metal that crossed his chest gleamed on a leather harness. The red cape would appear overdone on a lesser man, but on him it looked perfect.

"You look beautiful," he said. His gaze ran up and down and paused at her feet. "Nice toes," he added with a quick grin. His face radiated pride, and something more. She didn't want to analyze what it could be.

"Ready?"

She nodded.

He keyed the lock. "Put your palm on the screen," he said quietly.

She did. After a few seconds of whirring and clicking, the door opened to her touch. She didn't know what to say. *Thank you,* wouldn't surface.

They walked quietly to the hangar. Outside Cal-Eb and Del-Am's apartment, the couple sat at a small table eating their supper during the soft sunset. They stood in respect for the prince. The egg lump in Del-Am's belly displayed prominently. She would deliver soon. A bit of envy crept into Aril's thoughts. That couple loved one another, and soon there would be the evidence of that love, an egg, then a child.

Aril put these thoughts out of her mind as she and the prince approached the sporty flier. Tim-Ell held the low door for her, and she stepped in. Ray-Tan hopped in the back. After reversing the craft from its place, Tim-Ell ascended above the complex and flew unusually slow, which would be outrageously fast to a normal person. The trip to the palace soared well above the spires and rooftops as if he delayed the arrival by piloting safely.

CHAPTER 42

Aril felt a bit of pity for Tim-Ell. He hadn't said anything to her, but he worried about the summons to the palace. He had his hand on his pommel the whole way from the hangar to the Throne Room.

"The guards answer to the Commander of the Army," he said as the sentries lifted their pikes.

"Meaning you," Aril responded.

"That's right," he muttered, as if it meant more than the words themselves.

Ray-Tan stood at the double doors as the guardsmen opened them. Tim-Ell and Aril-Ess walked through the portal.

The King and Queen sat on ornate chairs in the middle of a draped and over-decorated room. Cadmia didn't, wouldn't, have such a garish place.

Tim-Ell had a strong hold on Aril's arm. She loosened his fingers a bit.

"Sorry," he whispered. He approached the throne and stopped at the Royal Emblem mosaic in the stone floor. He bowed low. "Father, King Jess-Reet, and Mother, Queen Ran-Cignar. I bid you greetings."

Aril bowed, saying nothing.

"Rise, son," The King commanded. "And your companion."

Tim-Ell's tension surrounded him like an aura.

"Approach," the King said.

The Crown Prince raised his head and stood tall. "You summoned me?"

"We did," the Queen said. "How is it you gave the Princess Sari-Van sanctuary? Why didn't you challenge that upstart guard to a duel? Imagine! Having the nerve to come here and then disgrace us. They should be punished."

Tim-Ell stiffened. "She declined to marry me, Mother. And that upstart guard was a skilled swordsman, the Captain of the Guards. Why would I risk my life for a woman who doesn't want me? Princess Sari-Van lost her title and her fortune. She won't be queen when I take the throne. Isn't that punishment enough?"

Ran-Cignar crossed her arms over her chest. "When I find them, there will be trouble."

Aril suppressed her smile. The royal couple didn't know the unroyal couple lived in the same complex as the prince. This kingdom didn't know what went on inside the confines of the city. Or as Jake Hill had said, "The left hand doesn't know what the right hand is doing." Or even more descriptive, "They don't know their elbow from their ass." Earth had such colorful sayings.

As king, what would Tim-Ell do to make life better in Protar? Could he?

"Is that it?" Tim-Ell said with a hint of annoyance. "Is that why you sent for me?"

"No." Ran-Cignar said. "Your summons represents an official decree. We will find another princess suitable for you."

"You mean another principality close by to enlarge our kingdom? No thank you."

The Queen turned red. "You have no say in the matter."

"Perhaps," Tim-Ell said.

"Come, come," King Jess-Reet said. "Let's not get upset over something that hasn't happened yet. Let's have dinner." He stood and extended his arm to the Queen. He led them out of the Throne Room and into a small antechamber set for a meal.

Servants brought platters and stood next to them to serve. The King laughed and clapped his hands. Eppo Zim came to the table carrying a tray with goblets sculpted in precious metals. He tasted one and gave it to the king. He put the other three wine goblets in front of the queen, Tim-Ell, and Aril. Then he spooned a bit from each platter and clearly swallowed the samples, nodding after each bite. Lowering the tray under his arm, he made a quick bow and left.

The King chuckled and cast a quick glance at Aril. "I love the look on his face when he serves as my taster. That never gets old." He winked at her.

King Jess-Reet smiled at Aril constantly, while Queen Ran-Cignar sneered equally often. When Tim-Ell suggested they leave after the meal, Aril whispered, "Thank you," to him. A first for her, words showing appreciation to her captor.

The trip home in the flier was quiet. The prince piloted the craft as if his thoughts focused deep, somewhere else, not engaging the mad low zigzagging of his normal flying. The atrium was empty and Aril felt unusually tired. When they reached the apartment, he halted at the door and let Aril open it. Did she really have freedom to come and go? At least she could control the door. Did her freedom include the front gate of the complex?

CHAPTER 43

Aril slept late the next morning. When she woke, her head ached and she felt sore all over. After washing up, she headed to the kitchen to make keela. The prince's harness lay on the stone table, where he'd taken it off the night before. She peeked into his room. He lay on his bed with his arm over his forehead. Maybe he suffered the same malady she felt.

She returned to the boiling kettle and sprinkled the grounds into the pot. The smell the steam produced when the water mixed with the roasted grounds pleased her. A flat pan on the stovetop heated waiting for a dollop of lakin butter to toast the bread she sliced. Toast and keela. That's all she could tolerate; her appetite did not require more. And her headache intensified.

Tim-Ell came from his room dressed in his usual sleep attire—the ankle dagger. He sat down hard on the stone bench adjacent to the table. "I feel like gant dung," he mumbled.

Aril pushed a cup of morning brew toward him. She put two slices of hot buttered bread on a plate next to the cup. It pained her arm to reach for the pot of tashberry jam.

Tim-Ell took a long sip from the cup and sighed. "You don't look so good, either."

She rested her chin on her hands and then looked at him. "You don't suppose…"

He made a face like it hurt him to think. "We all ate from the same platter, the ones Eppo Zim tasted. My mother wants to marry me off again, so I can't believe we've been poisoned."

Ray-Tan banged on the glass door.

"Come," Tim-Ell shouted.

Aril covered her ears. The noise rang in her head.

Ray-Tan walked smartly to the table and brought his fist to his chest and out again. "The groom has brought your gant."

Tim-Ell shook his head. "Put it in the stable with Fin-Dal's gants. I won't be going to the fort today."

With a similar salute, Ray-Tan left.

"I'll be training and riding my new gant," Tim-Ell said. "I have a feeling you know how to pilot, so you can use the flier."

That bit of news took attention away from her pain. "I can use the flier?"

He took a bite from the bread. "Don't go far." Grabbing her gaze, he added. "It isn't safe for you."

"It isn't safe from your spies?"

"I'm not in the mood for this, Aril. There are no spies." He pushed up from his seat and padded into the bedroom. Despite his typical open-door policy, he slammed the heavy door shut.

Aril-Ess dumped the remainder of the keela pot into the sink and stacked the few dirty dishes. Head pounding, she retired to her bedroom, closing the door to keep out the light. Sleep came in fits. Her slender cot offered little comfort to the tossing and turning.

As dusk settled in, Tim-Ell pushed open her door. "It's so hot in this apartment. Hot in here, too."

She had to agree. Sweat dotted her brow and the back of her neck.

"Can I open your window?" he asked.

"Yes," she said, hoping the air would cool the room. A high window, she rarely thought about it. To open or close it required a chair. Tim-Ell stretched his arms, and elevating on tiptoe, he reached the handle. Light illuminated his muscles, taut and elongated from his long reach. She couldn't take her gaze from his body. Shadows dipping and rising from his skin, accentuating his perfect physique, made her tingle. Shutting her eyes did little to dispel her desire.

He turned to her. "Are you all right?"

"Not really," she whispered, hoping he would leave.

But he didn't leave and sat on the edge of her bed, saying nothing.

Pure willpower kept her frozen to her spot, her mouth clamped tight, her eyes closed. He touched her shoulder; she felt like she would explode.

No longer frozen, she pulled up and into his arms. He put his lips to hers and a passion unimagined took over. His iron grip sent shock waves of energy and desire through her veins. The heat hadn't been from the room, it had been building inside them, a geothermal vent. They rolled and tossed, kissing and nipping, rubbing and pawing until there was only one way to satiate the demand.

Aril felt movement inside her, a cramp, and she stopped Tim-Ell for a moment. Glancing at his erection and noting the extra size, she let out a cry. She knew what had happened. The cramp she felt was an egg that had formed overnight, and his elongated erection was to make sure that egg would come into contact with what it needed to be fertilized. They had sipped the nectar, and nothing would stop the process. Her body took control, and the animal instincts the nectar imparted turned them into puppets, magnetized and programmed. He entered her with long, forceful thrusts, movements she wanted and demanded.

Their orgasms left them spent, basking in a hormonal glow from the nectar for the fertilization process. They slept in each other's arms.

CHAPTER 44

Aril awoke, refreshed from the morning coolness, without headache or pain. Physically, she felt fit and exhilarated. Her mood didn't match. She rose and pushed Tim-Ell onto the floor.

"How could you do that to me? It's the equivalent of rape." She kicked his side and kicked him again.

"Hey!" he said and rolled away from her swinging foot. "What's the matter with you?"

"Get out! Beast! Liar! Degenerate!"

"I don't know what you mean."

She punched his arm, th

en sent punches to his abdomen as she pushed him out the door. "You, you… How could you do that? Is nothing sacred? Have you no morals whatsoever? Dirt! You're worse than dirt. Dirt has value. You have none!"

"What has gotten into you? Have you gone crazy?" Tim-Ell stood in the doorway.

She slammed the door in his face. Stomping to the cot, she sat so hard the bed moved. From the other side of the door, muffled words questioned her behavior.

"Aril? What is wrong?"

She heavy-stepped to the door and opened it. "I never thought you would stoop so low for a deep orgasm."

He scratched his head. "That was unbelievable what happened last night, but I don't know what you are going on so about."

"Do you think I'm that stupid? You put nectar, or what serves as nectar in this trash kingdom, so you could enjoy the sacred experience. It's rape! Pure and simple. And you should be executed for it."

"Nectar? What are you talking about? I didn't put anything into anything."

"Get out. I hate you. You are worse than gant dung. Go. Leave. Now."

He crossed his arms over his chest. "I give you my word. I know nothing about nectar."

She slammed the door again. Her thoughts strayed from what Jake Hill would do to Tim-Ell's to the possibility, the probability, that she carried a fertilized egg. Their species had depended on the nectar, and it rarely failed. Her shoulders sagged. Having a child represented the highest morality in the union between Life-Mates. Especially in traditional countries, where couples took a long time to consider and prepare. In Cadmia, the couple went into the wilderness and gathered the flowers. They asked not to be disturbed while they carefully made tea from the white petals. Some couples gathered their closest friends and family to announce their decision. They drank the tea and waited for the results: the egg to form and drop and the intense lovemaking, the powerful and passionate union, almost always resulting in a fertilized egg. There were women who sold their bodies to men using the nectar as an aphrodisiac, and then aborted the egg. That illegal practice brought a severe punishment, and if caught before the abortion, the woman had to follow through and have her egg taken from her. The shame of the act never subsided. After a maximum sentence of slavery by the meanest sort, these women usually moved away to start a new life. What would happen to Aril? Under no circumstances would she let her egg die. The child would be forced to live in shame with her. She would fight to keep this child because she doubted anyone would want the bastard child from a slave. Not in Protar. Would Cadmia be more forgiving? How could she face the Hill clan, the royal family? The family the entire, almost the entire, planet admired and looked up to?

She went into the kitchen. Silence. Tim-Ell had left. Good. She imagined him riding the new gant. Maybe it would throw him and give the man a good stomping.

A noise outside caught her attention. Kye-Ren put her hand to the lock on her glass door. Aril flashed to the door pressed her palm on the screen. Aril had to open it first before the silver wench had time to key in the code. Small victories, but victories nonetheless.

The glass whispered soft sounds as it slid into its channel.

Aril's mood, still grim, manifested. "What do you want?"

Kye-Ren pulled her lips back to show the pointy incisors, her way of saying *Greetings, I hate you.* "To remind you to help Princess Sari-Van. Ray-Tan gave me the message from the prince."

"Hmpph," Aril snorted, "ex-princess."

"That sounds like something you'd say," Kye-Ren said. "At least Sari-Van isn't a slave."

"Slaves? Like me and *you*?"

Kye-Ren's lips showed more teeth as she sneered. "I delivered the message." She hissed and turned, stomping out the door.

CHAPTER 45

Helping Sari Van would give Aril something to do. Also, it worked into her plans because she could steer the conversation to when the soldiers and entourage who would return to their country would visit to say farewell. Aril had written several notes and felt at least one would get back to Cadmia.

Opening the door with her palm to the outside brought a half-smile. Crossing the wide atrium felt good, a bit of freedom that she relished. She eyed her herb garden and admired how it flourished. She'd plant an assortment of vegetables, too. Not that she planned to still be in Protar when they bloomed

She knocked gently on the glass door.

Sari-Van answered at once. She did a once-over appraisal and stepped aside, sending an unspoken consent for Aril to enter. "You are the Crown Prince's slave," she said, not as a question but as a commentary. "Good, I need you. This place is a mess."

Aril looked from side to side. There had been a gathering, and nothing had been cleaned. Various boxes of food in pieces and whole portions crowded the tabletop. More containers lay on the floor next to the couch.

As a slave, Aril knew she shouldn't ask questions until the conversation required her input, but the expression on her face must have prompted an explanation from Sari-Van.

"My guards and ladies-in-waiting visited last night. Most of them are returning to Crocess. She sighed. The rest must get employment here in Protar. They won't be able to clean up. I'm so glad the prince sent you."

Clean up? Did Sari-Van expect to use Aril as her servant? It might be difficult to be a high princess one day and later be a commoner, but this ex-princess needed a jolt of reality. "My Lady," the proper title for a slave to address a master, "the prince sent me to show you how to run a household."

Sari-Van's face crinkled into outrage. "You're a slave. You work. Now get to work."

Aril stiffened and tried to keep her words mild. "I am prince Tim-Ell's slave," not what she wanted to admit, but what needed to be said. "He sent me to help you learn how to be…" she ran out of appropriateness, "…a regular person, one who takes care of herself and her family."

Sari-Van's hand shot up to slap Aril, but Aril caught the swift wrist and held it firm. Obviously Cross masters mistreated their slaves as Protar did.

Sari-Van twisted her hand away from Aril's grip. "Are you saying you refuse to work for me?"

"I will gladly show you how to manage your household. I will not do the work for you."

Sari-Van stamped her foot, twice like a spoiled child. "Get out, you worthless slime. The prince will hear of this. I will demand he beat you for your insolence." She slammed her hand on the handle of the glass as if hitting it would open it faster. "Out!" she demanded. A short silence followed

As Aril crossed the atrium, she wondered how Prince Tim-Ell would react. *Bring it! Give me a sword. I'll defend myself.* Then the other part of the conversation with Sari-Van hit her. Blood drained from her face. While she and the prince had been in the grips of the nectar, Sari-Van's people had come to say goodbye. There went the chances for the Excaliburian Knights to get a message to Jake Hill. She stopped near the herb garden and hung her head. She would have to work on Dr. Fil-Set. He looked like her only hope.

Tim-Ell did not return that evening. He stayed away the following day as well. Dusting the house and cleaning where the rooms needed no attention, Aril entered Tim-Ell's bedroom. In his closet he had an extra sword in a new scabbard. In the top drawer of his bureau, three small leather bags bulged with money. And now she had access to the outside, including the flier. She didn't understand the change in her liberties. Had the prince tired of her? Did he want her to escape?

Working in the garden might lift her mood. She laid a towel on the edge of the neat rows that thrived on the kitchen compost and the water from the bath. While she weeded, sitting on the towel, four women were admitted by the front gate and proceeded to Sari-Van's apartment. Shortly thereafter Sari-Van came to the atrium, where she sat in the sunlight, relaxing. By the time Aril had finished weeding and trimming, she looked up to see Sari-Van staring at her. The ex-royal's nose went into the air, and she headed to her apartment. Later, as Aril dusted her hands, ready to return to her own place, Sari-Van, dressed head to toe in a bright yellow riding outfit that shone in the sunlight, headed toward the stable. A groom brought out a fine gant, most likely the one she had ridden with Fin-Dal. She petted the animal, gave it a treat, and with a boost from the groom, took the animal past the garden and out the front gate.

A flush of anger swept through Aril. Obviously the four women were cleaning the apartment while Sari-Van took a jaunt on her gant. Still a princess? Who paid for the cleaning ladies? Who paid for the gant feed? Aril slapped her own knee. It had been her idea to let the defecting couple live in the complex.

She returned to her apartment, made keela, cut slices of bread, and spread tashberry butter and jam. Even that purest of comfort food gave her little consolation. After consuming half of the sandwich, she was surprised by a knock on the door. One of the women who had gone to Sari-Van's waited outside. Aril shook her head. What now? Were they going to demand she help them?

Aril opened the door and didn't try to conceal the scowl on her face.

"Ma'am?" the lady said.

Ma'am? No one called a slave that. Who was this person?

"What do you want?" Aril asked.

"Your laundry."

"What?"

"I'm your laundress. I do the laundry for the," She moved her gaze next door, "woman," she carefully avoided saying, "the sylph." and pointed to Sari-Van's apartment. "The complex owner said to pick up the laundry here, too."

For a few seconds, Aril processed what the laundress said.

"Ma'am?"

That title, again.

Aril did not want to let an opportunity like that disappear. "Hold on," she said. "I'll gather the laundry." She hurriedly stripped the beds, gathered towels and everything she could think of and brought them to the woman who waited.

"Thank you," the woman said.

"Thank you!" Aril answered, grateful she wouldn't be washing clothes in the tub and hanging them out in the sunroom. Odd. Very odd. In a few hours the laundress gave Aril a basket with neatly folded, clean laundry.

Tim-Ell came later that afternoon. "Do you need anything?" he asked flatly, as if ready to duck a fist or a kick.

"Did you send a laundress?"

"Yes. Ray-Tan hired one for Kye-Ren. Fin-Dal took an advance on his captain's pay to hire help for Sari-Van."

Aril looked down at her hands. "About that."

"You don't have to deal with Sari-Van. She misunderstood what I offered. Fin-Dal understands. He had been a commoner who worked his way up the military steps. Sari-Van is his mate and his problem."

Should she thank him? Her hatred had waned a bit, but it still resonated.

"Aril-Ess. I don't know what happened between us regarding the nectar, but that's beside the point. If Kye-Ren and Sari-Van have help, you deserve it, too."

"You don't know what happened?" The rage surfaced. "Liar. And now you give me freedom. I've figured it out. If I have a fertilized egg, you know I won't risk getting hurt. Very clever. Freedom that means nothing."

Tim-Ell shot up from his place at the table, grabbed Aril by the wrist and, in a firm grip, pulled her inches from his face. "You had better believe me, for this is the last time I'll say it. I had nothing to do with what happened about the nectar. I'm as much a victim as you."

His jaw set hard, his face radiated seriousness, and his light blue eyes had become the color of alnata. Jake Hill had told his family members to listen to their gut. Aril's gut said clearly Tim-Ell told the truth. She believed him.

She stared into his eyes and nodded. He released his grip. They both sat at the table and watched each other for a few minutes.

"What happens next?" Tim-Ell asked.

She bit her lip. "I'll know in a few days if the egg is fertile."

He didn't ask how. She didn't go into detail, except to say, "In half a year, the egg will deliver, and it will be incubated for another half year."

"Oh. Right." He rose and headed for the door. "If you go out, be careful," he said. "I'll be back in a few days."

She leaned against the stone bench that served as a long seat for the table. Even if he didn't put the nectar in the food—probably the wine at the palace—someone did, but why?

CHAPTER 46

For the next few days, Aril busied herself in the garden, planting the seeds she'd bought at the market, the day she chose the melon-colored outfit. As she patted the soil over the rows, she spoke to the plants, telling them she hoped she would not see them blossom into the beans and tubers that would come. Maybe Cal-Eb's wife would enjoy them. The thought that Del-Am's husband, the loyal captain, might not live to taste them, or even see his child, saddened her. Men would die because of her. Good men, loyal to their leader and country, men who had nothing to do with her captivity. The ones who deserved death she wasted no pity upon, but the men, like the Swordmaster from Linter, Captain Fin-Dal, and Cal-Eb, would bravely face Jake Hill's men, and the finest blood of Cadmia would spill, as well. She stood and brushed dirt from her hands and shook the towel that had protected her from the pebbly ground.

Movement caught Aril's eye. Sari-Van, arrayed in her fine riding habit, soft, shiny fabric like a sunrise, walked smartly, carrying a quirt. Today she wore a matching scarf that tied a yellow wide-brimmed hat in place. The groom held the animal while the ex-princess, the woman who hadn't quite adapted to her new status, mounted the fine steed.

Calling for the outside guard to open the gate, Sari-Van urged the gant into a medium gallop and barely cleared the opening of the front gate. It had been a long time since Aril enjoyed a ride like that. She thought of her morning outings with Jerr-Lan, racing their gants. He always won. The memory brought a smile, then a deep wave of sadness. Why hadn't she married Jerr-Lan? Her sense of logic asserted itself. She liked Jerr-Lan deeply, admired and trusted him. He said he loved her, but she didn't feel the same depth of devotion she needed to join him as a Life-Mate. Maybe she never would experience that. Suitors had called her cold, unfeeling. Could it be true? Arba-Lora, grandsire's mate, loved him dearly, a love that had transcended the fact that when the Earthman crashed on the planet, he had nothing to offer the high princess. Word had it, Arba-Lora threatened her father that she would not eat or leave her room until the king relented and agreed to their mating. Grandsire had said many times that Aril was most like his mate. Arba-Lora loved deeply. Could Aril?

She put the thoughts behind her and returned to the apartment. After washing, she lay down on her cot. A cramp in her belly preceded a movement— the path of a small knot that moved from its place deep within to the chamber where it would develop. She carried a fertile egg.

Mixed emotions surfaced. She dismissed them one by one. She would be a mother, and needed to be strong, keep her wits about her, and most of all, stay safe. No longer did she have only herself to protect; she also had her future child. Running her hand over her belly, she searched for the small knot. Locating the barely discernable bump, she spoke to it, promising to take as good care as she could, and give it all the love a child needed. Love! Did she say that? She had, and it made her smile. She felt love, and it was good.

Late that afternoon, Tim-Ell made an appearance. "How are you?" He asked.

"I am well. You need to know I carry an egg. Your child."

What looked like the same mixed emotions she'd experienced, showed on his face. "Oh," he said. "Should you see a doctor?"

"I'm not sick." She stopped short. Maybe she did need to see Fil-Set. By now she knew the man wasn't the type who took risks, but Tim-Ell left money in his bureau and perhaps the slave doctor could be tempted to travel to Cadmia for a sum, if not for a favor to her.

Aril prepared dinner using some of the herbs she'd picked earlier. She'd eaten the last of the bread for lunch and made a batter bread, not as tasty as the wonderful redgrain Protar offered, but adequate. Maybe she would venture out tomorrow in the flier to shop. The idea of the small freedom to leave the complex pleased her. She turned away from the prince, so he couldn't see her take pleasure in that thought.

Without explanation, Tim-Ell spent the night there, once again with his bedroom door ajar.

In the morning, as Aril served the keela and the leftover batter bread, she asked if the prince would be back for supper.

He said he would be training his new gant, and yes, since he stabled the animal there in the complex he would be returning.

"I am going to the market tomorrow," she said. "I think I'd enjoy some wild fowl. Now that I can go outside," she let the words sink in. "I can roast it in the firepit, like Cal-Eb does." She referred to the several evenings when the captain and his wife dined outside at sunset.

"I haven't eaten roasted wild fowl since the last time I went out with a regiment on maneuvers," Tim-Ell said. "We brought down almost an entire flock of Greentails. Wonderful."

She sniffed at him. "With bow and arrows, right?"

"No. We netted them. But I can take down all I see with arrows, like I said earlier."

"Right." She put her hands on her hips and raised her eyebrow at him. "I'll clean and roast as many as you can shoot with an arrow. Leave the arrows in them."

"Deal," he said. He strapped on his sword and went to the stable. Shortly after, he called to the guard at the gate and galloped his new gant. Aril watched as he left. The gant, a mottled gray that faded to white on its belly, was one of the most attractive she had seen, and the gait looked smooth. Those pliable hooves would surely give the rider a silky-smooth run. Even Jake Hill's personal mount did not match the beauty and quality of this one.

CHAPTER 47

It had been several days since Aril-Es had seen Tim-Ell. Early in the afternoon he stumbled through the door and fell onto the floor, the armload of Greentails scattering around him.

Aril ran to see what was happening. "Prince, what's wrong?" She turned him on his back, kicked a bird out of the way, and gasped at his face. A large red welt on his cheek dwarfed the rosy specks dotting his face. As she ran her gaze over his body the welts and wheals plus the bits of redgrain still stuck to the bird feathers revealed the malady.

Redworms, the larval form of insects that lived on the plants when they flowered, pollinated the blossoms into grain. Redworms were a necessary evil, and those who worked in the fields knew about them and how to prevent being infested with the larvae that needed a blood meal to reproduce. Normally the maggots attached to vermin that thrived in the brush. After engorging, the young insects dropped off their hosts, pupated in the soil, then became the flying insects that left their eggs on the grain to repeat the cycle. The vermin were mildly affected by the infestation, but other species, like gants, and people, suffered and frequently died a horrible death as the worms bore inward, not laterally like they did in the small warm-blooded animals. Tim-Ell was being eaten alive by the worms that had burrowed inside him.

Aril left him on the floor and hurried to the herb garden, snatching leaves and pulling plants into a towel until the cloth was filled and spilling. She ran back into the kitchen and put water on to boil while she separated the herbs. She couldn't let the man moaning on the floor distract her. She threw the ingredients into the pot and sprinted next door to bang on the neighbor's back glass door.

Kye-Ren slid the glass back and pulled her lips apart, showing the small, pointed incisors at Aril. "Ray-Tan isn't here," she said.

"I know. You have to help me."

The sylph, turning a slight shade of purple, began to move the door shut, but Aril put her foot on the track. "Kye-Ren, you have to get the slave doctor, Fil-Set."

The smaller woman hissed, turning a bit darker. "I don't have to do anything for you."

"Yes, you do. Find a call box—"

"Go away." Kye-Ren tried to close the door.

"Look, if you don't help me, I will tell Ray-Tan you refused to give aid in an emergency. How do you think he'll feel about that, about you?"

Kye-Ren darkened and cast her gaze to the ground. "All right, for Ray-Tan, not for you."

Aril pushed the door wide. "Do it now. No time to waste. Go. Go!" She pulled on Kye-Ren's shoulder to hasten her departure. "Run!" She watched until the sylph turned into the arched gate. Hurrying back inside, she heard the pot gurgle, sending a swampy aroma around the room like bad incense. It needed to reduce more.

She went down on one knee to check, running her fingers over the large pulsating cyst on his cheek. "You walked through a redgrain field to hunt Greentails?"

Tim-Ell moaned. "Ohhh," Tim-Ell groaned. "Rode. My gant."

Aril shot up and found a piece of paper. She scribbled a note then grabbed a small, inked stamp. Rolling Tim-Ell's signet ring over the stamp, she pressed the paper over the insignia.

"What did I just decree?" Tim-Ell said, wincing.

"The execution of the gant you rode. It is experiencing what you are, too."

"Execute…"

"It can't be saved."

She ran out the door to see Kye-Ren combing back. "Kye-Ren! You made the call?" Kye-Ren nodded. Aril grabbed her arm and pushed the note in it. "Now, take this to Sari-Van. Tell her to get it to Fin-Dal." The sylph balked. Aril added, "It's an order from Tim-Ell."

Kye-Ren rolled her eyes with a stare like storm clouds but headed toward Sari-Van's.

Aril hurried back to the apartment, sorting her thoughts and organizing her moves. She left the door slightly opened. After releasing the lock, she stood over Tim-Ell, silently listing priorities. She kicked three Greentails out of the way, grabbed his hands, and pulled. Straining, she managed a slow move from the kitchen to her room, where the skylight offered good illumination. Getting him up on the cot took a lot of her energy. She had no time to rest.

In the kitchen, after checking on the bubbling mixture, she shifted it from the burner into the cool box, where she removed a bottle of erbate. She quickly assembled her tools, including a cup for the erbate and a number of towels. Running to the garden she hurriedly picked a small basket of fat duncan leaves, their astringent smell wafting in the gentle wind.

Back in the apartment she took the basket of aromatic leaves and crushed one in her hand releasing more of the biting tang. She wiped his face with the moist leaf. He moaned as the juice seeped into the flesh of the wounds.

"I'll need your dagger," she said as she slipped it from his ankle holder. She unbuckled his harness and eased him from the leather straps. Using the dagger, she cut through the short pants.

Aril took a breath and started to push the dagger tip into the large wheal on his face. Tim-Ell cried out.

"Hold still. The worm has teeth that attach to the muscle. I'll have to pull hard." Cutting and pulling, half of the worm emerged. "This isn't going to work," she muttered and strode hard swift steps to the cool box.

The liquid was still hot, but it would have to be used. Pouring it in a cup she brought it to the cot and helped him sit up. "Drink this. It will make you sleep. That way I can probe deeper and you won't suffer."

"You will put me to sleep?" His blue-eyed stare grabbed her.

She could read the stare. "No harm will come to you. I give you my word. Do you trust me?"

He nodded and sipped, the decaying vegetable smell wafting from the cup as he choked the mixture down. She paced the room until his breathing became slow and regular. The rest of that worm was her target. With Tim-Ell asleep, it was easier to probe and pull. The pieces went straight into the cup of erbate, which would kill the worms.

As she finished the few red mounds on his face, she heard the door slide back. Leaning, she saw Dr. Fil-Set enter.

"In here," she called.

He hurried in. "Where are you hurt? What can I do?"

"It's not me," she said.

"But the sylph said—"

"I told her to have you come to help me, but not because I'm hurt, because I'm trying to save the prince." She pointed to the pulsating red masses that grew by the minute. "Redworms."

Fil-Set's eyebrows went up. "He's unconscious?"

"Anesthetized. I've given him a sedative."

"What did you give him?"

"A mixture of makitterick, cadigan, and kij."

"Gunn?"

"Yes, a bit of that, too. From my herb garden. I've been cultivating them."

"A powerful mixture. Well done, clever slave woman!"

Aril-Ess put the bloody-ended dagger down. "I'm free to come and go."

"Free. Perfect! Now all we have to do is let him die. In a few hours some of those worms will work into a major organ, maybe his brain. I'll certify we did everything we could to save him. You can leave this place and be with me as my assistant."

"You'd let him die? You took an oath."

Dr. Fil-Set directed his gaze to the man on the cot. "I can rescind my oath when it comes to saving the life of a cruel captor."

Aril-Ess took a long look at the slow rise and fall of Tim-Ell's chest. *He was never cruel to me.* "He's not my captor right now, Doctor. He's a helpless patient who is suffering. I gave my word no harm would come to him."

"I don't understand you."

"A long line of people don't understand me. I'm in that line as well." She looked at the medical bag he held. "I hope you have some good tweezers."

While the doctor worked on Tim-Ell's body, Aril concentrated on his face. Her gut said someone in the palace tricked him into hunting in the redgrain field without protection. Field workers rubbed the leaves of a succulent plant, a weed that that grows near the grainfields, which repels the larva. Farmers and field workers know about the repellant, but would a warrior, one who had concentrated his life learning martial arts? He should. She did, but there were many things about Protar that needed fixing. Field danger was obviously one of them. She treated his face first. The people responsible for this, probably expecting him to die before he reached home or the barracks, would be looking for evidence of his vulnerability. If she could save him, she wanted as little as possible of his infirmity to show.

Aril made small incisions, and using a large set of tweezers provided by Fil-Set, probed to find the head of the worm, or the tail if the creature had burrowed inward, the hardest position to remove. As the hours ticked away, the worms that had time to feed had engorged and became even more difficult to grasp and remove. Spines on their tubular bodies gripped tissue, and the larger they were, the harder she had to pull.

Twice Tim-Ell groaned and fluttered his eyes. She put the cup of sedative to his lips and let the liquid roll down his throat. Each time Fil-Set sent her a look of disgust. Cups of erbate overflowed with gyrating bloody worms, some of them taking a long time to succumb to the alcohol bath. By morning, Aril and Dr. Fil-Set had removed most of the infestation, leaving a few thumb-sized wheals to deal with.

Ray-Tan came in as they attacked the last two wounds. The cuts to get to the worms were so large, they needed stitches. Tim-Ell lay on his stomach, the last areas being on his buttocks.

Ray-Tan rushed to his friend, hovered over him. "Hey! What are you doing?"

"Do you know what Red Worms are?" Aril asked as she yanked on the purple head of the large worm.

"I've heard of them. Is that what it is?" He pointed to the creature Aril struggled to dislodge.

"Yes. I think someone took Tim-Ell hunting for Greentails," she said, indicating with her head the dead birds lying on the floor, "at a time when the insects are in their worm state. There are plenty of Greentails available because people know not to be in the fields." She looked at the bleeding wounds, some that oozed from the stitches. "Tim-Ell clearly didn't know about the insects. Just like he doesn't know anything about ruling a kingdom." *Or raising a child.*

Ray-Tan's face glowered, his eyebrows formed a Vee. "*I* didn't know about that. We don't go into the fields. I remember him saying he was going hunting with some men who guaranteed a huge catch of Greentails. He wanted to take the birds with his bow."

A wave of grief coursed through Aril. She had challenged him, offering to cook as many as he could take with bow and arrows. He had left the apartment days ago after she accused him of tricking her into sipping the nectar. She knew he wasn't responsible for that.

Tim-Ell moaned. It wouldn't be good to give him another round of sedative. He would have to awaken, at least for a while, before he could handle more.

Ray-Tan looked at the doctor. "Why did you call the slave doctor? There are excellent doctors at the palace."

"Because," she said, threading the needle to close the wound. "Those doctors would be watched. The people who planned this would know if the prince lived, or how badly he was wounded. This needs to stay secret. He needs to be up and around as soon as possible so the criminals can be hunted down and interrogated."

Ray-Tan took a step back, surprise on his face. He nodded, a look of admiration preceding his response. "As soon as he can tell me what happened and who these men are, I'll start an investigation."

"The gant?" Aril asked.

"Taken care of. The prince's new mount. That will hurt him."

"Not as much as when he awakens from this. Dr. Fil-Set, what do you have for pain?"

Fil-Set opened his bag. "Not much, actually. I'm low on medicine."

Ray-Tan hurried from the apartment and returned in a few minutes with a leather purse. "Here. Use what you have for the prince and buy more later."

Fil-Set took the specie but reached into his bag slowly with an obvious reluctance. "The slaves have very little. The prince has everything."

Ray-Tan's hand went to his pommel.

Fil-Set pulled out a glass vial and a hypodermic.

Aril had a moment of panic. She knew Fil-Set hated Tim-Ell. Would he try to hurt him after spending the night working so hard to save him?

Aril grabbed the bottle, read the label, then returned it to the doctor. He injected Tim-Ell.

Aril stood and stretched. "Thank you, Dr. Fil-Set. I appreciate your dedication. Perhaps the Crown Prince will reward you for your service. Certainly, you will be paid for your time and the supplies. I'm sorry that I have taken you from your duties and service to the slaves who need you so badly."

The doctor's eyebrows came together. "You are dismissing me?"

"I don't wish to detain you further," she said as sweetly as she could fake.

He nodded and shot a look at Ray-Tan. "Very well. I'll be off. I'll check on him tomorrow. Call me if anything changes." He gathered his instruments, snapped his bag together and hurried out.

Ray-Tan escorted Fil-Set to the door. When it clicked shut, her turned to her. "That was abrupt, Aril-Ess."

She was tired, having worked all night and worrying about multiple problems, the biggest one being she watched Fil-Set to make sure he didn't do something to Tim-Ell. How should she answer Ray-Tan? His comment didn't require a response. "I have one more wound to close. After that, will you sit with him? I need to sleep. He'll need the sedative in a few hours, too."

"Of course. Aril-Ess, what is happening here?"

"I don't know, Ray-Tan, but you once said to me that Tim-Ell is in danger from all sorts of places, including the palace."

Ray-Tan let out a breath and nodded slowly.

Aril used the prince's dagger to recut the large red gouge on his cheek. Making two straight incisions, she pulled them together and took tiny stitches. "This looks like a wound from sword practice. It will be easy to explain. He should wear his dress uniform because it covers more of his body. He needs to be seen as if nothing happened out of the ordinary."

Ray-Tan put his hand on Aril's shoulder. "I thank you. I know he will be grateful. Take a rest. We can't do anything until Tim-Ell tells us what happened. But, if the men who brought him hunting suspects he lives, they will be long gone."

Aril retired to Tim-Ell's room and lay on the generous soft bed. Thoughts jumbled in her mind. She could have let Fil-Set carry out an easy death for Tim-Ell, but she would never let that happen, not to anyone helpless and trusting her. Within those jumbled thoughts, she turned over images and feelings associated with her capture. Tim-Ell had had set her free, but not really. He hadn't given her the papers he held with her slave status. And carrying an egg, she couldn't return to Cadmia. Wasn't she still a slave? She hadn't said anything to Fil-Set about messages to Cadmia because they had been so busy and then Ray-Tan had come. And the doctor hadn't volunteered any comments. She would wait until tomorrow to see if Fil-Set checked on the prince. Would he help her?

CHAPTER 48

Aril slept long into the day. When she awoke, hunger overwhelmed her. The Greentails had begun to stink but not enough to affect her need to eat. She asked Ray-Tan to dispose of the dead birds and as soon as he did that would he buy bread and a few other things. When he returned with the bread, she cut hunks and spread them with tashberry butter and jam. Thanking the Great Spirit in a quick thought, she shared the comfort food and put on a kettle for keela. Ray-Tan sat at the dining table and accepted a cup. They drank quietly, turning every so often to the sounds of Tim-Ell's moans.

"He'll be coming out of it soon," Aril said. "I'll pick some herbs and make him a soothing draft. But it won't be enough to take away the pain. He's going to hurt."

Ray-Tan nodded and placed his hand on the stone tabletop. "Thank you for saving him, Aril. You're the best thing that ever happened to him."

Aril half choked on the sip of keela. *What did that mean?* How could she be good for him? Yes, she'd saved his life, but she would have done that for anyone. Hadn't she saved the little silver bitch from her cut? No one knew about the nectar.

She hoped Jake Hill would come before anyone knew about the egg. Maybe she could take Tim-Ell's craft and head in the direction of Cadmia, but she only thought she knew where Cadmia was and wouldn't risk hurting her unborn child. Or perhaps she could ask for asylum by invoking sanctuary in a Rotner Monk monastery and have one of them contact Jake Hill. It would be too risky in

Protar, but in another kingdom, a neighboring country, they might not ask too many questions before she could get to the monastery.

Further thoughts were interrupted by a long cry from the bedroom. Ray-Tan rose from his seat and hurried toward the room. Aril followed, pausing at the door to watch Ray-Tan help Tim-Ell as he struggled to sit. She joined them, fluffed a pillow, and put it behind his back. Aril sat next to him on the bed.

"Thirsty," Tim-Ell rasped.

"I'll get you some water," Ray-Tan said.

"Erbate," Tim-Ell managed words from parched lips.

"Water," Aril said.

Tim-Ell's face grimaced in pain. His tanned skin had paled, and the ugly red wounds contrasted with his usually healthy appearance. The discomfort of the injuries didn't compare to the torture the toxins left by the worms; the acids exuded from their bodies to break down the tissue for nourishment. He would feel the internal agonies of the healing tissue for weeks to come. It hurt her to think about it. At least the gant had been put out of its misery. Her thoughts jumbled again. She rose, but Tim-Ell grabbed her wrist.

"Thank you," he whispered. "I knew you would help me."

What could she say? How close had he come to dying at the hand of Fil-Set? Even field medicine practitioners like she had been, took a vow not to harm. *How could Fil-Set go against his vow?* But he treated slaves when few doctors would.

"Aril?" Tim-Ell wanted her to say something.

"You'll be all right. You are going to hurt for a long time, though. I'll try to make something that will help, but it will only take the edge off. Understand?"

He nodded. Ray-Tan brought in a glass of water. He held the pillow forward while Aril put the glass to Tim-Ell's lips.

"Who took you hunting in that field?" Ray-Tan asked.

"Their names were Levit-Wel, and Gori-Uhl. It was my brother's field."

"Your brother? Sen-Mak?" Ray-Tan's voice went up a notch.

"No, Alor-Bit, my youngest brother. I don't think he would try to kill me. There's no reason. He is happy as a farmer, staying away from the palace or politics."

"You saw him a few weeks ago," Ray-Tan said, "when you spent the day with your father and brothers."

"Yes. We had a good time and agreed to do it again. Those men came to me outside of the palace and invited me to go hunting."

"You need to stay here for a while," Aril said. "But as soon as you can get around, you need to be seen. You have to show whoever is trying to hurt you that it won't be easy."

Tim-Ell said, "Those men should be easy to find. One had a purplish mark on his neck—very distinctive—shaped like a feather. The other had a turned foot."

Aril sucked in a breath. Those descriptions fit the men that watched the apartment complex, the ones she accused Tim-Ell of keeping track of her. *I told you we were being watched."*

Ray-Tan paced. "I've seen those men—messengers for Eppo-Zim."

CHAPTER 49

Two days later, Tim-Ell, still in pain, with assistance from Ray-Tan and Aril, dressed in his official uniform, the one that covered his arms and legs. The wound on his cheek, a slit closed with tiny stitches gave him a somber look.

"Shouldn't he cover that wound?" Ray-Tan asked.

"No," Aril said. "If someone asks, give them a plausible answer." She rolled her lip. "You can always say he sparred with the swordsman from Linter."

Ray-Tan laughed, but seeing that Tim-Ell scowled, his laughter faded, and he cleared his throat.

As Tim-Ell left the apartment, Aril pressed a small bottle into his hand. "When the pain gets too bad, take a swallow of this. Not too much; it can make you sleepy. And don't ride a gant. Let Ray-Tan pilot you."

Tim-Ell nodded. He paused and took her hand. "Thank you," he said quietly.

She looked over his shoulder. "You're welcome."

Later, when they returned, Ray-Tan helped the prince into the apartment and to his room. Aril gently unbuckled his harness and lifted the tunic over his head. He moaned when they touched him. She checked the bottle she'd given him. He had used half. "Drink the rest; it will help you sleep."

She held the bottle to his lips while Tim-Ell choked the liquid down. Aril touched his mouth with a small towel and helped Ray-Tan ease the prince into bed.

"Do you need anything?" Ray-Tan asked, looking out the backdoor glass. Kye-Ren waited outside.

"No, thank you, Aril said. "After the medicine takes effect, he won't stir until morning."

Ray-Tan pushed at the door. Aril put her hand on his arm. "You are a good friend. He is lucky to have you."'

"I see it the other way around," Ray-Tan said and left.

The friendship reminded her of Jerr-Lan and her brother. Was Protar all that different from Cadmia?

"Aril!" Tim-Ell called hoarsely from the room.

She ran to the room. "What is it, Prince?"

"I'm putting extra guards around the complex. And even though I said you could use the flier, I don't want you to leave the grounds. Understand?"

"I understand my freedom is short lived."

"Aril…"

"Speaking of freedom. Have you given Ray-Tan Kye-Ren's papers?"

"Papers?"

"The owner papers you received when you bought her and me. You don't want to keep her."

Tim-Ell's words sounded thick, the result of the pain reliever. "He doesn't want a slave. He told me that."

"You can be so dense, especially to other people's needs. It's obvious he's in love. He'll want those papers. Offer them to him."

His lips parted in surprise, then pursed in a tight line. He managed to raise his arm. "There's a wooden box in the bottom drawer."

She knew about the box as she knew about the money and anything else hidden.

"Get it," he said. He added, "Please."

She brought the box to him. With difficulty he rifled through various sheets, some folded, some in envelopes. He pulled out a parchment. "I can't read it because it's in legal language, but I think this is the one."

Aril read it over. "It's the one."

"You read the legal language?"

"I paid attention in school, Prince. As a future ruler you need to be able to read important documents."

He yawned. "That's why we have True Witness Scribes."

"And rotten untrustworthy viziers who cheat you regularly."

"My father can read the documents."

"Does he? Or does he sign where his advisors tell him?"

Tim-Ell didn't answer. "Where should I sign to give Ray-Tan his sylph?"

Aril went into the kitchen and brought back a pen. She wrote a sentence on the bottom of the scroll and drew a line. "This says you are turning over ownership to Ray-Tan. To free a slave, you need a different form. Ray-Tan can take care of that detail."

Tim-Ell scribbled his name on the document, wiped ink on his signet ring and pressed it on the paper. He fell back on the pillow and closed his eyes.

Aril blew on the ink and brought the paper out to the table. She sighed. It would be a quiet night.

In the morning at the sounds of Tim-Ell's stirring, she brought him a light breakfast on a tray and put it down on a small table near the bed. She put a new bottle of pain reliever next to the food. He took a swig from the bottle.

"Sit," he said, and patted a space on the mattress. "Please."

She sat.

"You saved my life and confounded at least one of my enemies. Let me do something for you."

She didn't hesitate. "Make me your Life-Mate so my child has a name."

"Your Life-Mate?"

"Do you have a hearing malady? Life-Mate. I don't want my child to suffer the shame of not having a name."

The prince ran his hand through his hair and winced at the movement. "I've been to the palace to consult with an old priest and also a trustworthy scribe regarding what you said about a second marriage contract. As I walked to the filer, those men approached me to go hunting."

"Don't change the subject. And don't try to say you can't do it because of whatever reason—"

He took her hand. "I'm not going to say that." Pressing her palm to his lips, he said, "I can take you as my Mate. I want to marry you. I love you, Aril."

A bit of his scent wafted passed her. She withdrew her hand from him and shot from her place on the mattress. "Love! You're out of your mind from the pain draft. And just so you know, I hate you." *Why did I say that?*

Tim-Ell looked at her with half-lidded eyes. "I'm sorry," he cast his gaze to the wall. His head drooped and as he let out a small sigh, he reached for the bottle of pain reliever and took another long sip.

She stepped back from the bed and stared at the man whose words took her by surprise. Quick steps took her from his room.

CHAPTER 50

The next morning at dawn, Tim-Ell dragged himself from the bed. He dressed, donned his harness with the royal emblem, buckled his sword, and left without breakfast or conversation. His body ached from the swollen, angry wounds he'd covered by wearing long sleeves. Every muscle screamed when he moved.

He flew low in his craft until he reached the monastery where the Rotner monks lived. Making a coin donation at the arched wooden doors of the stone building with the crenellated top, he asked to enter. The door swung wide.

"I need the services of a monk," he said to the shabbily clothed man who still had his hands on the metal door handle.

The man nodded. "I am at your service, Sir." He eyed the prince's emblem but did not amend his address. "When do you need me?"

"Now."

"Certainly, Sir. I will follow you."

The prince led the priest to the flier and flew sedately. He landed in the middle of the atrium.

Most of the residents had not left, and the changing of the guard, more of them than before, offered the only activity in the place.

The priest waited at the patio table where Tim-Ell directed. Tim-Ell knocked on Ray-Tan's door.

Ray-Tan answered, "Yes, Prince?" He added, "Is there something wrong?"

"Not wrong, friend. Would you gather the residents and meet me in the courtyard table?"

"Of course. Immediately."

Tim-Ell let himself in to the apartment and rapped on Aril-Ess's room door.

She opened it, "What is it?" she stared at him, looking surprised at his appearance. "You should be in bed resting."

"Get dressed," he said flatly.

She slammed the door, and he sat down at the kitchen table, the cold stone increasing the pain in his muscles. A few minutes later, Aril-Ess came out of her room.

"What do you want," she asked.

"Come with me." He stood and pushed open the door.

With her arms crossed, she followed him to the grassy expanse that served as the courtyard.

He noted that the grass grew there by her design, the bath and kitchen water that would have seeped into dry ground on the outside had provided the moisture for the now lush garden and bushes that enhanced the complex.

As they walked, he thought about her. *Who was she?* He didn't believe the made-up story from the slave market. She had been medical practitioner, herbalist, and excellent cook, and she read and wrote legal language.

"What is this?" Aril asked.

Tim-Ell didn't answer. He continued to approach the table where the monk waited. Two by two, the residents came from their apartments. Several of the guards came as well. When enough witnesses arrived, Tim-Ell spoke to the Rotner monk.

"I wish to take this woman as my Life-Mate." He whispered to Aril, "At your convenience I will release you from the vow."

Officiating the rite, the monk described the years the couple would be together, how they should care for one another, be loyal, never stray, and love each other under all circumstances. The simple admonitions expected of partners concluded in a few minutes, followed by the question the monk asked, meaning would they pledge their lives to one another.

Tim-Ell painfully straightened his shoulders and promised the witnesses he would adhere to the oath.

Aril-Ess, speaking in a near-whisper, promised the same.

The monk proclaimed them wed, asked for paper and pen, and created the document certifying the legality. The witnesses signed it. "Take this to a True Witness Scribe," the monk advised, "to have it registered."

Quietly the witnesses, including Sari-Van and her mate Fin-Dal, Captain Cal-Eb and Del-Am, Ray-Tan, and a subdued Kye-Ren returned to their homes. Tim-Ell escorted Aril back to the apartment, picked up the slave paper he saw on the table, and left without discussion.

He knocked on Ray-Tan's door again. Kye-Ren answered and advised that Ray-Tan was almost ready to go to the fort. Tim-Ell handed her the scroll. "This is for him," he said and put the document in the sylph's hand. "I'll take the monk back to the monastery and return for Ray-Tan."

Kye-Ren opened the paper, but obviously didn't recognize what it was. "All right," she said.

"Kye-Ren, it's your slave paper, for Ray-Tan."

Kye-Ren's mouth opened. Her pointed teeth showed as she pulled back her lips into a smile, the first time Tim-Ell had seen the expression. Aril knew, why hadn't he? Aril-Ess represented the finest and most intelligent person he had ever met

He hoped he would feel better about it all the morning, but for now, the pain from his injuries overwhelmed his emotions.

Joining the monk who waited in the atrium, he offered a small leather purse to him. The monk dumped the specie out onto the table, picked out a few coins, and returned the money to Tim-Ell.

The prince brought the monk back to the monastery and landed the flier outside of Ray-Tan's door.

Ray-Tan held the slave paper. He cleared his throat. "Thank you. When you can spare me for a few hours, I'm going to free her."

"Will she go back to her home?"

"No," Ray-Tan said in a surprised tone. "She'll stay here, eventually as my Life-Mate."

Life-Mate? Tim-Ell had never heard of a Commonfolk taking a sylph to mate. "You'll wed her?"

"After she's free."

Tim-Ell let out a breath. He hadn't thought about that. The ceremony this morning mated him to his slave, and she would retain the slave title forever. Kye-Ren would be a free woman marrying a free man.

"I'm sorry," he whispered.

CHAPTER 51

The gratitude Aril felt that her child had a name did not nullify the fact she remained a slave. She walked stiffly back to the apartment from which she could freely come and go.

Tim-Ell came back into the apartment quietly. He sat down at the table, wincing. "Fin-Dal has thanked me many times for allowing him a place in the Army. Sari-Van has not adjusted so easily. Fin-Dal barely makes enough salary to support her needs."

Rankling at her status as slave and now the memory of how Sari-Van treated her, Aril *hmphed*. "The needs of a princess? You mean her household help? Her need for fashionable riding clothes? Fin-Dal might get better value from his salary if he hired someone to teach her how to clean and cook. You provide grooms to take care of the gants in the stable. Fin-Dal can't afford a flier, but his mate gets domestics?"

"Yes." He moved stiffly on the bench. "She's asked Fin-Dal to get her a slave."

Heat seared through Aril's body. "What?" She couldn't summon words, but her face was on fire.

"Hold on," Tim-Ell said. "I told Fin-Dal no. I knew how you would feel about it."

Phrases choked in her throat.

Tim-Ell put his hand on her shoulder. "Relax. There will be no slaves in the apartment complex."

She found her voice. "Other than me and Kye-Ren?"

He turned his head from her view. "Actually Ray-Tan has freed Kye-Ren."

Aril stomped into the bedroom. She was the slave in the complex, the Mate of the Crown Prince. She sat on the bed, crossing her arms in almost a self-hug.

Tim-Ell came quietly to her. "I didn't want to tell you that, but you needed to know. He will wed a free woman. I'm sorry I messed things up. I beg your forgiveness. My brother Sen-Mak is a lawyer, I will ask him how to get your slave status reversed now that you are mated."

Aril snarled. "If laws in Protar are the same as in other countries, the only way to change the status of a mated woman is a royal decree."

He took her hand in his. "That doesn't sound impossible, you know. My father is fond of you."

Aril touched the knot in her belly and glared at him. "We need to keep this union quiet, and asking for a decree would draw attention, maybe danger."

He hung his head. "You deserve better, Aril. I understand how you feel about me."

She didn't move. He left the room and by the noises he made, it sounded like he was ready to leave. She left her room and walked to the door.

Tim-Ell stood before her on his way out. "Goodbye. I will be at the fort."

Time slipped away as she stared at the glass watching his rigid stride. Shaking herself out of her mental maelstrom, she cleared the table. From her periphery vision, movement in the courtyard caught her attention. She put the dishes in the sink and stood at the glass door. A small flier landed in the middle on the grass, grown by the diverted wastewater from the apartments. Few places as this existed in Protar.

A man dressed as a warrior helped three women out of the flier. The women carried baskets like cleaning personnel in Cadmia used. One woman went to Sari-Van's apartment, the second to Del-Am's.

Aril poured a second cup of keela and put her hand on her belly. "Sorry, egg, I need another cup." An old wife's tale warned that two cups of keela in the morning for a fertilized woman would grow hair on the baby's back. Then she laughed. Because of her genetics, her baby *might* have hair on its back. She could always blame it on the keela!

Her thoughts were interrupted by a knock on the door. She turned to see one of the ladies from the flier standing outside holding a cleaning basket.

Aril put her palm on the lock. The door whirred open. A flash of anger blew through her mind. Was Sari-Van behind this in some way? "Yes?" Aril said, her nostrils flaring. "What do you want?"

"Excuse me," the woman said and cast her gaze to the ground, the action of a domestic to royalty. "Wife of the Crown Prince? If you will allow me, I am your maid."

Aril had a laundress. Now more help? "You are my maid?"

"Yes, ma'am. If I don't please you, perhaps you would like someone else to do your work?"

Aril let go of the stiffness her anger produced. "Please, come in." Of course, Tim-Ell hired this woman to help. Albeit secret, next to the Queen, the wife of the crown prince held the top status of women in Protar. Tim-Ell was seeing to it that Aril was treated as she should be, even if in small increments. A hired helper would do the chores. Aril could take life easier, rest like many egg-bearing upper-level women did.

The time would come when she would wear loose clothing to hide her condition. The neighbors would eventually know, but they would keep the secret. Tim-Ell had surrounded them with loyal people, even Kye-Ren, who was most likely lonelier than Aril. No one but a sylph befriended another sylph, and Kye-Ren was the only one around. Would Ray-Tan hire a maid? What maid would work for a sylph? Things, *equality*, needed an overhaul. Not just in Protar but planetwide.

Aril sat at the table in the apartment sorting out what had happened in the last few months. Protar's Crown Prince Tim-Ell had just pledged his life to her. She had demanded he do so, but she hadn't expected him to comply. Her child had a name. And the prince indicated he would rescind the marriage when she requested. Dissolution of marriage didn't occur often in Cronanta, or maybe Cadmian couples kept together longer than in other countries. In all her studies, marriage had not been considered an important topic for analysis.

Tim-Ell had been gravely injured. She hadn't hesitated to help him, but she hadn't hesitated to help Kye-Ren either. That had nothing to do with how she felt about either one of them. Jake Hill had told his family if you don't know what to do, and it's not an emergency, wait. Things often sort themselves out. She hoped his advice would turn out to be true because she didn't know what to do or how to feel.

She busied herself with cleaning the kitchen cupboards, first thinking she should have her maid do it, but then grateful for something to do. She muttered to herself how far she had fallen from high princess to slave-wife, oddly now welcoming a bit of cleaning.

Maybe she should have been a little kinder to Sari-Van. Could she have made a friend? The ex-princess had no experience being a commoner. At least

Jake Hill had thought to prepare his progeny for hardships by requiring them to serve in the military and take on public service positions for a few years. It appeared that the only thing Sari-Van knew how to do was ride a gant, which she did each morning. Aril longed for a ride. Maybe she should swallow her pride and ask if Sari-Van would like some riding company. She instantly dismissed the thought. Most likely the haughty ex-princess would say no.

After the maid left, Aril spent a few hours in the garden. Some of the seeds she'd planted when they first moved there had small yellow tubers at an edible stage, early and very tender. The smaller leaves at the top of the plant would be a crisp spicy green for salad. The prince preferred meat for his meals. She laughed derisively regarding the dinner—was she making plans for her wedding feast? A bit of braised lakin, yellow vegetables, and leaf salad? Not what she'd pictured as a celebration meal. Actually, she'd never thought about it at all, not even when Jerr-Lan had hinted at their union.

Later that afternoon, Ray-Tan came to the apartment. She invited him to join her in a cup of keela, which he accepted.

"Aril-Ess, the prince gave me ownership to Kye-Ren. I'm sure you had a hand in that. I want to apologize to you. I'm ashamed that I took part in that slave business. I pledged on the symbol of Excalibur to uphold the values of the Knighthood. I didn't. I had turned my back on morality, and you shamed me that day. Having Kye-Ren gave me a new perspective on slavery, and now she is free. Thank you. I will try to make her understand what you've done for her...us."

"You're welcome, Ray-Tan. I doubt you'll be able to change her mind about me, but who knows?"

"The other reason I'm here is to find out what you need. The prince said I should get a list and he'll make sure you are taken care of."

Aril processed his words. It meant Tim-Ell would be staying at the fort. She'd be alone. She could move about the complex but not be able to leave. The new Life-Mate of the Crown Prince remained a slave, title intact. She believed he'd been a victim of the nectar, and he had done right by her. She treated him with disrespect, going so far as to say she hated him. What did she expect?

"Thank you, Ray-Tan. I'll give you a list later. Good luck with your relationship with Kye-Ren. I know you love her."

When Ray-Tan left, Aril felt more alone than she could remember. She patted the tiny knot in her abdomen. "At least I have you."

Days went by. On her list she'd put books, and Ray-Tan brought her a lot of them. He didn't ask about the ones that described the care of an egg. Most females learned how to care for eggs when they attended school, but Aril wanted to know more—and she had plenty of time.

Two weeks after the Life-Mate ceremony, Tim-Ell came to the apartment. She couldn't help the feeling of pleasure at seeing him, if only for a bit of company. The scar on his cheek had become a fine line. The army surgeon must have removed his stitches because she hadn't. Most of the visible wounds showed as pink marks and he appeared to move with less pain.

A rarity for her, she found no words to greet him.

He spoke first. "We've been summoned to the palace." His tone resembled the last time he had been required to appear before the King. And he definitely said, "We."

She found her voice. "When?"

"Tomorrow morning."

Before she could ask a question, he added, "I'll be here two hours after dawn to get you. Please be ready. Do you need anything?"

She hung her head for a few seconds. "No. I can wear the outfit from the last time. I'm good with everything else."

He stood, gave a short bow of his head and left.

She felt empty. Why didn't she invite him to stay for a meal? If he refused, would she have felt worse? She doubted she could feel any lower. Then she wondered what the summons meant. He didn't seem overjoyed to be called. What would happen?

In the morning, she offered him keela and he drank a cup without discussion. He didn't mention she looked nice or make any commentary to her appearance. In fact, he didn't look at her at all, keeping his focus on the cup, the table, or sometimes the wall. When he finished the keela, he put the cup in the sink. "It's time."

She followed him out to the flier that he left close to the back door. The ride was slow, like the last time, with ample room given for the spires and rooftops.

As they made their way to the palace, the guards saluted smartly, some of them saying, "Hail, Prince," or bowing their heads in a respectful manner. She wanted to comment on the difference of the guards' reaction.

He stopped and faced her. "I've been spending more time getting to know the palace warriors. Good men, ones I overlooked earlier."

She admired the tactic. Warriors who respect and admire their superiors are more dependable, fight harder. Tim-Ell had not been a shallow, inept leader. Ray-Tan had said it to her earlier. His men regarded him with esteem, and bad leaders never earned that.

The guards at the throne room brought their pikes up in unison. "My Prince," they both said as the spears snapped upward.

"Greetings, men," the prince said as the pages opened the wide wooden doors.

Tim-Ell stiffened his shoulders with a slight wince, then stood tall like a man facing trouble square-on. She did the same until they stopped at the emblem on the floor, the place where visitors did not proceed until invited. They both bowed low.

"Hello, my son," the King said. "Aril-Ess."

The Queen, with her usual glower didn't speak, but Aril suspected the woman bided her time.

"Approach," Jess-Reet said.

They stepped closer but were not invited to sit in the soft chairs near the throne.

Jess-Reet raised his hand. "Word has come to us that the two of you have joined. You have become Life-Mates. Is this a silly rumor? I need to hear it from you."

Tim-Ell cleared his throat. "You have heard correctly. News travels fast."

Queen Ran-Cignar said, her tone shrill and threatening. "Bad news travels. You know it is illegal. We have been searching for a suitable wife for you."

Tim-Ell spoke clearly and firmly. "My union is legal and there is nothing you can do about it. I have documentation that describes the law, which says since I had been declined by the contracted party by way of defection, and sanctuary granted, I am not obligated to a second contract."

The Queen's voice went up in pitch. "Sanctuary granted by you! Not us."

"I am able to grant sanctuary, Mother. I am a member of the Royal Family and have that ability. Princess Sari-Van abdicated her royal position and pleaded for sanctuary. I granted it. She married her guard captain, and I offered him a position in the army because of his excellence. Once I was unbound from the princess, I was able to choose my Life-Mate. I did. Aril-Ess."

"Your slave!" Now the Queen's voice hit a stabbing pitch. "A whore! We know nothing about her."

"You don't need to know anything other than I chose her. And there is nothing you can do."

The Queen's eyes narrowed. "There are always things that can be done."

Tim-Ell's hand went to the pommel of his sword. The guards around the throne put their hands on their swords. He looked at one and then the others. No one moved. "If that is all you wanted to say to me, then I ask to be excused."

"Arrest her," the Queen said.

"Father," Tim-Ell stepped closer. "You are the King. Isn't it time you made the decisions?"

The King let out a long breath. "Yes. And I think you made a good choice for a mate. I understand why you chose to marry quietly. We could never have given permission to such a union. But I'm glad it can't be undone." He cast a glare to his wife. "Let it be, Ran."

Queen Ran-Cignar hit the arm of the throne with her fist. "A slave for Queen? Never. Mark my words."

The King put his hand over her fist. "Enough." He looked at Tim-Ell. "You are excused, my son."

The quiet flight back to the complex unsettled Aril. Tim-Ell escorted her to the door and paused.

She pressed her hand against the lock, waiting for the door to wheeze and open. Instead of proceeding she turned and caught his gaze. "You said you loved me. Why don't you stay here?"

"How is that?" Tim-Ell asked.

"I'm alone. You live at the fort."

"I said I loved you, and nothing has changed. My regard for you requires me not to force you to tolerate someone you hate."

Words escaped her. She shook her head. "I should not have said that because it isn't true. I don't hate you."

"And?"

"And I don't want to be alone. Please stay here. I will be your wife in every way."

Only a muscle in his cheek moved. His face stoic, he said, "I have commitments at the fort. I will be back tomorrow."

"To stay?"

He nodded. "To stay. As your husband."

The wind blew, bringing a trace of his scent. A shiver ran up her spine.

"Tomorrow, then," she said, hoping the effect of his musk didn't show.

"Tomorrow," he said.

CHAPTER 52

After exercising in the sunroom, Aril spent the next morning weeding the garden, harvesting small tubers, and clipping greens. She needed to banish the thoughts of Tim-Ell returning, those thoughts bouncing from excitement to dread. At noon she rearranged the stones around the herb area and tied vines to trellises, taking care not to dislodge the fruit that, now green, would turn red in a few weeks. Would she still be here?

Running her hand over the small knot in her belly, she whispered, "I know grandsire will find me. And you. I want you to be in Cadmia, at the palace, and know safety and love."

Seeing movement from the corner of her eye, she turned. She lowered her head in the proper slave position and waited.

Del-Am stood over her, smiling. "Good afternoon, Wife of Crown Prince Tim-Ell."

Aril brought her head up and smiled back. Of course! She had a new title, and this woman had initiated a conversation. Not with a slave, but the mate to an important person.

"Good afternoon…" They had not been introduced. Aril, usually sure of herself, didn't know the next step.

Del-Am held her hand out. Aril rose and shook garden dirt from her smock.

Del-Am kept her hand toward Aril. "We haven't met officially, but I hope my actions aren't forward. I'm Del-Am, wife of Cal-Eb." She laughed lightly.

"Don't worry about the dirt. I come from a large family of farmers. Soil means honest effort." The woman took a step and grasped Aril's hands.

"Lady Del-Am," Aril said hesitantly.

"No title. Just Del-Am. And you are Aril-Ess? Wife of our splendid prince."

Wife of the Prince. A second, excellent title that allowed anyone to approach her.

"Yes, I am Aril-Ess. Thank you." Aril read the face of the kind woman before her. Del-Am had selected Aril for company.

"Would you care for some keela, Aril-Ess? I've made a cake."

How long had it been since someone offered to serve her? Treat her like a person? And how long had it been since she had been taken prisoner? Although the time had gone slowly, like years, it had been less than one year.

"Aril-Ess?"

"Oh, yes. I'd love some keela and cake. Thank you. Out here?" She pointed to the table in the courtyard.

"In my apartment, if that suits you."

Does it suit me? "Yes, thank you." She brushed off the smock again.

"I have a sink. You can tidy up there," Del-Am said soothingly. "Come."

Aril threw the tools she used in a small basket and placed them behind a bush in the shade. Waves of gratitude and pleasure washed over her as she followed Del-Am. The sun produced shadows, accentuating the bump in Del-Am's dress, the bump made by an egg soon to be delivered.

Del-Am caught Aril staring. "Yes. It won't be long now. I can hardly wait." She put her hand on her door lock pad and the glass slid open. "After you," she said allowing Aril to walk first.

The apartment conveyed warmth and happiness. Rich magenta drapes covered the windows. Sofa pillows in various colors coordinated with the furnishings. Aril had given no thoughts to furnishings or color matches in her apartment. Why would she? Thoughts spun in her mind.

"The bathroom is down the hall. I would think the same design as your apartment," Del-Am said.

"Uh, yes. Of course," Aril stammered. Her hostess had just reminded her to wash up. Aril had a moment of indecision regarding her situation. Who was she? A high-born princess, a slave, the wife of the Crown Prince of Protar? All of that plus a dirt-ridden gardener, one who had just made a friend.

She padded down the hallway into the bathroom. In her own apartment, the tub sat in the middle of the tiled floor with the sink against the wall. This bathroom, although identical, had a curtain circling the tub. Lush towels served as décor, and sweet-smelling soaps molded in flower designs added to the feeling of care and hominess. Del-Am and her mate had made a home for themselves and the new one that would be delivered.

After washing, Aril returned to the kitchen and sat at the long stone table, like her own, but draped with an embroidered cloth, set with a vase of flowers. A bowl of fruit gave color and cordiality.

Del-Am placed a kettle on the stove and took cups and dishes from the cabinet. The dishes matched—blue background with painted designs. Pretty. Elegant.

For a moment, emotions ranging from homesickness to longing for domestication overwhelmed Aril. Is this what her life would have been like had she had wed Jerr-Lan? But she had a husband now. Should she try to decorate the apartment? Get pretty dishes? Put flowers on the table? A flush of anger made her take a shallow breath. She didn't have time to waste on decorating. Aril had to get out, return to Cadmia. That needed to be a first priority. When Jake Hill came, none of this would matter. Would Jake Hill spare Cal-Eb? Not likely. All of Protar would feel the Planetary Prince's wrath. This good woman who fussed about her kitchen, wanting to make Aril's day better, would wind up a widow, and the egg she carried would never know its father.

"Is something wrong?" Del-Am asked.

"No. I'm fine, thank you

Del-Am placed dishes with cake and cups for the keela on the table.

"When do you expect to deliver?"

Del-Am smiled wide. "Within a few weeks. Would you like to see the room for the egg?"

Aril followed her new friend down the hall and into the room which, in her apartment, served as her room. A sturdy platform held a metal box, the incubator. Conflicting with the warm decoration of the room, the incubator seemed plain and ordinary. Aril had seen many incubators, especially in the palace, where the boxes kept warm by a pipe connected to the geothermic steam from underground sources. Many of the boxes in Cadmia's palace were beautifully wrought with precious metals and gemstones, often with delicate designs flanking the glass sides.

"I know," Del-Am said, "it's rather dull. But it's mine, meaning what my mother used for me. I'd rather have this than a fancy one." She chuckled. "Imagine what it must have been like before mothers had these and carried the egg with them in a sling."

Aril laughed. Centuries before the invention of the incubators, women kept their eggs with them. Some naturalists still did. What would she do for her own egg? She dismissed the question. By then she would be back in the palace in Cadmia. What would become of Tim-Ell?

Del-Am placed her hand on Aril's shoulder, shattering the vision of Tim-Ell and Cal-Eb lying dead at the hand of her revered ancestor, whom no man had defeated in battle.

They returned to the kitchen. The keela was brewed and ready. The cake tasted wonderful, and the keela, a different roast from what Aril made, paired with the pastry perfectly.

Del-Am had a calming way and chatted easily. Aril relaxed for the first time since she'd been in Protar. "You said you came from a farming family?"

"Yes, north of here. My father raises lakins and has a dairy. When I was younger, Cal-Eb hired on as a farm hand. I loved him immediately, as he did me. My father wouldn't consent to our mating until Cal-Eb proved worthy. To my surprise Cal-Eb joined the military, which suited him better than shoveling lakin dung. He went up through the ranks, and when he made Captain, my father consented."

"What a lovely story."

"And now, we live in a fine place, with a prince as our neighbor." She smiled. "Along with his beautiful wife." She patted her bump. "In addition, our love has come to its natural apex—we will have a child."

The relaxation Aril felt dissolved. *Love's natural apex?* Not for her. "Thank you for the cake, the keela, and the story," she said. "But it's time I went back to my place." *Her place?* Nothing was hers.

"Come over anytime," Del-Am said, escorting her to the door. "If I see you in the garden, may I visit with you?"

The question made her stop. *She's asking permission to talk with me?* "Yes, of course."

Del-Am bowed her head. "Thank you. I've enjoyed our time, Wife of the Prince."

Saying Wife of the Prince offered Aril a reminder that she wasn't a common slave now. Although she retained the title of slave, it had been superseded by her new one. Aril had a feeling Del-Am would make sure everyone knew it. She turned and smiled at her new friend. "Thank you."

Aril returned to the garden, picked up her tools, and went into her apartment. She ran the water in the tub, put fragrant oils in the water, and took a luxurious bath.

CHAPTER 53

At sundown, Tim-Ell returned. His belt, harness, and weapons, save the ankle dagger, made a splatting noise as he hefted them on to the eston tabletop. Dust from the articles floated in the last rays streaming in from the glass of the back door.

Aril-Ess left the stove, took the prince's items into the bedroom, and stowed them in the closet under his uniforms. For a moment, she pondered the space where the clothing hung on pegs. Would she move her few garments into the closet? She had promised to be his wife, implying she would sleep with him. But would she share the room in everything? Her parents shared a room. What kind of living arrangements would she have? But she had other things to ponder.

Dinner consisted of meats and vegetables left over from the last few days. Adding the things she'd gathered from the garden, she set the table with the dishes that, after seeing Del-Am's lovely set, seemed coarse and mismatched.

Tim-Ell sat at the table and waited for Aril to serve. He said few words as he ate, and she didn't initiate conversation, either. While Aril cleaned up after dinner, Tim-Ell bathed and got ready for bed.

He came out to the kitchen as she put away the last dish. He announced he was ready for bed.

Was she?

"I've had a hard day. I'm tired. Good night," Tim-Ell said and went into the bedroom. Leaving the door open, he fluffed the pillow, lay down and turned on his side.

Aril entered the room, stood next to the bed, and watched for a few moments, unsure of what had happened. His back toward her, no scent wafted in the air. In a short while, his breathing became long and regular. He had fallen asleep. Giving him a little more time to drop deeper into the slumber, she took care not to move the mattress as she took her place next to him.

Sleep did not come as easily for her. Thoughts about the day circled and landed. New images such as incubators, draperies, and fine linens flooded her mind. She put her hand on the tiny knot under her navel. The time spent with Del-Am had been valuable. The Great Spirit…did it arrange these occurrences for a reason? Jake Hill said the Spirit took care of people who believed. She rarely thought about it, trusting what her grandsire taught. But then…Why would a beneficent being allow wars? Crime? Suffering and death to innocent people? Grandsire said that was part of Free Will, and that Commonfolk, like Earth folk, brought on their own miseries. Aril had not brought on the crash, or the slave status. She had been mapping little known areas to help sky mariners navigate to find their way.

Tim-Ell made soft sounds as his chest moved up and down. His weapons hung in the closet and were not close at hand; the ankle dagger offered his only defense. He trusted her. Did she trust him? He had never hurt her. Did he really love her?

After hours of thought, she floated to sleep. In the morning, bird calls from the bushes in the garden awakened her. She sat up to find Tim-Ell, his legs up, and elbows resting on his knees staring at her. The fine oily mist on his neck perfumed the air with his scent.

Oh, no. She came fully awake in an instant. The urge for his touch swept over her like a desert sandstorm, the kind that materialized without warning and blasted across the land. Deep inside she felt like the steam pits when a searing column of mist pushed and pressured its way upward searching for a fissure to detonate into the sky.

In the early morning shadows, the grin forming on his face excited her further. He leaned over her. "You are beautiful, even in your sleep."

She pulled away to the edge of the bed.

"I know you're not afraid of me. Why do you pull away?"

How could she tell him she was afraid of her reaction? It was too late to get away from his scent. The attraction lured her closer to his body, and she felt like a thirsty animal at the watering hole.

Taking her in his arms, he kissed her, sending shockwaves of heat through her body and turning her rock resolve into vapor.

He stopped, pulled back and cocked his head. "I'm not drunk." Engaging her attention, he added, "Right?"

"Yes," she said quietly.

"Say it."

"Say what?"

"Tell me you know I'm not under the influence of drink."

Her heart beat like a herd of thundering gants. "You aren't drunk," she whispered.

"No spiked wine, right? No nectar."

"No."

"Say it."

The thundering rang in her ears. "No nectar."

"You want this? Me?"

"Tim-Ell…"

"Say it." He brought her face close to his. "Tell me."

Breathlessly she whispered, "I want you to make love to me."

"Again."

She looked away, willing the booming within her to quiet. It didn't. She stared at him. "Make love to me. Now."

The last word blended into a long kiss. She felt like she would come out of her skin. The drive to have him brought back the memories of his previous touch, the lovemaking, the intense pleasures. She embraced the movements, the sensuality.

As she peaked, she cried out.

"Prince?" a man's voice said. Ray-Tan had come into the apartment.

"Wait for me outside," Tim-Ell shouted. "I'm sorry," he whispered, then moaned with his own pleasure.

They lay in each other's arms for a quiet time.

"I didn't know how late it is," he said. "They're waiting for me outside."

She didn't want to move, basking in the blush of the lovemaking.

Tim-Ell slid out of bed. She rolled on her side and pushed against the pillow. Muffled noises from the kitchen made her think about what Ray-Tan might have heard. Would he ask Tim-Ell? Did men talk about their intimacies? Did women?

Quick noises in the bathroom were followed by the whoosh of the back door closing, the sign Tim-Ell had left. Aril got up and ran to the glass door. Key-Ren shot from the apartment next door to give Ray-Tan a goodbye kiss, not a quick peck, a full-on deep kiss.

Would she ever kiss Tim-Ell goodbye with such ardor?

CHAPTER 54

Toast in hand, Aril lingered at the glass door and scanned the atrium. The men, Tim-Ell, Ray-Tan, Cal-Eb, and Fin-Dal had not yet left for the fort. They approached the gants waiting at the stable, the part of the hangar converted to keep the animals. Grooms held the snorting mounts. Tim-Ell accepted a medium sized gant. Not a sleek, beautiful steed, this gant appeared tired, unspirited. Maybe that was best, considering the prince was still recovering from his injuries, especially in light of the workout he had experienced with her that morning. The warriors left the atrium and disappeared from her sight. She remembered when the soldiers of Cadmia brought their gants home to break them in. Fliers remained in their hangars until the mounts had been fully trained and bonded with their riders.

Her blood still surged from Tim-Ell's earlier stimulation. She needed to calm down. Out in the sunroom, she went through her exercises, taking care not to bang or disturb her abdomen. She wondered how long she could or should be active like this. Nothing in the books about caring for an egg told her about what precautions should be taken before the delivery. Was that something a woman knew instinctively? Taking a break, she sat on a low bench carved into the wall. She regarded the apartment. It had been well designed, functional, and as Del-Am had shown, easily made comfortable and attractive. For a moment, Aril thought about how their apartment could be decorated, changed into a place that reflected her tastes and style. She laughed at herself and dismissed the notion. When Jake Hill found her...How long had it been? She had been lost for months and experienced so many deviations from her normal life. The Crown Prince had embraced her and pledged his love. She sniffed, dismissing her feelings as leftovers from the pheromones that manipulated her. Her gaze fell to the floor. Jake Hill would slay Tim-Ell and hold him responsible for her captivity and the child. There would be no reasoning with him.

She directed her musings to her child to be. After showering, she spent the remainder of the morning reading the books on caring for an egg. The knot in her abdomen, implanted deeply, could be felt by pressing in. She tried to assess whether it had grown but at this point, there would be no way to know. Patience! She had never been one to wait.

After a light lunch she took her garden tools and headed for the herb patch. Working outside surrounded by greenery always provided comfort. Even back at the palace in Cadmia, she often helped the herbalist, listening to his instructions and helping cultivate the plants. The love of botanical learning had propelled her into field of medicine, the discipline that served her well in the military. The experience of treating the injured from a battle had been enough for her to be against war, and she had vowed that if she could help prevent wars, she would do so. No matter how she turned it over, it came out the same… Jake Hill would challenge Tim-Ell, Tim-Ell would die at grandsire's hand, then the soldiers loyal to the Crown Prince would attack. Many would die.

She sniffed back a tear. Unusual for her to cry. If she could get away and go to Cadmia…maybe she could be safe in her country and not tell grandsire the background. Stubbornness came easy to her. She smiled at that thought because her obstinacy had been inherited from the Earthman. He would have to understand.

Leaning against the stone bench, she turned over plans. Hadn't she promised Tim-Ell she'd be his wife in every way? Even placing blame on the hormones for the attraction, their time together had been enjoyable. Perhaps if she told him who she was and what he would face…No. He said he loved her, but the fear of Jake Hill's wrath might lead to her death. Not from Tim-Ell, but from someone who would learn of her heritage. She couldn't take that chance. Not now, with the egg inside her.

"Hello."

A familiar voice shook her out of her thoughts.

"You look far away," Del-Am said.

"Oh, sorry. I guess I was far away."

"How about some keela?"

"Sounds good," Aril said. "I don't have cake, but I could serve the keela."

"Thank you," Del-Am extended her hand to help Aril up. "I don't wish to sound too forward, but I'm glad the prince has returned. It isn't good for a couple to be separated."

Del-Am knew the prince had slept at the barracks for those weeks. Did the residents pay attention to what happens?

Del-Am put her hand to her mouth. "Oh, I'm sorry. I can tell by your expression I shouldn't have said that. Forgive me."

Aril wasn't sure how to respond. Touching Del-Am's hand, she said, "Thank you for your concern. I'm glad he's back, too." Did she just say that? She meant it. She hadn't felt this good in a long time. "Come. I have some fresh redgrain bread I'll toast with butter and papiset spice."

A memory tugged at her. Jake Hill served her sweetened papiset toast when she was little. He said it reminded him of Earth cinnamon toast, a common treat on his home planet. The urge to confess all that weighed on her to this friendly woman almost forced words from her, but the same anxiety that Del-Am would react from fear of Cadmian retribution stayed Aril's confession.

The fact that the door slid away from her palm gave her a little comfort, but entering the undecorated, plain apartment canceled that bit of positive feeling. Not that Del-Am would judge or comment, but…

Aril swept her hand in the air. "The prince—"

Del-Am nodded. "Being a warrior, he likes his apartment to resemble the fort. Cal-Eb is the same. If left to him, we'd have no curtains, and the walls would be painted tan to match the color of the plains." She laughed. "It's a good thing my mate is of common blood. That way, I can override his decorating decisions."

A wave of gratitude coursed through Aril. Del-Am understood.

Aril prepared the simple snack and served it on her unmatched dinnerware.

Halfway through, Del-Am bent over and let out a groan. "I think I'm about to expel my egg," she whispered.

Even though Aril had been trained for battlefield emergencies, she became flustered at her friend's predicament. "Do you need to lie down? Shall I send for the doctor?"

With her hand over the bump in her belly, Del-Am smiled. "Help me back to my apartment, please. Send one of the soldiers to get the Fort surgeon and notify Cal-Eb."

Aril, arm around Del-Am, helped her friend as they made their way across the courtyard.

The gate swung wide as Sari-Van galloped her gant past them. The ex-princess turned her mount and circled them. She smiled at Del-Am and scowled at Aril. "Are you all right, Del-Am?"

"Yes, Sari-Van. The Crown Prince's Wife is taking good care of me."

The realization that Aril-Ess had been elevated to royal status showed on her face and made the ex-princess flinch. Her scowl deepened. "Is there anything I can do?"

"Yes. Tell one of the soldiers to contact the fort." Del-Am told Sari-Van whom to notify. Sari-Van turned her mount toward the gate guards.

In the apartment, Aril eased Del-Am onto her bed, helped her remove her clothes, and assisted her into a loose nightdress.

A pain bent the woman over. When it subsided, she asked for water and a basket from the cool box.

Aril brought the water and basket. She busied in the bathroom dampening washcloths and selecting towels to put underneath Del-Am.

Del-Am lifted her torso from the mattress while Aril arranged the toweling. "Will you stay with me? You don't have to watch, just be near me, in place of my mother."

"Of course. I'm honored, Del-Am."

"I can feel it moving! I hope the surgeon gets here in time," Del-Am took a sip of water and bit down on one of the root vegetables from the basket.

Aril pulled the covers away. "Let me see." Del-Am parted her legs.

"The egg is showing," Aril said. "It won't be long. We'll do this together."

The gray-white oval of the egg's rounded end moved further out. With each muscle ripple, the egg progressed until it showed halfway. The soft shell undulated as the child within reacted to the pressure.

"It's moving, Del-Am! That's excellent."

"Yes." She let out a tired sigh. "I am running out of strength."

"Don't worry," Aril assured her. "You'll both be fine." With the next contraction, Aril wrapped a small blanket around the soft egg and gave a tug. The egg came out. The towel under Del-Am absorbed bloody liquid. Aril removed the towel with one hand and held the wrapped egg with the other. After helping her friend sit up, she put the bundle in the woman's arms.

Del-Am parted the blanket and kissed the exposed part of the egg. "Who needs doctors, right? I'm so glad you were here."

"Shall I get the incubator?"

"No. I want to hold it until the shell hardens." Del-Am unwrapped her egg. The thin supple shell in its leathery stage showed movement inside. "Thank you, Wife of—"

"Aril. Please call me by my name." She sat on the bed next to Del-Am. She ran her hand over the egg that began to form ridges from top to bottom, looking like a melon. She laughed. "We're close now."

Del-Am took Aril's hand and kissed it. "Yes, we are. I'll never forget this."

Slave, royalty, those ranks meant little as the rank of friend rose to its lofty station. Even in Cadmia, Aril couldn't treasure this friendship more. They stayed quiet until voices in the hallway meant people had arrived.

Cal-Eb pushed aside the door and hurried to Del-Am's bedside. The doctor followed closely behind. Aril left the room and waited on the living room couch, which had a velvety fur cover, the color blending with the other furniture and accessories.

Cal-Eb came to her. "Thank you for helping my mate. She can't sing your praises any higher. I am indebted to you." He bowed his head as if he spoke to royalty, the way she had been addressed in Cadmia.

In the palace, she would have nodded, said nothing to the person addressing her, the appropriate response. This called for something different. "It is my honor, Cal-Eb. I thank the Goddess I could help."

He smiled. "Yes, just so." He looked toward the bedroom with the closed door. Undoubtedly the surgeon was making his examination. "I should get the incubator now."

"Of course," Aril said. She knew his statement was a request for privacy. "If there is anything I can do to help, I'm right over there." She pointed in the direction of her apartment. The plain, warrior-like, undecorated apartment would soon undergo a few changes.

"Thank you," Cal-Eb said.

As she headed toward her place, she put her hand on her belly. Movement caught her attention. Kye-Ren, taking her daily sunbath, changed positions on the stone bench. The silver demon put her nose in the air, sniffing her distaste for her neighbor. Would Aril ever be the Wife of the Crown Prince to the awful little sylph?

But now she had a good friend, Del-Am.

CHAPTER 55

Tim-Ell came home early that afternoon. He unbuckled his weapon belt, and as he placed it on the table, he chuckled. "You're quite the hero, you know."

Aril-Ess leaned against the cool box with a bottle of erbate in her hand. "Me?"

He angled close, placed a kiss on her cheek, and removed the bottle from her grasp. "You delivered Del-Am's egg." He saluted her with the bottle. "Well done."

She added, "Good and faithful servant." It was a line from a revered Earth book. She could quote a number of lines from what Jake Hill had told her.

Tim-Ell frowned. He couldn't have known about the book. It must have sounded like a bitter reminder of her slave designation. "I'm sorry about that, Aril." He looked at the bottle and put it on the table. "I should have given you your freedom."

Yes, you should have. But she should have asked for it when she reacted to his offer of a favor. Both of them shared the oversight.

She managed a smile. "I'm Wife of the Crown Prince, now."

He pulled her into an embrace. "Yes, you are. Beloved by him in addition to being the hero of the day."

She leaned into his embrace, enjoying his closeness, feeling his affection, appreciating the soft kisses he placed on her forehead.

"I'm so proud of you, my dearest," he whispered.

How many times had her mother and father said that? Jake Hill had told her the same on countless occasions. Coming from Tim-Ell, the words had a special effect. "Because?"

He broke from the embrace and looked at her. "Because of the times you have rendered service to others: the sylph, me, and now the wife of my high captain. You are a treasure—to me and to Protar." He chuckled gently. "If I believed in a deity, I'd say the Goddess sent you."

Sent by the Goddess! He had no idea what that goddess had done to them. She should tell him everything—her heritage, her training, the tragedies she would bring to Protar. She should beg him to send her away, back to Cadmia with the promise she would not tell the Planetary Prince where she had been and who had kept her from her family for so long. The time had come. She took a breath and sorted her words...

The rapping on the door broke her concentration. Ray-Tan let himself in, deep-inhaling to catch his breath. "Prince, Linter has captured two spies and managed to subdue them."

Blood drained from Aril's face. *Spies? From Cadmia?*

Tim-Ell gave Ray-Tan his bottle of erbate. Ray-Tan accepted. He wiped his mouth. "Linter said the spies had infiltrated the ranks. He heard their accents, familiar to him from his wife's family in Lanosse."

"We have no quarrel with the people of Lanosse," Tim-Ell said. "Although they weren't happy when we annexed the Forest of Akeetovin, the piece of land had been taken from them by my mother's country."

Ray-Tan finished the erbate before he added, "The country that almost doubled the size of Protar when the Queen joined forces with your father."

Aril relaxed. The spies didn't come from Cadmia. It took a few moments to understand the threat of the spies from Lanosse. Would there be war?

"The spies?" Tim-Ell asked.

Ray-Tan shook his head. "One dead, the other in too poor shape to talk. Linter served us well."

Aril put her hand on Tim-Ell's arm. "Linter has a wife?"

"Prince?" asked Ray-Tan.

Tim-Ell let out a sigh. "He must have when he left his country to fight. She probably thinks he's dead, and now he's joined our army and living up to his pledge to put his life on the line for Protar."

"He must be an Excaliburian Knight," Aril said.

Both Tim-Ell and Ray-Tan turned their view to her. They didn't speak, but the look they gave each other agreed with her statement.

"I know you won't give Linter freedom to return to his own country," Aril said, trying not to sound caustic, "but perhaps you can arrange to bring his wife and family, if he still has one, here to be with him."

Tim-Ell pulled at his chin. "Ray-Tan, send for our best surgeon to save the spy who lives so we can question him when he's able. Then speak with Linter. Make him the offer, which my brilliant mate suggested. If Linter agrees and thinks his wife will come here without divulging his whereabouts, we will send emissaries to his country to speak with her."

Ray-Tan left. Tim-Ell sat on the table bench. "I'm aware of how much you admire the Excaliburian Knights."

Remembering how she had hurled accusations about the abuse of the Knighthood when she first met the Prince, Aril carefully chose her words. "I do. Linter pledged his allegiance to Protar. He could have let the spies take information back to a country that would spare him during a war, but his oath overcame his desire to return to his country. Training makes a man powerful and righteous."

Tim-Ell crossed his arms over his chest. "From the powerful and righteous Jake Hill?"

Aril looked down to obscure the anger that might show in response to his slur.

He took her back into his arms. "Never mind, my love. Let us talk of other things."

The time for disclosures had ended. She would wait for another chance to tell him her secrets.

Aril prepared the evening meal. The apartment stayed quiet while she and Tim-Ell ate and kept their thoughts to themselves. Later that night, Aril succumbed easily to the scents Tim-Ell provided. She slept deeply and well.

The next morning, she lingered by the door. Tim-Ell fastened his sword belt, then kissed her cheek. "The dressmaker will come by this afternoon." He motioned his head at her smock. "It's time you wore something else."

She shrugged. "These garments suit me."

He smiled. "When you work in the garden, I suppose. But you are the mate of a prince." He avoided the word "Princess," which could have been her title had he given her freedom before the marriage. "Tell the dressmaker what you want." He laughed. "Not that I worry you won't."

She blocked the doorway, her arm sweeping the air to indicate the area around her. "Furnishings? New dishes?"

He cocked his head. "Of course." He looked surprised. "You're the Wife—"

"Of the Crown Prince. I know. It's all right with you if I make changes?"

He spread his arms. "I don't care what you change here. Have fun. Keep busy." He kissed her cheek again. "Just don't get spoiled. I like you just the way you are."

She backed away from the door and watched him join Ray-Tan and Fin-Dal, who waited on their gants, holding the rein of the sluggish animal from the day before. As they headed to the fort, Aril crossed the atrium to visit Del-Am. Cal-Eb answered the door and invited her in. He showed her into the bedroom, where Del-Am sat next to the incubator. The glass sides of the holder, its gentle light radiating on the now hardened egg, showed soft gaps between bright white ribs. The gaps would allow growth, while the ribs gave strength. What had been oval and smaller than Del-Am's head yesterday had taken on a rounded appearance, resembling a snowy melon. In Cadmia, egg births were events often celebrated with loved ones in attendance to lend support to the new mother. Aril had been present for her cousin's delivery. Over the following months she'd watched the egg expand and been summoned to observe as the egg cracked, and the child stepped out into the arms of the parents. Aril's thoughts naturally worked into her own state. What would her future bring with her own egg, and later, her child?

Aril stayed for a short while, chatting with Del-Am. She left when Cal-Eb stuck his head in the doorway to ask if it was time to nourish the egg.

When Aril returned to the atrium, passing Kye-Ren, who lounged on the stone bench for her morning sunshine, the sylph let out a quick hiss. Ignoring the jeer, Aril sped toward her apartment. As she put her palm on the lock, a man called out to her.

"Wife of the Crown Prince."

It was Leb-Brit, the overweight, fuzzy-haired Royal Dressmaker. His young apprentice, carrying an armload of equipment and fabric samples, hurried to keep up. As soon as the fat little man recognized her, his face screwed up into an expression of distaste. "You? Wife of the Crown Prince?"

Aril would not tolerate this man. On the other hand, perhaps she'd put up with a small amount of arrogance when she thought of his wonderful design and workmanship. "Yes, it is I," she'd love to say princess just to make the man squirm, but she couldn't, not here in Protar. "I am the wife of Prince Tim-Ell. It doesn't make a difference what my status was in the past, so remember your manners."

The man frowned, then recovered. "Yes, yes. Shall we get on to business? I've brought dress designs. You can choose the ones you like and then match them with samples of fabric."

She invited the man and the boy into the apartment. This time, she noticed he looked around at the lackluster surroundings. Why did his disdain bother her? Without giving an invitation for him or his assistant to sit, Aril asked to see the designs. He handed her his device. She dismissed page after page, until three designs remained. Using the attached stylus, she made changes. The dressmaker had trouble keeping his annoyance from showing. Once she'd transformed the outfits to her liking, she examined the fabric samples. She ordered five outfits, loose-fitting for later when she needed them to conceal her condition.

"Wife of Crown Prince Tim-Ell," Leb-Brit began his argument. "Why don't you order two or three, and then if the designs suit you, you can have many outfits."

"I want them as soon as possible. You understand that concept, correct?"

"Of course," he countered.

"There are no budget restraints, correct?"

He waivered a bit, "No."

"Then take my order and get them to me right away." Aril gathered the samples and put them into the boy's hands. "Any questions?" She used her most dismissive tone. She added, "I hope what you create meets the quality of the gown you made for me to wear at the palace. Its beauty is beyond compare." The comment lessened the tension.

Leb-Brit smiled. "Of course, my lady." *My lady. That sounds perfect. Royal enough.* "Thank you," she said softly. "You are indeed an artist. I look forward to seeing the garments." She saw the two visitors to the door. "Oh, by the way, I will decorate the apartment soon. May I call upon you for suggestions?"

Leb-Brit turned and surveyed what he could see. "Yes, of course, my lady. I am at your disposal."

Did she just make another friend? Not that she would keep company with such a fussy, arrogant person, but with Del-Am busy adjusting to her situation, this man would no doubt provide a wealth of information. She watched him head to the gate and thought how deeply she was becoming invested in the society that had abused her.

CHAPTER 56

The weeks passed. She saw Del-Am occasionally. Sari-Van avoided her, and when they did encounter each other, the ex-princess tolerated her with strained apathy. Kye-Ren openly hissed, Aril's new status, notwithstanding.

Leb-Brit brought her new clothes. They didn't disappoint, being as beautifully made as her palace gown, so nice she couldn't bring herself to wear them around the complex. She ordered plainer items for everyday use. Leb-Brit also brought drawings of his ideas for the apartment. Aril selected several choices for the rooms, including soft furs and satiny fabrics that shone with a subtle richness. With each change, Tim-Ell complimented her taste. The Royal Dressmaker also sent a potter, who brought samples of his dinnerware. This offered her, the person who loved to learn new things, a chance to participate in fashion, something she had not concerned herself with before. Not thinking herself as being domesticated, she enjoyed decorating the apartment she shared with the prince. Adding to her pleasure, the egg she carried grew until it became a discernable knot in her belly.

Although Tim-Ell spent most of his time at the fort, when she asked him to take her to the large market on the edge of town or go on a picnic to the lake in the south, he rearranged his schedule to be with her. Each day he never failed to tell her how much he loved her, mentioning the irony of his gratitude to Eppo-Zim, who told him about the slave auction. Slave market references annoyed her, but Tim-Ell's appreciation, softened the outrage. She focused on her future, projecting images of raising a son or daughter.

One afternoon when she was alone Dr. Fil-Set visited. "May I come in, Aril, Wife of Crown Prince?"

She had pegged him as a coward and knew he wouldn't travel to Cadmia or take a chance giving a message to someone else. She opened the door. "Just call me Aril-Ess, if you don't mind."

He raised his eyebrows. "Princess?"

"No. I'm still the prince's slave. Please don't call me Princess."

"I see," Fil-Set said.

"I don't think you do, but it doesn't matter."

Fil-Set drew close and touched the area around her eyes. "Are you sleeping well?"

"What?"

He took her to the door where the light shone through. "The tissue around your eyes is…puffy." He ran his hand over her belly. "You have an egg!" His face screwed up as if he had seen something terrible. "That monster!" He shook his head and drew a breath. "Did you *agree* to this?"

"No," she said, "but you don't understand—"

"I understand perfectly. For the ultimate orgasm he forced you to take nectar."

"No, it wasn't like that. He didn't force me."

"You said you didn't agree. So, which is it?"

Aril hesitated. How much information did she need to share with the man who would have bought her, just as Tim-Ell did? "I, that is, we…it was an accident."

Fil-Set moved his head in deliberate swings. "Beast. But the deed is done. How are you feeling? Any nausea? Dizziness? Mood swings? Have you seen a doctor?" He felt the knot again. "Halfway through?"

She thought for a moment, unable to come up with a date. "You are my only doctor." That would remain true because she couldn't risk another doctor seeing her body hair. "I guess I'm about halfway along. I've had a bit of nausea, no dizziness. Oh, and the mood swings. Plenty of them." Did he need to know her moods had been good ones?

"I should examine you. Come, lay down on your bed, and let's have a look."

"I'm fine." Her bed? Fil-Set might not be able to handle the fact that she willingly shared the bed with her mate, Crown Prince Tim-Ell. The fact gave her a pause. Willingly. She enjoyed sleeping with him. And it had little to do with his attractive scent. "I don't need an exam. If I have problems, I will send for you."

"You will call me, right? I will check on you from time to time. I'll mark my calendar."

She hustled him out the door. After he left, she sat and thought about the time of conception and consulted her books about the egg's development. In about four revolutions of the greater moon, she should be ready to deliver the egg.

That evening over supper, Aril thought the time had come to discuss the event.

"The egg is due in a few months."

Tim-Ell nodded. "That should be interesting."

"It is important to have proof that the egg is ours."

"Who else would claim it?"

"Although you are in line to be king, I don't want the child to claim heir to the throne."

Tim-Ell pulled on his chin. "I don't want to be heir myself. But I am, and that makes my child heir."

"I want his heritage to be yours. You know what kind of stigma goes with a fatherless child."

"It won't be fatherless. I want the child to have my family name."

"Your family might not be so generous."

Tim-Ell sighed. "I wish I could argue that. Mother hasn't accepted you as my mate. Imagine what she'll think we she learns about this." He patted the knot in Aril's belly.

"What shall we do?"

Tim-Ell put his hand on her shoulder. "Don't worry. I'll ask a Rotner Monk to stand by as witness. Then I'll hire a fair scribe to be present." He raised his eyebrows. "They, the monk and the scribe, may demand to watch if they are going to certify the birth."

"Whatever," Aril said. "I think we should have someone from the palace, someone who you trust and can keep quiet about it, be here, too."

He ran his hand from her shoulder to her wrist and kissed it. "I'll give it some thought. You are right, though. Our egg needs to be marked by officials, so when it hatches, the marks identify the child as the product of the egg—the one that came from you, and certified as my blood."

"Thank you," she whispered.

CHAPTER 57

One morning as Tim-Ell buckled his sword belt, a rapid knocking on the back door brought Aril from the kitchen to check. She answered the anxious tapping.

Cal-Eb, ignoring the prince, spoke directly to Aril, "Our egg is cracking. Del-Am wishes you to be there."

Aril took a quick breath. "You've called the doctor?"

He nodded. "She wants you to be there."

"I understand," Aril said. "In place of her mother, or sister."

"Just so." Cal-Eb ran his hand over his chin. "You will come?"

She patted his arm. "Of course. I'll be right over."

Tim-Ell walked outside with her. He took the gant from the groom, and holding the reins kissed her cheek. "Have a good day," he whispered.

She'd been with him long enough to read more from his words, meaning she should enjoy her time with her friend and become comfortable knowing what she would be facing in time.

"You, too," she whispered back.

When she crossed the courtyard, Cal-Eb waited, holding his door. "Please," he said in a jittery voice, "be with us."

Aril made her way into the bedroom. Del-Am, sitting in the middle of the bed, looked anxious, but smiling. Her nervous hands twisted a soft towel on her lap. The army surgeon sat in a chair between the incubator and Del-Am. Cal-Eb leaned stiff-bodied against the doorframe. Aril pulled a chair up on the other side of the bed.

Del-Am grabbed Aril's hand. "Thank you for coming."

"Of course," Aril said.

"Poor Cal-Eb," Del-Am said, sending a smile his way. "It doesn't matter how much experience he's had on the battlefield. This is almost more than he can handle."

Aril laughed. Her cousin's mate, a fierce warrior, had the same reaction. Jake Hill had to take the man out of the palace for a long walk.

"It's time," the doctor said. He removed the large egg from the incubator and placed it on the towel on Del-Am's lap.

The egg rolled onto the bed and a small crack enlarged. Fluid dripped from the fissure as the fracture expanded. Del-Am dabbed at the leak as small fingertips emerged from the break. "Oh!" Del-Am said.

As a reflex, Aril put her hand on her stomach.

Del-Am relaxed and fixed her stare on Aril. She opened her mouth as one does when discovering something amazing. Cocking her head, she sent a questioned look. Aril nodded. Del-Am grinned for a moment, then focused her attention on the bed, where the egg swayed and rolled, each movement splitting and cracking wider, until a curly-haired girl pushed away the last piece of shell.

Although Aril had seen egg-births before, like the other times, she was amazed how an egg the size of a large oval melon could hold a child tall enough to reach above her knees.

The child batted her eyes at the light and, adjusting her view, looked around. Cal-Eb approached and picked the child up. He held her as Del-Am toweled their daughter dry, then wrapped her in a blanket. Cal-Eb assisted his mate to a rocking chair and put the child into her mother's arms. He kneeled next to them.

Aril choked at the sight. The air in the room held a thick veil of love. While the doctor took his medical bag over to the happy group and unwrapping the blanket used his instruments to check on the child, Aril tidied the bed.

The happiness occurring in the corner blurred as thoughts coalesced in Aril's mind. It wouldn't be long until the delivery of her own egg. At first, she struggled to accept the fact she carried it, but now she wanted it, wanted to be a mother, wanted to share the responsibility of raising a child with her mate, Tim-Ell. The Crown Prince would be a good father, as he had become a good husband. The emotions she choked back moments before surfaced, and she said a silent thanks that the other people in the room focused on the new life and not her reactions.

"Aril?" Del-Am extended her arm, inviting Aril to join them.

Aril quickly wiped the moisture from her eyes and hurried to be part of the admirers. The child took up most of Del-Am's lap, the golden curls drying against the daughter's pale face.

The doctor, having pronounced his good wishes, packed his equipment and left.

Aril touched the child's cheek. "She's beautiful." Unable to come up with anything else, she rolled her lip, keeping her tears at bay.

"Thank you," Del-Am said. "I am grateful for your friendship."

Aril nodded, still lacking words, a state unusual for her.

"Cal-Eb," Del-Am said, "would you like to make the announcement?"

He stood up and gave a short bow to his wife and child. He left without speaking.

Aril understood the silence, believing if the man spoke, he might break down with emotion.

Del-Am ran her fingers through the child's hair. Sending her soft stare at Aril, she said, "Soon for you?"

Aril patted her bump. "I think so. A few weeks, maybe."

"I know it isn't much, but would you care to use my incubator?"

A pulse of warmth ran through Aril. The intimacy of the gesture touched her. Only the closest friend or relative made that offer. "I will be honored. Thank you, Del-Am." The knot in her throat expanded. It took a few moments before she could speak again. "Do you have a name for her?"

"We spent hours laboring over a name. Sel-Aspree, after our grandmothers. They will be thrilled when they learn of it."

"How lovely," Aril said. "Her name rolls off the tongue." She had a vision of when she and Tim-Ell would discuss the names, traditionally done when the egg is placed in the incubator. Her life had changed to something she cherished. Was there a Great Spirit, as Jake Hill taught? If a Great Spirit existed, it had a warped sense of humor. What kind of benevolent being bestows that kind of compassion? Did the Spirit have a streak of cruelty?

"Aril?"

"Oh, sorry, Del-Am, I started thinking…"

"Of course! You can't wait to hold your own child. I understand."

Aril sent a quick, silent thank-you to the Great Spirit for what it *had* provided, this kind and gentle woman. "Can I do anything for you? Get you anything?"

Del-Am smiled. "I will let Cal-Eb do those things. He needs to stay busy until we have adjusted to our new roles. Why don't you go back to your place and rest? You will need your strength for the delivery."

Over Del-Am's protests, Aril prepared the afternoon meal, serving the food on trays she delivered to their bedroom, where the parents softly spoke with their child, telling her of their love. The child didn't understand the words, but the tone soothed her, and she fell asleep in Cal-Eb's arms. A child's first hours provided stability and trust, most important as the introduction to family life. Aril tried to stay in the background, helping but not distracting.

When Tim-Ell returned from the fort at sundown, he paid a visit to the new family. He escorted Aril back to the apartment, where they shared a light supper.

"It won't be long before the egg comes, Tim-Ell."

He extended his hand and caressed her shoulder. "What about a doctor?"

"If I need one, we can call Fil-Set," she said.

"Him? Why would you use a slave doctor? There are other doctors, ones who serve nobility."

She couldn't tell him the real reason—that Fil-Set knew of her heritage and that he kept her secret. Even if she hid the body hair, she couldn't take a chance the egg would have an anomaly from the Earth gene. Some of the eggs from Jake Hill's lineage had marks. Although these marks were not well known, she wouldn't risk that a doctor, who had traveled or had anything to do with Cadmia, would know.

Tim-Ell made a face. "I don't approve of that man, but if that's what you want, we'll call him. What's important is this," he said, putting his hand on Aril's abdomen, "and you."

"I can take a few days off. Actually, things couldn't be better at the fort. Ray-Tan can handle it."

"Thank you." Aril took comfort knowing Tim-Ell would be with her in the coming days. Ray-Tan could handle everyday army affairs.

Suddenly, a twinge like a knife in her back bent her over.

"Aril?"

"It's all right. The egg moves. A little, nothing wrong, in fact, it reassures of the life inside."

Tim-Ell rubbed his hand over the oval protrusion. "Feels good. I never thought about being a father." He scratched his head. "We need to certify the egg. But I'm not sure how to do it."

"Of course, you do. First a Rotner Monk must witness the delivery, and before the shell hardens, stamp and date it with his symbol. They are above reproach." She angled her head in his direction. "Even in the palace."

"We don't have them in the palace," he said.

"Precisely. Find a Rotner Monk who will agree to attend."

Tim-Ell nodded. "And?"

"Find a True Witness Scribe. Not from the palace. One who can record the description of the birth, witnesses, who did what and when. The monk and the Witness will sign the document and register the birth at the Hall of Records." She sent a quick glare. "Protar *does* have a Hall of Records, right?"

He rolled his lip. "Uh, yes. Uh, of course."

Her eyebrows shot up. "You don't know? The Crown Prince?"

"I'm sure we have a Hall of Records. I just don't know where it is. But I'll find out." He adjusted his emblem. "Do we need anyone else? You know, to certify the birth?"

"One more. Someone you can trust from the palace, someone who would swear as an observer and would put a mark on the egg along with the other witnesses." She dropped her chin and lowered her voice. "Someone who could convince the King and Queen that the egg is mine."

He stepped closer and put his lips to her ear. "And mine." Brushing a curl from her forehead, he whispered, "Don't worry. I'll find someone from the palace we can trust."

"Thank you. I worry about the child."

"I know. We will do as much as we can for his, or her, safety. I should order an incubator. I can ask the Royal Metalsmith."

Aril pulled away and glared. "No! Nothing from the palace. The secret would be out faster than an arrow. Plus, I don't trust anyone from the palace. The Vizier uses the metalsmith, I'm sure."

"He does. You're right."

"I already have an incubator. Del-Am has offered hers."

Tim-Ell's expression softened. "Truly?"

He understands the significance. Good. "She has been kind to me. I am lucky to have her as a neighbor and friend."

"Cal-Eb says she is fond of you."

Aril couldn't stop the smile that took over. "Not like silver-girl next door. She hasn't forgiven me for the shocks when I stood up to the matron."

Tim-Ell laughed. "No. Not at all like Kye-Ren. I wonder if you will ever win her over."

"Maybe if I had a knife stuck in my back."

Tim-Ell pulled her close. "That is not going to happen. Understand?"

She didn't pull away. "Yes. Thank you." He would guard her with his life. And their child.

CHAPTER 58

Aril's back ached as she bid Tim-Ell goodbye in the morning. The small buzzing pains circling her waist increased hourly, and by mid-afternoon she thought today would be important.

With careful steps Aril approached the gate guard and asked him to send for Tim-Ell and Fil-Set. She left the glass door open a crack, then returned to the bedroom and lay down on the bed. The pains became regular, more powerful. At the end of a prolonged contraction, Aril recognized the errant sounds as knocking on the door. When she could speak, she called, "Come in."

Tim-Ell peeked in, then pushed the door wide. A man, somewhat shorter and resembling Tim-Ell stood next to him.

"Aril-Ess, meet my brother, Sen-Mak."

Sen-Mak? The brother who wanted to be king? The man who resented Tim-Ell for being first in line to the throne? What should she say? Why was he here? *Tim-Ell, are you really that stupid?*

A new contraction diverted her deliberation.

I won't let anyone from the palace see me weak. I won't cry out. Not in front of those rotten people. "Oooh," she grunted, and stopped mid-squeal. *Be strong.*

Tim-Ell rushed to her side and sat on the edge of the bed. "Sen-Mak, meet my Mate, Aril-Ess, the woman I love. Who is about to deliver our egg."

Sen-Mak took a jerky step backward. "An egg? You brought me here to witness a birth?" His lips parted, but only an unintelligible babble followed.

Crooking his finger, Tim-Ell beckoned Sen-Mak closer. "Yes. I need you. You are my brother. Who else would I want to be here from the palace?"

Sen-Mak's noises formed words. "I guess there isn't another at the palace. Oh, Tim-Ell," he said pulling the last word out into a long roll. "Mother... Oh, Goddess, when—"

Tim-Ell jumped up and grabbed Sen-Mak's arm. "Mother can't know. Not yet. And I trust you to keep the secret. You will put your mark on the egg so everyone in Protar will know this is a royal child."

Sen-Mak nodded. The look of admiration turned into a smile. "Well done, brother. I always knew you were a superb warrior, but I underestimated your intellect."

Another contraction came, interrupting the laugh that Aril couldn't suppress. "Intellect?" She writhed and crushed a ball of bed sheet in her hand.

Tim-Ell bent over her and pushed back a sweaty curl. "I have to fetch the scribe and the Rotner Monk. Ray-Tan, Cal-Eb, and Fin-Dal are guarding the door. Sen-Mak will be my Honor Man and will look after you until I get back." He shot a serious look at Sen-Mak. "Won't you?"

Sen-Mak's smile broadened. "Of course. I will protect her and the egg with my life. I serve."

Warmth pulsed through Aril's body. The request of Honor Man was the same here in Protar as in Cadmia. Maybe the birth pledge was planetwide. She had never thought about it. A father can ask allegiance of a man he trusts at the birth of his egg, and the man is honor bound to make the promise—and keep it. Sen-Mak agreed! Perhaps he recognized the situation and paid homage to his brother, both in words of admiration and in his promise to protect and serve.

"I'll be back as soon as I can," Tim-Ell said, and left.

"Have a seat, Brother-of-the-Crown-Prince."

"Please. Call me Sen-Mak. May I address you as Aril-Ess?"

Aril braced for pain. It didn't come, which worried her. "Yes, please. Aril is fine." The pain caught up with her. She placed one hand over her swollen belly, grabbing a wad of sheet with the other. "Why didn't he send *you* for the scribe and monk?"

"He wanted me to guard you. As I promised."

"Thank you, Sen-Mak. I won't hold you to it."

"You should, and you can. I've given my word of honor. Which, around the palace is a rare thing. Tim-Ell dignified me with his trust."

She got the words out before the next pain took over. "I don't know what to say, but thank you." She shut her eyes and clamped her teeth.

"Is there anything I can do? Water? Another pillow? Something?"

"No," she said, letting out the breath she held. "It's not that bad. Have you attended a birth before?"

Sen-Mak let out short breath. "No. It's all new to me, especially my brother's attitude. We've never been close." He scratched the back of his head. "All I remember about my other, younger, brother is that my father stayed with Mother and held her hand."

"Yet, *my* mate leaves me with almost a stranger."

Sen-Mak laughed. "Father speaks highly of you. He said you had a detached sort of humor."

"He has spoken of me?"

"Not much around Mother, but yes. He approves of Tim-Ell's Life-Mate. My father mentioned how you have brought about a change in Tim-Ell, and in how he, the King, looks at things. He said Tim-Ell is smarter than he lets on. I believe it, too." He laughed again. "You're the one he didn't give away."

She waited until the next pain subsided. *Right. Tim-Ell gave his slaves away when he tired of them.*

Sen-Mak's first reaction was a smile. He pulled his eyebrows together. "Sorry about that. I meant no disrespect."

Aril put her hand up in the sign of *No problem.* "It's all right, Sen-Mak." The importance of what was about to happen meant this was not a day for conflict. And Tim-Ell had asked his younger brother for help. Sen-Mak had accepted the invitation to attend the egg delivery as a royal witness.

An ache in her back struck like an arrow. "Goddess! That was a bad one. Tim-Ell better hurry."

"Um, don't you have a friend, you know, a lady to be with you? Isn't that what women in labor do?"

"In a few minutes, you can ask to Cal-Eb to send Del-Am here. She can join the festivities, 'the let's watch Aril-Ess scream, open her legs wide, and push that egg out' party. Everyone gets to see."

Sen-Mak stepped close to the bed. "No privacy. Right. So, the child can be claimed royal when it breaks the shell. That is noble of you, Aril."

"Noble? You are aware I am a slave?"

He pushed a chair next to the bed and leaned closer. "I know nobility when I see it."

Those words made her pause. What did he mean? Surely, he didn't know. The only person who knew was Doctor Fil-Set. Would Tim-Ell summon the doctor? Of course. Aril had asked for him. The arrow pierced her again. She suppress her cry.

Out of breath, she rasped, "Sen-Mak, will you ask for Del-Am, please."

"Yes, yes, of course." He sprinted out of the room and was back in time for the end of the grimace. "She'll be here right away."

Time became muddled. All at once, people were flooding through the apartment and into the bedroom. Del-Am headed the parade and after her, a robed monk, the True Witness Scribe with his pen, ink, and scroll, Tim-Ell, and at the end, Dr. Fil-Set.

Del-Am sat on the bed and took Aril's hand. "Bad?"

"Not terrible. I'm not as brave as you were."

"You thought I was brave?" Del-Am chuckled.

"You hardly groaned. So, yes, I think you were brave."

"I didn't groan because it didn't hurt. I chewed *churro root*." She took a small linen from her pocket and unfolded it, exposing a finger-sized orange root with a bright green frilly top. "Care for a bite?"

"Yes!" Aril took the root and bit a chunk of the sweet fibrous thing. Chewing released juices, a tangy syrup imparting a soothing cascade of peace. "How much?"

"All is good. It won't hurt you. It reduces your ability to feel below your hips."

How is it, that I, a field medic didn't know about this vegetable? Cadmia is the leader in medicine and science. But Protar, a backwater nation, knows? A barely perceptible cramp fluttered her belly.

Doctor Fil-Set made his way to the bedside. He took the root from Aril's hand. "Churro? Good. I brought some paste, but fresh is better." He passed the vegetable to Del-Am and pulled back the sheet covering Aril. "I need to see." He parted her legs and lifted her buttocks for examination. "The white is showing. We'll have this egg within the hour."

"Hour! Goddess! Give me the rest of that root."

The thickness of the room's tension impeded conversations. Now that she no longer cried out, Aril liked the quiet. She could feel her hipbones giving way to the egg. How dignified. Emotions flooded her mind. Between the spasms of pushing and cramping, she allowed the feelings to surface—anger for being captured and sold like an asset, having to hide her true status, allowing strangers into her bedroom to stare at her shaved interiors just to satisfy the public knowledge of her child's heritage. Aril cringed. She would never allow her son, or daughter, to rule in Protar. Even if Tim-Ell changed the palace's dirty dealing, her child wouldn't be there to take over. What about Jake Hill? She willed those thoughts away. Not the right time.

The next cramp created a long push. Doctor Fil-Set, grim-faced, nodded. "A few more pushes."

"Let's get this done," Aril said, and bore down. The egg slid onto the sheet, oval and ribbed, like one of the pale melons at the market.

Fil-Set picked it up and held it high. "A royal egg," he pronounced and pointed to the fine red, blue, and purple line traces along the ribs.

"Of course, it's royal," Tim-Ell said. "It's from me."

Aril hoped that Fil-Set bit his lip to keep from saying the shell of the egg reflects the mother's ancestry. The egg *was* royal, and Fil-Set knew the background. She held her breath, fearing he would follow Tim-Ell's statement by commenting on the shell's markings.

Tim-Ell took the egg from the doctor and invited the visitors to put their seals on it with the date. The scribe had been writing the stages of labor and what had been said regarding the birth. The air dried the egg, and the ribs became less noticeable. The space between the ribs would allow it to grow.

Cab-El brought in the incubator and placed it on a small table that Ray-Tan had placed next to the bed.

"I want to hold it for a while," Aril said.

Del-Am dusted imaginary particles from her incubator. "Of course, you do." She spread her arms in a herding gesture to the visitors. "You've done your duty; now let's give the new mother some time."

One by one the visitors left, except Tim-Ell and Sen-Mak. Del-Am pointed to Sen-Mak, "Not too long, Prince, all right?"

"Just a few minutes alone with my brother and his mate."

Del-Am closed the door behind her.

Aril held the egg against her chest. She scooted over in the bed to let Tim-Ell join her. Sen-Mak came to the bedside and patted Tim-Ell on the shoulder. "I will go, now. Thank you for the honor you bestowed on me. You have my allegiance and my best wishes. I envy you, my brother."

"Me?" Tim-Ell asked.

"Not because you are in line for the throne, but for what I see here."

CHAPTER 59

The following morning after Tim-Ell left for the fort, Doctor Fil Set visited. "How are you doing? Any problems?"

"No. I'm a little sore. A little blood."

"That should be expected. It will last for a few days. I want to examine you and check the egg."

Aril wasn't keen on the examination, but she knew it should be done. On rare occasions, mothers had internal damage which should be attended to immediately to avoid problems with future deliveries.

She went into the bedroom and lay down on the bed, the one she shared with Tim-Ell. The stubble from the area she shaved before the birth had not yet appeared. Would Doctor Fil-Set remark on the missing body hair?

He didn't but probed and pushed. "Everything looks good. I'll check the egg." He removed the glass dome from the incubator and placed his monitor on the shell. "Sounds good. All is in order." He closed the dome.

"Thank you, doctor."

Fil-Set extended his hand and helped her sit up. His face contorted into a scowl. "He should be executed for what he did to you."

Although she didn't want to explain to the doctor, she also didn't want him to make similar comments in the future. "It isn't like you think. He didn't rape me. He is a perfect pheromone match. When he scented, I responded. Because of the chemical attraction, I had no control."

"What are you talking about?"

"Hormonal matches." She tapped her nose. "Perfect. When I breathed his scent, the instinct took over. I couldn't help it."

"You think hormones control mating?"

"Of course. That's how it works. A perfect match is so strong it can't be overcome by... anything."

"That's ridiculous, Aril-Ess. Where did you get such an idea?"

"I learned it." Where did she learn it? She thought about her medical training. Scents and attraction hadn't been covered in detail during that training. Field medicine had more to do with battlefield emergencies. She couldn't recall where she learned about hormones and attraction.

"Look," Doctor Fil-Set said, grim-faced. "If a woman is repulsed by a man, and he is a perfect match, nothing can *make* her mate with him. Unless he *forced* you into having sex, you would have rejected him, probably fighting. Why are you covering for him? Has he threatened the child if you say he raped you?"

Aril shook her head. "He would never do that. How do *you* know about scenting and attraction?"

"In Medical School, in *Cadmia*, by the way, I wrote a dissertation about it. I am the planet expert on scenting and attraction. That research became a book, which is used in medical schools planetwide. The book provides my main earnings because healing slaves and low-income people wouldn't support me."

The information about scenting made her dizzy. Fil-Set was wrong. She had hated Tim-Ell and had not been attracted to him—until she reacted to his scent. Then, she had no control. That is *exactly* how it happened.

"Aril-Ess," Fil-Set said. "What is wrong?"

She couldn't think fast enough to give a reasonable answer. "I feel dizzy."

He fluffed a pillow. "Here, lie down. You are probably still overwrought regarding the delivery."

She reclined.

"I'll stay for a while and monitor you. Have you fed the egg yet?"

"No, nothing has happened. Can I have keela?"

"It usually takes a day or so before the feeding starts. You can have keela. Don't overdo." He folded his arms in front of his chest. "What about the blood feeding? I don't recommend you offer both milk and blood. I can find someone who can be a blood feeder."

How should she answer? Fil-Set was her doctor by her own demand. This new information confused her, yet another instance of her not having control of her situation. How much did Fil-Set need to know for her and the egg's care? "I thank you Doctor, for your concern and care, but Prince Tim-Ell has not been violent with me. I won't explain the circumstances of our relationship. And I won't need a surrogate."

"He bought you, Aril, and you were his slave. That is all I need to understand. You told me you didn't willingly sip the nectar. There must be something he holds over you to protect him. What am I to believe?"

"Just tend to my medical needs and keep my secret. That is all I ask."

"What will happen when Jake Hill finds you?"

Even with the good feelings associated with motherhood engulfing her, she couldn't stop her barbed response. "It is less likely to happen since you didn't help me contact him." She brushed his hand away and got up from the bed. "Don't concern yourself about what will happen. Rest assured *you* will be safe."

Fil-Set didn't speak for a moment. "Thank you." He picked up his equipment and quietly stowed it in his bag. "I'll check on you again." With rigid strides he left the room.

She sat on the bed next to the incubator and raised the dome. Placing her cheek next to the warm shell, she sighed. She needed to banish the bad thoughts and concentrate on the child-to-be depending on her for its care.

That evening, after Tim-Ell returned and they had dinner, she took him into the bedroom to talk about the care for the egg and what to expect. She removed it from the incubator and held it next to her body.

A slight movement from the top of the egg, made her smile. "Watch," she said.

Tim-Ell pulled back in a reflex. "What's happening?"

"Just watch" A small crack formed at the top and a hole the size of a fingertip formed. It moved. A funnel-shaped object pushed up, trailing a white tube. Aril removed her tunic and sat still while the funnel waved atop the tube. The small white object worked its way closer to her and rested against her abdomen. She guided the piece to her nipple, where it latched on.

"Oh!"

"What?" Tim-Ell asked. "What's going on?"

She made a face and grimaced as the funnel began to draw on her breast. "It's feeding. I didn't know how sensitive this would be. It, ouch! Hurts." She put her hand around the funnel. "It will be all right. I have to adjust." Then she laughed. "Wait until it's *your* turn!"

Tim-Ell blanched, "My turn?" He put his hand up to his chest.

"Not there. From your arm. You have brothers and a sister. Have you never seen feeding an egg?"

He pulled back a few inches. "No. Why would I want to see that? We had servants and the Vizir hired women to feed and take care of us."

"Really? Your mother and father didn't feed their eggs? The child inside needs to hear voices, become accustomed to the surroundings so they won't be frightened when they emerge."

His face reflected confusion. "I don't know anything about this part of childhood."

"Well," she said, moving against the pillow to get comfortable. "You will be learning this evening. Stick around."

After a few minutes, Aril moved the funnel to the other breast, and the child fed until the funnel dropped off and retracted.

"That's it?" Tim-Ell asked.

"For this part. Give it some time. There's more."

"Are you all right? You said it hurt."

"Just at the beginning. Once the milk came, it got easier."

Tim-Ell stroked the top of the shell. "You know a lot more than I do about care."

She laughed. "I've been reading. Although I've seen this before with my relatives." She stopped because she had never mentioned family and it might bring questions, ones she wasn't ready to discuss. She would have to tell him sometime, but not now.

"There!" She pointed to another area on the top of the shell. A point, looking like an arrowhead emerged. Like the funnel, it snaked up on a tube. "Give me your arm."

After a moment, Tim-Ell put out his arm. Aril guided the arrow point to his inner elbow. "Brace yourself, Warrior," she advised with a smile.

"Uh, all right," Tim-Ell said and stiffened.

The tip, its sharp hollow point, buried under Tim-Ell's skin. "Hey! Ow!"

"Be still; it is finding a blood vessel."

Tim-Ell didn't flinch but looked at his arm, then at Aril. 'What is happening?"

"The child inside takes milk from me several times a day, and blood from you once, usually at night. That is the traditional way. If you don't want to feed it, I can give it my blood."

"I want to give it *my* blood. I want to be part of this." He leaned over and kissed her.

Tears manifested in Aril's eyes, but she suppressed them. Hormones do things to new mothers, she mentally explained to herself. Before she had carried the egg, she never imagined how the scenario of feeding her child would be.

The child's first blood meal didn't last as long as the milk feeding. The tube retracted, and Tim-Ell gently replaced the egg in the incubator.

"Interesting," he said. "I didn't know about the blood. Is erbate out of the picture?"

Aril laughed. "You can still enjoy your erbate. Don't over-enjoy."

He nodded in a solemn move. "Right." He moved his gaze to her breasts. "You are beautiful. Have I told you that lately?"

A lump caught in her throat.

Tim-Ell bent and kissed her breast. "Thank *you*," he whispered. "I'm not a man of fancy words. I don't know what else to say."

She pulled his face to hers and said in quiet words, "That is perfect." She scooted into his arms and relaxed into his embrace. They lay together on the bed and fell asleep enjoined.

The next morning, Aril brought the egg into bed and fed it.

"I'll make breakfast and bring it to you." Tim-Ell said.

Surprised, Aril thanked him. The Crown Prince of Protar was making breakfast for *her*.

By the time he came into the room with a tray, she had finished and put the egg back into the crèche.

They sat together and ate.

Tim-Ell took a bite of toasted bread. "How does the egg expand?"

"The ribs expand as the child grows. The hard shell keeps filling between the ribs. When it gets big enough," she spread her arms to indicate the end size, "then it stops growing and the child inside undergoes the last of the changes, including muscle development. The ribs become brittle, and when the child is strong enough, it pushes against the sides until the shell cracks. We'll see the cracks and wait for the hatching."

"You said about half a year?"

"Yes," she took a sip of the keela. "It takes about that long."

"I feel like I should know this, but I didn't pay attention when my brothers and sister were born. What happens when they come out?"

"The child will have to work the muscles for a few hours to stand and then walk, but he or she must be taught to speak. We are in charge of our child's education, starting with the basics."

He threw a fond look at the white oval under the dome. "You will be a good mother. I hope I can acquit myself with honor."

A wave of pleasure spread through her. "You will be a fine father." She laughed. "Or you will experience a misery you've never dreamed of!"

He laughed and kissed the top of her head. "I better go. It's not good for the Commander of the Army to be late."

The pleasure she felt receded instantly. How would this commander acquit himself when facing the Army of Cadmia when that time came?

CHAPTER 60

Aril's pleasure of nurturing her egg and speculating on what her child would be like alternated with fear of being found out. She didn't question the loyalty of her neighbors, Sen-Mak, and the few others who knew about the egg, but secrets get out.

She had dismissed the maid right after the egg delivered. At that time, she suggested the woman work for Kye-Ren because the silver girl had not taken to household duties. The maid sternly refused, saying no respectable person would clean for a sylph. The only reason a laundress served that apartment was because she laundered Ray-Tan's clothing, little though there was for a warrior, and his linens. Kye-Ren had to wash her own clothing.

In a moment of weakness one day, after feeding the egg, Aril knocked on Kye-Ren's door with the idea she would help.

Kye-Ren cracked the door and glared at Aril. "What do you want? Unless it's an emergency, leave me alone."

Aril peered over the shoulder of the small woman at the kitchen in disarray. "From what I see, it *is* an emergency."

Kye-Ren hissed and bared her teeth. "We like it just fine. Go home. Mind your own business." Having turned a slightly darker purple shade of silver, she slammed the door shut and pulled a curtain across the glass.

"No surprise there," Aril muttered and returned home to attend to her own housework and to prepare the apartment for Leb Brit and his assistant, to install draperies. Today would be like the other times—Aril, on pins and needles that one of the men would see the incubator. She kept the door to the bedroom closed, and thus the windows in there remained unadorned, but the rest of the apartment showed tasteful splendor fit for a warrior prince and his mate. And their egg.

Months later, the apartment, less the bedroom, had been decorated. Dinnerware in a fine cream-colored pattern, and eating utensils in a simple, but elegant design, graced the place. Aril, for the first time in her nonroyal life, hosted a luncheon, inviting Del-Am, Sari-Van, and Kye-Ren.

Kye-Ren declined with a sneer. When she invited Sari-Van, the first question was, would the sylph be there. Aril felt a wave of guilt in the reassurance that no sylph would be in attendance. Del-Am, delighted, said it would be a good experience for Sel-Aspree.

The luncheon went well, but Sari-Van remained frosty to Aril, not having changed her opinion of slaves mingling with royalty. Aril had more right to claim royal status and it rankled the ex-princess. The strata Jake Hill disliked would be hard to dislodge, and from her experience, Aril knew things had to change. It would happen in small steps, perhaps like ladies of different stations having tea. Adding sylphs to the process would take larger, bolder steps.

As the egg grew, Aril came to appreciate Tim-Ell. He made a point to return home at blood-feeding time with only a few evenings where being Commander of the Army kept him away.

After one such incidence, where Tim-Ell had been gone for three days, he asked to take Aril on a day out, a surprise, and said he had already asked Del-Am to care for the egg, that is, if Aril could leave enough milk in a feeding device that could substitute for her. Getting a day's supply of milk into the feeding device presented no problem. Being away from her egg, did, even though she trusted Del-Am. Tim-Ell urged her to go, and she acquiesced. He told her to pack food for the day.

The flier, packed with its small cargo and two passengers, headed south toward the lovely lake situated within the borders of Protar. Passing over the lake, it descended to a low altitude and headed east.

Aril didn't enjoy surprises. "Where are we going?"

"To the oasis. The Burnettia are ready to pick."

"This is the long way. Why aren't we using the route near the gant ranch? It's so much shorter."

"I can't navigate backward from the gant ranch. Once we get into the desert the landmarks are different. I can only navigate *from* the oasis *to* the gant ranch. The sands move making it impossible to find the way without rock formations, and they are low, sometimes covered. The oasis is protected by the two ridges that form an oval. The sand doesn't go past the ridges, keeping the oasis free of drifting sand. Not only that, it is virtually hidden. Few people know about it, and fewer know how to find it using the rock formations as navigation points. The former Commander of the Army showed it to me, saying I might need a getaway to think. But it is unknown because it is difficult to find."

She tried to keep the tone of rebuke out of her question. "What about navigation instruments?"

"They don't always work. I'm not sure why. In fact, the flier may have some problems staying aloft. I will have to keep it low and slow. I usually go there by gantback. But we don't want to be away from the egg all day, thus, the flier and our low, slow route to the oasis."

The image of the blue sand came to mind. "Large deposits of alnata can do that to instrumentation. The color of the sands on the way say alnata is present."

He looked at her sideways. "Yes. I remember your comments. You know a lot of things about rocks and sands."

She didn't respond to his comment. "But the bluish cast indicated *some* alnata. The large deposits must be under the surface."

"After we've picked the fruit, we can check out the area. I will navigate back by way of the gant farm and the ridge of hills behind it to guide the way."

As predicted, the flier bucked and coughed as it made its way to the rock formations. Although she trusted Tim-Ell's judgement about being able to fly to the destination, her heart pounded on several occasions when the sleek little flier skimmed the sandy terrain, sending out ripples of dust.

Tim-Ell guided the craft over the ridge and down to the bubbling fountain. Some trees still held blossoms, perfuming the air. Many trees had fruits in varying degrees of ripeness. Enough trees held the rich brown fruits ready to pick, and there were even a few trees where the treasures had dried, making them sweet and slightly chewy—her favorite state.

After picking enough to fill the back end of the flier, they ate the sandwiches and cheese she had packed. A dip in the warm spring left her relaxed and limp, but her muscles came to full attention when the breeze brought Tim-Ell's scent to her. She still believed the attraction resulted from the hormones. And she still enjoyed the physical pleasure those hormones helped deliver.

They napped by the spring until late afternoon.

Tim-Ell shook her shoulder. "We should go."

The flier took altitude. Just beyond the ridge of the oasis, Tim-Ell pointed at the sky. "Look at the dust storm over the ridge."

Aril squinted at the sky. "Dust? It looks more like steam."

"I don't think so. Steam in that tight a cloud doesn't exist naturally."

"True, I've never seen it like that. Steam with that much force would blow out the rock and escape in a fine mist."

"That's how I've always seen the geothermal vents." He pulled at his chin. "A chimney?"

"That's what I would say. Someone has harnessed the steam and has an industry. I would bet they are mining for alnata. You said no one comes here?"

"No. I would know about that." He held his palm up to prevent her from a reproach about his knowledge of Protar. "Since you have pointed out my weakness in knowledge about what's going on around me, I've spent time learning about the country, the resources, and other things. I'm sure there's no industry out here; that is, *royally sanctioned* industry."

"We should check that out."

"We will. But with the unreliability of the navigation, we must take special care not to get lost."

Aril's face blanched. His good intention of bringing her to the oasis for a day of relaxation and fruit-gathering may have turned into a dangerous outing, one that may cost them being lost, or worse. Whoever ran the illegal mining would not want them to make it back to the city.

Tim-Ell swiveled in his seat. "We need to check this out, but I worry about the navigation. Do you have something to draw this horizon?"

Aril kept a tablet with her provided by Leb-Brit to make notes on clothes or decoration. She used the attached stylus to make an exact line of what the sand dunes, hills, and rocks looked like at their exact location. It was the best they could do to find their way through this dangerous territory that didn't allow instruments for guidance.

Diverting toward the direction of the steam cloud, they traveled through a narrow pass of high dunes.

"Tim-Ell! That looks like a man!"

Advancing as fast as the flier could go and still keep aloft, Tim-Ell flew toward the still body lying in the sand. Landing, they rushed to find a man barely clinging to life. Tim-Ell held him up while Aril put a canteen to his lips. He drank and fluttered his eyes open. "Princess?" He moaned and passed out.

Aril flushed. He looked familiar.

Tim-Ell helped the man sit upright. Pulling his hand away from the man's back, Tim-Ell stared at the bloody smears, and splashed water on the man's face. The man came to.

Tim-Ell trickled water on the man's neck. "You've been beaten and thrown into the sand to die. Who are you?"

"Randor-Kin," the man whispered.

Aril cringed. The cook on the *Nautol!*

Tim-Ell put the canteen to the man's mouth, and again the man took long sips and opened his eyes fully. "What happened?"

Randor-Kin turned his gaze from Aril to Tim-Ell. "I don't remember much, but I was wounded, and the doctor in a slave camp kept me alive where I was bought by Eppo-Zim. Like many other captives, I was purchased to work in the mines. I fell ill, and when beating didn't make me work, according to his policy, they threw me away. He will find someone to replace me."

"No, he won't," Tim-Ell said between clenched teeth. "We will get you to Protar, and I will put a stop to Eppo-Zim."

They jettisoned all the fruit and put Randor-Kin in the back seat. Tim-Ell turned the flier in the direction from where they came, but he couldn't locate the oasis.

After several hours, Aril recognized the horizon. "Look, it matches my drawing. We are near the east ridge of the oasis. We can get back to Protar."

Tim-Ell cast a grim glance at the man in the back seat. "I hope it's in time to save his life."

Hours after sundown, hurtling past the rich grain fields and the gant ranch, they reached the city limits and flew straight to a medical center. The medical staff took the man. Aril couldn't get home fast enough; she had been away from the egg all day. Tim-Ell set the craft down on the grass behind their back door. Aril ran to it and put her palm on the lock; it wheezed open and she flew inside.

Del-Am met her in the kitchen. "Did you have a good day? All is well here. The egg took all the milk, and I gave it my blood just an hour ago."

"You fed my egg?"

Del-Am's eyebrows went up as she blanched. "Oh, forgive me. I meant no disrespect. The feeding tube emerged. I couldn't let it be hungry. I'm so sorry!"

Aril put her hand on Del-Am's arm. "Thank you. I don't know what to say. It's so kind of you to offer your blood for my child."

"Wouldn't you do that for me? Cal-Eb would die for the prince, you, or the royal children. Giving a small amount of blood is insignificant in comparison. I just wasn't sure you would approve of my…common…blood."

"Common?" The word took Aril by surprise. Del-Am had no title, but as far as Del-Am knew, Aril was as low as one could get—a slave.

As if Del-Am read Aril's mind, she said in a gentle tone. "You are royalty, Aril-Ess, inside. Nobility is not just a title."

Aril choked back a lump in her throat and said goodnight to the woman who had taken care of the most precious thing Aril had ever had.

Tim-Ell and Aril bathed and went to bed.

At breakfast the next morning, Tim-Ell finished his keela. His face said an apology would follow. "I'm sorry, Aril. I may be late or not come back at all for the next few days. I must—"

"I know what you must do. I'll manage. It's important you take over that mine and find Eppo-Zim. I would imagine the Treasurer is in on this, too."

"Just so. My life and my country have changed because of you."

Aril sighed. If Randor-Kin survived, would his memory return? Would he let out that the slave-wife of the Crown Prince was the high Princess of the Hill Family?

CHAPTER 61

Tim-Ell spent the next day with his troops out in the desert. Using sentries within view of telescopes, he stationed them in a line toward the mine, starting at the place where the horizon matched Aril's drawing.

Tim-Ell and his men easily overcame and arrested the mine guards, marching them back to the fort for interrogation. All work at the mine ceased. The slaves needing medical attention were evacuated by gant wagons and taken to the surgeons at the fort. Tim-Ell provided the remaining slaves with good food and rest. They were only too happy to relate the details of the abuse heaped upon them by Eppo-Zim and his crew. The slaves added that although the mine supervisors kept things going, Eppo-Zim hadn't been seen in weeks. After the mine had been established, he came once a week to check on things, especially the amount of ore that his wagons took away. None of the slaves knew what happened to the ore.

Ray-Tan said, "I'd be willing to bet that in another area of the desert, there is a smelting facility. He'd keep the structures small, the mining center and the smelter, able to fit between ridges. Because of the alnata interference, fliers wouldn't spot the buildings. Ore would be transported by gant-wagon to the smelter and from there to where the instrumentation wouldn't affect fliers. Then the material could be flown away for sale. No one would see anything."

Tim-Ell nodded. "Except for a steam cloud, that my intelligent mate saw and recognized as industry."

Tired from the events of the day, Tim-Ell stayed at the fort. He would travel to the palace in the morning.

A steward brought a tray to his office, where he discussed the matter of a rotten Vizier with Ray-Tan. "I have to go to the palace tomorrow and speak with my fath—the King."

Ray-Tan put his hand to his chest in a salute. "My friend, Crown Prince, and Commander of the Army. You have come a long way."

Puzzled, Tim-Ell returned the salute. "What do you mean?"

"You have separated your relationship to the King. You act, not as his son, but the man who serves him and the country."

"Thank you," Tim-Ell said quietly. "I hope I can serve him and my country well enough to bring us out of this mess…and messes yet to come."

Later, when he arrived at the palace, Sen-Mak met him at the hangar.

"I got your message, Tim-Ell. I am curious that you have asked me to meet with you and Father."

"I need your help," Tim-Ell said and quickened his pace.

Without further commentary, Sen-Mak matched the stride and entered the throne room.

Jess-Reet sat on the throne alone, grim-faced. "Greetings, my sons," he said without cheer.

In short, to-the-point words Tim-Ell told the King about the illegal mining and slave labor. "I have ordered the arrests of Eppo-Zim and his followers. That leaves us without a Vizier or Treasurer. As Commander of the Army, I have many powers, but I can't appoint positions in the palace. I, can, however, suggest."

"What is your suggestion, Commander of the Army?" Jess-Reet addressed Tim-Ell by his title, understanding this was not a father-son forum, but an official council for serious discussion.

"I suggest you appoint a dual designation, of Vizier-Treasurer, and I suggest that person be Sen-Mak."

The King nodded and cast his gaze to his second son. "So be it, if you are willing to accept."

Sen-Mak blinked. "I am once again honored by my brother. I accept the responsibilities and swear to do my best by my country."

The King smiled. "No one could ask for more."

Sen-Mak's lips thinned. "When was the last time you visited the vault, Father?"

"When your brother didn't wed the Princess of Crocess. I personally oversaw the dowry being stored in the vault."

Sen-Mak shook his head. "I suspect Eppo-Zim and our wily Treasurer, Ark-Dal, are gone. I wonder how much of the royal fortune remains behind the thick doors. I will check, but we may be insolvent."

Tim-Ell put his hand on Sen-Mak's shoulder. "Once you arrange to sell the alnata ore, we will have plenty of wealth."

"Yes," Sen-Mak said. "I will see to the mines and foundries. We have a lot of work to do."

Jess-Reet looked away and back at his sons with alternating expressions of shame and pride. "I have been a poor king. But I have been blessed with competent sons."

"It is not too late for you, Father," Sen-Mak said. He cast his gaze to Tim-Ell. "I see greatness in this man."

"It is fortunate one came along who brought out that greatness."

Tim-Ell nodded. "I am aware of that more each day, Father."

CHAPTER 62

Alone that day, Aril provided both milk and blood for the egg, which had grown enough to almost touch the sides of the incubator. She struggled to enlarge the frame of the creche and slid the glass out to its fullest capacity.

She had just enough milk, the egg suckling longer each day. That night, when Tim-Ell struggled home, dirty and tired, she drew a bath for him and helped him into bed.

"I must feed the egg," he said wearily.

"No. You must rest and be ready for tomorrow. I'll take care of the blood feeding." She paused. "Randor-Kin?"

"Too late for him. If only we'd gotten to him before. He will be honored, even if we don't know much about him. He could have told us so much."

Aril flushed. Randor Kin recognized her. The image of the *Nautol* crash surfaced. She remembered how bravely he fought, taking arrows like Jerr-Lan. Miraculously, Randor-Kin survived. Who else could have survived the deadly attack?

"Aril?" Tim-Ell said.

"All the deaths and injuries…" She shook herself out of the hideous images. "You need to sleep now. There will be much to do."

He didn't argue but lay down on the bed and within minutes, breathed the deep inhalations of one who slipped into a profound sleep.

At the sounds of her mate's deep sleep, Aril opened the glass of the incubator and allowed the arrowhead of the tube to find a vein at the bend of her elbow.

The egg drank for a long time. She ignored the light-headedness as she took her place next to her mate.

When she awoke the next morning, Tim-Ell had already left. She spent the day grieving for her countryman and the others who had perished on the *Nautol*.

In the evening of the next day, Ray-Tan rapped at the back door.

Aril beckoned him in with a wave.

"Good evening, Aril. Tim-Ell will not be home tonight., nor Fin-Dal, or Cal-Eb. He sent me to check on things. You are well?"

"I am, Ray-Tan, thank you."

"Aril… would you allow me to feed the egg tonight?"

"Tim-Ell sent you to give your blood?"

"No. I am asking for that honor. He knows you have been taking his place and he also trusts you to know when to ask for help. I *want* to do it."

Aril, not knowing how to respond, put her hand over her mouth. After a pause, she nodded. "Come with me." She led him to the bedroom and to the creche where the egg almost filled the box.

"Sit," she said and opened the front of the incubator. "Give me your arm."

Ray-Tan extended his arm, watching intently as she guided it near the egg. At once the white oval shimmied in its toweling and sent the arrow-headed tube toward Ray-Tan's arm.

"Be still while it finds a spot," she said.

The warrior flinched as the point dove beneath his flesh. The white of the tube turned pink as the hollow inside gorged with the lifeblood of this man, the friend, the brave warrior. As the egg fed, Aril removed the soiled towel from underneath it and replaced it with a fresh one.

"Do you know when it will hatch?" Ray-Tan asked, every so often staring at the place where the point disappeared in his arm.

"Not too much longer, I hope. It has almost outgrown the box. I don't know what I will do if the glass in the incubator breaks because the egg has grown so much."

Ray-Tan had no suggestions and sat quietly until point eased out, and the tube went limp.

A few drops of blood oozed from his arm.

Aril pressed a cloth against it. "Keep a little pressure."

Ray-Tan pressed the cloth against his arm and stood. "Thank you for allowing me to help," he said in a quiet tone.

Aril could only respond with, "You are welcome, my warrior friend."

Tim-Ell did not return the next night, but Cal-Eb came to the apartment, asking permission to feed the egg. The night after that, Fin-Dal came.

Protar, the place that kept her a prisoner had become her home, with people she loved and who loved her.

CHAPTER 63

After a week of absence, Tim-Ell returned home. Tired and dirty, he greeted Aril with a long hug before taking off his gear. "How are you?" He laid a bumpy bag on the stone table.

"I'm well. You look worn out."

"I feel better just being here. So many things have happened. Sen-Mak acquitted himself admirably. He temporarily closed down the mine and hired workers. He has audited the treasury records, which," he said, laughing, "you won't be surprised, have been horribly altered. He works at sorting out how the soldiers and palace workers will be paid. The vault has little treasure left, only half of what Sari-Van's country gave as her dowry. Eppo-Zim and Ark-Dal are on the run." His voice hardened into a sneering threat. "They had better run far."

"I have what's left of dinner," Aril said.

"Anything will be fine." He tapped the bag. "I have something for you, too." He opened the drawstring and dumped a load of burnettia on the table.

She laughed, picked up a fruit and tossed it in the air. He caught it and put it to her mouth while she took a bite. While the fruit, sweet and gooey, melted on her tongue, she admired Tim-Ell, patched with sand and sweat, his leather worn and stained. She had seen Jake Hill like that. The Planetary Prince got sweaty and dirty and served his people well.

As Tim-Ell washed up, she heated the leftovers.

"Aril! Come quick!"

She hurried into the bedroom.

Tim-Ell held the incubator box as it teetered off its pedestal. "It almost fell. There's a crack in the shell."

Aril grabbed towels and put them on the bed. "You'd better summon the witnesses. The egg stopped feeding two nights ago. That's the sign it's ready to hatch. Take it out of the box and put it on the towels, first."

Tim-Ell hefted the egg to the bed, then hurried next door to ask Ray-Tan to round up the scribe, the Rotner Monk, and Sen-Mak.

He returned to the bedroom, where Aril sat next to white oblate form moving erratically next to her, a single crack radiating down from the feeding tube dimple toward the bottom. Yellowish water oozed. The signatures and marks left by the witnesses a half-year before were hazy but recognizable. Tim-Ell and Aril took turns holding the wobbling ovoid, and each time they switched, the clicking became more pronounced, as the cracks lengthened, and the faint salty smell announced the child inside pushed with strength and endurance to enter the world.

Sen-Mak entered first, and a few minutes later, the scribe. A Rotner monk followed shortly, and all noted their marks on the shifting egg's surface. The scribe made notes regarding each witness's testimony that the marks were genuine. This is the egg they saw come from Aril, the Life-Mate of the Crown Prince.

Cracks on the shell toward the top converged into a triangle. The piece moved outward, showing small fingers.

"I can't stand it," Tim-Ell said, and took his dagger from its holder at his ankle.

"What are you doing!" Aril shouted.

"Trust me," he said, positioning the blade at the apex of the missing piece. He pried open at the new crack forming. Another piece popped off. Aril dabbed at the dripping cracks, while Tim-Ell helped the fissures separate. The room filled. Del-Am, Cab-El, Fin-Dal, with Sari-Van hanging back in the living room. Ray-Tan, without Kye-Ren, stood next to the bed and cheered each time a piece broke off or was pried away by Tim-Ell.

When most of the upper half of the egg had been expelled, the room grew quiet. A dark, curly head peeked out and scanned the room with large eyes. The apartment exploded in murmurs and hoorays. Tim-Ell lifted the child, a well-formed boy, and put him into Aril's lap. The boy's head reached her chin. She toweled him, and he eyed the well-wishers as she spoke softly to him. When dried to her satisfaction, Aril wrapped him in a soft blanket.

Tim-Ell picked him up and held him for all to see. "Please welcome Prince Jes-Ell."

The witnesses and well-wishers left. Tim-Ell and Aril held their child for a long time in silence.

The child squirmed out of their embrace and stretched.

"We need to help him stand," Aril said. Speaking to the boy softly, she took his arm, bending and kneading it. She did the same to the other arm and then both legs. "Hold him up and let him down carefully until his feet touch the floor."

Tim-Ell followed her orders, and within minutes the boy could hold his weight. He looked at them quizzically, and they praised him with words and caresses. Aril would like to have told her mate how much the son resembled the Planetary Prince. The telltale hair would not appear for a few years at adolescence. The boy, whose head towered over her knees, was already muscled at the shoulders and legs.

That evening, they brought the boy to bed with them. He slept snugly between his parents.

In the morning, Jes-Ell left the bed. Startled awake, Tim-Ell hurried him into the bathroom to give him one of his first lessons.

Aril rushed to make breakfast, how to eat being the second lesson for the child.

With the boy cleaned and dressed in a small smock, they brought him to the table, speaking to him as they offered food and lakin milk.

"Tell him everything you do," Aril said. "It will take him a few months to learn to speak, but he will understand the words before he can say them. We will have to train him for everything."

"This looks like it will be one of my most challenging missions," Tim-Ell said with a smile. "One I look forward to. Thank you, Aril."

Should she say *you're welcome*? A course of life she had not chosen made her a mate and a mother. Now, if she could change it, she wouldn't. Was there a goddess watching over people, guiding them? She could not answer that, but if that is what happened, then she gratefully accepted it. A flash of worry interrupted the warm thoughts. What would happen in the future?

For the next few months, Aril and Tim-Ell spent their time happily training their son.

Aril could not remember a time when she felt so fulfilled.

CHAPTER 64

Jes-Ell stared out the glass of the back door. His mother had been taking him into the garden, talking to him and training him with words, pointing out the sky, grass, birds, and plants. He still hadn't spoken his first word, but she felt he understood.

"Jes-Ell," she said behind him. He turned. "You know your name!" She put her hand under his chin. "Let's get your jacket. We'll go for a walk."

He didn't move, but she thought she detected a look of anticipation, the face that showed the eyes of his father.

She pulled his jacket from the pegs near the door. He extended one arm.

"Yes! Good boy. You know I'm going to put this on you."

Jes-Ell waited, watching as Aril put on her own wrap. She opened the door and took his hand. The boy paused outside and then pointed to the atrium arch.

She inhaled quickly. He wanted to see what was outside the complex. How could she refuse his silent request? The wind blew a sudden gust of nippy air. "All right, my darling. We'll go for a short walk. I know, we can go to the small market a few blocks away. We'll get a treat, maybe a freshly baked cake."

She gave a light pull on his hand as she turned toward the gate. The two guards, their pikes held high, nodded and opened the thick wooden doors. Jes-Ell paused, looking right and then left. He looked at her, his eyes wide.

"It's all right, precious. Come."

He nodded.

"You understand! Oh, thank the Goddess. You will be talking in no time. Wait until your father comes home. What news we will have."

As they walked, Aril pointed all around and named the items. She laughed. "You are destined to be the strong silent type, no doubt. The part of me that takes in the surroundings is evident. You have your father's taciturn attitude."

At the market, the boy moved slowly, examining the items on the shelves. He stopped at the shelf that held breads and cakes and breathed in.

"Smells good," Aril said.

The boy moved closer and inhaled the aroma. She could barely contain her delight. She selected a loaf of redgrain bread, the shiny crust covered with toasted seeds, and also chose a dark cake flavored with carnott. For a moment, she had a memory of Jake Hill slicing a piece of cake for her, saying carnott tasted like Earth chocolate, the grandest of all Earth's flavors. Someday she would have to disclose her heritage to Tim-Ell.

She had kept the secret for so long, she had put it away in her mind. It had been over two years. How could it have been so long? Of course, Jake Hill searched for her. Had he been told she was dead? He would not be satisfied with a report. He would seek out the truth and not believe it until he received unmitigated proof, and there was no way he could get that. She lived. This day represented a happy time, and she would not allow her thoughts to get in the way. She took her purchases, and with Jes-Ell's hand in hers, left the store. They had been out long enough. Time to return to the complex.

The wind had increased. Aril turned the collar up against her son's neck, worried he would become chilled. Their pace increased as they headed back down one long road ending with a short turn. In the middle of that long road, a figure, large and unkempt, appeared frozen to the spot. Her gaze focused on the man, for the figure had the stance and bulk of a warrior, but wild and ferocious. The worn leather sheath at his side meant a long, powerful sword. She stopped, her gut telling her this wasn't right. Taking note of her surroundings, her mind raced, thinking about cover and protection. Seeing none, she estimated how far they were from the market. Jes-Ell didn't understand enough to run there. Instinctively she knew this man did not belong to Protar. And he was focused on them, an unblinking, staring concentration. Aril felt for the small dagger she kept at her waist. She'd not used it since Tim-Ell had given it to her, along with a thin blade hidden in a hair ornament. Jake Hill had required all of the family, including the females, to be armed at all times. She tensed, moving her hand to the dagger handle and unsnapped the strap that held it safely in the leather case.

The man hurtled forward in a run. She stood her ground, putting her son behind her. As the man neared, she recognized something about him. Astonishment replaced her fear. He came close enough that she could see the details of his face and the sad state of his clothing.

"Jerr-Lan! How could this be?"

His long, shaggy hair blew in the wind. He bowed low. "Princess. I have found you. Please forgive the amount of time that you have been lost to me. I will take you to Cadmia."

She didn't know what to say.

"May I approach you?"

"Yes. Yes! It's been so long. I thought you were dead."

He took a step closer. "I would have been if not for a band of travelers who took pity on me and the engineer who survived the attack."

A band of travelers? Aril had heard there were still itinerant groups who had no home, but who moved about the planet. They were people of legend, who supported themselves by many means, entertainment, dancing baccurs, fortune telling, and sales of substances frowned upon by city people.

"A band of travelers rescued you?"

"And treated my wounds with marvelous ointments." He moved aside the ragged fabric of his tunic, revealing large scars, ones that would have come from multiple arrows, as she remembered.

"I have become one of them. After I deliver you to Cadmia I will take my place as a leader in the band."

Aril knew him well enough to realize the sound of his words indicated more than their usual meaning. "There is a woman?"

"There is, but she understands I cannot commit until I have fulfilled my promise to find you. The promise I sent to Jake Hill."

"Jake Hill knows where I am?"

"Not yet. I have tracked you to this area. Now that I have found you…"

Jes-Ell peeked around her waist.

Jerr-Lan pointed at him. "The child?"

"My son," Aril said with hesitation, the pause not lost on the man who had known her so well.

Jerr-Lan's face turned harsh. "I heard you had been taken as a slave."

He said it like a question, and the answer she would give would be the solution to other questions.

"I was sold as a slave."

"Owned by a powerful prince," Jerr-Lan said.

"Yes, but—"

Jerr-Lan's hand went to the pommel of his sword. "I will make him pay for what he has done to you. And then I will give him to Jake Hill to be finished."

Aril put her hand out. "You don't understand, Jerr-Lan."

"I understand perfectly because I have already encountered the woman who had been the artist on the *Nautol*. She told me where to look for you as she lay dying. The woman had been mistreated by her…master." He spit the word *master* out like sour fruit. "Come with me."

She pulled away from his hand.

A whoosh above her head took her attention. Tim-Ell's flier descended, and he hopped out before it completely landed. "Aril! Aril!"

"Please, Tim-Ell. Stay where you are. I must talk with this man."

Jerr-Lan sneered. "Is this him? The man who purchased you? Who abused you for his pleasures?" He pulled his sword out, the blade shining in the sunlight. He tossed his words in Tim-Ell's direction. "Defend yourself."

"No! Jerr-Lan. Don't challenge him."

Tim-Ell drew his sword and took swift steps forward.

"No, Tim-Ell. Stop."

The prince stopped but shook his head, frustrated.

Jerr-Lan spoke in low, mean words. "I will avenge you, but not completely. Jake Hill would want his turn."

She touched the top of the sword. "Do not engage the prince. I don't want to frighten my son. And Tim-Ell is a good swordsman. You might be killed."

"My equal?"

"Perhaps better. But I don't want either of you hurt." Her hand moved from Jerr-Lan's sword to her heart. "And I love him." She cast her gaze to Tim-Ell. She whispered to herself. "I should have told him that long ago."

Jerr-Lan shook his head. "He is not the prince who bought you at the slave market?"

How could she explain? "He is, Jerr-Lan. And the father of my child. But in spite of that, he is a good man." She tapped the sword. "Are you still my champion?"

"Yes, my life is yours to command."

"Then stand down. You have fulfilled your promise. You have found me. Where is your woman?"

He returned his sword to its scabbard. "She waits near a lake south of here."

Aril relaxed. "Go and pledge your life to her."

He crossed his arms over his chest. "I must report to Jake Hill."

"I ask that you wait. Give me some time to think."

Jerr-Lan's lips quivered as they changed from aggressor to understanding friend. "My people and I will travel to Cadmia, where I will deliver the information."

"How do you travel?"

"By convoy—wagons pulled by gants. We walk beside them."

"How long will that take?"

"By the time of the Shortest Day."

That meant more than half a year. "Then that is how long I will need," she said.

Tim-Ell returned his sword to its leather scabbard and approached. Aril put her hand out to him. As he took his place next to her, two policemen on gantback thundered toward them.

Tim-Ell motioned them over. He addressed Jerr-Lan. "Did I hear you say something about gant trains and walking?"

Aril and Jerr-Lan exchanged looks. Tim-Ell hadn't heard the whole conversation. Aril answered. "Jerr-Lan is an old friend. He belongs to a group of wanderers. They're headed north."

Tim-Ell pointed to one of the patrolmen. "Give this man your gant." He looked at Jerr-Lan. "Let me help speed you on your way." His delivery was frosty, but not unkind.

Aril wound her arm around the prince's waist. "Thank you."

The patrolman handed Jerr-Lan the reins. With hesitation, Jerr-Lan took them and glanced to Aril. "Until the Shortest Day."

She nodded. Tim-Ell dismissed the patrolmen.

Aril pulled Jes-Ell from behind her. "Thank you for giving me space. How is it you appeared?"

Tim-Ell's fingers brushed the top of his son's curls. "Two reasons. One, I heard you had left the complex with Jes-Ell."

"You have spies watching me?"

"If you mean do my guards keep track of you for your safety? Then yes. A gate guard sent notice you had left. But two, I received a summons from the palace. We must appear tomorrow."

She didn't know which event caused her the most concern, the summons or Jerr-Lan's appearance. It was time to tell him who she was and where she came from. "Can you stay home for a while? I need to talk to you."

"If you're about to dress me down for having you watched, then I must tell you that while I have enemies, you have more. It's not safe for you to go out unattended."

"No, that wasn't what I need to talk with you about."

"If you want to explain that unsavory character who just left on one of Protar's gants, then I will say I have been expecting something like this."

"What?"

"Even though he was disheveled, he wore the metal of Cadmia. You are a descendant of Jake Hill."

A burn coursed through her. "How did you know?"

"I have eyes, my dearest one. You are outstanding in many ways, including the fine line of hair in an interesting place."

"You knew about the genetic marker?"

"I didn't until I asked the head surgeon about what would cause it. He said only the relatives of the Earthman possess that trait."

"Why didn't you say anything?"

"You would tell me at your own time. I have been building the army to prepare for the inevitable."

The burn turned to fear. "No. There can be no war. It's not right. So many people will suffer."

"It is right by Jake Hill's view. Perhaps we can come to an understanding."

She dropped her head. "You don't know him. He can be a gentle soul, but when it comes to his family, I fear there will be no mercy. Especially for you."

Tim-Ell put his arm around her. "What happens, happens, my beautiful mate. I have been happier than a man has a right to be. I feel that pleasures have been stolen from other men and have been given to me. No one man deserves what I have—you—and from you a son. Beloved, I must face my fate. Let Jake Hill avenge you with my life. Perhaps it will save some of those who are innocent and don't deserve to die because of my folly."

He added, "What you need to think about now is our summons to the Palace. Summons rarely result in pleasantness."

"Tim-Ell? I have something else to tell you. I love you."

He smiled. "That's another thing I knew."

CHAPTER 65

Tim-Ell escorted his family back to the apartment. He nodded his thanks to the guards at the gate. Fine men, he thought. The Protar Army would defend him and his family with their lives. Hopefully, the soldiers stationed at the Palace lent their loyalty to him as well. Not that they wouldn't give their lives for any of the royal family, but if they had to choose, and he deeply hoped it would never come to that, the guards would take his side in a family conflict. He had handpicked the men for that reason. Palace duty was the pinnacle of posts, the men would be grateful and loyal to him. His guards kept him abreast of what went on in the palace. Jess-Reet and Ran-Cignar were in no danger. Tim-Ell had seen to that, but the grand page, and the royal messengers, his men, had been alerted to watch carefully. There were enemies in the palace, some who had not shown their hand.

Seeing his mate and son safely back, he returned to the fort. He had many things to ponder, including why they had been summoned for the following day, but he couldn't leave Jes-Ell home. The boy would accompany them to the palace. He had hoped the boy would talk before being presented to the court. Now it was out of his hands.

The warrior who tracked Aril-Ess down was not a worry. He could have taken him. Maybe not easily, but that did not pose a problem. Jake Hill was a problem.

Since the time of their life mating, he had learned of Aril-Ess's heritage. And that was when he decided to offer his life to prevent war. Would it be enough for the Planetary Prince? Aril would try to interfere. She was headstrong, and smart.

He'd listen to what she had to say, but ultimately it was his fight. One he had brought upon himself, and he if could help it, he would take care of it with his life, the only thing he believed would satisfy the esteemed Earthman.

CHAPTER 66

At the palace, Aril's heart pounded so heavily she feared it would show. Tim-Ell said they were safe. She had to trust him. The King approved of her; even Sen-Mak said so. They did not get permission to sip the nectar and had managed to keep the egg a secret, but now the palace dwellers knew about Jes-Ell.

"Bring the child to me," Jes-Reet said.

Aril stepped in front, guarding him.

Jes-Reet stood at his throne. "You fear me, Mate-of-the Crown Prince?"

She swallowed, "Not for myself."

The King left his chair. As he made the three steps to where they stood, Tim-Ell took his place in front of Aril and the boy.

The King looked at his son. "Do you fear for your child?"

Tim-Ell squared his shoulders and looked down the few inches to his father's eyes. "No, Sire. I can defend my family should I need to."

Jes-Reet laughed. He peeked around Aril to see Jes-Ell. "You have no worries from me, my son. I would like to meet my grandchild."

Tim-Ell gently pulled Jes-Ell from his spot behind Aril. "May I present my son, Jes-Ell of Protar."

Jes-Reet squatted to be eye-level. "Hello, there. Do you know how to greet your king?"

The boy didn't flinch, but he looked from Jes-Reet, to Tim-Ell, to Aril, and then gave a long stare at Queen Ran-Cignar.

The King stood and addressed Tim-Ell. "Does he talk?"

"Not yet. We wished to wait until he could communicate to present him."

"But you kept the egg a secret from us?"

"Yes, Father. A would-be target is better protected if unknown."

Jes-Reet looked over his shoulder at his mate, then back to Tim-Ell. He sighed. "Understood. But we know about him now. He needs to be officially acknowledged."

Aril stayed where she was.

Tim-Ell took Jes-Ell by the hand and led him up the steps to the throne. After a pause to allow the King to take his seat, Tim-Ell cleared his throat; in a sure, firm voice he made the introduction. "King Jes-Reet, Queen Ran-Cignar, Mother, Father, citizens of the Realm, this is Jes-Ell, my son, second heir to the throne of Protar."

"Never!" the Queen screamed. She shot up from the chair and stomped out of the Throne Room.

Jes-Reet curled his fingers to bring Jes-Ell close. Tim-Ell led the boy to the King, who patted the boy's shoulders. "We'll let the Queen settle down. I'll send for her later. Now, let's get to know this handsome, fine young man."

Aril kept her place, observing the three generations of Protarian royalty. She had seen similar presentations in Cadmia. No queen, however, had acted like that. Aril had to watch her back. But the Queen's bad reaction might serve Aril's purpose. To make her status more palatable to Ran-Cignar, the King might make a proclamation reversing her slave status and promote Aril to Princess.

After a few minutes, Jes-Reet beckoned Aril to join them. Although Jes-Ell appeared not to react to the activities around him, he moved his head, and wide-eyed, watched, occasionally searching with his gaze for her. She smiled to reassure him.

The King stood and clapped his hands. "Those of you in attendance, approach the throne. Come. Admire my new grandson and second heir."

A hum developed and echoed from the shiny stone walls and pillars as the crowd moved forward.

The boy took a step closer to Aril, who moved closer to Tim-Ell.

"So many people," she whispered.

"Don't worry," he said so only she could hear. "The guards are mine."

Jake Hill had said that often when he visited outside of Cadmia. More and more Tim-Ell reminded her of her great warrior ancestor.

When Jes-Ell turned to Aril and buried his face in her skirt, the King smiled.

"Perhaps, we should retire to a smaller room. Come." He patted Aril's arm as an invitation to follow him.

The King paused at the door to an anteroom. "We are entertaining an important ambassador. You might want to meet him, my son."

He led the way into a smaller, but no less ornate, chamber, where Queen Ran-Cignar spoke with a man whose back was to them.

Turning, Ran-Cignar's pink face transformed into sour red. Her attention shot to Aril. She pointed and spoke in a volume heard around the room. "This is my reception room. Get that whore-slave out of here. And that bastard child with her."

The visitor turned to look at what caused the commotion.

Aril sucked in a breath. She knew the man standing with the Queen. Abon-Kel was the Cadmia Master of the Excalibur Order. His look turned from confusion, to recognition, and back to confusion.

As King Jes-Reet hurried to quiet the queen, Aril quickly put her finger to her lips as a signal to Abon-Kel not to say anything.

Aril grabbed Jes-Ell's hand and hurried out. Without commenting, Tim-Ell followed her. He caught up with her. "I'm sorry, Aril."

Along the way to the flier, the guards saluted, bringing their fists smartly to their chests. Tim-Ell returned the salutes, slowing them down.

In the flier, Aril could barely speak. When they soared over rooftops and spires, she put her hand on Tim-Ell's arm. "The man in your mother's reception room comes from Cadmia. He is a close friend of my grandsire. We are doomed."

CHAPTER 67

Tim-Ell immediately tripled the guard at the complex. The next morning at breakfast, he barely ate. "My agents at the palace said the ambassador left abruptly. I would imagine by tomorrow he will be in Cadmia."

Aril hadn't touched her food. "And an hour later, he will have an audience with Jake Hill."

Tim-Ell said nothing.

"Oh, Tim-Ell! Jake Hill will waste no time coming here."

"That may be, but even the best commander can't move any faster than his troops can travel. How large is the infantry?"

She shook her head. "Small in comparison to Protar's infantry."

"Truly? How can that be?"

"Because most of Jake Hill's army is cavalry."

"Mounted?"

"And thousands of air ships. Some large vessels bristling with steam cannons. Others with high sides for the archers. There are one-man fliers piloted by skilled fighters."

"Then, my dear, that is what we will face. The question most of my mind is will he avert war if I offer myself?"

"No!" She shot from her seat and paced. "I don't know." She turned to him. "Please. Let me think." She swallowed the knot that formed in her throat. "I believe he will leave the bulk of the soldiers outside of the main city. He and a small guard will go to the palace to speak to the King and announce his intentions."

Tim-Ell pushed his finger around the rim of his cup. "Such a gentleman."

"Believe it," Aril said. "He will want to know where I am and rescue me before the fighting starts."

"Then he has my blessing," Tim-Ell said. "You and our boy are my first concern."

Aril put her head back and closed her eyes. "As soon as the Cadmia Army is spotted, I need to know. And when Jake Hill goes to the palace, I must know that, too."

CHAPTER 68

"Del-Am, I need your help."

"Of course. What can I do?"

"I will need Sari-Van to help, as well."

The look on Del-Am's face said such a request would not be easy. She nodded.

"Then," Aril took a long breath, "I will need Kye-Ren to help."

The look on Del-Am's face now said it would be close to impossible.

"Del-Am, Kye-Ren likes you. You have been kind to her."

Del-Am shook her head. "I doubt the sylph likes anyone. I have only spoken to her. We aren't friendly."

"You haven't shunned her, like Sari-Van and others have. She might listen to you. And this has to be confidential. You can't tell Cal-Eb. You will have to convince Kye-Ren not to say anything to Ray-Tan."

"But Ray-Tan could get her to do just about anything."

Aril sighed again. "Agreed, but he can't know. No one can. Just us, you, me, Sari-Van, and Kye-Ren. We need to start riding in the afternoon; that is, you, me, and Sari-Van. You will have to trust Kye-Ren with Sel-Aspree." She rolled her lip letting her request sink in.

"You wish the sylph to care for Sel-Aspree while I ride?"

"Yes. I don't care for Kye-Ren very much, truthfully, and she hates me. But I don't think she would let any harm come to children. I think she would be kind and caring to your daughter—if *you* asked her. I have to trust people, and I'll start with Kye-Ren."

Del-Am made a sour face. "You are asking her to watch *your* child, too?"

Aril sighed, understanding the difficulty she faced. "Yes. But one more thing. Please ask Sari-Van if we can wear her riding clothes. Including her matching hats."

Del-Am stretched her neck and looked to the sky. "I haven't ridden for years."

"You know how to ride, don't you?"

"I was raised on a farm. I can ride. I just never did it as entertainment. I don't understand what the attraction is, to go out for an hour, put a gant into a trot, then a canter, then a gallop, and come home. What's the point?"

"The point is, it will help me. And maybe save some lives." She put her hand up to stop questions. "It will be better if you don't know some of this. Do you trust me?"

"I do. My husband has vowed his life to the prince and the royal family. Asking me to go for a gant ride in the afternoons seems trifling. Well, except for the part where I trust my child to a sylph."

"The sylph has a name, and we need to forget that she is of a different race. We are all in this together."

Del-Am nodded. "I will do anything you ask. First let me work on Sari-Van. When do you want to start riding?"

Aril spread her hands. "Tomorrow?"

"I should get going, then. First, Sari-Van. Then," she gulped, "Kye-Ren, our silvery neighbor."

Aril grabbed Del-Am's hand and kissed it. "Thank you. You are a true friend. And thank you for not asking questions."

Del-Am patted Aril's cheek. "I have a feeling it's better I don't know."

Aril squared her shoulders and marched to Kye-Ren's apartment. At the door, the sylph bared her teeth. Jes-Ell shrank back behind Aril's leg.

Kye-Ren's eyebrows came together. Did she realize that she had frightened the boy? In an unexpected, gentle tone, she said. "What do you want?"

Aril swallowed and selected the words she rehearsed for the last hour. "I need your help." She put up her hand to stop Kye-Ren's refusal. "Please listen first."

Jes-Ell peeked around Aril's side and stared at Kye-Ren.

"Speak," Kye-Ren said.

"It is very important, believe me, Kye-Ren, very important, that you…" She wet her lips. "That you babysit for me and Del-Am an hour each day starting tomorrow."

Kye-Ren's eyebrows went up in the precursor to a smirk and a haughty refusal.

"Wait!" Aril said. "I know it sounds foolish, but it isn't, and it might save many lives. No questions. Just agree, please. For Tim-Ell, and maybe Ray-Tan. He would want you to help." She suspected Ray-Tan had mentioned possible problems with Cadmia.

A war waged in the sylph's mind. Her face softened, and she bent down near Jes-Ell. "Hello, Jes-Ell. You are a beautiful child. Would you like to come in and visit?"

Aril wasn't sure Jes-Ell knew what the words meant, but she took his hand and led him inside while Kye-Ren held the door. As she passed the sylph, the look in her neighbor's eye said nothing had changed between *them*. That was fine with Aril. Kye-Ren only had to be nice to the children. Aril sat back and let Kye-Ren talk to Jes-Ell. Kye-Ren offered him a sweet, putting it in his hand, then guiding it to his mouth. He bit and smiled.

They stayed for an hour. On the way out, Aril caught Kye-Ren's eye. "Thank you," she said, and took Jes-Ell home. Later that afternoon, Del-Am, hand in hand with Sel-Aspree, made a visit to the sylph. Aril timed it. They stayed an hour.

The first part of the plan had been accomplished.

Sari-Van sent over a bright orange silken riding habit, along with its matching hat. Aril pulled the waist ribbon and admired the fit in the mirror. Although she would never choose something so gaudy, the bright color suited her plan well. Jes-Ell did a doubletake when Aril went to wake him from his nap in her old room. "Right. Your mom looks strange. I agree." She gave him his afternoon snack and dreaded what she was about to do.

It was difficult to take Jes-Ell to Kye-Ren and more difficult to leave him there, especially when he made whimpering sounds. Aril hardened her resolve, and along with Del-Am, dressed in bright yellow, handed her child over to a dour-faced, half-sized woman.

Sari-Van waited at the stable already mounted, wearing glowing red. They donned wide-brimmed riding hats, the generous ribbons tying under their chins, almost hiding their faces. Aril smiled.

Aril and Del-Am trotted behind the smooth-paced gray gant the ex-princess rode every day, the one she had been on next to Fin-Dal the first time Aril saw her. Sari-Van had a regal bearing, one that her plunge to commoner would never change. The ride lasted a long hour, but Aril was happy with the outcome. She also appreciated the joy Jes-Ell displayed when she appeared at Kye-Ren's.

Tim-Ell did not return that night. She had decided not to tell him what she had planned until after the first run. Now she could not discuss it because he was not home.

The rides went well the following two days. Sari-Van led them in several directions, the usual routes she had taken since she moved into the complex. Tim-Ell stayed busy at the fort. Aril wished he would return so she could let him know what she'd set in motion.

The next day, after lunchtime, Ray Tan rapped on the glass with a cadence suggesting importance. Aril hurried to the door and let him in.

"My agents say the Cadmian army is camped to the north, and Jake Hill, with a small contingent on gantback, heads toward Protar, most likely the palace."

Working to keep the quiver from her voice, she said, "Your men have done well."

Ray-Tan nodded.

"I need two things," she said. "First, send a message to the fort and tell Tim-Ell he must take Jes-Ell on a camping trip." She held her palm toward him to stay any questions. "Second, I need you to take me to the palace so I can wait at Sen-Mak's apartment. Can you get me admitted?"

Ray-Tan looked at her sideways. "Yes, I go to the palace on military business; the guards will let me in. But the Queen. . ."

Aril's voice-quiver became more difficult to suppress. "That's why I need Sen-Mak. And you must return to the fort as soon as you gain entrance for me." Her face muscles tightened. "You will be needed there. In case. . ."

He looked away for a moment and turned back, understanding in his eyes. *In case of war.*

"I hope Sen-Mak is at the palace." She recognized the confusion on his face, but by now Ray-Tan, Tim-Ell's closest friend, trusted her and would support her requests.

The warrior lifted his shoulders in the manner of the Knighthood. "I will send a courier to the fort. When do you want to go to the palace?"

Aril lifted her shoulders in the same way. "Now." She cast a glance at Jes-Ell, who sat at the table examining large puzzle pieces. "I need to talk to Del-Am."

Ray-Tan looked over at the boy. "If Del-Am can't watch him, Kye-Ren will."

"Are you sure? I mean, she already—"

"Look," Ray-Tan said, "Kye-Ren maintains her, um, distaste for you, but she doesn't hold it against your son. She's not a total bitch."

Aril's mood lifted for a moment. The man loved his sharp-tongued, often nasty, sylph. He accepted her personality and didn't cover for her. Aril's admiration for this man climbed to a new level.

"Thank you," she said. "Send the messenger, then come back." He left.

Aril called to her son. "Jes-Ell?" The boy looked up. "Come with me."

It took a moment for him to process her command, but he had been learning, and he knew this one. He stood.

She took his hand and gently pulled him to her side. "We are going to see Del-Am. You like her. And you can play with Sel-Aspree. We'll go now, all right?"

Jes-Ell offered no resistance. They walked across the courtyard.

Del-Am answered the knock on her glass door. "Oh, you're early, Aril. Hello, Jes-Ell."

Aril softly pushed Jes-Ell into the playroom, where Sel-Aspree sat at a pile of building blocks. Aril treasured the image of her child as he rambled toward the girl.

She turned to Del-Am. "I won't be riding today. Could he stay here until I return? I'm not sure how long I will be gone."

Del-Am's smile faded.

Aril counted on their strength of their friendship. By now this woman should understand a serious request.

Del-Am's smile returned. "Of course. Whatever you need."

"Thank you. And, please, ride today like always. It's important."

"All right."

Bless Del-Am!

Aril stepped into the playroom, pulled her boy close, and kissed his silky head, whispering, "I love you." She needed an extra shot of will to leave, but she detached from the boy and left, picking up her pace across the courtyard, where Ray-Tan waited. They both headed for the hangar.

Ray-Tan must have taking flying lessons from Tim-Ell. He flew the sleek little craft low and fast, skimming the spires and rooftops, coming to an air-skid at the top of the palace hangers, descending to the dedicated slot for the Crown Prince's flier.

Guards appeared. They chest-saluted Ray-Tan, Second-in-Command of the Protar Army.

Aril admired this man, a commoner who had come up the ranks, and through merit and skill, attained his position, another example of how Tim-Ell resembled

Jake Hill. Grandsire banned military rank by family, opening lead positions to men and women who earned their commissions.

Ray-Tan escorted Aril through the palace at a fast clip, but turned where the main hallway branched, heading to the royal apartments.

Sen-Mak answered his door with surprise. "Well, hello," he said, mildly stunned. "Come in."

"I must leave," Ray-Tan said. "You will take care of her?"

Sen-Mak's voice dropped into a grave tone. "I gave my pledge."

In an unusual gesture, Ray-Tan kissed Aril's cheek and whispered, "Good luck."

Aril swallowed hard. Even not knowing what she had planned, Ray-Tan trusted her. The friendship and faith here in Protar equaled what she experienced in Cadmia. She must stop the coming war.

Sen-Mak cleared his throat. "Sister?"

She could reveal the plan. "You must trust me. Jake Hill is on his way to the palace, and I want to be there when he comes."

"Jake Hill? Why is *he* here, and how do you know this?"

"Tim-Ell had the border watched. And I need to speak to the King. Will you just take that explanation?"

Sen-Mak scratched at his forehead. "All right. I have confidence that my brother has things in control. And I have come to know *you* well enough to believe you have his best interest at heart."

She hadn't expected that, and words she had ready to convince him faded, along with an appropriate response to his compliment. For an awkward, silent moment she gathered her thoughts.

Aril stepped close. "Where can I wait so I know when Jake Hill comes? Will he meet resistance by the guards?"

"The first question is easy. There is a small antechamber off the Throne Room, where you can sit. If you pull a curtain away you can watch and hear through a small window. The second part, I don't know. It depends on the Planetary Prince's arrival."

Aril looked away. She returned her gaze to her brother-in-law. "You're right. A small contingent would mean he will request, strongly, an audience with the King." What she didn't say was it wouldn't make a difference. Everyone knew the appearance of the Earthman from the hair on his arms and legs. No one would deny him. If they did, they would perish.

CHAPTER 69

When the messenger told Sen-Mak the palace was buzzing from an important guest, he took Aril's elbow and hurried her through a passage in the wall, a shortcut to the antechamber. He pointed to a seat next to a curtain and pulled it back, revealing a round window. Aril appreciated the subterfuge. She had been in the Throne Room several times. The decor on the walls had concealed this watching place. It assisted her now.

Droning sounds in the Throne Room became louder as King Jess-Reet and Queen Ran-Cignar took their places.

Minutes after they settled onto the ornate seats, the double doors burst open. Guards with lances pointed their weapons and stepped in front of the royal couple. More guards rushed through the entry and ran to form a line protecting the King and Queen, their points forward.

Aril's heart skipped beats. Jake Hill didn't break stride as he approached the guards. He dropped his sword on the floor with a resounding clang and waved his arm at the guards to stand down. His waist dagger bounced on the floor, sending the message he was no threat—not yet. The guards looked to their leader, the captain in the middle of the line, who turned his head for the King's call.

"Enter," King Jess-Reet said.

The guards kept their lances low but stepped back a few paces, closer to the throne.

Jake Hill approached the speaking circle but did not bow. He stood with arms crossed over his burly chest, staring at the royal couple.

Aril left her seat and ran into the throne room. She passed the circle, where Jake Hill stood like a threatening statue, ducked between the guards, and kneeled at the king's feet. Turning her head and engaging Jake Hill's surprised stare, she shook her head in a barely perceptible motion, sending him a silent message not to react.

Queen Ran-Cignar yelled, "Get that piece of trash out of here!"

Aril tapped the King's foot and whispered. "Time to be a King."

The King's eyebrows went up. He nodded.

The Queen screamed again. "You, Captain, throw this dirty slut out of the palace."

Once again Aril met Jake Hill's gaze and shook her head against a reaction.

King Jess-Reet summoned the captain and the guard next to him. "Escort the Queen to her chambers."

Queen Ran-Cignar pulled in a hoarse breath.

Before she could say a word, the King held his palm up at her. "Leave or I will have you forcibly removed."

The men approached the Queen, whose skin paled rapidly.

"Not another word, Ran," the King added. "Not one."

Crestfallen, shocked, the Queen stood and shuffled away between the two guards.

Jake Hill took a step, one pace over the circle, a gesture flaunting his power. "I demand you turn over Crown Prince Tim-Ell to me immediately."

Aril tapped the King's foot again, whispering. "Don't do it. You are the King of Protar. Be the King."

King Jess-Reet cast his gaze down to Aril, "Who *are* you?"

"A woman," she whispered, "who loves your son. Please, don't give him up."

Jess-Reet straightened in his ornate seat. He addressed Jake Hill. "I have not invited you to my country, but I have allowed you to enter my palace. Please state your business and your reason for wanting one of my citizens, my son, my successor."

Aril sent a silent eye message to her grandsire. He gave a slight nod but took another step toward the throne. "The Crown Prince has transgressed the law of the planet and offended Cadmia. For this he will pay. With his life. Avoid war, turn him over to me."

King Jess-Reet paled but recovered. "I will not give anyone to you until I know the circumstances. This is a diplomatic incident and requires discussion. I invite you to stay here until we can meet, discuss, and work in a civilized manner."

Taking a step closer, Jake Hill stood a few feet away from Aril. "I will stay at my camp on your border. I will speak with you but make no mistake. You son will face me. If he hides, we will find him." With one more glance at Aril, Jake Hill stepped sharply away from the throne, retrieved his weapons, and his footsteps echoed on the shiny stone floors on his way out. The six warriors in Cadmian uniforms who waited by the doors separated as he broke through their line. They formed a Vee and followed him.

Sen-Mak, wearing a tunic with the royal emblem, stepped in front of a Cadmian warrior on the end of the line. The warrior drew his blade. Sen-Mak handed the man a note. "This is for the Planetary Prince. Please see he gets it."

Aril had written the note earlier, asking Jake Hill to come to her apartment the next day, alone and unarmed. She knew he would come.

The room remained soundless.

Jess-Reet stood, bent down, and took Aril's hand to help her rise. "Now, dear girl, so foolishly brave to come into my presence and give orders, explain yourself."

"Forgive me, King. I am your son's mate. . . and slave."

"Mate and slave, eh?" He squeezed her hand. "You've made me a real King today, young woman. And as the King, I decree you are Mate, but no longer slave."

"You are freeing me?"

"I am. Now tell me what's going on."

Aril swallowed hard. "Please. Allow me a few days?"

Jess-Reet let go of her hand and sat hard on the rich fabric of the throne seat. "I should trust you with this crisis?"

She nodded. "Yes." She pleaded, "Please."

He tipped the crown back on his head. "I must allow *another* woman to be my sovereign?" He cast a glance at the direction that the Queen had taken on her way out.

"For a few days, my King." The words, *my King* gave her a ripple of realization that she had fully adopted Protar as her country.

As if he understood her realization, he nodded. "You might be my only hope to save my country. And my son." The King slumped. "Hope."

Aril leaned over and kissed his cheek. "We must have hope."

She left the throne room and met Sen-Mak at the double doors. "Will you take me home?"

"Of course," Sen-Mak said.

In the quiet of the flier, she went over her plan. *Hope,* the thin thread left when Luck turned its back and Fate faced you.

CHAPTER 70

When Sen-Mak landed at the apartment complex, Tim-Ell came out of the hangar, grim-faced, his usual good-natured relaxation changed into tight-lipped determination. The brothers clasped arms in a way that encouraged Aril. Sen-Mak had kept his pledge as Honor Man and would continue the support.

Tim-Ell slid his arm around her and took her away from earshot of others. "I don't want to leave, but I will at your request. I have two gants that can make the trip to the oasis. Their saddlebags are packed. I can leave in the morning."

"No! You must leave now." She paused to let the feel of his arm at her waist sink into her memory, then hurried to Ray-Tan's apartment, where Kye-Ren attended Sel-Aspree and Jes-Ell. Warmth spread through her when her son looked up and smiled. He had been learning so much and was reacting to her.

"Thank you, Kye-Ren," she said sincerely. "You take good care of the children. I think Jes-Ell is fond of you."

Kye-Ren said nothing in response, but she didn't hiss, snarl, or bare her teeth, either. Progress?

Aril took Jes-Ell by the hand. She looked at Kye-Ren. "He will come with me now. I missed the afternoon gant ride with the other women. Sel-Aspree will have to play alone until her mother comes for her."

Kye-Ren didn't respond to that, either. Aril-Ess had no time to waste. She hurried her boy from the apartment and brought him to the hangar where Tim-Ell checked the gants' hard fleshy feet.

Tim-Ell led the two animals from the stall and motioned to the guards at the gate. In a smooth, graceful motion, he mounted the larger gant and bent low, extending his arms to Jes-Ell.

Aril squatted eye-level with her son. "Go with your father." She pointed to Tim-Ell and waited for acknowledgement. The boy backed up a few inches from the gant.

For the first time that day, Aril fought fear. How could they take a child quietly away to hide if he didn't cooperate? Jes-Ell didn't talk, yet. But he could cry and scream. He was only beginning to understand words. He had progressed faster than she had expected, but there hadn't been enough time.

Aril gave her son a gentle push toward the large gant. Taking his hand in hers, they stroked the animal's soft flank. The gant's head, with large brown eyes and a long snout, turned toward them. Aril tensed, waiting for Jes-Ell to cry, but he stepped closer to the gant and stroked the sinewy neck on his own.

"See?" Aril cast a glance to Tim-Ell. She kissed her son's cheek. "Nice gant. She won't hurt you." Pointing to the saddle, she whispered, "Ride with your father. You'll have fun. Right?"

Aril gently backed Jes-Ell closer to the warm animal's side. Tim-Ell bent further and picked their son up, pulling him onto the saddle. Jes-Ell leaned forward and stroked the line of hair running down from the animal's ears to where the saddle began.

"Good boy!" Aril said. "My wonderful, good boy." She looked at her mate and barely choked out, "My wonderful boys." She took the reins of the second gant and handed them to Tim-Ell. "Be careful. I love you."

Tim-Ell nudged the haunch of the large gant with his riding boot. The animal trotted, picking up speed, followed by the second gant. Aril ran alongside until they left the gate. When the gates closed, she watched through a slit in the wooden enclosures until they were out of sight.

She returned to her place and did something she rarely did before coming to Protar.

She wept.

CHAPTER 71

Aril woke from a fitful sleep, remembering the dream about pushing her face into a protective, hairy chest and thick muscular arms. Grandsire would come—she knew it.

The morning dragged by, with little sounds normally unnoticed making her flinch. She checked the kitchen timepiece often, waiting for the prescribed hour. Jake Hill would appear at the appointed time. Nothing she could do would calm her.

A few minutes before his scheduled time, she went to the gate. The thick wooden sections lay open, per her instructions to the guards. As she stood in the middle of the portal, waiting, the sound of gants pounding on the road preceded the appearance. Precisely as she asked, a squad of twenty warriors rode behind Jake Hill.

The events unfolded as she wished. Jake Hill dismounted and strode toward her. His men got down from their animals and approached the complex's protectors. The Cadmian warriors spread out, stopped in front of the Protar warriors, and each pair slowly drew their weapons placing the pieces on the ground. They faced each other a few feet apart, the Protar soldiers facing forward, the Cadmian soldiers facing the complex. Aril couldn't see the sides or the back of the complex, but knew it was the same all around the building.

Jake Hill strode to her. Her heart pounded. She wanted to throw herself into his protective arms, but this was not the place or the moment.

She bowed her head. "Grandsire," her voice shook. "Come with me."

Without words, Jake Hill followed Aril into the apartment. When the door made its distinctive click, she gave in to her desire and pressed against him. As his arms went around her, she let out a sigh and the sob she had held back surfaced. He tightened his grip around her until she stopped shaking.

Aril disengaged from his hold, moved the orange riding silk she had placed in full view and pulled a handkerchief from her pocket. After a moment of composure, she addressed him. "Grandsire, I—"

"Yes," he said, "it is good to see you, too. Now you will explain why I could not take you with me when I saw you at the palace. I ache to dispatch the criminal who defiled you before we leave."

The shake returned to her voice. "I don't want anyone to die over this." Those weren't the words she wanted, but the momentous occasion left her confused.

"At least one person will die, my dear girl, of that you can be sure."

"No! That is why I asked you to come here. I need to explain what has happened in the two years I've been gone."

"You were taken captive and sold as a slave?"

"Yes."

"You have a child?"

"Yes."

"Did you want to have a child?"

"No, but that's what I wanted—"

"That is explanation enough. The child will have my name and I will take both of you back to Cadmia. The people involved will be punished as the law allows. Your abuser will face *me.*"

Aril shook off the shiver that pierced her like a lance.

"Grandsire, would you please have some keela with me?"

An offer to share food or drink meant more than eating. It meant willingness to sit at a table and be open to discussion.

"If that is what you wish, granddaughter. Don't fear. Your adversities are over."

Oh, if only that were true.

"Thank you. Please sit at the table while I prepare the keela."

She had the brew ready before she asked, part of the plan. She brought out the cups, cream and sweet granules, and poured. "First please tell me of my parents, my brother, and Grand Dame Arba-Lora. They are well?"

Jake Hill splashed cream into his drink. "Much better now that you have been located. We searched everywhere for you when we found the remains of the *Nautol*. We uncovered no clues to your whereabouts, no witnesses, nothing until the Excaliburian Ambassador came back to Cadmia." He took a sip. "Now, calm yourself and tell me what happened."

With a shake in her hands, she sipped and put the cup down. "While we mapped an area not well known, we were shot down by a group of slavers. Many lives were lost." She sorted her words carefully lest Jake Hill ask about Jerr-Lan. Talk-dancing was one thing, but she would not lie to him, and she certainly did not want him to know she spoke with the warrior a week before. "The female members of the team were taken to a center where people from all over the planet were sold as slaves. I was paired with a sylph and put up for auction."

"A sylph?"

"Yes." Aril unfurled the tale up to the part where Tim-Ell purchased her and gave Kye-Ren to his friend.

Jake Hill put his cup onto the saucer with a heavy clack "Illegal slave purchase is one matter, punishable by law to its fullest. Rape is a capital crime, punished by execution. I will be happy to carry out that sentence."

"Other criminals, the real culprits, have fled. Oh, grandsire, the Prince *rescued* me."

"If he *rescued* you, he would have brought you back to Cadmia."

She let out a short breath. Her first try shot down by her wily ancestor. She took several long sips to ponder her next move in the discussion.

"Where is your child? He, correct?"

Aril nodded.

"He is my descendant. I want to see him."

"Jes-Ell, my son, isn't home right now."

Jake Hill turned his head sideways and glared under lowered brows. "His father, the Prince, has taken him from you? He will die slowly, I assure you."

"They are...away. Camping."

"You mean the coward has taken the child hostage and has gone into hiding."

This was not going well. She had to steer the conversation to her advantage.

"No. The Crown Prince checks his borders every so often and thought the child should have the experience."

"Of escaping justice," Jake Hill said. "I'll find him. I have one-man fliers out now, as we speak."

She suppressed her smile. *You won't find him.*

"He's no coward, grandsire. He keeps close watch on his country, including the borders."

She hoped the clue, *borders*, would prompt Jake Hill to send the searchers in many directions. No one would be able to locate the oasis.

"What does he hold over you? Has he threatened the child? Why do you defend him? Do not fear. I have come to deliver you to safety."

"If you want me to feel safe, go home. Don't stalk the prince. Don't threaten war."

Jake Hill jerked back and stared for a minute. "You speak to the Planetary Prince in that tone?"

"Yes. I can't let more lives be lost. Enough good people have perished."

The Planetary Prince softened his voice and took her hand. "My dear granddaughter, you have been mistreated and suffer from fear and confusion."

She could not deny her mistreatment at the slave camp. "Yes, I am afraid, but I suffer no confusion."

He let go of her hand and pounded the table with his fist. "Criminals must pay for their actions."

"Yes!" Aril said. "Start with the slave camp. Arrest those who capture and sell innocent people. If you need directions to that place *outside* of Protar, they will be provided."

"All in good time, my dear. But I begin at the most egregious crime—the man who brutalized you with nectar. Two crimes executable—rape and murder—and he, the Crown Prince of this country, is patently guilty of one, and involved in some way with the other."

"Grandsire, I beg you to drop your quest to punish Tim-Ell."

"Request denied," Jake Hill said in a firm voice.

Aril glanced the timepiece on the kitchen wall. She stood and extended her hand. "Revered ancestor, I ask that you come again tomorrow at the same time."

His full eyebrows came together. "*Tomorrow?* I came to bring you back with me."

"I have plans."

He stood up stiffly. "You are *dismissing* me?"

She threw her arms around him and buried her face against the leather harness that crossed his hairy chest. Her hand went to the metal emblem set at the apex of the straps, the emblem displaying the family crest and the symbol of the Knighthood. "Grandsire, I lived a cold, haughty life inaccessible to feelings and love. Please know how much I adore you and my family in Cadmia."

"I have always known you loved us. My unfortunate dear young woman. If you need another day to prepare to return, I will grant you the time."

Aril disengaged from his embrace. "Take your squad of guards with you."

"I have brought them to protect you."

"My guards are in place for that. The only danger I face would be from your warriors. I ordered the Protar guards to drop their weapons, which is why I asked you to have your men do the same."

"*You* asked the guards to drop their weapons?" He scratched at his chin. "How is it that a slave can give orders to the army?"

"Tomorrow, grandsire. Come at the same time."

Jake Hill sideways-glanced at her as he did when questioning a decision. "Tomorrow, then."

She kissed his cheek and gave him another hug.

Jake Hill left. Aril donned her riding suit.

CHAPTER 72

Sari-Van and Del-Am, mounted on their gants, waited for her at the stable. A groom held her saddled gant.

The three riders, clad in brightly colored silks, rode east, as Aril asked. When they reached the watering spot, Sari-Van slid off her animal and stood with her arms pushed out against her side, eyes intent on Aril. "You said no questions about the ride. But from my door I saw him, the hairy Planetary Prince go into your apartment. I want to know what is going on."

Aril swallowed. "I am from Cadmia."

Sari-Van shook her head at the answer. "Jake Hill has come to take back a slave from Cadmia?"

A sigh wobbled Aril's shoulder. "Jake Hill has come to take his great granddaughter back to Cadmia."

Del-Am dismounted. "A princess!"

Aril reached out her arm and placed it on Del-Am's shoulder. "Your friend."

Sari-Van stomped her foot. "You are colluding with Jake Hill, giving him information so he can have the advantage in battle."

"No!" Aril said.

Del-Am stood between Sari-Van and Aril. "Don't you see, Sari-Van? She is negotiating to prevent war. Jake Hill would have already attacked." Del-Am went down on her knee and kissed Aril's hand.

"Del-Am! Please don't kneel. I'm just a woman, your neighbor."

"I'm not kneeling for your royal station. I am thanking you for trying to save the lives of our men." She cast a look at Sari-Van. "My mate, and Fin-Dal." She stood. "How can we help you?"

"By riding with me in the afternoons and not asking questions."

With the gants refreshed, they mounted and returned. As they parted, Sari-Van threw a whisper to Aril. "Thank you, Princess."

CHAPTER 73

In the morning, Jake Hill returned. He sat at the eston table and drank keela for a few minutes before speaking. His gaze went to the open door of the bedroom where Aril had camping supplies poorly covered with a tarp. Her orange riding silks lay nearby.

Jake Hill fixed his stare on her. "Do you still defend the prince against his crimes? What does he have over you? Why are you protecting him? My men search for him. Do you know where he hides?"

Aril played with the spoon in her cup. "He isn't hiding. I asked him to leave, to give me an opportunity to talk with you."

Once again Jake Hill brought down his fist on the stone tabletop. "I know what happened. You were enslaved, bought by a villain, and kept as prisoner to serve as his plaything, I trained you myself. You could have dispatched him when he wasn't looking. He must have had a waist wire on you. Did you wear a wire?"

She could not lie. "Yes, but only for a short while."

His eyes narrowed. "In countries that keep illegal slavery, escapees are killed, their bodies displayed for other slaves to see." He clenched his jaw. "He tricked you into sipping the nectar for his ultimate pleasure, the equivalent of rape. He must die."

"It was an accident, grandsire."

"Accident? You didn't agree to the nectar, right?"

She shook her head.

"Then you were tricked. Rape. There are no accidents with the nectar."

Aril was ready with Plan two. "There *are* accidents, grandsire, as you *well know*."

He pulled back a few inches from the tabletop. "What do you mean by that?"

"When your spacecraft entered the unknown worm hole, you crashed in the desert outside of Cadmia. The remains of the craft have become a national shrine."

Jake Hill waved his hairy arm, flapping with his hand. "Yes, yes. Old history. Everyone knows the story."

"And when you crawled from the wreckage, you saw a huge sandstorm passing by and a one-person flier emerged from the dark dust. The damaged craft made a landing near you."

"This is common knowledge. Get on with it."

"Arba-Lora stepped out of the craft. Her beauty grabbed you."

Jake Hill sighed. "Gob-stopped," he said, smiling.

"But as you admired her, a group of eight Hordesmen—"

"Six Hordesmen. Let's get this story accurate."

"All right, six men rode over the hill with the idea that a woman who flew such a high-classed craft would be rich and they could hold her for ransom. But when they tried to take her, she fought, and you had to help. So, you grabbed a piece of metal from your wreck and lit into the first man who held her down. Your denser muscles and strength dispatched him easily and using the dead man's sword you took care of the other five."

"So what?" Jake Hill said. "Are you trying to flatter me? What does this ancient history have to do with why I am here?"

"I'm getting to that. It was a long way, and both of you had to walk. You fell in love on your way back to Cadmia. One night you slept in a meadow. That meadow had little white flowers in full bloom. The perfume didn't affect you, but Arba-Lora breathed it all night. Two nights later, she craved your touch, and you accommodated her wishes. By the time she returned to her palace, she knew she wanted, and needed, to take you as her Life-Mate. But you were a freak to the King, her father. He didn't know what to do with you but couldn't lock you up because you had rescued his daughter. She went on a hunger strike, and after she fainted from dehydration, the King gave in and let her wed you."

Jake Hill's eye twitched. He had trained her well and she knew the *tell*. More importantly, he did not deny the story.

"I don't know where you would get such an outrageous notion," he grumbled.

Still not a denial.

Aril laughed quietly. "I didn't spend all of my time with you, grandsire. I kept company with Grand Dame on occasion."

His face darkened. "She would never tell you such a thing."

"Because it was your secret?"

He did not claim the supposition was false. Frequently when training his offspring, he said the silent lie was the most powerful lie. She recognized the silent lie— the absence of denial.

"So, you see, grandsire, you weren't held accountable for the effects of the nectar, and neither should Prince Tim-Ell."

"I did not take Arba-Lora as a slave, make her wear a tortuous wire, or mistreat her."

Aril leaned in toward him. "Tim-Ell is guilty of illegally buying a slave. That is all."

"He stopped the slave auction to buy you because he was the prince? Using his royalty to get what he wanted? The nectar? The deaths of good Cadmian men? The list goes on."

She shook her head. "Circumstantial and not his fault." She cast her glance to the timepiece on the wall. "Please come back tomorrow."

"Again? Who do you think you deal with? I am the Planetary Prince."

"Oh, so using a royal status is wrong for some but right for others? I thought I was addressing my revered ancestor, the man who helped raise me and provided my values."

Jake Hill's face went red. She had him. For now.

"Please, grandsire. I have something very important to do."

He eyed the open door of the bedroom. "Very well. Tomorrow. But if my men find him, I will haul him to the center of town and challenge him to combat."

Aril walked him to the door. She kissed his cheek and put her head against his chest. "Please don't, Sire. Our child…"

"I won't do anything in front of the child."

She stood in the atrium as he left. Outside the gate, he called to his men, who faced the guards surrounding the complex. The Cadmian warriors picked up their weapons. She held her breath that neither a hothead from Protar or Cadmia would start trouble.

Leaving the gate open so Jake Hill's spies could readily see, she returned to the apartment, and dressed in the orange riding silks and wide hat, brought an armload of supplies out to the waiting gant.

On this day, the brightly dressed riders left early, headed to a market south of their complex. Leaving their gants at a hitching post, they hurried into the crowd. A cage of birds spilled open next to the gant post, birds that when taking flight spooked the many gants tied there. Gants pulled from their tethers and went in all directions. While groom-attendants and owners hurried to catch their mounts, Cal-Eb, dressed as a groom, took three gants around the other side of the marketplace. The rider in orange with the heavily laden supply gant went north, the rider in red, east, and the yellow-clad rider on Sari-Van's elegant gray gant, galloped south.

The elegant gant twitched and balked, not being accustomed to the new rider. After a few minutes, the rider gave the gant its head and the animal eased into a comfortable stride at a fast pace toward the shifting sands of Protar's desert.

She glanced behind her, wondering if the ruse had worked. It had. No one followed her. With a sigh of relief, Aril, who had exchanged her orange silk for the yellow, urged the animal into a gallop.

Aril pulled the gant up to a desert outpost where Ray-Tan waited with Tim-Ell's flier. He asked no questions, as she wished, and handed the flier over to her. He mounted Sari-Van's gant and headed to the rendezvous, the gant farm outside of Protar's main city.

CHAPTER 74

Aril flew the craft inches over the sandy terrain until she saw the rock formation that resembled a religious symbol. Making the turn, she headed toward the second of the rocks, no longer with the same appearance, now blue, full of alnata ore. She panicked when the flier's instruments swirled and blurred. The craft pointed its nose downward, then it skimmed the surface, making scraping noises on the rocky ground. If the craft stalled, she wasn't sure she could get it started again. Even at full throttle, the craft lumbered along, the buoyancy tanks wheezing and hesitating.

She breathed a short sigh of relief when the profile of a sleeping lady appeared on the horizon. The craft shook and shot forward, free of the alnata influence. She aimed for the cleavage between the sleeping lady's breasts and laughed into the wind when she viewed the ridge. Breeching the crest, she saw the line of sparkling waters, the grove of trees, and the narrow verdant strip that marked the oasis. Flying in low and fast, she brought the craft in near a tent. The gants grazing on the lush plants cast lazy eyes toward her. Tim-Ell came from around a hedge of fronds growing along the stream. He waved and ran to her. Jes-Ell followed close behind.

Tim-Ell gathered her in his arms and swung her around. He bent her backward into a long, hard kiss. "My darling," he whispered. "You are all right?"

"Yes, of course." She would not sully the moment by telling him Jake Hill would challenge him.

As she sorted her words, Jes-Ell approached her. "Mother?"

Her worries and fears abated. "You speak! Oh, my precious." She looked at Tim-Ell. "You've been teaching him."

He smiled at the boy. "I'm not sure about the speech, but he's a natural gantsman. You should see him ride!" He took her hand. "You must be hot and tired. Flying here is dangerous. I should scold you for coming, but I am so glad to see you."

He needed to know the truth. "I can only stay for an hour. I had to see you and Jes-Ell. The negotiations with Jake Hill don't go as I wish. That stubborn man!"

He kissed her again. "I had the impression you *liked* stubborn men."

"I *love* two stubborn men. I wish one didn't want to kill the other."

"I must face him, my love."

"Not yet. Please! Give me more time."

"You will do the right thing, Aril."

She nodded, accepting his statement.

The time to leave came too quickly. Tim-Ell reminded her of the way back to the gant farm and where the instrumentation might falter. She climbed into the flier.

Toward sundown she spotted the verdant grain fields and beyond them the gant farm. Sari-Van, in orange, and Del-Am, in red, waited for her alongside Ray-Tan, who exchanged the gant for the flier. The three colorful riders headed back to their complex in the dark.

CHAPTER 75

In the morning, Aril recognized Jake Hill's stern face as she met him at the gate. It meant his spies had not been able to follow her.

"That was a neat trick," he said as she held the apartment door for him.

"I learned from the best."

"You can't keep this up."

"Tim-Ell is a good man. He hasn't hurt me. I love him. We love our child."

All traces of emotion drained from the Planetary Prince's face. The stony countenance of a judge passing sentence blended with his stern gray eyes. "I can't show favoritism. The law extends to all people. No one is exempt. Not even someone my favorite granddaughter wishes to protect."

"So," Aril said, grabbing at straws, "you would condemn your beloved Arba-Lora if she killed someone?"

"We are not speaking of Arba-Lora. She wouldn't murder or rape anyone. And, yes, if that came to pass, she would be the first to insist on fair punishment."

Her voice went up in a panicked pitch. "Grandsire! I love him."

"You must deliver him to me. The time for talking is over."

"You will challenge him?"

"He can always kneel for mercy."

As hard as she could, the image of Tim-Ell laying his sword on the ground, kneeling on it, and putting his hands in the air over his bowed head would not form.

"Would *you* do that, grandsire?"

"Only if someone I loved would be spared." He pointed at her. "And *you* are not in danger."

Aril pushed away from the table. She glared at him. "If you kill my Life-Mate, I will claim revenge and challenge you."

He shook his head. "I will not raise my blade to you."

"Then you will die, grandsire, and I will be hated around the planet."

"But it would be legal and fair."

She got closer, her face inches from his. "Don't you see? Legal and fair aren't always right."

Jake Hill pushed out of his seat and took her in his arms. "I must make an example of this man. It's my right and duty."

She hung her head. "He agrees, grandsire."

He kissed her forehead. "Then you will bring him to me."

"I will bring you to him under my conditions."

"The mate of a condemned man tells the executioner how to carry out his job?"

She ignored his comment. "You will inform your spies not to follow. You will accompany me alone with your sword as your only weapon."

"My sword is all I need. You are not the kind to lay traps. We leave this afternoon?"

"Yes. On gantback. I have your word you agree to the terms?"

"You need my word?"

She looked him in the eye. "You did not admit that my story about you and the nectar meadow was accurate."

"Well done. Although I don't believe my Life-Mate would tell you, I will admit the story is true. Do you need my sworn word on either of those things?"

She sighed. "No, Sire. I trust you."

Aril called to a Protar guard to get her mount ready while Jake Hill gave orders to his men. The Cadmian warriors picked up their weapons and headed back to the camp. Only the Protar guards surrounded the complex.

As Aril and Jake Hill traversed the atrium, Del-Am and Sari-Van came out of their apartments and gave mournful waves, as if they knew why Aril was leaving. Aril nodded to them, hoping they would translate the gesture to mean their men were safe and there would be no war. Tim-Ell would sacrifice his life to spare others. It was the right thing to do, and Aril was making it happen.

The ride progressed in silence, past the outpost, turning at the first rock formation, and turning again at the second. The sleeping lady reminded Aril of a dead lady now. The sun beat down, sweat wetting Aril's simple dress over a leather under-harness. She carried a dagger in her leather belt, and a strong pin-blade hidden in a hair ornament, the weapon Jake Hill insisted the women in his family keep on their bodies.

The ridge appeared on the horizon. She forced herself to continue. At the crest, she lingered, this time not taking in the beauty of the quiet oasis but cursing the situation where she led her lover's assassin.

"Down there," she pointed.

"I see the tents."

Tim-Ell came out of the large tent, behind him Jes-Ell. At the sight of them, she ached to hold them and kicked the gant's side for speed. At the tent, Tim-Ell caught her after she launched from the back of her mount.

Jake Hill bounded to the camp. "You are Prince Tim-Ell?"

Tim-Ell disengaged Aril's grip, pushed her aside, and stood erect to face the Planetary Prince.

"I am. You will challenge me?"

"To the death," Jake Hill said without emotion in his tone.

Aril stepped between Tim-Ell and Jake Hill. "No! You will have to go through me if you challenge him."

From behind her, Tim-Ell put his hands on her shoulders and pulled her touching his body to hers. With his lips next to her ear, he said in a low, calm voice, "Take Jes-Ell and leave."

Aril turned into his arms and buried her face into his chest. "I can't leave you."

Kissing her hair softly, he then pushed her a few inches away, engaging her gaze. "You must. This is between the Planetary Prince and me. I am responsible for what happened, and I will face the challenge." He swept a dark curl from her moist forehead and smiled. "I wouldn't change anything. Circumstances, right or wrong, brought you to me and provided more than I ever dreamed of."

She pressed against him. "I wouldn't change it either. Even if for a short time, I have known love." She chuckled sadly. "Thank you for buying me." Tears ran down her cheek and trickled onto her lip as a small smile broke through her sorrow. "Even if you had to take Kye-Ren in the bargain."

He laughed. "Ah, your acid wit is one of the things I adore. Go, my love. It's the right thing. That has always been one of your strong points—doing the right thing."

Jake Hill stepped closer, his eyes flashing. "The prince gives good advice. Go now, granddaughter. Take your child."

Tim-Ell pushed Aril gently toward the gants. "Let Jes-Ell ride my gant. He can handle the animal."

Aril extended her hand and called to Jes-Ell, where the boy waited by the tent door. When they clasped hands, she turned to look at Tim-Ell.

"Go," Tim-Ell said. "As your Life-Mate, I tell you to go."

Aril stopped and shook her head.

Tim-Ell pointed to the gants. "You are a citizen of Protar, and I am your sovereign. You must obey."

Jake Hill looked at Tim-Ell for a moment. Then he spoke to Aril. "A citizen of Protar?"

Aril squared her shoulders and stood stiff, tall. "Yes. Protar is my country. I will obey my prince. My love." She clasped Jes-Ell's hand and headed toward the gants. After helping the boy onto his mount, she pulled up onto hers and urged the animals away from the camp.

CHAPTER 76

Tim-Ell, taller and leaner than Jake Hill, stood proud like Aril had done. "My mate is a singular woman, and if I have you to thank, then you deserve my greatest admiration."

Jake Hill took a few steps back, as if preparing for a duel. Instead of giving the salute that precedes a challenge, he put his hands on his hips. "I believe I also provided her stubborn streak."

Tim-Ell had to chuckle. "For that, I'm not sure if admiration is the proper emotion." Then he stiffened. "Let's do this. It does no good to keep my country waiting. They don't deserve war."

Jake Hill did not change his stance. "No war. You are the one I came for. But not here. I want no questions about our challenge. It will be public. You will go with me into the city where all can see."

Tim-Ell shook his head. "You will not take me prisoner."

Jake Hill shrugged. "Then go voluntarily."

Who was this man? Were all Cadmians unpredictable? The old warrior sent Aril and Jes-Ell away so they wouldn't see the fight. Now the man wants everyone to see the fight?

Jake Hill's face showed no change of emotion. "My granddaughter says you are no coward. If you are a man of principle, you will come with me. Our challenge will be honorable, public, and verifiable."

Tim-Ell could not understand Jake Hill's demand, but what difference did it make where they fought? No man had ever beaten the Earthman in combat or challenge. "I will go with you." He added, "on my own accord."

Jake Hill bowed his head and swept his arm toward the two gants.

CHAPTER 77

At first Aril kept the gant's pace slow, confused and unhappy to leave Tim-Ell behind. But she *had* left him—to die at grandsire's hand. Emotions circled inside her, love for Tim-Ell, hate for Jake Hill, understanding the justice and how unfair justice can be. Admiration for Tim-Ell's bravery surfaced from the emotional mire. His death that would save his country from war sent a message to those who participated in the ugly, brutal business of illegal slavery. Many lives, both warrior and slave, would continue because of the noble sacrifice. She sat up on the plodding animal, grasping that scrap of pride, knowing her mate would fight well and with purpose. Not allowing the image of the combat to form, she focused on her grandsire, how she would never speak to him again or return to Cadmia. Justice be damned. Jake Hill would return to his country without her or Jes-Ell. She dug her heel into the gant's side to speed the pace. Tim-Ell had taught Jes-Ell well, because within seconds he was at her side grinning, enjoying the increased velocity. Like his father.

They kept the long, fast stride until verdant fields of redgrain came into view. Past the fields and the gant farm, they reached the outpost. She pulled her mount, its side heaving from the run, to a watering trough. Before she could help him, Jes-Ell slid from his father's oversized, worn saddle.

Aril squatted and embraced the boy. She had hardly spoken with him since she arrived at the oasis, and she had few words now. Overwhelmed, she could only hold him close. After a long embrace, she sensed someone nearby. She turned.

"Princess." A man dressed in a Cadmian uniform stood close. "I've come to escort you to camp."

Her anger flared. "Jake Hill gave me his word we wouldn't be followed!" *He wouldn't lie to me.*

"Come with us," the warrior said, indicating a group of men appearing from behind a low building.

The men approached swiftly. Despite her grief, she kept wary, protecting her son. Something wasn't right. The man had a uniform, but not the Knight emblem. His hair was bushy, not the short, almost shaved cut of Jake Hill's personal guard. Grandsire would never send anyone to escort her but his own guard. She scanned the six men who approached. They weren't Cadmian soldiers, no matter what uniforms they wore.

"Leave me be. I know my way back to my home."

The man sneered and grabbed Jes-Ell. "Well, you won't be going home."

Another false warrior locked Jes-Ell's arms, and five grabbed Aril, who struggled, kicking one in the groin. That one went down, but four were enough to subdue her. A swift punch to her cheek made the world go black.

When she awoke, her head throbbing and vision blurry, her hands were bound behind and a rough piece of cloth drew tightly over her mouth. Jes-Ell lay next to her on the bottom of a medium flier, his mouth gagged, and his hands tied in front. Her indistinct sight functioned enough to discern the terror in the boy's eyes. When she tried to speak to him, words came out as garbled moans. She needed time to think. Moving caused pain. It would do no good to try to sit up, better to lie quietly as if she remained passed out. Maybe she could hear something important. As she rested motionless, her vision cleared enough to see five men, the one who caught Jes-Ell and the four who captured her seated in the flier. Biting the gag, she wished the man she'd kicked, absent in the flier, was still writhing on the ground.

Keeping her eyes slitted, pretending to be closed but seeing, she examined each man, noting their weapons, their size, or anything that could give her an advantage in defense. None had the physique of a warrior. These men were soft, probably given to drink and excess, but there were five of them. Where did they get the uniforms? She silently sniffed her derision. It couldn't have been one-on-one to steal a uniform. A Cadmian fighting man could take two of these flabby weaklings without breaking a sweat. Perhaps the quartermaster's store had been broken into, the reason for the absence of the Knighthood badge.

What weapon did she have when she got the chance to free Jes-Ell and escape? Surely, they took her dagger. She rotated on the flier's floor at the next air bump. Her scabbard held nothing, pressing softly against her side. At the next ship bounce, she tested for the hair ornament. It was still there. She had something. When the next air current jolted the craft, she rolled on her side and started working at the leather bond that held her hands. She hoped for a long ride, one that would allow her wrists to expand the thong enough to move her fingers against the knots. This had been part of Jake Hill's early training. The trainees had contests to see how long it took to untie knots, which became increasingly complex. At that time, it had been fun, but Jake Hill told them as relatives to a world leader, they were subject to abduction, and they should be prepared in case of capture. A tear fought its way from her eye. So many times he had been right. But, with Tim-Ell, he showed how wrong he could be. The vision of Tim-Ell's valiant defense inserted its horror into her mind. No matter how she tried to stop it, the image of his fight with Lintor, the huge sword master, melded into a visualization of Jake Hill advancing, wielding his sword in whistling cuts through the air, backing Tim-Ell further until the bloody end. For her sake, she thought grandsire would make it quick. If he didn't . . . Would she challenge him as she had threatened earlier?

One of the men spoke, taking her out of her vengeful thoughts. Had he said they were almost there?

The craft slowed and lost altitude.

CHAPTER 78

As they galloped through the desert toward the gant farm outpost, Tim-Ell kept his gant behind the Planetary Prince. Although the gesture represented the proper etiquette for the leader of the world, Tim-Ell did not care about that. He didn't want to have his back undefended. Even if Aril claimed the man was one of honor and trust, this was not a circumstance of letting down the defenses a warrior trained for.

Everyone on Cronanta could recognize the Earthman. No other person had arm or chest hair like him. The muscles on his legs, powerful and developed, were swathed in a coating of slick, sweaty fur. Even without the dark matted cover, he stood out. Most warriors were taller, leaner. This man, almost a head shorter than the average Cronantan fighting man, was thick and muscled. Legendary accounts claimed he had faced multiple foes in confrontations many times. But it had also been said that the man sometimes granted mercy to those who kneeled and begged. Tim-Ell would acquit himself to the best of his ability. He would not let his people down behaving as a coward, begging for his life. It would be a good, honorable death, one his mate, and more importantly, his son, could call worthy.

The gants took the last desert ridge. The vista of fields, rows of plants with heads of grain bending in the wind, came into view. Beyond that, the gant ranch, then onward until they came to the outpost, where the road would take them into the city of Protar. Travelers usually stopped here to water their animals.

"We should give the animals a rest," Tim-Ell said, pointing to the trough.

"Agreed," Jake Hill said, and touched the reins on his gant's neck to turn.

"Wait!" Tim-Ell shouted. "Those animals at the trough. That's my gant, and the one Aril-Ess rode. They are here."

The outpost consisted of a small, squat eston shack with a few tables under a roof. The shack's wide, open entry revealed its emptiness. No one was there.

Tim-Ell slid off his mount and checked the area. "Marks in the sand," he said, examining grooves in the sandy ground. "A flier was here." He glared at Jake Hill. "Your men took her?"

Jake Hill strode hard to where Tim-Ell stood. "No. I gave orders no one was to follow or hinder Aril-Ess."

Tim-Ell closed his eyes. His hands became fists. "Eppo-Zim. They couldn't get me, so they took her, and Jes-Ell."

"Who is Eppo-Zim?"

"The ex-Vizier of Protar. We shut down his illegal mining operation, freeing the slaves. I thought he fled, but I've underestimated him." He flashed his glare at the Planetary Prince. "Goddess knows what he will do with the boy. He will kill Aril."

Jake Hill sneered and patted his sword. "Then we will find him. I have an army at my service."

"I think I know where he is, but we will have to sneak up on him, and we can't do that with an army."

"Then it will be you and me," Jake Hill said.

With water still dripping from their gants' mouths, the men climbed into the saddles and galloped on the road.

"East," Tim-Ell pointed when the road forked. "We will bypass the city to the farthest end of Protar."

Jake Hill nodded and rode alongside.

Tim-Ell squinted in the sunlight at the man next to him. "Just like that?"

"What do you mean?"

"What if I'm leading you into a trap? An ambush? What if Aril has set this up so we can leave Protar and live somewhere else? You follow me because I've said Aril and my son are in trouble?"

"My granddaughter would not be part of something so heinous. She would not love a man who is a coward."

"But she would love a criminal, which you think I am."

"You have committed crimes, so yes. And you are not off the hook."

"What?"

"An Earth expression. She assured me of your honor, which means you will still face me when we have rescued the woman and child who are beloved to both of us."

Within minutes they reached a small out-of-town settlement. Tim-Ell left his mount and approached a man who tended his lakins. "You, there. I need your flier."

The man bowed his head, recognizing Tim-Ell. "Yes, Your Highness." Then he did a doubletake when he saw the hairy man sitting on the gant. "Oh! I heard the Cadmian army had camped north of here. I. . . that man —"

"Yes, the man on the gant is the Planetary Prince."

"You're still alive! We heard the Planetary Prince searched for you."

"As you can see, he found me."

"But. . . you're still alive!"

"Yes. I still live. Listen carefully. We have business in the east. You must get a message to General Ray-Tan. Use your neighbor's flier." Tim-Ell pointed to a flier parked a few houses away. "Tell Ray-Tan to take a squad to the forest that borders Malmetemp. He will know what I want."

"Yes, Your Highness. Right away." The man stared at Jake Hill for a few moments, then scurried toward the neighbor's flier.

Tim-Ell and Jake Hill turned the gants into the pasture and jumped into the farmer's flier. The older craft wheezed as Tim-Ell pushed it to its limit, wishing he had his fast, sleek little vessel. Eppo-Zim had a villa on the borderland of Protar. Tim-Ell programmed the course that would take him to Malmetemp, Eppo-Zim's fortress. The estate enjoyed a natural barrier of protection provided by a dense forest that gave way to open savannah, then desert that surrounded the walled manor. Tim-Ell had been there once as a boy and had wondered why someone needed guards who walked the parapet. Aril knew he was a villain the moment she met Eppo-Zim. Why hadn't he, the Commander of the Army, questioned why someone would need such fortification? His family had been lazy and careless, letting power corrupt their vizier. Now they were paying for it. Aril and Jes-Ell would pay dearly.

Tim-Ell hung his head. Perhaps he should be executed for that alone.

He pushed the old flier hard, staying low. Jake Hill stared at the landscape below and tapped his sword pommel. Tim-Ell understood the Planetary Prince's nervousness. Even a monstrous foe was better than an unknown one. How many warriors worked for Eppo-Zim? Was the man at his fortress? How long would it take for Ray-Tan to get the forces there?

CHAPTER 79

Aril lay still, but Jes-Ell made sounds through the gag. The flier silently bumped down, and the engine whined to a stop. The craft had landed. Aril's opportunity to untie the knot that held her hands had come to an end.

The boy had awakened.

Rough hands pulled her to a sitting position. Her vision had returned, and as her scan revealed the locale, her heart skipped a beat. She recognized the place.

A whooshing overhead turned her attention to the dock. An open flier landed next to them. The distinct voice of Eppo-Zim gave Aril's stomach a turn. Her chances of escape had notched down. Words from her past pushed their way through her worry. *If you live you have a chance to flee.* This advice from Jake Hill during his training of escaping an abduction restored her courage. Observing the surroundings gave her a bit of encouragement. The place was a wreck.

Eppo-Zim stomped out of his flier. A man, bloodied and limping, came from the building where doors were ajar, and window glass lay shattered

Red-faced, Eppo-Zim's arms flailed. "What happened? Where are my guards?"

The injured man, a wound in his neck, struggled to speak. "Yesterday a band of Wanderers led by a warrior with Cadmian insignia attacked. They fought the guards. They took the slaves and medical people with them."

Eppo-Zim turned from red to purple. "Wanderers! There's no such thing. Cadmian warrior? The Cadmians are camped in Protar. Liar. Tell me what really happened."

The man swayed and looked as if he would drop. "I speak the truth. Wanderers led by a Cadmian warrior took down the camp. I'm the only one alive."

Aril heard the report. The irony gave her a smile, difficult because of the gag. Jerr-Lan and his new people had tracked down the camp from the artist on the *Nautol*, the woman who had told him where to find Aril. Jerr-Lan not only freed the slaves, but slowed his own journey back to Cadmia, unaware that Jake Hill had found Aril from the Excalibur emissary who had seen her in the palace at Protar.

Eppo-Zim, face darkened, stomped to where Aril stood, held fast by one of the captors. "Cadmia! This has everything to do with you." He slapped her, sending her backward with such force that her guard took a whack from her head.

Jes-Ell made a muffled cry. Aril sent him a look, hoping he interpreted the gesture to lessen his fear.

Eppo-Zim turned to the injured guard. "What about my brother?"

The guard pulled in a breath, sending his shoulders up and down. "He escaped. I don't know where."

Eppo-Zim flared his nostrils. "I know where he is. Malmetemp. Load them back into the flier. I will accompany you so nothing happens to *them*." He gestured to Aril and the boy. "You," he said, pointing to the treasurer and the guard he displaced in the medium-sized flier. "Follow me."

Two guards grabbed Aril and Jes-Ell, pushing them into the back of the flier, onto the floor. Aril had another chance to work at the leather thong that held her hands.

As the craft whizzed through the air, Aril worked on the knot, keeping her movements as still as she could. Every so often, Eppo-Zim would turn his head and glare at her with the unspoken promise of pain and death.

Aril had no idea what Malmetemp was until the pilot of the craft mentioned Eppo-Zim's well-fortified estate. The more the pilot spoke, the more she knew getting free from the evil Vizier would not be easy. However, her first step had been accomplished. She had untied the bond. Her next move began. She retied the knot in a special configuration Jake Hill had taught, one that appeared secure, but pulling one loop disengaged the entire restraint. At least she had that.

By her reckoning, the flight took less than a half hour, and judging by the speed of the craft, and the position of the smallest moon in the sky, a pale crescent sliver, they were north, maybe fifty miles. Although she might not have a use for that, she had been taught in the military to gather as much information as possible. By now she knew the sound of the captor's voices, especially the hollow gravely bellow of Eppo Zim. She would know them in the dark, easily identified as they begged for their lives in her imagination.

This time on the bottom of the flier, she could almost touch Jes-Ell. The boy shifted until their gaze met. Sending him an *it's going to be all right* look, she hoped he believed her. She would die trying.

Judging by the conversation, they were close to landing. Aril tensed. The whooshing of the other craft faded, meaning it had docked. Then the whine of her ship's engine stopped. They had docked. When she was roughly pulled to her feet, she studied the stronghold's edifice, plainly structured with eston, lacking decoration. Instead of beauty, the estate radiated strength. She wanted to deny the simple elegance because of the man who owned it. Her thoughts focused on the sturdy thin blade keeping her curls in place, hidden by a simple, unadorned hair pin.

A small man met them on the landing platform inside the high wall surrounding the property. Immediately Aril recognized him, Guar-Gul, the man at the slave camp, the one who delighted when his partner died after his attempt to take pleasure from her. Now she knew why Eppo-Zim looked familiar when she first saw him in the palace at Protar. Although not the same size in body, their faces could not deny their relationship. They had to be brothers. It all made sense. The smaller brother ran the slave camp, and Eppo-Zim took the males to work the mining operations. The brother sold the females and the young boys. Her heart pounded.

Two men hoisted Jes-Ell onto the landing dock while the craft hovered alongside.

The smaller man stepped close to the boy. "He's a bit old for the training, but he'll learn." The man pointed to the guards on either side of Jes-Ell. "Take him to my quarters."

Aril could do nothing. She could take out one or two, but there were at least six guards from the two ships and more coming out of the building. She had one move. She collapsed.

Two guards bent to help her up. She let her weight fall to the left and while one guard tried to take the load, she threw him off balance. With a slight shove, he fell from the dock and plummeted to the rocky ground, a height of two men. When she hurled the second guard over the dock, Eppo-Zim shot her with a stun dart. The last thing she heard before passing out was Jes-Ell's cries as they took him away.

She came to lying on a bed in a room with rich furnishings and gauzy draperies. The quarters contradicted the Spartan architecture outside. Looking to her right, Eppo-Zim stood with his hands folded in front with a vicious smile on his face.

"Nice try, Princess. I will kill you, eventually. First, I will take what I deserve. And if Jake Hill doesn't find the prince, then I will. I knew there was something different about you. Certainly, the idiot son of the idiot king couldn't have become a leader by himself. And what other woman, besides a Hill relative, would have the nerve to boss a prince around? With your spit and vinegar, I thought for sure you would throttle him when you discovered the nectar had made you fertile. I can't understand how he survived your wrath. But you are finished with thwarting my plans."

With her hands still tied, Aril struggled to sit up. "So, you plan to take pleasure from me? Not very manly to take me while I'm bound."

"True. But only you and I will know that. And I'm not that stupid to turn your hands loose." Eppo-Zim took off his robe, and let it drop to the floor.

Aril laughed. "It's going to be difficult for you to do anything with that huge belly!"

"Bitch. Don't worry, I have plenty enough for you." He stripped off his undergarments, an erection forming. "See."

"What I see is a twig. I am accustomed to a branch. I might not even feel *that!*"

"Feel this," he slapped her face.

She let out a cry. The slap stung, but the cry was to make him think she couldn't take the roughness.

Eppo-Zim kneeled on the bed. He slapped her again.

She cried. Pretending to pull herself together, she sniffed loud and juicy. "Look. Please. Jake Hill has great wealth. Tell me what you want. He will give it to you. Spare me and my son."

"If I cared to, I could sell you back to Jake Hill. But I've already given the boy to my brother. What an attractive child. He's just perfect for what we provide."

It took everything she had not to fly up and stick him through the neck with her hair blade. But he wasn't close enough. Maybe her fake plea had worked against her.

"Although it sounds tempting to exact a fortune from the Planetary Prince, I won't do anything to invite that animal close. But I will have some fun with you. That is, while you live." He moved closer and pressed his erection against her leg.

Now he was close enough.

Eril put her thumb into the loop that bound her wrist, releasing the leather strip. Swiftly she banged her forehead against Eppo Zim's confusing him long enough for her to remove the thin blade fixed to her curls. She didn't give him a second to understand the situation—she sliced from one side of his neck to the other. Before blood pumped out of his throat, she tucked the sharp weapon back into her hair to work at the lock on the door. She peeked out, seeing a guard at the end of the hall. He turned away to look down the stairs. Aril leaped down the hall in giant strides, pulling her slender knife from its place. Blade at the ready, she caught the guard as he spun around, his mouth agape. With the momentum of her speed, she hurled herself at his mass, slamming the man against the wall. She knew well where the heart was, and with surgical precision plunged the weapon deep within. He slid to the floor, grasping his chest. She had to find Jes-Ell and get them both out of the complex.

An elderly man carrying a box appeared from one of the rooms. Bloody blade held as a warning, Aril approached him.

He dropped the box. "Please, no." His elbows went up in a defense position. Aril swallowed hard. The old man was probably a slave, accustomed to physical violence. She stood over him but let the knife point down, unthreatening. "There is a new boy here, dark curly hair, well formed. Where is he?"

The old man nodded. He pointed to the last door down the hallway, a few doors from where she had emerged. "I will come back for you if you are lying."

The man's eyes grew big. Her gut told her he had given her the truth as he knew it. Without another word, she flew, stopped at the door, and silently tried the knob. No surprise. The lock didn't give. She leaned against the wall. How could she get the door open? She already knew what she would do to Eppo-Zim's brother. As she pondered, movement caught her side vision. She tensed, ready to take on whoever attacked. It was the old man, not with the box but with his hand open, showing a shiny piece of metal. He grinned and slipped the metal key in the lock, which suggested he had been trained to be silent and not disturb the master. He stepped back and nodded. Aril motioned for him to go, but he stepped backward, folding his arms over his thin chest.

Aril kicked the door open. Inside was Gual-Gur trying to feed a sweet to Jes-Ell, who clearly didn't want the confection. Guar-Gul made a move to press a button on the wall, but he did not make it. She grabbed him and snapped his neck. He fell to the floor, jerking and kicking.

"Come, Jes-Ell. We're getting out of here." She took his hand and fast-walked out the door. The old man, grinning with what teeth he had left, clapped his hands together and bowed to her. She nodded and urged Jes-Ell to hurry, running toward the stairs. Men's voices echoed up the stairwell. More than three. She pulled her boy back from the steps.

The old man padded up to them. He put his finger to his lips and gestured for her to wait. With difficulty, he took the treads one by one.

Aril didn't want to wait. But she didn't know how many guards were down there. A soft voice called, and the voices stopped. She heard the names Eppo-Zim and Guar-Gul then heard the men shuffle outside.

The old man stuck his head into the stairwell and smiled up to her.

She breathed out a sigh. At least it was safe down there. But what about outside? Come what may, she was as ready. Aril and Jes-Ell took the stairs in double-steps. Although she wished she could hug the old slave, she didn't have time. She looked around. The old man pointed to double glass doors. He headed that way, and she caught up to him. But what she could see beyond the doors stopped her. At least a dozen guards with swords drawn were checking the landing dock, and she bet there were more on the other side of the building. The dock! It had fliers tethered to hooks. She just had to get to one. She doubted she could run fast enough to make it to nearest flier, unhook the tiedown, and get speed before the guards saw her. Moreso, the old man shadowed her, probably wanting to escape too. He would slow them down. Taking her blade from her hair, she opened the door and said to Jes-Ell, "We are going to run to that green flier. Do you see it?" The boy wrinkled his brow, then nodded. She prayed to a Goddess she did not believe in to help her save the boy, the child from her Mate, a portion of the man she loved. *Now or never.* She grabbed Jes-Ell's hand with her free one and yanked him into large strides. They reached the flier, and she released the stern tie-down. She pushed her son into the craft and swiftly moved to undo the bow tie down. But not quickly enough. A guard came flying toward her, his sword ready to strike. She held her tiny weapon in a white-knuckle grip, taking the wide-foot stance of defense. Her step aside didn't save her, but the guard tumbled over the dock and onto the rock-strewn bottom. The old man had body-slammed the warrior, knocking him over and down.

Two warriors replaced the overturned attacker. They bypassed the elderly man lying sideway on the dock, heaving for breath. They headed for Aril. She waited, thin knife in hand. A brown bottle hit one warrior's head and bounced off. That warrior halted and turned. Two more bottles hurled his way, and one hit his forehead. The old slave's ammunition came from a cold box left on the pier. He took two more bottles and threw one at a warrior, then hit another warrior close up. The erbate bottle shattered and the elderly man made good use of the jagged pieces. As the warrior went down, the slave removed the warrior's dagger and took the sword that clanked to the wooden dock. He threw the dagger at the man who charged Aril. The blade hit home.

More guards came, angry and shouting. Aril snatched the sword from the downed warrior and had just enough time to get his dagger. Now she stood a better chance of defense. She yelled, "Two of you against a woman? Cowards."

Sneering, one guard held back and leaned on his sword to let the other one fight. Guards, working for decent or nefarious reasons still had their pride. The second guard reached Aril, a man twice her size. She would not use words on him but stepped forward. He swung; she stepped aside and plunged the dagger into his ribs. As if she had hit him with a pebble, he winced and drew his sword back. She didn't wait, anticipating his move, and jumped out of his arc. It was her turn. Low and fast, while he recovered from the powerful swing, she got him in the belly, his muscles so hardened she had to lay into the push as if going through stone.

Before he hit the ground, the other guard stepped up. He wasn't as brawny as his companion but smirked. "Your luck has run out, woman."

She backed up a few steps to buy her time. The adrenaline trickled inside her, not roaring like it had been. So many things that happened that had day drained her.

His sword swung out. She parried but just barely. One had to have strength to use metal to stop metal. Her strength waned, but she couldn't let him best her. He held his sword high as if to come down on her head, but she recognized the trick and threw her sword at his, knocking it out of his grasp. She plunged forward and took him out with the dagger, starting at his throat and slicing down as far as his bones let her. He fell.

Drained and spent, she summoned energy from that inner source that everyone has but rarely taps. Only a little energy coursed through her veins. Maybe she had been tapping the hidden treasure all along. Two more guards came from around the corner of the platform surrounding the house. She rested for a moment and took her stance. She would do what she could.

Two of them engaged her. Small, but swifter than the average warrior, she held them at bay for a timeless blur. She barely heard the whoosh of another ship landing. Her faculties focused on the swordsmen backing her up to the wall of the house.

"She's magnificent!" came one voice.

"So, she is," another voice declared.

Aril could not take her attention away from her combat. Two warriors joined her. They rousted the guards within a few moments.

More guards, roaring from the side of the building, assembled to engage.

Tim-Ell held his sword aloft. "This is ended. You won't live. Drop your weapons." As the last word emerged, he glanced up at the roof. An archer had pulled back his bow. Tim-Ell kicked Jake Hill out of the way, inches from where the arrow vibrated on the wooden plank.

Jake Hill rose, flashed a thank you to Tim-Ell, then in his hairy glory, held up his sword. "The Crown Prince is right. Stop while you still have breath. My sword has barely tasted blood and is hungry for more."

The guards mumbled. Jake Hill's reputation protected him and his family like a shield. Only fools tried to overcome him. The guards threw down their weapons, the metal clanking, reverberating against the stone walls.

Aril's knee buckled. Tim-Ell caught her and pulled her close. "Eppo Zim?"

"Dead," she whispered having little breath to spare.

She cast her gaze to the boat where Jes-Ell and the old man sat. The elderly slave gave them a wide, almost toothless smile. "He helped," she said in a half gasp.

Jake Hill started gathering weaponry while Tim-Ell caressed his mate.

After he loaded his second batch of blades into the craft, the Planetary Prince spoke. "Take her back to your home. I'll talk to you later. I can hold these unarmed fools until your army comes."

Tim-El didn't argue. He motioned the old man to move over, then gently sat Aril in the flier's bench. Jake Hill unlatched the holding loop. Backing out slowly, Tim-El went full-throttle, the voyage turning into a zooming dash. Aril held Jes-Ell close and tight until he broke from her, wanting to sit in the passenger seat up front. It wasn't safe for him to change seats, but he grinned as the air blew his curls and attempted to block his progress. Clearly, the boy enjoyed the speed and the near misses of the spires.

When Tim-Ell set the craft on the green sward in front of his apartment, neighbors and guards came running. He helped Aril out of her seat, then offered the old man his assistance.

Aril turned to the elderly slave. "We couldn't have done this without your help. How did you manage your accuracy with the knife and the bottles?"

"I was once a Lancer in the Cadmian army. I won medals for the accuracy of my javelins. As a slave I practiced at every opportunity to keep my skill. That Guar-Gul, may he suffer in the pits of fire and agony." He grinned. "Today was my first chance to use my skill. I knew when my Planetary Prince arrived, we were all saved."

Aril kissed his cheek and whispered, "It goes without saying, but I need to tell you not only are you free, but—"

He held his hand up to stop her. "That is all I desire."

She nodded and took Jes-Ell by the hand. He shook her off, pointing to the gathering of men in the atrium. Aril understood. She put her palm on the lock, left the catch unfastened, and went inside. She flopped on the couch, sinking into the thick furs she had ordered. *Perfect.* Now she started to hurt. All over, including a splitting headache.

The door pushed open. "Aril?" a woman's voice called.

"On the couch," Aril responded.

Del-Am came to her. "Although I'm delighted to see you, I have to say you look awful. Can I bring you broth? Something sweet? Keela? Give you a bath?"

"Maybe an erbate can help my head," Aril said with a sigh in her voice.

Del-Am dashed into the kitchen. She returned with a frosty brown bottle and spun the cap. "Here." She left the room.

Aril sipped the unpleasant brew. *Why do men like this?* Water gushed in the bathroom. Spicy, floral aromas of oil and unguents drifted through the air. *A bath!* That was precisely what she needed.

In a few minutes, Del-Am helped her to the bathroom and stripped away ragged clothing full of dirt and blood. Del-Am dabbed ointment on the many cuts and nicks then helped Aril sink up to her neck in the water. The woman emptied a large sponge above Aril, pulling the sponge over her arm, a foot, a knee. *How long has it been since someone did this for me?* Del-Am pointed to Aril's abdomen. "You have hair there." Then she smiled. "Of course, you are a Hill descendent."

"You won't hold that against me?"

Del-Am shook her head. "I believe you saved Cadmia and Protar from war. Even if you were silver from head to toe and had pointy little teeth, I would adore you. You are the most wonderful person on Cronanta."

"Thank you," Aril said.

"Are you ready to get out?"

Aril shook her head. "In a few minutes, when it gets cool."

"I'll make tea. Do you keep sheeran in your herbs?"

That is exactly what I need. "Yes, it is marked in a little tin."

While the tea steeped, Del-Am helped Aril from the tub and dried her. She took Aril's robe from the closet and put it on her.

They both went into the kitchen and sipped the tea. The taste took Aril back to her youth. When she got into trouble, her mother would serve her the sheeran tea and discuss the situation. Aril pretended to listen and agreed with every word, but in her heart, she laughed at the ineffectual lecture. That memory brought up the worst recollection of her childhood. Aril had lied and got caught. Grandsire would not tolerate liars. Dishonesty topped the list of bad behavior and gave ground for corporal punishment. A family castigation almost never happened, but when it did, everyone attended. Her mother sat in a chair with Aril hanging over her lap. The woman wept, not wanting to hurt her child. "Begin," grandsire commanded. The lady's hand came down on Aril's buttocks, much like a butterfly landing to take nectar. Aril felt shame, having the whole family know her crime and watch her punishment. And she wanted to get it over with. "Mother," Aril said. "Stop whimpering and do your duty." She pulled up her garment to encourage the proceeding. Her mother gently pushed Aril away and sobbed. "I cannot hurt my child." She rushed out of the room. Aril stood next to the chair and broke down into tears. "I'm so sorry," she said to the family. Then she approached grandsire who sat next to Arba-Lora. "Grandsire, Grand Dame, I'm sorry. I hurt my mother. I won't ever lie again." Grand Dame took Aril in her arms. "I know you won't." After great sobs Aril looked up. The room was empty except for Jake Hill and Arba-Lora.

Jake Hill had cleared his throat. "That really hurt you."

"No. I didn't feel a thing."

Arba-Lora touched Aril's chest. "It hurt here. Heartache is the worst kind of pain."

It was true. The spanking would have been nothing, but the specter of her mother in tears had torn at her. Heartaches were the cruelest pain.

The memory flushed her with panic. "Tim-Ell!" Aril called out.

"I'll get him." Del-Am kissed Aril's cheek. "Good night, great friend."

Aril nodded and hoped Tim-Ell would come soon.

Jes-Ell trailed Tim-Ell into the apartment. Aril pushed into her mate's arms, almost burying into his skin. She drank deeply of his man-smell. *Perfect.*

Tim-Ell tilted her face up. "Ray-Tan cleaned out both strongholds. The ones in charge are dead or imprisoned." He kissed her forehead. "I'll get me and Jes-Ell cleaned up. Wait for me in bed."

She nodded, turned off the lights in the kitchen and living room, then got into bed, shedding the robe first. When her mate entered the room, he didn't wear his ankle dagger.

They made slow, sensitive love, unaware of time. When the peak shook her to her core, she wept.

The Planetary Prince would visit them in the morning.

CHAPTER 80

Mid-morning, after they had breakfast, they waited, then jerked at the pounding on the door. Aril summoned her dignity and opened the glass door. Grandsire stepped in.

He spoke to Aril. "You, your mate, and boy will come with me to the Protarian Palace. We will conduct our business there, publicly." He turned to Tim-Ell. "You will fly us there in your craft. Now."

Aril ran words through her mind, but she knew nothing would change grandsire's mind.

Grimly, Aril, Tim-Ell, and Jes-Ell trudged to the hanger. The boy hopped over the gunwale and sat in the front.

Jake Hill touched Aril' hand. "It's all right. He can sit with his father. Besides I have some questions for you, Granddaughter."

She turned away, staring at the bleak scenes below the craft. Her mate seemed to be extra-cautious in his piloting, flying over spires with plenty of space.

The Planetary Prince tapped her shoulder. "Aril? How did you know about the nectar meadow? I don't believe Arba-Lora shared our secret."

Why not? How could things get worse? "When I was younger, I went to see the crash monument. On the way back, I saw the meadow in full bloom. A couple was picking the flowers. Going over the story, it seemed unlikely a king would give his daughter to a hairy freak, even *if* she loved him. There had to be a stronger reason for the quick nuptials."

"You based your suppositions on that evidence?"

"You taught us how to observe facts, apply logic, and listen to our guts. That is what I did and it felt solid."

No further conversations occurred until they touched down on the reserved parking space for the Crown Prince. Tim-Ell saluted the guards all the way to the chambers where the king and queen conducted business.

When Queen Ran-Cignar saw Aril, she pointed. "No! Get that slave-slut out of here."

Obviously, the information regarding Aril's birth-right had stayed secret in their compound.

"Mother," Tim-Ell said in a harsh tone. "You will not speak of my wife in that manner."

Ran-Cignar brought her lips together when Jake Hill stomped to the first step of the throne. "I second that." He turned to Jess-Reel. "Can you keep her quiet?"

The king of Protar nodded. "I can do that, Planetary Prince."

Jake Hill curled his fingers at Aril-Ess, meaning she should come forward. She stood next to him on the step.

"Your mate is a worthy man. Unfortunate for him, he chose you as his slave."

"I chose him, Grandsire. I could have left when he freed me."

"It doesn't matter. Although it's a shame to waste such a warrior and leader, the law is not to be bent. When I became the Planetary Prince, one of the changes brought was equal justice to all people, race, creed, and nation. I must apply that equality here."

Aril-Ess stood with her arms crossing her chest. "I used to think you were flawless. But now I can see that you have allowed pride in your sense of justice to overwhelm your sense of mercy." She paced down, then up again and turned to him. "I will have to take this to a higher level and make an appeal."

"There is no higher level."

"Well, then, I need advice as to what I can do for an appeal. I will travel to Cadmia and seek an audience with one who may have a suggestion."

"I don't know who you think can help you."

"Grand Dame. I will explain the situation to her, liken our histories, see what she—"

"Arba-Lora? You would embarrass her with your accusation?"

"An embarrassment compared to a life? Yes, I would do that."

Jake Hill's cheeks flushed. His eyes narrowed, then he cast his gaze downward. When he raised his head and engaged her, no smile appeared but the look on his face mingled admiration with concession. "So much like her. You have always been her favorite."

"I know, but that is because I am so much like you, Grandsire. Therein lies the attraction. And I believe I have found another flaw. You aren't the highest power. There is one with more authority, and she keeps that status because she knows the appropriate time to wield it."

"When did you acquire such wisdom, Granddaughter?" He sighed. "You are correct. Perhaps my sense of mercy has been overshadowed. Arba-Lora would no doubt intercede for you and your mate despite the shame she would be forced to admit. Let us spare her."

He called to the guard outside. The warrior rushed in. "Sire?"

"Alert the appropriate people to gather in the palace tomorrow at sun-high. I will make my proclamations."

"And you," he said to Aril-Ess, using his Warlord voice, "will be there to hear what I have decided."

Aril carefully blanked her face of relief, lest it show disrespect to the Planetary Prince. "Yes, Sire." Then she pleaded sincerely, "And Tim-Ell?"

"He shall be there as well. And your son."

"Yes, Sire." She stood frozen and could not help the tear that formed.

In a grandfatherly gesture, Jake Hill put his arm around her. "After tomorrow," he said, his voice warm and soothing, "we will return to family. We will put our enmities aside."

She wished his words would end her fears, but he didn't say that all would be well.

Jake Hill bowed to the king and queen and announced his departure. The queen had not said a word, possibly because she put her hand to her mouth at the first evidence of Aril's lineage.

Jake Hill had a gant waiting for him outside the palace. He rode back to the camp.

After the gant disappeared, Aril, Tim-Ell, and Jes-Ell flew back to their apartment. The three of them went to bed early and shared the big bed.

At the appointed hour the next day, the throne room of the palace pulsed with tension. Officers of both nations stood cramped together next to royals and dignitaries. The king and queen sat nervously on their raised seats. As soon as Cadmian guards got sight of Tim-Ell, they surrounded him, and the group moved smoothly to a place near the far wall.

Aril raised tiptoe to see him but could not get close because of the crowd.

Jake Hill strode into the room. People parted to make way. He stopped in front of the royal dais.

"I have accepted Crown Prince Tim-Ell's surrender and am gratified to report neither side lost warriors. However, violations of planetary laws must be recompensed. You, King and Queen, will quit your rule. You will take over the estate in the far corner of your land and oversee the upbringing of the group of boys who have been confined there. A commission will be formed to find the mothers, who will then help raise the children to adulthood.

"You." He pointed to Tim-Ell. The guards came to attention. "Will not inherit the throne as your punishment of misconducts."

Aril closed her eyes in relief. Jake Hill had not publicly announced Tim-Ell's crimes, and further she did not want anyone to see her pleasure that her mate would not be expected to take over the rule.

Jake Hill continued. "The next in line to the throne will succeed and will be advised by a cabinet agreed upon by the new king and the governor of Cadmia whom I will appoint until such time as the cabinet unanimously approves that the leader is worthy of administering to the wellbeing of the country.

"Also—" Again Jake Hill directed his words to Tim-Ell. "You and your mate will take the responsibility to end the planetwide illegal slavery trade."

To relieve Tim-Ell of ruling pleased her, but to travel the planet for the sake of finding illegal slavery meant he would have to relinquish the command of the army. An outrage! Some of that outrage being that Kye-Ren, a sylph! would take Aril's place. Although Tim-Ell would live, his punishment turned out to be loss of his military status. Further, Aril's punishment for standing up to the Planetary Prince meant she would travel as a pseudo-ambassador who must root out corrupt slave dealers. Neither of them had dodged Jake Hill's wrath. And Tim-El had no title.

Grandsire had won, as usual. After their mission, what would happen to Aril and Tim-Ell? Could she tolerate living in Protar? In Cadmia? As what? What role would Tim-Ell have? Aril was no longer Wife of the Crown Prince, and that nasty sylph would be Mate to the Commander of the Army. Ray-Tan and Kye-Ren had announced their nuptial would be held the next day.

In the palace, when papers were signed and the changes set in motion, Aril sought the audience of the Planetary Prince.

He came to her. "You have something to say about my sentencing?"

Aril ground her teeth. "So many words I do not know where to start." She inhaled, sorting her grievances. "You always win, don't you? You spared Tim-Ell's life, not because of your great mercy. *You owed him your life.* He pushed you away from the archer's arrow. His only crime was buying a slave. Now he has to eradicate illegal slavery? You took away his position of Commander of the Army for that? In Cadmia a minor judge would have fined the offender and released the slave."

"Granddaughter—"

"Let me finish. You have taken many steps to protect your loved ones from enemies. *You* are my enemy and there is nothing that protects me from *you*, a stubborn, prideful, and cruel man. I will always love you, but for what you have done to me and my mate, I turn my back on you and Cadmia."

Aril stood like a statue while she allowed the enormity of her harshness to sink in. She assaulted the loftiest person on the planet. But he was also a family member. She wasn't sure which of the two designations she had addressed. What did it matter? She dropped her head and turned to leave.

Jake Hill stepped to her and wound his hand around her arm. "Aril-Ess, my beloved girl, forgive me."

She choked back tears and met his gaze.

He kissed her hand. "Your voice rings of Arba-Lora. What you say is true. In my rage to avenge you I have been wrong."

His words shook Aril. *Grandsire? Admitting he is wrong?*

"I am sorry. Your mate is a fine man, worthy of you, my best and favorite. I live because of him."

A moment of silence hovered over them.

Jake Hill pulled Aril into an embrace. "You and he must oversee the mission of a traveling council to all countries not closely aligned with Cadmia to seek out illegal slavery. You can stay in Protar and facilitate from here. I will publicly restore Tim-Ell as the Commander of the Army. But he will not be king, as I said before. Nor will he be prince."

She pushed away from his arms. "And since I am now a Protarian, I will no longer be a princess."

They locked gazes.

Anger welled up inside her. "And who are you to take away royal titles?"

He tapped his chest. "I am the Planetary Prince, with dominion over all countries."

Aril crossed her arms over her chest. "The man who wants to remove royal titles uses his title to decree new laws? How does *that* work?"

Jake Hill's eyebrows came together as a scowl formed. The skin of his hairy cheek flinched. "Perhaps I should be the one to cast my title into the dust as an example. I will be called the Planetary Adviser."

Aril's words formed slowly. "Tim-Ell and I will follow your example. And, Grandsire, perhaps before you discard your position, you will decree that those who currently have royal designations can volunteer to drop them. However, for those who don't, their future offspring will not inherit the titles."

Jake Hill closed his eyes and nodded, his face expressing his admiration.

Tears flooded her cheeks. She pushed in to his arms and wept on his chest.

The man who held her whispered soothing words like he had when she was a child. When her tears abated, he let her go. "I understand something unusual will happen in your apartment atrium this afternoon. Do you think I could get an invitation to the wedding of a warrior to a sylph?"

"Grandsire, you wish to be a guest at the mating ceremony?"

"Yes. Perhaps it is time to include the sylphs as equal members of the races on Cronanta. If an honored warrior mates with a sylph, there has to be something valuable about the woman."

There's something about that sylph indeed. "Grandsire, I believe that can be arranged. You constantly surprise me."

"As you do me," he said. "Life pushes forward, or it goes the wrong way."

Tim-Ell strode toward them. He bowed his head. "Planetary Prince."

"Grandsire, if you please."

Tim-Ell bounced his gaze from Jake Hill to Aril. "Yes, Grandsire."

Jake Hill took their arms and walked between them out of the palace. "We have work to do. Free the illegal slaves, mend the flaws in the Excaliburian Knighthood, ally Protar with Cadmia..." All of his ideas spilled out as they got into Tim-El's elegant flier and continued as they headed to the apartment complex.

After the wedding, where Kye-Ren's smiles exposed the tiny, pointed incisors, one of the warrior guests eagerly volunteered to take the Planetary Adviser back to the camp.

The guests left, and the residents returned to their apartments.

Aril-Es, her mate, and her son sat at the eston table and shared tea, like any family in Cronanta. A lot of events were behind them, and now they looked forward to what was to come.

THE END

ABOUT THE AUTHOR
Patricia Crumpler
AUTHOR, EDITOR, AND ILLUSTRATOR

A retired high school art teacher, librarian and so much more.

She writes in several genres including children's books, science fiction, fantasy, and romance. She has five books published by World Castle and several self-published books. She enjoys illustrating her own children's books. She grew up in south Florida and loves the beach and all things under the sea. Patricia counts her many pets as her best friend, especially Ramp, the dog dear to heart who inspired an upcoming book about pet adoption. She would love to hear from her readers.

Now collaborating with DeanaBean to create and publish her children's books!

Visit my website and follow my blog at carpewordum.com

Find more books from Patricia Crumpler at Amazon!

amzn.to/3UOG96T

scan me

Made in United States
Cleveland, OH
25 April 2025